Land of Shadows

LAND OF SHADOWS

SHADOWS

Rachel Howzell Hall

A TOM DOHERTY ASSOCIATES BOOK
NEW YORK

LAND OF SHADOWS

Copyright © 2014 by Rachel Howzell Hall

Designed by Mary A. Wirth

A Forge Book
Published by Tom Doherty Associates, LLC
175 Fifth Avenue
New York, NY 10010

www.tor-forge.com

Forge® is a registered trademark of Tom Doherty Associates, LLC.

Library of Congress Cataloging-in-Publication Data

Hall, Rachel Howzell.
    Land of shadows / Rachel Howzell Hall.—First edition.
        p. cm.
    "A Tom Doherty Associates Book."
    ISBN 978-0-7653-3635-4 (hardcover)
    ISBN 978-1-4668-2819-3 (e-book)
    1. Teenage girls—Crimes against—Fiction.   2. Police—California—Los
Angeles—Fiction.   3. Los Angeles (Calif.)—Fiction.   I. Title.
PS3608.A548L36 2014
813'.6—dc23

                                                            2013029609

Forge books may be purchased for educational, business, or promotional use.
For information on bulk purchases, please contact Macmillan Corporate
and Premium Sales Department at 1-800-221-7945, extension 5442,
or write specialmarkets@macmillan.com.

First Edition: June 2014

Printed in the United States of America

0 9 8 7 6 5 4 3 2 1

For Maya Grace

Acknowledgments

Jill Marsal, thanks for being a superagent and being "on it" so often that I never have time to fully commit to my role as impatient, neurotic author.

Kristin Sevick, my editor, you're so funny and you're so smart. Thanks for loving Lou and helping to make her shine. And big thanks to the folks at Forge, including Bess, Seth, and Julie. Oh, the places we'll go!

Thanks to my friends (a.k.a. my victims). You know I'm paying close attention to everything you do—and yet, you still do it, knowing that it will eventually make it into print. I love you, man!

Thanks to Terry, Gretchen, and Jason for being perfect siblings and great friends. I appreciate your advice and glimpses into other worlds. Terry: all things law. Gretchen: Ransom Unique. Jason: Visine and unattended cocktails. There are so many "Really? Are you kidding me?" nuggets of crazy that you drop to help create the world found in these pages. And thanks for having great kids who now serve as my ambassadors to "The Youths." Now tell them to get off my lawn and turn down that music!

To my parents, Nate and Jackie, thank you for nurturing my need to surround myself with books—even when that meant schlepping crates of them up and down the coast for four years. More than that, thank you for not forcing me to be "normal"—as though that's even possible in our family.

David, my first reader and toughest critic, thanks for encouraging me to go further and farther. And! Thanks for buying me video games to play when I'm tired of thinking and just want to wander a pixilated world in search of treasure chests. And also, thanks for never rolling your eyes when I ask, "When is the next *Fable* coming out?" which is all the time.

And thank you, Maya Grace, for being my sweet girl. Thank you for watching *The Golden Girls* with me every single night, for always filling my water bottle, and for asking permission before using my fancy pencils. You are my greatest creation and my favorite heroine. I look forward to witnessing every chapter of your extraordinary life.

Twenty-four hours a day somebody is running, somebody else is trying to catch him.

—RAYMOND CHANDLER, *The Long Goodbye*

Wednesday, June 19

Two hundred and six bones make up the adult human skeleton.

And on a Wednesday night in June, I was perfecting my hammer fist, an efficient strike that could break at least four of those bones.

Fifteen minutes into my Krav Maga class, the bell tower rang—a ring tone chosen for Lieutenant Zak Rodriguez. And even though I was hammer fisting; even though, a yard away, my friend Lena was flirting with Avarim as he taught her how to break from a choke hold; even though I was off duty and needed this workout and was observing the tradition known as "having a personal life"—duty called.

For whom the bell tolled.

Elouise Norton, LAPD Homicide Detective, Southwest Division.

I excused myself from my trainer, Seth, and padded over to the mirrored wall. I scrutinized my abs, a part of my body that rarely saw the sun and was always hidden beneath silk shirts and six pounds of Kevlar. Not to brag, but my belly looked awesome in this light.

I grabbed my iPhone and towel from the floor and glanced at the phone's picture of a middle-aged Latino with smoke-colored eyes and a Clark Gable mustache.

And the bell tolled again.

I took a deep breath, then said, "Lou here."

"You're not answering your radio," Lieutenant Rodriguez shouted. Sirens blared in the background.

"Because it's in the car."

"And why aren't you in the car?"

"Because I'm on the Westside, getting in some exercise."

Lena, also getting in some "exercise," was now sticking her ass into Avarim's crotch and cooing, "Like this? Like this?" Newly divorced,

Lena was tiny and dazzling. More than that, she could filet men like a hungry grizzly could filet salmon.

I swiped the towel across my sweaty forehead. "What's up, LT?"

"A Jane Doe hanging in a closet."

Unimpressed, I lifted my left knee to my chest and held it for two seconds. "Oh, yeah?"

In this city, Jane Does were always found hanging around. In closets, off bridges, in shower stalls . . .

"Yeah. A security guard found her in one of those condos over on Santa Rosalia near the Jungle, the ones still under construction. You know 'em, right?"

I had started to lift my right knee but froze. My grip tightened around the phone because yeah, I knew Santa Rosalia, and yeah, I knew the Jungle. From age three and on to my eighteenth birthday, I had lived in that part of black Los Angeles. Worse, my big sister, Victoria, had been snatched off those streets, never to be seen again. I hated the Jungle, and yet I had never left.

"From what the first officer told me," Lieutenant Rodriguez was saying, "she's pretty ripe, more than five hours old, and . . . Hey, you there?"

I stifled a sigh. "Yep. I'm . . . good." But his words must have spooked me—Lena had abandoned sexy Avarim to come stand beside me. Big brown eyes wide with worry, she touched my wrist and whispered, "You okay?"

I nodded, even though, no, I wasn't okay, not entirely. "I don't understand," I said to my boss. "Why am I catching this? Last time I scanned the board, there were blank spaces by Guerrero's and Dolby's names."

"First," he said, "you know the people in that area better than Guerrero and Dolby, so it won't take thirty years for you to figure out your ass from your elbow. Second: Guerrero and Dolby are on everybody's shit list for screwing up that Sizzler robbery, and this Jane Doe in a closet could be something, and I really don't wanna read in the *Times* that two Southwest Division dicks forgot to fingerprint the scene. I swear those two are SOS."

He paused, then added, "I know you have two cases simmering right now, but *you* know and *I* know that our clearance rate is shit right now. I need the A-Team on this."

"One more question," I said. "May I ask why you're heading out to a suicide? Not that I don't enjoy your company."

"Again: she's on Napoleon Crase's property. That worries me."

Yeah. That worried me, too.

"I just want everything done right," he said. "I already called Taggert and he's en route to the scene. He's an ass, but he's now *your* ass, so be nice to him, all right?"

"I'm always nice," I said with a smirk.

He chuckled. "Oh, yeah. You're a black Marie Osmond. Meet you over there."

Lena had returned to grappling or . . . whatever she had been doing with Avarim.

"I caught a case," I told her. "A suicide. So I gotta bail."

Eyes on her trainer, Lena puckered her lips. "Lovely. Go protect and serve. Be a hero. Join the Navy." Then, she shooed me away—she was now able to flirt with Avarim without worry or judgment from her personal Jiminy Cricket.

Four minutes later, I strode from the locker room to the exit, wearing the blue pinstriped pantsuit and white silk shirt I had just ditched twenty minutes before but had Febreze'd after Lieutenant Rodriguez's call.

In the space of ten miles, buildings along Olympic Boulevard transformed from glass and marble towers named after powerful lawyers and bankers to burned-out medical offices and bail bond joints, storefront churches and liquor stores, lots of liquor stores. The billboards changed, too—from Nicole Kidman selling Chanel N°5 to people-less Rémy Martin and "Have you been tested for HIV?" ads.

I sped past it all in my silver Porsche Cayenne SUV, a beast of a car even at thirty-five miles per hour. Behind the wheel of my Porsche, I became That Asshole, ducking and dodging, revving and tailgating—so different from the Other Lou who used to drive a Jeep Cherokee before she caught her husband banging an E3 booth babe while he was *supposed* to be attending a seminar on next-gen video games for tween girls and so, as penance, had to buy his wife a $90,000 sports car.

Tonight, I had a reason to be That Asshole. The ripe Jane Doe hanging in a closet wasn't gonna cut herself down, was she?

The condo site over on Santa Rosalia Drive sat at the base of Baldwin Hills and on a plot of land that had been vacant just a year ago. When I was a kid, pick-up-snake churches, speak-in-tongue churches, and go-to-church-every-day-of-the-week churches had pitched large white tents there for revivals. At the end of the week, the portable organ played "Take Me to the Water" as sinners and their mothers trudged to the altar for redemption and a dunk in the rollaway baptismal pool. My family attended a few of those week-long extravaganzas, but after Dad abandoned us and after Tori had disappeared, Mom stopped talking to God. For the two remaining members of the Starr family, "churches" became Church's, the fast-food joint that sold fried chicken and hush puppies.

The revival tents disappeared completely after April 1992, when twelve angry white people acquitted three LAPD officers of using excessive force. Black and brown folks, pissed off at that verdict, burned down the city. And then, two years later, a 6.7 magnitude earthquake finished the demolition, knocking down the charred remains, including much of the Santa Barbara Plaza off Santa Rosalia. No more shops and nightclubs, gas stations and burger stands. There had been talk of rebuilding the plaza and some initial efforts had succeeded—Earvin "Magic" Johnson opened a movie theater that prohibited men from wearing baseball caps, and across the way, Walmart bought space in the irrelevant shopping mall. But none of this brought the sexy back, and blacks with money, the ones who lived in the surrounding hills, found fancier parts of Los Angeles to shop and dine.

My Motorola radio, now riding shotgun, squawked. "Where you at, partner?" Colin Taggert's slow baritone filled the car.

I grabbed the radio and keyed the mike. "Five minutes away."

"I'll go ahead and—"

"No, you won't."

"I've done this before—"

"That was then. This is now. You *will* wait for me."

Colin had lived in Colorado Springs all of his life. His daddy was an Air Force colonel and his mommy was married to an Air Force colonel. Colin hated flying, and so he had chosen to pound the pavement for the Colorado Springs Police Department. After four years on patrol and some strings pulled by his father, Colin made detective at just twenty-eight years old.

"Jane Doe ain't going nowhere," I told him now, "unless you have magical resurrection powers. Do you have said powers?"

Colin sighed, then said, "No one's here, and—"

"That doesn't make sense," I said, narrowing my eyes. "What address do you have?"

"I'm at the condos on Stocker."

"You're supposed to be at the condos *off* Stocker." Then, I gave him new directions to Crase Parc and Promenade.

Two years ago, a businessman named Napoleon Crase and his partners wrote a check to purchase the old plaza. Wonder of wonders, the check didn't bounce (like prior checks from other developers had), and the Santa Barbara Plaza revitalization effort was resurrected.

The Crase Parc and Promenade would soon house Buppies and young white couples looking for cheap yet swanky condominiums in a soon-to-be-gentrified neighborhood. A neighborhood that had already seen its only Starbucks close and the crime rate double. No worries, though. The fancy "c" in "Parc" would act as an invisibility cloak, hiding the chickenheads, wackjobs, and gangbangers roaming the ruins of the Plaza just a block away.

One of those abandoned stores in the dead shopping center had been Crase Liquor Emporium, Crase's first business and the last place where I had seen my sister alive. Twenty-five years had passed since that day at the liquor store, and I still didn't know how to answer a very simple question: *Did your sister die?* Didn't know, because the case had never been solved.

Colin stood near his Crown Vic, now talking with Lieutenant Rodriguez. He had a burger in one hand and waved at me with the other. My new partner had dirty-blond hair, steely blue eyes, and a swimmer's body. He also had a too-square jaw, a hawkish nose, and ears as big as sails. He was almost hot but then, in the LAPD's candy shop, perfection didn't matter.

Not many black female police officers worked in Colorado Springs, and so Colin didn't know how to deal with me. On our first day together—just three days before this Jane Doe suicide—I took him for coffee and broke it down. "I'm sassy, but not Florence-the-Jeffersons'-maid sassy. Nor am I ultrareligious. I'm sure as hell not an earth mother, so there's *that* to remember, too. *Actually,* you'd be better off seeking comfort from that palm tree across the street before coming to me.

"Also: I hate watermelon but I love chicken. I can say 'nigga' but I will break every bone in your face if I hear you say it." I squinted at him. "And you look like someone who's been around people who say it *a lot*. So be careful, please." I sipped my Venti drip, then added, "On a lighter note: yes, the myth is true. The blacker the berry and so forth and so on."

He had gaped at me *what's this about berries?*

It had been a very long week.

The sun was now dropping behind the hills, leaving Santa Rosalia Drive in shadow. There was a chill in the air. Typical June gloom: overcast with a high of seventy degrees. Not too cold but cold enough to slow death's decay. There weren't many looky-loos standing on the sidewalks yet. Just an old black couple, a guy wearing khaki Dickies, and his tatted-up girlfriend in a sequined halter top.

Two separate buildings made up the under-construction Crase condominiums. No concrete had been poured yet over the dirt to make sidewalks and driveways, and white paint had been slapped only on the south-facing walls. The burgundy sign nailed to the construction trailer showed renderings of one- and two-bedroom units. *Starting at only $400,000!*

"Almost half a mil to live here?" I mumbled, gazing at the buildings. "Not even open yet, and the place is already in the shit."

I slipped on my shoulder holster full of Glock, pulled on my suit jacket, and clipped my gold shield to my belt. Then, I whispered a quick prayer—God was like my mother's ex-boyfriend who I still liked, and so I snuck quick conversations with Him because, sometimes, He did cool things for me.

Colin, finishing the last of his meal, ambled toward me, smiling his all-American smile and *I'm the Shit* eking from his pores. "That dispatcher," he said, shaking his head. "Who the hell gave *her* a radio?"

"Oh," I said, "it's *her* fault that you were about to bust down the wrong door."

He wore a wool suit too heavy for Southern California, a red-and-gray striped tie he had worn in prep school, and black cowboy boots that were shinier than the detective's shield hanging from his neck. He crumpled the burger's wax paper as he admired the Porsche's curves and sexiness. Then, he smiled at me, bit his lip, and tilted his square head.

That was a thing of his. A gesture that was supposed to make me rip off my slacks and lie spread-eagled on one of those Crown Victorias.

"You look exhausted," he said to me, before tipping a plastic container of orange Tic Tacs to his lips.

I grimaced as the tiny candies rattled, as his teeth crunched, as he shook the little box again before slipping it into his pants pocket. "And you look like you're going to a bar mitzvah at the Ponderosa. You just eat?"

He nodded. "Fatburger. Damn good."

"We're about to see a body."

"Yup."

I gaped at him—damn good or not, filling your stomach full of burger, then going to a death site wasn't the smartest thing to do. "Where's the RO?"

A light-skinned black patrol cop stepped away from the small group of bystanders and shouted, "That's me."

I grabbed my leather organizer from the passenger seat of the Porsche and pulled out a pen. "So, what's the deal—?" The responding officer's name tag read SHEPARD.

"The site's security guard called in saying he had found a body," Shepard explained. "I arrived at 7:05 P.M., and got a statement from the guard. His name is James Mason and he says he was doing rounds when he noticed that the front door to unit 1B was open. He went inside, smelled it, looked around, and found Jane Doe hanging in the closet of the master bedroom."

"He touch her?" I asked.

"He says no," Shepard stated. "I reached the unit at 7:08 P.M., found the girl, then came back down to notify Lieutenant Rodriguez. Then I called Dispatch to send an ambulance, even though it was clear the victim was dead."

"And how did you know she was dead?" Colin asked, a pen poised over his steno pad.

Shepard's eyes flitted down to Colin's rep tie and fancy boots. He chuckled but couldn't respond out of deference to Colin's rank.

So, I responded to Colin for him. "Don't know what goes on in Colorado, but living people in *this* state don't smell like rotten pot roast."

Colin's cheeks reddened. "I know that. Just askin' a question. Just doin' my job."

Shepard turned back to me. "After notifying the coroner, me and my partner secured the scene."

"This guy Mason got a jacket?" I asked.

"A deuce and a 415."

Drunk driving and general disturbance went together like chips and dip.

"Did you FI this Mason guy?" I asked.

"Yep," Shepard said, then nodded to the quartet behind the yellow tape. "Now I'm interviewing the folks over there, but so far no one's seen anything strange. My partner's inside."

Colin said, "Good job."

Shepard rolled his eyes, all *This guy* . . .

I turned to my partner. "Ready to meet the dead?"

Colin did that smile-bite-thing. "I'm always ready."

Yeah. That's what they all say. Especially the ones with their guts filled with meat. And then they fall to their knees and land facedown in a pool of their own vomit.

3

Shepard's partner, a weasel-like cop with slicked-back hair, guarded unit 1B. According to him, no one had entered the condo since his and Shepard's initial search. And even though this was now my investigation, he told Colin (because Colin had a penis) about entering the condo.

I frowned and snapped my fingers in the uniform's face. "Hey. This is *my* crime scene, understand?"

Weasel Cop's nostrils flared as he offered a solemn nod.

Freakin' broads were taking over the LAPD. What next? Pink Glocks and Spanx instead of bulletproof vests and all-steel Walther PPKs?

Weasel Cop finished his daring tale of finding Jane Doe in the closet and glowered at me, certain that I'd lose my shit at the scene, screw everything up—it was just a matter of time.

I placed a hand on Colin's elbow. "Okay, so don't figure nothing out yet. Just look, all right? Can't have tunnel vision going in."

"It's a suicide, not an assassination. No grassy knolls here, my friend." He pulled away from me. "You don't have to hold my hand—I'm not a crime scene virgin, all right? And didn't you say somethin' the other day about finding solace from a pine tree?"

"*Palm* tree." Jerk. I pulled a travel-sized jar of Noxzema from my jacket pocket and slid a coat of cream beneath my nostrils. "Need some?"

Colin said, "Nope," then plucked a pair of latex gloves from his own jacket pocket.

"Just keep doin' you, Rough Rider." I tried not to laugh as I plucked gloves and a Mini Maglite from my other magic pocket. "Ladies first."

No one thought Colin would last a week in the Southwest. A generous soul, I gave him a month. In his first three days as an LAPD detective, the angels had been on his side. Day one: a stop 'n rob got hit, but the banger who did it forgot to wear a stocking and so we all saw the sprawling BLOOD 4 LIFE prison tattoo beneath his eyes. Patrol cops picked him up two hours later. Day two: a shooting left a hooker nicknamed Hoo (short for Hoover because of her . . . ahem . . . *specialty*) bleeding out in an alley off Coliseum. Vice caught the john, a social worker who immediately confessed. And day three, today: a Jane Doe suicide.

Twelve years as a cop and I still wasn't accustomed to the sickly-sweet smell of death. "Dead" had a taste—like you've eaten globs of rotting hamburger meat while sucking on pennies. That flavor clung to your taste buds, impervious to Listerine and obliterated only by time. But I put on my big-girl panties at every body dump and dealt with the horror. That smell, though . . . It bothered me. And I *wanted* it to bother me because it reminded me that this rotting corpse used to be someone's kid, used to be someone's mom, used to be *someone.*

My eyes watered from the smell as Colin and I stepped across the threshold of unit 1B.

I wrinkled my nose. "Is it me, or do you smell something weird?" I winked at my partner.

Colin didn't answer—he was sipping air like a guppy trapped in a dirty tank.

I clapped him on the back. "You okay, bro?"

He wasn't okay, but he nodded and clicked on his flashlight.

"Maybe you shouldn't have stuffed your face before coming here," I scolded before clicking on my own flashlight.

The condo was near move-in condition, only needing appliances, carpet, and faceplates for the electrical outlets. But you could check "buzz of a thousand blowflies" off that list, because this condo had plenty of buzz. Ten steps from the front door through the tiny living room was the patio. And the view from that patio? The Sears at the mall across the street. Some view for $400,000.

"You look over here and I'll look over there," I instructed.

A rookie detective, Colin shone his light at the ceiling.

"Hope floats," I said, "but blood and bone drop."

Puzzled, he scrunched his eyebrows. "What?"

I pointed to the concrete ground. "Scan down here, too, Colombo. Because there's this thing called 'gravity.'"

He blinked at me. "Oh. Yeah. Of course."

I shone my flashlight on the tiny foyer's ground. No skid marks. No blood. In the living room, the size of a decent walk-in closet, I crouched on the balls of my feet and peered closer. Some parts of the concrete appeared cleaner than other parts. Darker. Like it had been recently wiped down. I directed a beam of light at the white floorboards, a place blood splatter could land. Clean.

At the entry to the master bedroom, I looked up, I looked down, I looked everywhere.

No blood.

In the middle of the room, I crouched into a catcher's stance again and scrutinized the concrete walls and floor. Nothing strange. Well, except for the intense drone of those flies.

I drew closer to the bedroom and the buzzing intensified. As I stepped across the threshold, dread filled the pit of my stomach. I took a step, and then another, toward that closed closet door.

As I reached out to touch the doorknob, I muttered a quick prayer. "Please help me to see."

On the morning of Valentine's Day 1988 (the fifth Valentine's Day without my father), my mother, Georgia, stood before the bureau mirror in her bedroom, holding a bottle of Tabu perfume. She sprayed her wrists, her long neck, and behind her knees. Then, she smiled the way a woman smiles when she knows another's nose will enjoy those scented places.

Days before, Tori and I had noticed the recent primping and perfuming. We had noticed the looseness in her shoulders, the late-night telephone calls, the smiles not meant for us. According to Tori, Mom of Perpetual Mourning now had a man.

And on this morning, she caught my reflection staring at her from the bedroom doorway. "Why don't you hang out with friends tonight?" she said. "Tori's going to a dance, and I . . . have plans."

I gawked at her—she never let me hang out with friends after sunset.

Mom lifted an eyebrow, then turned around to face me. "You *do* have friends, don't you?" She sounded just like Tori.

Dumbstruck, I nodded. "Shawnee said I could come over whenever I wanted." Shawnee lived in the Tahitian Towers just a few blocks south of my apartment building.

"Think I can trust you to sleep over there tonight? You're almost thirteen. I think it's time." She sat the perfume bottle on the dresser. "Just as long as that little whore ain't there."

After school, I walked home with Shawnee. Kimya (six months pregnant and rechristened "that little whore" by moms everywhere) sat on the porch of Shawnee's apartment unit. Kimya's tight New Edition T-shirt rode high, showing a belly striped with stretch marks and bulging with a kid she'd already named Ransom Unique. "Dang, y'all took forever," she complained. "I been sittin' here since two."

Shawnee slipped a key into the front door lock. "We get out later than St. Anne's, remember?" St. Anne's was the School for the Colored and Knocked Up.

Shawnee's mother, Miss Linda, worked as a clerk at Paramount Studios, and their apartment reflected her devotion to Hollywood. Framed posters—*Fatal Attraction, The Golden Child, Crocodile Dundee*, and on and on—hung on every wall, and countless videotapes and screenplays were crammed into cabinets and piled high on every flat surface.

For dinner that night, Miss Linda ordered us Chinese food and sat cans of Shasta on the kitchen table already crowded with yellow legal pads of her own scripts. Before leaving for her date, she gave us each a tiny box of Godiva chocolates and told us to "be good." And once Miss Linda's old Honda Civic rumbled out of the carport behind the apartment, we carried our dinner from the kitchen and to the coffee table in the living room.

Kimya shoved her can of soda between the couch cushions. "I'm thirsty."

"We got sweet tea if you want some of that," Shawnee said as she pushed *Eddie Murphy Raw* into the VCR.

Kimya frowned. "I want a *real* drink. A grown-up drink."

"Who a grown-up?" I asked, nibbling an eggroll.

"If you can have a baby," Kimya reasoned, "then you a grown-up. And if you a grown-up, then you can have something stronger than a stupid-ass soda." She rubbed her belly. "Both of y'all can have babies, so y'all is grown-ups."

Shawnee chewed on her knuckles, then sighed. "Follow me."

Our journey ended in the dining room and in front of a filled liquor cabinet. "What you want?" Shawnee asked.

"Let Lulu choose," Kimya said.

"Umm . . ." I grabbed the only alcohol that I knew—the purple velvet bag of Crown Royal whisky. My father's brand.

On my third glass of 80-proof Canadian whisky and Shasta cola, I staggered to the bathroom and vomited in the toilet. Then I passed out.

The next time my eyes opened, the digital clock on Shawnee's desk read 8:43 P.M. Tori stood over me. Her lipstick and eyeliner were smeared, and her breath reeked of cigarettes and beer. "Get your bag and come on," she spat, pulling me from the bed.

Shawnee and Kimya had disappeared, and Miss Linda, arms crossed and frown in place, saw Tori and me to the front door. Each step I took tore a chunk out of my flesh—I'd be a Lilliputian by the time I climbed into my own bed.

"Thank you, Miss Linda," Tori shouted as we headed to the side-walk. "Sorry for the trouble."

The fresh air made it easier to breathe—I wanted to drink it and then bathe in it. My knees wobbled and the top part of me moved ahead of my lower half, like a fanned-out deck of cards.

Tori trudged several steps ahead, actively ignoring me while rapping the lyrics of "Fuck Tha Police."

"Mom home?" I croaked.

She glared back at me. "What do *you* think?" One of her boyfriends had needed a good chew after dinner, and had left a fresh hickey as purple as a huckleberry on Tori's neck. She grabbed a lighter and a pack of Kools from her purse and lit up. The cigarette's fiery tip bobbed in the dark and smoke snaked around her head.

"You think I'm stupid, don't you?" I asked.

Tori said nothing and pulled on the cigarette.

"Well, I'm not. My stomach was empty."

She blew smoke into the air, then, in her best Joan Collins voice, said, "You, darling, are a spoiled *bore*. Overprotected and scared of Jesus and mom and your own shadow. Can't even get fucked up properly without needing somebody else to rescue you. You're lucky I was home when Linda called."

Her words hit me in the gut, and just like that, tears and snot gushed down my face and onto my T-shirt already crusted with vomit, whisky, and soy sauce.

Tori threw her cigarette into the street and reached into her purse again, this time pulling out a wad of tissues. She handed them to me and watched as I dried my face. "I have so much to teach you, Lulu."

At home, we retreated to our bedroom. "Take a hot shower," my sister instructed as she pulled a set of my pajamas from the dresser. "So hot that it hurts. Then, pop three aspirin before you get into bed. Oh—brush your teeth. Twice."

Lessons one, two, and three.

The next morning, the bright sun pulled me from sleep just five minutes later than my regular waking time. My head didn't pound and my breath . . . well, it stank but not like a corpse had been reanimated behind my molars.

I followed the fragrance of toast and bacon to the kitchen. Tori sat at the counter, dumping ketchup over her eggs. She wore the tank top version of her green-and-white Dorsey High cheer outfit.

"Hey," I said, climbing onto the empty stool, "I don't feel hung over."

The hickey on her neck no longer existed, courtesy of mom's bottle of Fashion Fair Copper Blaze foundation. "How the hell would *you* know how 'hung over' feels?"

I dropped my eyes—I didn't know—and stared at the tattoo on her left biceps. "When did you get that?" I asked, jabbing at the black, swirling letters. "Who's G-Dog?"

She slapped at my hand. "So what's your story? Mom's gonna want to know why you came home last night. And if you say that Miss Linda brought you, then she's gonna call over there and thank her. And if you say *I* brought you . . . You can't say that I brought you."

I stared at the countertop. "I . . . umm . . ."

Tori stuffed her mouth with eggs. "Tell her a version of the truth but leave out the parts where you fucked up. She'll believe you—she *always* believes you. I bet that she'll throw you a parade."

"Okay," I said, eyes burning with tears. "But I don't know how . . . What . . . ?" A tear slipped down my cheek.

Tori dropped her fork, then used a napkin to wipe my face. "This is what you'll say . . ."

Ten minutes later, I was deep into my fish story. "And when they pulled out the whiskey bottle," I was saying to Mom, wide-eyed, "I knew it wasn't right. Shawnee listened to me but Kimya didn't—and I swear that I didn't even *know* that Kimya was gonna be there. So I left and ran home."

Mom poured coffee into her mug, then squinted at me with blood-shot eyes. "Good. That was a brave thing to do. I'm still not happy that Kimya—"

Tori sashayed into the kitchen, opened the fridge, and grabbed an orange from the crisper. She was now wearing her long-sleeved cheer uniform.

"Victoria," Mom said.

Tori turned and her green-and-white pleated skirt went *whee!*

"Did Lulu tell you about her adventure last night?"

Tori rolled her eyes. "I don't think I care about Lulu's adventures. By the way, I still need fifty dollars to pay off my class ring."

Mom frowned. "By when?"

"By today."

"Today?" Mom screeched. "Tori, why the hell—?"

"Don't you have somewhere to be?" Tori asked me.

I nodded. To Mom, I said, "Leadership Class has a field trip to City Hall today, remember?"

Mom, eyes hot on Tori, waved her hand: I was dismissed. "Victoria, what is your problem? You are becoming more and more . . ."

Before leaving the kitchen, I glanced back at my big sister and mouthed, "Thanks."

Tori glared at me, then winked.

There she was, my newest Jane Doe, hanging in the closet just like I had been told. A black girl, couldn't have been older than twenty-one, her body teeming with wriggling maggots and blowflies. Some of the hair behind her right ear looked gummy and matted. *Blood?* Even though she was now bloated with gas, I could still tell that she had been a little thing. She wore a blue-and-yellow cheerleader's uniform, the tank top with the word VIKINGS printed in white, and a white-striped skirt torn at the hem. Stained white anklets. No sneakers.

Where are your shoes? How did your skirt tear? Why are you here?

Her legs were splayed before her and her hands had been tied behind her back with a yellow Vikings scarf.

My mind scrolled through a list of Los Angeles–area high school mascots. *Who are the Vikings?*

Jane Doe also wore a green-and-red Gucci web belt around her neck, pulled so tight that her eyes had bugged and her tongue stuck out from between her lips. The rest of the belt had been looped around the closet's crossbar. An iPhone sat near her left foot.

For just a moment, my heart broke and I almost dropped to my knees—I had wanted all of this to be a mistake, a practical joke, or even a modern-day Lazarus story that ended with Jane Doe coming to and explaining that she and her buddies were just fucking around and it all got a little out of hand.

But I've never experienced those stories. I'm labeled "homicide" for a reason.

And as a homicide detective in a big city, I had visited hundreds of crime scenes starring dead, black teenage girls. But this one girl . . . This cheerleader . . .

Tori.

I swiped at the slick cream beneath my nostrils to reactivate its scent but more to collect myself. "How long have you been here, sweetie?" I whispered.

The bigger larvae would help determine time of death—flies had found her and had lain eggs quicker than it takes a microwave to cook a frozen pizza.

Stiff-legged, I backed away from her and returned to fresher air in the kitchen.

Colin was writing in his notepad—he was the Usain Bolt of good report writing, and I almost hated to interrupt him. But I did. "Your turn."

Without a word, he headed toward the bedroom.

As a cop—hell, as a decent human being—you try to make sense of horrors like this. Murder or suicide, though, a dead girl just *shouldn't exist*.

In less than two minutes, Colin plodded from the master bedroom and found me sketching the condo's layout in my binder.

"I'll have Zucca do 3D scans of the condo inside and out," I said. "Once we leave, none of this will ever be the same again. And . . ." I looked up from my diagram.

His face was flushed and his eyes were moist. There was a chunk of who-knows-what on his chin.

"Oh, crap," I said, tossing my pen on the counter. "You throw up in there?"

He steadied himself against the counter. "A little. But not in the closet. Near the window."

"Am I supposed to give you a gold star for discretion?" I muttered a curse, then scribbled a note about his vomiting on the crime scene.

He rubbed his neck, then murmured, "Poor girl."

"Yeah. Fancy belt for a hanging."

"Is it real?"

"The belt? From just eyeballing it, yeah, it's real." Back in the olden days, I used to patrol the garment district in downtown Los Angeles, a mecca for knockoff Gucci, Louis Vuitton, and Coach products. I could spot a fake Chanel handbag quicker than I could spot a hooker on fire.

"School's out, right?" he asked.

"Yep." I tapped the pen against the counter. "So was she going to or coming from a special pep rally or something? Hanging out with other cheerleaders just because or . . . ?"

He shrugged. "You see the phone?"

"Yep. We'll tag and bag it later. And I'll have Joey check out the latest missing persons reports—she may be in there."

He hid a burp behind his hand, then said, "So?"

"*So*, we need to find the Bad Guy. And our chances of that are cut in half if we don't catch a lead by Friday."

He squinted at me. "Bad guy?"

I closed my binder and headed to the door. "Congratulations, Colin Taggert. This is your first murder."

As soon as we stepped into the lobby, I took several gulps of fresh air, then slowly exhaled through clenched teeth.

"But how is this murder?" Colin asked.

"Her hands," I said, barely hearing myself over the phantom fly-buzzing and the roar of blood churning in my ears.

"They were tied behind her back. So what?"

"How the hell could she bind her hands like that? Is she a contortionist?"

"I dated this chick," Colin said, "who could wrap her ankles around her neck, and then do this weird, scooting thing with her hands."

I scratched my eyebrow. "And you're sharing this with me because . . . ?"

"*Because*, from my experience with hot yoga instructors, I know that it's possible that the victim could've tied her own hands. She's a cheerleader, right? So she's stretchy. Hell, kids these days do all kinds of Cirque du Soleil shit. Doin' the Dougie and what-not."

"The Dougie," I drawled. "*Ri-ii-ght*."

The huddle of looky-loos had grown, and now close to twenty people held up their cell phones, taking pictures to text and post in cyberspace. My eyes tried to scan each face in that group, but after leaving the condo I had run out of memory. Fortunately, another patrol officer was photographing the crowd.

"Lou! Taggert! Over here." Lieutenant Rodriguez towered over his black Crown Vic as he consulted with Shepard and Joey Jackson, the redheaded dick who sat across from me back at the station.

Before joining the LAPD, Lieutenant Rodriguez had played linebacker for USC. At six-foot-six and almost ten tons, he had been damned good. In his junior season, he had made sixty-seven tackles, with ten of those resulting in the other team's loss, and had been selected for First Team All-Pac-10. But then, his mother was diagnosed with non-Hodgkin's lymphoma and he dropped out to care for her. She died along with his dreams of playing for the Raiders.

Joey Jackson leered at me as Colin and I joined the huddle. But then, Joey had just two expressions: leering and smirky. "What's up, *Elouise*?" He grinned at Colin as though we'd been caught making out behind the school auditorium.

"She dead?" Lieutenant Rodriguez asked me.

"No doubt," I said. "But not how we thought. So, no one goes back in until the techs and the medical examiner get here."

Lieutenant Rodriguez considered me for a moment. "One-eighty-seven?"

I nodded. "In my always humble opinion."

He gave Colin the up-and-down, stopping at his cowboy boots. "What about you, John Wayne?"

"I'm not as convinced as Detective Norton, sir," Colin stated.

Lieutenant Rodriguez grunted—he didn't care about Colin's opinion and was just being polite to the new kid. He grabbed his radio from the car's rooftop and called it in.

"Shepard," I said, "where's this night guard, Mason?"

"The Li'l Debbie over there." Shepard pointed to a patrol car. An obviously shaken fat guy wearing a cheap, blue uniform sat in the backseat.

"Taggert and I will talk to Mr. Mason," I said, eyes on the guard. "Joey, check the latest missing persons reports, and Lieutenant Rodriguez, could you pull me, please, when the CSIs get here?"

The security guard was wheezing, and his dark skin glistened with the sweat of a man who drove a Segway to take a crap. His cheap tin shield, now caught between his boobs and gut, probably said SHERIFF, DODGE CITY.

I stooped beside him. "Sir, do you need medical attention?"

"Naw," he panted. "I'm"—*pant*—"all"—*pant*—"right." *Pant-pant-pant.* "Whew."

It took almost ten minutes for Colin to take down his bio because of all the pants and whews. Eventually, we learned that James Mason was thirty-two years old, an Aquarius who lived off Buckingham Place on the other side of King Boulevard. He had worked for Jenkins Security for almost two months.

As he talked and wheezed, I leaned in close, sniffed, then squinted at him. "Sir, have you been drinking?"

His eyes dropped to his lap. "Naw. Well, yeah. Just a beer at lunch."

A beer at lunch, another beer at lunch, and then, a whole case of beer after lunch.

"Mr. Mason," I said, "can you tell me what you were doing—?"

"Look, homeboy," Colin interrupted. "Did you kill the girl? Just admit it, all right? We ain't got all day."

I glared at my partner. *What the hell are you doing?*

Mason's eyes bugged. "Naw. Hell, naw. I ain't killed nobody."

"And why should I believe you?" Colin asked, getting in Mason's face. "You sittin' there, all oiled up, drunk as fuck. We ain't stupid, all right? You can lie to my partner all day if you want, but you can't pull *shit* on me."

The guard leaned back, his eyes now filled with fear. "I swear, I ain't . . ."

I threw Colin another glare, then said to Mason, "What were you doing before you found her?"

"I was doin' my rounds." The guard swiped at the sweat dripping down his temples. "Usually, I start on the top, level two, and work my way down, but not today. Condo 1A was cool, locked up, nothin' unusual. I get to 1B, though, and the door was cracked open."

"So what happened next?" Colin asked, but then held up a hand. "No. Wait. Lemme guess: you opened up another forty-ounce?"

"I went in," Mason said, his voice firm. "Shouted, 'Anybody in here?' Nobody answered. But there was that smell comin' from the master bedroom. Man, I ain't never smelled nothin' like that before in my life. I thought some dog had died up in there. Or a possum. We get possum 'round here all the time. That's what I was expectin', but shit, man . . . She was just hangin' there, all dead and shit."

"So," I said, "the closet door was open when you came in?"

"Yeah," Mason said. "I closed it just a little cuz . . . Just seemed right."

"Did you turn on any lights?" I asked.

"Naw. Just used my flashlight."

"Were lights on in the unit?"

"Naw. It ain't been wired for power yet."

"Other than the front door and closet door in the master bedroom, did you open or close any other doors? Did you move anything at all?"

"Naw. I ain't touched shit."

"What about windows?"

"They was all closed."

"Is there a surveillance system?"

"Naw. They took it down cuz niggas was stealin' the cameras and shit."

"Do you know the victim?" Colin asked. "Tell the truth, homie, cuz we'll find out if you're lying, and then you'll be *totally* fucked."

Mason shook his head. "Naw, man. I ain't never seen her before."

"Did you see anything weird tonight," I asked, "or over the last few days?"

"Not really." The guard swiped at his sweaty forehead again. "I get here 'round six, right when the construction crew be wrappin' up for the day."

"Wouldn't the crew have noticed a dead girl in the closet?" Colin asked. "Or did they hire the Blind Boys of Alabama to do the spackling?"

"They been working in the back units," Mason explained. "Ain't nobody been up in the front since last week."

"So no strange people around?" I asked again. "No strange cars?"

"Crackheads and shit hang across the street, in the Plaza," Mason said. "Sometimes they wander over here, but it's too early in the day for them zombie muthafuckas to come out. Zombie muthafuckas start rolling out around eleven when the bangers collect their money from the skanks, and when the tweakers pick up their last Fatburger 'fore it close for the night."

"And what time is your shift over?" I asked the guard.

"I get off at three A.M.," he said.

The victim had been killed during this guy's watch.

"Where were you around midnight last night and three in the morning today?" I asked.

Mason frowned. "Where was . . . ? I was . . . Umm . . . Usually, I'm in the lobby."

"Doing what?" I asked.

"My *job*," he snapped. "Guardin' shit."

Colin and I exchanged looks—*a little defensive now?*

"You go to the bathroom while you're working?" I asked.

"Yeah," he said. "I go to the bathroom."

"When did you go last night?"

"Hell, I don't know."

"*Where* do you go?"

"In the outhouse by the trailer." He narrowed his eyes as he thought, then said, "Yeah, I remember goin'. My stomach was messed up. Had them five-for-five-dollar hot dogs from Wienerschnitzel. So yeah, I was in the can 'round one. And then again at two somethin'."

"Did you ever leave the premises?" I asked.

"Naw," he said, dumb-eyed. "I didn't leave."

Everyone lies: the first lesson you learn as a homicide detective.

"Mr. Mason," I said, crossing my arms. "I'm losing patience."

Colin leaned in with a grin. "Keep lying, buddy, and we'll get a crane to hoist your ass into Men's Central."

Mason swallowed hard, then croaked, "I left for a minute."

"When?" I asked.

"Before I took a dump that first time, I drove to Taco Bell across the street to get a few of them chalupas, cuz I was hungry. Them dogs went through me like Roto-Rooter."

"So you had your midnight chalupa," I said. "Anybody stand out at Taco Bell?"

Mason chuckled. "Ain't nobody 'cept weird muthafuckas at Taco Bell that time of night."

"Strange and evil, though," I said, shaking my head, "those are different types of weird." But I was now convinced that James Mason wouldn't know the difference between Carrot Top and John Wayne Gacy.

The guard shrugged. "There were a coupla black guys there. Black hair, tall, umm . . . Tennis shoes . . ."

"So the starting lineup of the Lakers," Colin said, rolling his eyes.

"Any kids there?" I asked. "Cheerleaders or guys that looked like high school ballplayers?"

"Nah," Mason said. "I ain't seen no kids."

"When did you get back to your post?" I asked.

Mason shrugged again. "Around one, one thirty."

A patrol officer held up the DO NOT CROSS yellow tape to allow the white-and-blue coroner's van to pull in. Dr. Spencer Brooks, my favorite ME, rode shotgun.

"So you were gone for an hour, almost two?" Colin asked Mason, wonder in his voice.

"Just about. Went home when my shift ended at three, then came back this evening at six." The guard folded his arms. "Nobody ain't never broke in here before."

"Until today," I pointed out. "And now, there's a dead girl hanging in the closet." I pulled a business card from my pocket and offered it to the guard. "If you remember anything else, call me. For now, though, stay around a bit. I may have more questions."

"Am I a suspect?" Mason asked, wide-eyed.

"I'm interested in what you've told us," I said, waving over Officer Shepard.

The guard offered a cautious smile. "Anything to help out a brother officer. Or, 'scuse me, a *sista* officer."

"Yeah," I said. "Sure. Why not."

Colin and I left Officer Shepard with James Mason, security guard extraordinaire. Shepard would take the man's picture, then help him to complete a witness statement card.

Chalupas.

Freakin' Taco Bell.

7

Because Colin was an ass, twenty-eight years old, *and* had the least se-
niority on the team, I assigned him Dumpster duty.

"You want me to dig through the *trash*?" he asked, mouth agape.

"Uh-huh. Look for anything that may possibly be related. Start with
that one." I pointed to the filthiest Dumpster on the building's north
side, the Dumpster with the waves of spoiled-food-cat-urine-and-dirty-
boxers stink wafting off it. "And mind the rats—don't want you comin'
down with hantavirus."

He scowled. "I didn't come all the way from Colorado to dig through
some trash can."

"And I didn't come all the way from the Westside to hear you bitch
about coming from Colorado." Then, I turned my back to him. "Next?"

Joey Jackson, who would've been assigned Dumpster duty the prior
week, clapped Colin on the shoulder and said, "Get to diggin', Cowboy."

Dr. Spencer Brooks, the medical examiner, was a close friend of my
sorority sister Syeeda McKay. He had the "black professor" thing going
on: small frame, wire-rimmed glasses, and less sense of humor than a
mortician. *But!* He was as bright as a supernova and had helped me clear
almost all of my cases. As I strode toward him, I shouted, "I am *so* glad to
see you."

"What do we have?" he asked, grabbing his tool kit from the van's
backseat. I briefed him as we headed to unit 1B, where Lieutenant Rodriguez, Joey Jackson, and Arturo Zucca, the lead criminalist, waited.

"But you don't think it's a suicide?" Brooks asked as Weasel Cop took
pictures of his shoe soles. "Because of the bound hands?"

"Gut feeling," I said, shaking my head. "Her hands, yeah, but there
are a few places on the ground that look like someone may have cleaned
a spill, and again . . . Trusting my gut here."

I led Brooks to the master bedroom, and the rest of my team followed. We watched silently as he approached Jane Doe.

Flashlight in hand, Brooks shone light up and down the girl's body, then stooped to start collecting fly larvae of every size. Once he had vialed enough specimens, he shone the beam of light on the victim's hands. "Rigor's set in . . . And look at her fingers. The tips are dark purple—the blood's settled. She's been dead for a while." Using a scalpel, he cut through the girl's tank top right above her waist. Then, he cut into her skin and stuck a long thermometer through the incision, deep enough to pierce her liver. After a few seconds, he checked the thermometer's gauge. "Sixty-nine point six . . . She's probably been dead for about twenty hours."

"Shit," Joey muttered. "A *day*, just about?"

Brooks shone his light on the victim's bound hands again.

She wore yellow acrylic fingernails.

"The tips have been cut off," I noted. "And one nail, the right middle, is totally gone." My eyes skipped around the closet. "And that one nail is presumably missing."

"Were they cut before or after she died?" Lieutenant Rodriguez asked.

Brooks said, "Don't know."

My sister would clip off the tips of her acrylics, then soak her fingers in acetone before going to the nail shop—the shop charged if they had to take them off. Back then, I had cringed as I watched my sister doing this, as nail carcasses flew here and there, sometimes hitting me in the eye, most times landing in the space between Tori's bent leg and thigh; Technicolored nasty things that held two weeks' worth of dirt, dead skin, and, on my sister's worse days, green fungus.

Had this (Jane Doe being frugal and doing some of the work herself) been the case here? Or did we have a monster who had watched episodes of *CSI* and knew that her fingernails held vital clues to his identity?

Brooks swabbed the girl's arms and neck with cotton swabs, in the hopes that the murderer had left behind saliva or semen. As he slipped the sticks into glass vials, he said, "I'll do a rape kit when we bring her in." He slowly exhaled. "So now, let's address this." He shone his flashlight on the girl's neck. "See how her facial skin tone is redder than the skin tone of her arms? Could be an indicator of strangulation. You see how the bruising around her neck is in a straight-ish line? If she had hung herself, that belt would have left a bruise shaped like an upside-down V." He studied the bruise, then shook his head. "He didn't have to choke her so damned hard."

"See the scratches?" I whispered, pointing at her face.

There was a scratch on her right cheek that ended near the top of her lip. There was another scratch above her left eyebrow.

"Did she fight him?" Joey asked.

"I sure as hell hope so," Lieutenant Rodriguez said.

"Could she have tied her hands herself?" I inquired.

Brooks narrowed his eyes, then cocked his head. "It's possible, but I don't think so."

I pointed to the spot near the back of her right ear. "Her hair back there . . . looks like she may have been bleeding." Brooks shone the light on that spot but didn't move her. He grunted, then nodded.

"We'll move her once Zucca gets what he needs." With that, he closed his kit and left the closet.

Lieutenant Rodriguez clicked his teeth, then said, "Lou?"

"After Zucca does his thing," I said, eyes still on the victim, "I wanna look around her again."

Arturo Zucca was a fat-thin Italian-American, one of those guys that looked chubby but wasn't—six months working out on an elliptical machine and eating bags of spinach would change everything. Zucca had the eyes of an eagle and the mind of Louis Pasteur: two advanced degrees in biology and chemistry and a grand master in the USPSA shooting competition. His love of guns and science made him perfect for a job in which an ordinary person strolls into an unoccupied condo and sees no blood, no signs of struggle, nothing. That person will scan the two bedrooms, the bathrooms, the kitchen, and still see nothing except empty holes for electrical sockets and a layer of dust and grit on the countertops. That ordinary person will return to the lobby, ruffle her hair, and say, "Other than the dead girl, the flies, and the cell phone, I didn't see anything." But Zucca saw everything because there was always something there. Every time you left a place, you left behind a little piece of you.

The condo was quiet, too quiet, even as seven people worked the scene. I heard my pulse racing and my shallow breathing. I heard

Lieutenant Rodriguez and a forensic tech whispering. I heard cameras pop and click. And then, there were the flies . . .

Too much quiet. Not enough noise. And so, I passed forensic techs dusting for prints on the front door and tiptoed to the hallway to clear my mind. I glanced out the narrow window at the north end of the hallway—the construction trailer, a medical building, and a dirt lot. I swiveled away from the window to stare down the hallway. At the south end, an exit sign hung above an emergency staircase.

I toggled the switch on my radio and called Colin. "Pull a uniform and search the emergency stairs off the second floor. The bad guy could've brought her up that way."

Zucca poked his head out of unit 1B. "Anytime, Lou."

The videographer, a hard-built woman with chopped-off gray hair, was recording a criminalist peering into the kitchen's drainage pipe. Another criminalist, this one in the second bedroom, inched in a slow clockwise spiral, searching for a strand of hair that shouldn't have been there. Countless yellow evidence tents had been dropped in the living room, near the threshold of the master bedroom, and at the patio window.

"Found some dust motes from the San Gabriel Valley?" I asked Zucca.

He surveyed the room. "Something like that."

"I didn't see any blood," I said, "but, of course, that doesn't mean that there isn't any."

"Once we move the girl," he said, "I'll use luminol." Which glowed blue once it acted with the iron found in blood.

"I didn't see any drag marks, either," I noted.

"Right. He must've carried her here."

"And you'll use ninhydrin to lift prints off the closet and bedroom walls?" I asked. "He could have placed his hands there to balance himself while hanging her."

"Yep," Zucca said. "And I'm assuming you'll want 3D scans, inside and out."

Pure white light burst in the world beyond the balcony.

My hand flew to my chest and I gave a small yelp. "Did the Russians just nuke us?"

"Someone finally switched on the halogens," Zucca said with a chuckle.

"I'll never get used to that." I saluted him, then returned to the brightly lit master bedroom for my second search of the closet.

A yellow tent now sat by the iPhone.

I pulled on a new pair of latex gloves, then picked up the device. Didn't see any fingerprints—didn't mean there weren't any. I pressed the power button and the phone's light filled the closet.

The wallpaper picture was a yellow dog, something small like a Shih Tzu.

The battery symbol indicated the phone was fully charged.

I wanted to study the call log but didn't want to smudge any possible fingerprints.

"Who the hell threw up?" one of the techs shouted from the bedroom.

"That would be my partner," I shouted back.

"You make a note?"

"Yeah. Sorry 'bout that."

I powered down the phone and sat it back by its little yellow tent. Needing a breath, I stepped back into the bedroom.

Over by the window, the techs were photographing Colin's vomit. Other than that, there was nothing else to photograph. No beer cans or cigarette butts, no half-smoked jays or used rubbers. Nothing to suggest a party or squatters hanging out and shooting up.

Back to the closet.

Nothing there except that phone, that belt, and that girl. There were no other items to move. No other doors to open. No couch cushions to search.

Who are you?

A Vikings cheerleader, sure.

She wasn't a strawberry, though: raggedy and desperate, giving head for crack.

No. Jane Doe had income—a fourth-generation iPhone cost $100, but then throw in the data plan . . . Nope, this girl wasn't poor. She was somebody's kid. She was that yellow dog's mom.

I ran my flashlight down to her feet.

And where are your shoes?

Tori had left behind one shoe, the left, a white Nike Huarache with a bloodstain the size of a quarter on the toe.

I ran the light up the girl's legs and up her torso.

Light reflected off an object stuck to the back of her shoulder.

I peered closer.

Gold cursive letters. BABY GIRL. A nameplate with no chain.

I stared into the girl's dead, half-mast eyes—3 percent of me still believed that the last image seen by a dying person remained fixed in her eyes. "Who did this to you, sweetie?" I didn't care about the "why." Fuck the "why." I wanted to know who had taken this girl's life. Unfortunately, there were no images of that monster in her cloudy corneas. There *were* specks of red, though. Blood.

"That's okay," I whispered. "I'll find that son-of-a-bitch." *For you. And for me.*

8

It had been three hours since my arrival to Crase Parc and Promenade. A dead girl (another dead girl) had entered my life, this one anonymous. She had possibly left little drops of herself on the lobby floor, dripping all the way to a condo unit on the first floor, drops that were now marked with miniature orange pylons. With that cheer uniform, she may have been the same age as my sister when she disappeared. And Jane Doe had also been victimized in the same neighborhood as Tori, with the name Crase featured prominently in the background. *Again*.

A part of me dismissed those similarities—*of course* there would be another dead black girl in this area, since no white ones lived here. Since the start of the new year, I had investigated a lot of murders starring this demographic. But this hadn't been a simple drug deal gone bad or a trick turned fatal. The larger part of me agreed with writer Emma Bull: *Coincidence is the word we use when we can't see the levers and pulleys*.

And now, I was punching through fog, grabbing for those pulleys but missing by miles, to explain away the coincidences. I squeezed shut my eyes—the halogens were too bright, my mind too fragmented, but I needed to get over it and focus. I shuffled through the field interview cards compiled by Officer Shepard. Correction: interview *card*. Just one from the security guard, who had been gnawing on chalupas and guzzling Budweiser while a girl was being strangled to death and hung in a closet.

Colin had abandoned the Dumpsters and was now chatting with Nancy Douglass, the tacky blonde reporter from the *Weekly*.

"What the hell?" My gut burned seeing him there at the tape, flapping his gums to the first hack he saw. *Dumb ass*. I barked his name.

He ended his conversation with the reporter and sauntered over to where I stood.

I wanted to rip out his trachea. "*You* don't talk to the press," I growled at him. "*I* talk to the press, and if you do it again, I'll pack your steam trunk myself and ship you off to fuckin' Provo, Utah."

He tried to explain himself and stammered about not saying much to Nancy, about being off the record and *blah-blah-blah*. But I had already gone deaf from anger.

After working all day and then being called back in, I needed a Billie Holiday. Vodka, grenadine, and ginger ale, all living happily ever after in my bloodstream. Unlike security guard James Mason, though, I didn't drink while on deck, so relief needed to come from a less-distilled source.

I pulled out my cell phone from my jacket pocket and moved past the black-and-whites and the coroner's van to the Porsche.

Lena had texted me a little after ten o'clock. *U ok? Told Sy about your dead girl. Oops. ;)*

I loved Syeeda, but she was still a journalist, freelance or not. She, too, had grown up in the Jungle and if anything dramatic occurred in this area, she had to look into it. "Looking into it" included sniffing around me and asking questions that I mostly couldn't answer on record. Hopefully, there would be no intrigue or multistory series because of tonight's murder.

Greg: he'd make me feel better. But his ringtone—pinballs—hadn't clanged since . . . since . . . that long.

I selected GREG'S CELL from my Favorites and listened as his line rang and rang.

For the last eleven years, my husband had served as confidant and court jester, coach and lover. When the boys acted like sexist jerks or I hit a roadblock in a case that seemed insurmountable, Greg would wave my bra in the air and tell me that Harriet Tubman didn't ride the bus with Madame C. J. Walker so that I could punk out. And as I stood at my car, punching through fog, grabbing for those pulleys and staring at orange pylons, that's what I needed: an "All your base are belong to us!" from the man I loved.

Greg was now in Tokyo, on day thirteen of his thirty-day stay. He was the Vice President of Creative Development for M80 Games and was now overseeing the script writing, artwork, and voice work for the company's new franchise *The Last Days*. I missed him and resented his absence, but who was I to complain? He had eaten many cartons of Drunken Noodles alone while I had spent my nights stepping in suspect pools of goop and interviewing new widows in roach-infested apartments. You know, living the glamorous life.

But Greg's phone kept ringing and ringing . . . ringing and ringing . . .

I glanced at my watch—11:07 P.M.—and tried his hotel room phone. Okay. Yeah. Tokyo was sixteen hours ahead of LA. Which meant that it was two in the afternoon there. Which meant that he was probably in meetings. But still . . . I was biting my nails now, and my heart was pounding, and the chaos around me had muted. Because where was he?

In meetings.

Why wasn't he answering?

Because it's two in the afternoon. Duh.

Was it happening again?

Umm . . .

Colin jogged over. "Guess what?"

I wanted to throw a hammer fist to his gullet. Instead, I snapped, "I'm on the phone," then left a message. "It's me, at a scene, call me when you can, don't know when I'll be home . . ." and so on. I turned my attention to Colin. "You had something to tell me? You find something in the Dumpsters?"

Colin frowned. "Other than diphtheria and possibly malaria? No, I didn't."

"What about that staircase? Find something there?"

"Possibly. Zucca dropped tents by invisible spots on a few of the steps. Oh, and some of the techs were looking at me like I was crazy. Guess you told them that I puked?"

I didn't blink. "Was I supposed to say something different?"

He smirked. "Then allow me to fuck up your day just a little bit more."

I opened the Porsche's trunk and grabbed a protein bar from my gym bag. Taught to share as a child, I offered him a bar.

He declined, taking out his Tic Tacs and rattling the box. "Zucca gave me permission to handle the vic's phone," he said as he crunched candy, "so I took a quick look through the call log. You know, who she called, what time, and what-have-you?"

"And?"

"And she's a girl with a phone," he said. "She called every-fucking-body yesterday, including Colin Powell and Taylor Swift. There's a pattern in some of the numbers, but I said, 'Fuck it, save it for later.' But the part that's gonna ruin your day? In the Notes app, I found the last entry she made. I wrote it down."

I chewed my protein bar—it tasted like planks and raisins.

Colin found the page in his notebook, then took a deep breath before reading.

Dear mom and dad,

Please I hope you will forgive me. I love you so much and I wanted so hard to make this go a different way but I couldn't. It's not like I didn't want to be around you anymore but I couldn't breath. And Derek and me, were compliated right now. We are friends and that's it. He gorges me. I hope Von will to. It was to soon to get married and I am tired of talking about it. I'm tired of everything and everybody. And mom I did not steal that money. I am not macie. you never believe me I love you anyway.

Peace and blessings
Your babygirl that will love you forever
Monie

PS please rake care of butter. I will miss her too

I had stopped eating my bar sometime after hearing "I'm tired of everything."

"Sounds like a suicide note to me," Colin speculated.

"Let me see that," I said, reaching for his notepad.

A plea for forgiveness, why she did it, one last request . . . Written on June 19 at 2:51 A.M. Early this morning.

"But you don't buy it," Colin said.

My gut was telling me not to believe it. My heart, though, ached for this girl named Monie who had parents, a dog named Butter, and people named Derek, Von, and Macie complicating her life. But I trusted my gut more. "This note's a ruse. I can't prove it but . . ." I handed Colin his pad. "Anything else?"

He nodded. "A patrol unit found an abandoned dark red 2012 Lexus parked at the Fatburger over at the mall. The officers went into the restaurant and asked if it belonged to a customer. But nobody claimed it."

"A Lexus in this neighborhood at this time of night," I said. "Sears is closed, so no late-night shopping by a desperate housewife. They check out Taco Bell?"

"Nobody stepped forward," he said. "But the plates were personalized. 'BabyGrl.'"

"I found a 'Baby Girl' nameplate on her shoulder."

"And the note on the phone," he added. "'Your babygirl that will love you forever.'" He flipped a page in his pad, then said, "They ran the plates, and the car's registered to Monique Darson, age seventeen. Lives on Garthwaite Avenue."

"That's over in Leimert Park," I said.

He handed me the slick telefax of her driver's license.

Monique Darson: born August 3, 1997, brown eyes, five-foot-one, one hundred pounds, organ donor.

A seventeen-year-old driving a Lexus . . . What was *that* about? Had she been dating a dealer? And Garthwaite Avenue: a nice street but definitely not fancy-pants Northridge Drive up in Windsor Hills. And: How had she moved from the car in the parking lot to the condos across the street? Did she walk? Was she carried? Was she alone?

Brooks would have to confirm officially, but Monique Darson was my Jane Doe. I sighed with relief and agitation—she had an identity now, but she also had people to mourn her death.

"The cheer outfit," I said.

Colin dumped more Tic Tacs in his mouth, and said, "What about it?"

"If she was on the right track, she would've just graduated from high school. Again: why was she wearing her uniform?"

Colin narrowed his eyes, then said, "Nostalgia?"

I folded my arms and dropped my chin to my chest. "She's too young to long for the good ol' days." I paused, then added, "Maybe someone she was with wanted to relive his."

And we both thought about that while trudging over to the mall's near-empty parking lot with Zucca and Officer Shepard.

My stomach tightened as I stood directly across the street from the ruins of the Santa Barbara Plaza.

A small crowd had gathered outside Fatburger and Taco Bell, abandoning their King Fats and 5-Layer Burritos, Dr Peppers and Mountain

Dews, to take pictures of the cops standing next to the abandoned Lexus. Wednesday night dinner theater in the hood.

We each clicked on our flashlights and searched the asphalt around the Lexus.

No blood. No ripped-off buttons. No bullet casings.

I pulled the shortest straw so I got to peek into the Lexus first.

The interior smelled of piña colada air freshener.

CDs lined the driver's-side sun visor.

A fuchsia, quilted Juicy Couture jacket and a little pink Bible sat on the passenger seat.

There was yellow dog hair on the cloth backseats.

There were no ashes in the ashtray—she didn't smoke. Just a receipt from the Ladera Center Petco. On Tuesday evening, at 7:13, someone had purchased a bag of Science Diet dog food and a doggie chew toy.

I popped open the trunk and found the food and toy. "If she wanted to kill herself, why buy food and leave it in the car you're about to abandon?" I took a step back and stared at the Lexus as though it would answer. Before it could, I spotted a pair of lemon-colored skinny jeans, a black tank top, and black Ugg boots in the shadows of the trunk.

"Think this is what she had on before changing into the cheerleader getup?" Colin asked.

I nodded. "So when did she change? Hell: *why* did she change?"

Colin searched the car's cabin next.

I turned to survey the entire parking lot. My gaze stopped on a dark green truck that slowly rolled north past the mall. The windows were tinted, so I couldn't see inside the cabin. Was this a looky-loo or—?

"Where's her purse?" Colin shouted.

I tore my eyes away from the green truck and said, "What?"

"Her purse," he repeated. "You know, the bag you ladies carry that's filled with a bunch of crap nobody needs."

Most teenage girls carried a purse stuffed with a phone, a bottle of perfume, a wallet, keys, earbuds, lipsticks, eyeliner, tampons, pens, chewing gum, a broken necklace, an earring without a back, and a book of matches. A field kit for surviving the City.

No shoes, and now, no purse? What was missing was just as important as what had been found.

"We'll log and collect everything," Zucca said. "Better to take too much than not enough."

I glanced toward the Fatburger. "Wonder if there's a surveillance camera that looks out to this part of the lot."

A minute later, Colin and I stood in the tiny back office of the burger joint. The manager, a rangy woman who didn't look like she'd eaten much of her product, rolled the videotape from the security system.

Lots of cars in, lots of cars out. Impalas, Corollas, minivans, SUVs. No dark red Lexus.

Back in the parking lot, I wandered around, flashlight up, in search of a camera that could've captured the moment when the Lexus had been abandoned. No cameras.

As I returned to my team, the coroner's van crept past the mall. Brooks sat shotgun as another ME drove Monique Darson to 1104 North Mission Road.

I squared my shoulders, knowing that I, too, would have to drive to the coroner's office for the girl's autopsy. And then, I would have to do the part I hated more than attending autopsies: notifying the family.

9

Times have changed since he left this neighborhood a day ago. The yellow tape around the girl's Lexus keeps him from being close to the scene. And now, there are people—from Taco Bell, from Fatburger—so many people pushing him to get a better view.

A view of what? The car? The detectives? What? The best pictures are being taken across the street, inside unit 1B. And once the coroner's van (*there it goes!*) reaches the county morgue, the best pictures will be taken of the girl on a cold, steel table. Anyway, he knows how she looks—what he left behind, what he took when he left—and all of those images will stay with him forever.

Well. Not forever.

On cue, the spider pokes from beneath the skin near his left eyebrow. The flickering red, white, and blue lights of the patrol cars make the spider skittish. The creature spins there, above his eyebrow, then skitters to his hairline before settling above his left ear.

He touches his temple and pushes.

Something there pops and gushes, numbing his brain.

A white detective wearing cowboy boots stands at the tape, talking to the night manager of the Taco Bell. What is the cop telling him? And what did the manager see last night?

A black woman, shoulder-length hair, pretty but too tall, stomps over to the cowboy and the cook. A gold badge sparkles off her hip. She touches the white boy's elbow, nods, then asks the manager a question. Then, she turns on her heel and stomps back to the car with the white detective following her, his eyes on her ass.

He smiles—he hates a bossy woman, but this woman . . . This detective . . .

He glances up at the LAPD helicopter circling the scene and opens his mouth to shout, "What the hell are you looking for?" But he clamps his lips together and makes an *mmm* sound. What *are* they looking for? A gun thrown on a rooftop? Another body in the trunk? *Him?* Well, he's down here with the great unwashed and he didn't use a gun. Never has. Never will.

The spider pokes again, this time from the bridge of his nose.

He closes his eyes; takes in a long, deep breath; then blows out air through gritted teeth.

When was the last time he'd slept?

The sides of his head tighten as he thinks . . . thinks . . .

The spider retreats behind his left ear.

He opens his eyes again and focuses—so hard to do now—and sees that the female detective is moving toward him and the group of bystanders. "Shit," he says.

The woman standing in front of him, the one holding a sleeping toddler, glares back at him. As though his curse is worse than her bringing a half-dressed, two-year-old girl to a crime scene. He glares at this bitch holding her ugly kid. She has the sense to turn back around.

Still, he had forgotten that he now stood in a public place—the spider makes him lose himself every now and then. Like that time when . . .

The detective stops and heads back to the Lexus.

He swipes the air. Tiny flies swirl around his head. *Maybe.* Or black spots that *look* like flies. *Probably.*

"Sunday," he says aloud. *That* had been the last day he'd slept. Four hours. *Maybe.*

The black detective directs a photographer to take pictures. Inside the car. Inside the trunk. Her partner wanders around the parking lot with a flashlight, still searching for a clue, head down, eyes on the ground.

Just keep lookin'.

His hands now shake and his fingers wriggle like one-winged butterflies, and he can't hear the rumble of the approaching tow truck or the helicopter or anything at all. He closes his eyes again—the spider is behaving badly today.

He shouldn't have come here with all the lights, all the noise, and all the people.

He bats at the flies (or the spots or whatever they are) and hits the toddler's hand. One of the girl's eyes opens. She studies him, then slowly falls back asleep.

The two detectives stand together while looking back at the condo, then at the tow truck pulling in back of the Lexus. The white boy rubs his forehead, puffs out his cheeks. The woman tugs at her ear, then folds her arms. They're stuck.

It's only a matter of time.

They *will* figure it out.

Then? Then, it will be over before it even begins. And if *he* doesn't end it, the spider will.

Thursday, June 20

10

Dawn was two hours away, and the longest day of the year was just beginning, even though it felt like it had already happened. I sat in the Porsche, completing the first report for Monique Darson's murder book—injury extent, who found her, evidence recovered. Then, I completed a search warrant request for the construction trailer. I called Joey Jackson over and told him to take the warrant request to the courthouse and hand it to Judge Keener as soon as she popped open her first can of Diet Coke. That part of my to-do list checked off, I screeched out of the mall parking lot and raced east on Martin Luther King Jr. Boulevard.

At 3:12 in the morning, the city still slept. Despite their neon beckoning, Jack in the Box and Alex Fish Market were closed until a reasonable time of the day. Jehovah's Witnesses weren't up and out, either, so no one wandered the streets wearing nylons and neckties. The bail bond joints were open, but then bail bond joints were always open and always filled with baby mamas hoisting sleepy toddlers on their hips or *abuelitas* clutching purses to chests, sick and tired of That Boy messing up again, muttering that *ésta es la última vez que ella venga aquí, no más, basta*, but knowing that she *would* come here again even though this time was *supposed* to be the last time.

I didn't turn on the car's stereo—the engine's muted roar always helped me plan Next Steps. Hard to do, though, because my head hurt, my stomach growled, and my husband hadn't called me back. So I drove in silence, racing through the city I had vowed to protect, my gaze always moving, always searching

Prostitute.

Wino.

Church, church, immigration lawyer, liquor store.

Repeat

I hopped on the 10 Freeway East, then exited off Caesar Chavez Boulevard in East LA.

Prostituta.

Un borracho.

Iglesia, iglesia, abogado de immigración, una licorería.

Repetir.

In a city with more than three million souls, you had a lot of dead—on average, fifty thousand people died in Los Angeles every year. From suspicious-looking heart attacks and strokes to gunshot and stab wounds, the Los Angeles County Department of Coroner saw them all. Everyone was welcome, no matter their race, religion, or political affiliation. Death accomplished something Mahatma Gandhi and other people of peace could never do: bring the world together.

The coroner's office never closed, either. Bodies rolled in, bodies rolled out. Death had no schedule.

Colin paced in the large, windowless autopsy chamber near the stainless-steel sinks. Like me, he wore powder blue scrubs, a hairnet, a disposable plastic face mask, and booties. This was his first postmortem exam as an LAPD detective. He nodded to me, clearly anxious (a rare state for him) behind that face mask.

There was a lot of activity in this room. One medical examiner was taking pictures of a tatted-up Crip who had been peppered to death by gunfire. Another ME was scrubbing up and preparing to examine a familiar-looking blonde (sitcom actress, maybe?) who had jaundice, bloody wrists, and what appeared to be a thing for sharp objects. Blondie had more scars than the gangbanger—scars beneath her boobs, armpits, ears, and chin. An eternal knife fight with a plastic surgeon.

I caught my reflection in one of the glass-front cabinets. At least, I *thought* it was me. Couldn't be sure with the hair cover and the face shield. I took a deep breath and exhaled—the new swipe of Noxzema beneath my nostrils wasn't working. I could still smell raw flesh and old blood mixed with Pine-Sol.

Brooks stood at the countertop, gathering scalpels, scoopers, and tweezers. A pair of scissors slipped from his grip and clattered to the orange tiled floor. He cursed, scooped up the scissors, then chucked them in the sink.

A naked Monique Darson lay on the stainless-steel table. Her limbs had relaxed as rigor mortis started to disappear. Brooks's assistant, Big

Reuben, a giant black dude plucked from the end zone of Cowboys stadium, was taking the last pictures of the girl—one of which I'd use for the family's notification. A blue body bag with MONIQUE DARSON written on the plastic sat on the only available examination table. Zucca would comb over the bag's insides in search of fibers or hair that had been left behind.

Brooks approached the table and said to me, "Didn't I just see you?"

I introduced Brooks to Colin. The pathologist barely acknowledged my partner's existence before asking me, "So what were you doing before you got the call?"

"At Krav Maga with Lena."

"Sy told me that Lena's there hunting for her next ex-husband."

I snorted. "Aren't we all?"

He reached for the hanging microphone and stated the date, time, and those in attendance. Then, he noted the girl's statistics—sixty-four inches, one hundred pounds, brown shoulder-length hair, and brown eyes. Then, he peered into those eyes. "Petechial hemorrhaging present in the conjuctival surfaces of the eyes." He stated that he was removing the Gucci belt, then said, "Two ligatures are present on the neck. Ligature A is the form of a V on the anterior of the neck. Ligature B is a bruise around the neck. Excessive hemorrhaging. Ligature A is right below the mandible and consistent with hanging. However, there is a lack of hemorrhaging, which indicates that the injury occurred postmortem."

He moved down to her torso. "Bruises on the sternum, right breast, and rib cage." He measured the length and width of each bruise.

Genitalia. "No evidence of external injury."

Arms and legs. "Abrasions along the wrist, biceps, and triceps."

Colin raised his hand.

Brooks clicked off the mike.

"What do you think made the scratches?" Colin asked.

Brooks, eyes still on those cuts, said, "Fingernails?" Then, he clicked on the mike and considered her left hand. "As we indicated earlier, the victim is wearing acrylic fingernails with yellow fingernail polish. The tips have been cut. On the right middle finger—that acrylic nail is missing."

Ankles. "Tattoo on the right ankle. Decorative letters spelling 'Baby Girl.'" And then, Brooks took a scalpel and made a Y incision from her shoulders to her abdomen. Big Reuben crunched through her rib cage with a tool that resembled gardening shears.

I jerked at the last crunch.

After Big Reuben removed the sternum, Brooks leaned closer to peer at the girl's internal organs. "No evidence of injury." Then, he extracted the heart, examined it for trauma, stepped to the countertop, weighed it, and cut a piece for microscopic examination. Then, he did the same for her lungs, liver, and kidneys.

He returned his focus to the girl's neck. He cut out her larynx, then pointed to a jagged bone just above her throat. It was covered in reddish tissue flecked with spots of purple. "The hyoid bone is fractured." He clicked off the microphone, then pointed to the bruises on her neck. "See how there's uneven hemorrhaging around the neck tissue? The belt wouldn't do that—the belt would've left even hemorrhaging. What you see here is manual strangulation."

"Why didn't anyone hear her screaming?" Colin asked, shaking his head.

"Probably because he got her right beneath the vocal cords," Brooks explained. "Her neck's not thick so that part probably happened very quickly. And just looking at the blood in the body cavity, I can see that there's no clotting. Again, that tells me that she died pretty quickly." He exhaled long and loud, and his mask fogged. "So the fun part: who wants to stay for the brain?"

I took a step back. "I've ODed on fun. But you'll remember to check out that possible skull injury?"

Brooks nodded. "Of course."

"I do have one more question before you break out the Stryker. How long has she been dead?"

For several moments, Brooks stood silent as he stared at the girl reposed before him. Then, he said, "The maggots I collected in the closet are now adult flies . . . So, she's been dead now for approximately twenty-six to twenty-eight hours."

I did the math in my head. "That means she was killed between midnight and two o'clock yesterday morning." I turned to Colin. "Which meant that she didn't write that suicide note you found on her phone. Whoever wrote it, wrote it fifty-one minutes too late." To Brooks, I asked, "And the apparent cause of death?"

"Asphyxiation due to strangulation." The pathologist's eyes met mine. "You were right, Lou. This is a homicide."

11

And she was *just* talking about Chi, too. Had told her friend Malia that he had been the best lover she had ever had. That once? He was so deep that the condom had come off and, like, afterward? She couldn't pull it out and had to drive to the student health clinic on campus and, like, have a nurse fish it out. That. Was. *Crazy!*

But after that night? He didn't call her again.

And she had been totally embarrassed and pissed and everything.

But then tonight happened. Okay. More like this morning. A four A.M. hook-up when she had class in three hours.

I must be on crack. But then sex with Chi? *Crack-tastic.*

Nikita didn't consider herself to be a beautiful woman. She was an ethnic mutt, long-limbed and tawny-skinned, with sharp cheekbones and a luscious mouth hiding teeth that were a little crooked. The retainer she wore at night would straighten them out. Until then, the teeth kept her humble—at nineteen years old, she already knew that she had the power to make grown men like Chi beg for mercy.

She smiles at her reflection in the golden doors of the hotel elevator. The Omni. Fancy. But then, Chi is rich and powerful, and she is Hott and deserves fancy.

A bellhop also stands in the car. He smiles and gazes at her, bottom to top.

Does he see through her pink trench coat? Does he see her red push-up bra, the one with the little black bows, and the tiny, red sheer skirt and . . . nothing else?

She winks at him, then purses her lips.

The bellhop blushes and gapes at the elevator doors.

Oh, yeah. He sees. And he knows why she's here.

The elevator stops. A bell dings and the doors open to the twenty-first floor.

She throws the hotel worker one of her sultriest looks, then says, "Sweet dreams."

His stare burns her ass long after the elevator doors close.

Alone now, Nikita's heart races as she sashays down the hallway in search of room 2109.

Will he, like, have Moët and that other stuff? *Paste? Pate?* Nasty but classy food a sophisticated woman would like, not some boring chick from Irvine studying education at Jesus-camp Chapman University. And she's just at Chapman because of her parents or whatever.

And here we are . . .

She takes a deep breath, wets her lips, and knocks twice on the door. *Maybe he'll make mimosas. And maybe he'll have strawberries. Big ones. Ooh! And Cool Whip.*

"It's unlocked," a man shouts from inside the room.

She opens the door and crosses the threshold. Bummer—he didn't choose a suite. Nice room, though. Big bed with thousands of pillows. Flat-screen television. A whirlpool tub in the bathroom.

Sweet.

Chi sits in the armchair at the windows, wearing suit pants and a blue, long-sleeved shirt. Behind him, the lights of Petco Park stadium shine.

She smiles as the trench coat slides off her body and lands on the thick blue carpet. "Someone order room service?" she coos.

Ohmygosh, that sounded so good!

His eyes move from her hips to her breasts and back to her face: "Long time no see," he says.

"And do you like what you see?" she asks.

He smiles and beckons her to come to him.

She takes one step and then another . . . another . . . until she stands over him.

His pupils are as big as pennies. And there's already white powder on his nostrils.

"You started the party without me?" she asks, fake pouting.

"Don't worry," he says. "I have everything you need. Sit."

Nikita straddles him, then leans back until her long hair brushes his knees.

"You miss me?" he asks, his voice thick, his fingers tracing her long neck.

She stiffens but nods: his hands are freezing and his fingers feel like sausages. Ugh.

"You're not scared, are you?" His crooked smile never reaches his eyes.

"I'm a big girl," she says. "I can handle what you got, baby." She bends forward to kiss him.

He grips her neck, keeps her from that kiss. "Still not scared?"

What was this? A hazing ritual? Why did she have to prove—?

"I asked you a question," he says, his hold tightening.

She squeezes out, "No," but now air comes by sips and gulps. Her heart beats double time. "Stop, baby. You're—"

Tighter.

And now, Nikita is on her back, on that thick blue carpet, with a view of the ceiling, most of it blocked by Chi's twitching, sweaty face.

Only Malia knew she was driving down to San Diego; and Malia won't worry if Nikita doesn't show up to their dorm room because—

Tighter.

She tries to push him off, to bat him away.

His free hand pins her left arm down and his knee pins down the right.

Tighter.

The light in the room . . . fuzzy . . . gray.

How long has she . . . ?

12

As I left the autopsy chamber with a photograph of Monique Darson in my hand, Brooks's Stryker saw buzzed to life. The tool sounded like a dentist's drill but louder, meaner. Even though I was thirty paces down the hallway, memory told me that I smelled hot-burning bone, that I heard the *pop* of the cranium separating like two halves of a honeydew melon. Memory can be a callous bitch sometimes.

Monique Darson's family needed to know that she had been murdered—it was four in the morning, though. Usually, horrific news was best delivered before breakfast, but not today. I couldn't do that to this family, who probably hadn't been concerned with her absence.

Growing up without Tori, I had freaked out every time the phone rang, every time someone knocked on our door. Would it be the police with news? Would it be Tori? Sometimes, it had been Detective Tommy Peet with an update—still no Tori. It had never been my sister knocking or calling. And it had never been my dad, who could have heard through the grapevine that his eldest daughter had disappeared and here he was, back from Wherever, to look for her . . . and to comfort me. No.

Some mouth-breather realtor had told Colin that the city of Glendale was just a twenty-minute drive over the hill to South Los Angeles. Genius didn't take into account . . . *Los Angeles*, with its overturned cement trucks, six-car fender-benders, and lost refrigerators blocking the left lanes of the freeway. And what about the road closures and the men working and the roving police chases? Unless the agent had meant twenty *football* minutes. Converted into real time, that would be . . . a six-hour drive. Sounded right.

The thought of driving all that way to Glendale and then, in three hours, driving back over the hill into Los Angeles, made Colin as weepy as a pastor's wife in a strip club. He kept staring at his car, and then, glowering at the foggy purple foothills to the north, back to the car, back to the hills, and on and on.

I watched Mr. Ready-Fire-Aim-Just-Do-It-Already for a moment, watched as his lips vanished and his eyes hollowed, watched as his inner Colin kneaded his sweater. Feeling charitable, I said, "Hey, you can shower and crash a moment at my place." Not waiting for his response, I climbed into the Porsche.

His face lit up as though I had just offered him a pot of gold and a Playboy Bunny with no gag reflex. And so he followed me home, past downtown, past the Jungle and Culver City, until we reached Cielo, my condo development just a stone's throw from the Pacific Ocean.

Three years ago, Greg and I had purchased a million-dollar three-bedroom, trilevel condominium right in the middle of this urban heaven On my salary, a million dollars was the same as a trillion dollars, but Greg had it like that: a six-figure salary, royalties from his graphic novels, no kids or ex-wives to pay. And he said that we would save in the long run since he worked only three blocks away. He claimed that a million dollars was a steal—this unit was detached, and at 3,200 square feet was larger than the average house. We had the Ballona Wetlands and the Pacific Ocean, a coffee shop, a dry cleaner, a sushi joint, and a market all around the corner. "And when the revolution begins," he had said, "you won't have to leave the block for milk and *uramaki*. Cielo truly is paradise."

It took an eleven-year-old girl dying after storing her mother's crystal meth in her vagina to make me sign the title. After catching that case, I had needed a retreat from evil, a Shangri-la far from nuts who lit loved ones on fire and drowned their babies in toilets.

Now, I pulled into my driveway at forty-five minutes past four in the morning. The sun's arrival was just an hour or so away, and the sky was still wet with marine layer. Light shone from a few windows but no televisions had started their whisperings of morning news and cartoons.

Colin, idling at the open garage door with a knapsack of fresh clothes, stretched and groaned as his muscles flexed. He closed his eyes and took a deep breath like a man who had been stuck all day in a musty elevator. "There's no circulation in Glendale," he said.

"I know: we stole the air when we stole the water." I pointed to his cowboy boots. "You gotta leave those shit-kickers out here. A happy home is one that does not smell of other people's death." Then, I slipped off my own shoes and carried them inside the house.

Greg's original artwork from his graphic novels and video games lined the walls. By the time Colin had wandered from the garage and through the game room, he had said "Wow" and "Hey, I played that game" about a hundred times. By the time we reached the guest room, he was in wide-eyed fanboy mode. "He illustrated all this?" he asked.

I nodded, annoyed with the cloaked goblins, big-titted Nazi hunt-resses, and zombie marines. I wanted Regular People's Art—fake Picassos sold at Ikea or real art found at those convention center shows, the ones where everybody's uncle had a booth and every painting looked Motel 6 ready. Alas, Greg's ego had hoarded all the wall space. Eleven years ago, when we had first met, I had found his creative confidence hella sexy. *Eleven years ago.*

"You should introduce me to your husband," Colin declared.

"Why?"

He shrugged and blushed and studied the charcoal sketch of a sexy she-elf. "I'm a cop—I could give him tips for making those games of his more realistic."

I stared at him—not only was I a cop, I was also married to the man. If he confabbed with *anybody*, it would be (and had been) me.

"I wanna do that consulting thing, you know?" Colin continued. "A lot of these games are all hat and no cattle, know what I mean? I wanna be the detective that Hollywood turns to. Makin' shit they come up with more real."

I sighed, then pointed to my left. "There's the bathroom. Towels are in the cabinet. If you need me, I'll be upstairs."

"So is that a no, you won't introduce me?"

"It's a 'there's the bathroom and towels are in the cabinet.'"

"Later then?"

As I turned to leave, Colin said, "Hey, Lou?" He was doing that squinty-eye-lip-bite thing that was supposed to get me all loose-limbed and fuck-friendly.

And with my shoes off like that, it was kind of working. "Yeah?"

"Thanks for not sending me over the hill."

I waited for more, but that was it. "Sure. No problem."

I left Colin to do his business and drifted to the kitchen to check voice mail: Mom (*Do I need to send out a search party for you?*), Syeeda (*Guess what I'm working on?*), and an automatic reminder from Arrowhead to leave my empty water bottles on the porch. No message from Greg, and it was now dinnertime in Japan. He couldn't have called before heading out for *teppanyaki*? What the hell was he doing?

You mean, who the hell is he doing?

Stop.

Where is he, then?

Working. In a meeting. Hasn't had the chance to call, is all.

Loafers in hand, I marched up the stairs to the sun deck and grabbed the can of Lysol that lived there. I sprayed three bursts of "clean linen" on the soles and the insteps, and then set the shoes on an Adirondack chair. Good footwear was the best tool I had, and I treated my shoes like a farm treated its best combine. Being a detective meant constantly walking, sometimes running, a lot of times stepping in blood that had the consistency of almost-there chocolate pudding.

Back to my room I went.

I slipped off my suit jacket, pants, and shirt for the second time in nine hours, then grabbed the bottle of Febreze from the nightstand. I gave my clothes a half-assed spritz, but changed my mind and shoved all of it into the bag of clothes that needed to be burned.

The bed was just as I had left it on Wednesday morning—tucked and neat. The cream carpet was free of charcoal pencils, little scraps of plastic wrapping, and Hawaiian Roll bread crumbs. More proof that Greg really wasn't home. I eyed *Heart of the Volcano*, my latest trashy romance novel waiting for me on the nightstand. But I had no time for fire priestesses and sexy gargoyles.

I padded to the walk-in closet. Since I didn't expect to encounter death again until the Darson case had ended or had been shoved to the back burner (like my other two cases) by a more exciting murder, I chose a linen, faux–St. John pantsuit and a yellow silk blouse. I glanced at the top shelf, at the document box stowed beneath a winter blanket.

I hung my outfit on the doorknob and pulled the box from its place. I held my breath as I slipped off the top.

Even though I had collected every report and statement that had been generated, Tori's case file was still as thick as a Pee-Chee folder on the first day of school. I had also taken Tori's senior yearbook and had found a copy of the school picture that Mom had given the police. There was also one newspaper clipping reporting her disappearance and a "Have you seen me?" flyer that had been designed by our church. For years Mom had kept Tori's things in our bedroom. Back then, Mom would always say, "Any day now, she'll be home." She signed the financial aid papers for Tori's first semester at Cal State Northridge and bought her a new knapsack. That first Christmas, she bought Tori a box set of Love's Baby Soft, a makeup bag, and blank cassette tapes. The presents sat beneath the tree, wrapped and waiting to be opened. Tori, of course, never opened them and those wrapped gifts disappeared on January 1.

Twenty-five years passed with no new developments or "aha" moments about Tori's disappearance. But I still hoped, even though that part of me was supposed to be extinct by now. After all this time, Tori's disappearance still hurt. On many occasions, Lena and Syeeda had asked me to talk about that first week without my sister. I would open my mouth to speak, but sorrow trampled clear thought. My eyes misted, my lips quivered, and defeated, I swallowed that pain. All I could offer them was a sad smile and a shake of my head. But on every November 12, Tori's birthday, they joined me and silently raised their glasses of wine to toast a woman they would never meet.

Greg: he was the only one who knew it all. And he was always the person sitting next to me on our bed on every July 17, waiting until I finished my conversation with Mom, holding me afterward as I cried and memorialized the day my sister disappeared. And before he had been pulled into the black hole that scientists had named It's All About Me, Greg had hired a private investigator to find my sister. The guy was a charlatan—he had sounded like a cop only because he had played one on TV.

Many cold cases have been solved because of the development of hadron colliders and new ways to split atoms. Maybe now, smart guys like Brooks and Zucca would pull a fingerprint off Tori's left-behind Nike. Maybe they could analyze that blood spot to see if it belonged to her or to the Bad Guy. Maybe . . .

I didn't open Tori's file—I knew that the first document there was the incident report taken by Detective Peet. The words there had been typed on an IBM Selectric with a worn ribbon. And now, time had stolen those words just as it had stolen the LAPD's interest. In that way, the monster who had taken my sister was winning, erasing her from all of life as though she had never existed. I would not let that devil enjoy this victory.

Beneath Peet's incident report was my witness statement—the ramblings of a frightened thirteen-year-old girl—along with the witness statements from Napoleon Crase, who had owned the liquor store, and from seventeen-year-old kids named Kesha Thompkins and Golden Lee, Tori's best friends.

I hadn't come face-to-face with Crase since that July afternoon, but I had cut out every article that mentioned him. I had taped those slips of paper into a notebook kept at my desk in the squad room—he didn't deserve to share a space in Tori's storage container, my only resting place for her. There had been the "good" stories about Crase—more stores purchased around the city, a car dealership opened, Man of the Year honors from churches and civic groups. And there had been the sordid stories: young women caught in compromising situations with him at parks and movie theaters, domestic disturbances between him and those girls now wearing layers of makeup and lipstick to hide the bruises, now taking it all back for jewelry, handbags, and another day aboveground.

It was an understatement to say that I saw Napoleon Crase in my sleep.

Kesha and Golden, though . . . I tried to recall their faces, but had no luck. Even though I recalled some of that day perfectly, my brain didn't want to remember all of Golden and Kesha. Fear killed memory, and sometimes I wondered if that day in July truly happened.

"Can I get something to drink?" Colin shouted from the kitchen.

I slammed the top back on the box as though he'd found me flipping through *Hustler*. "Yeah," I shouted back. "I'll be down in a minute."

Fifteen minutes later, I jogged downstairs showered, dressed, and smelling of Flowerbomb.

Colin stood in the den, bent before my bookcase as he read the books' spines. "*A Wicked Liaison, The Playboy Sheikh's Virgin Stable Girl, The Naked Duke* . . ." He squinted at me. "Didn't figure you for the cheesy romance novel type." He had changed into crisp khakis and a white long-sleeved Oxford shirt. His still-damp blond hair stuck to his scalp, and lather hid in his right ear.

"Virgin stable girls get my mind off murder," I said. "Coffee?"

"Please." He now stood before my wedding portrait. "He's a good-looking guy."

"Yes, he's aware," I said, rolling my eyes. Skin medium-toasted, pecan-colored eyes, barely there mustache and goatee, lopsided smile, six-foot-three, 215 pounds. Yes, Greg and the entire world had noted his looks. Then, they all told me that I was a lucky girl. Yep, as lucky as Nancy Reagan getting lost in Watts on New Year's Eve.

I glanced back at Colin and caught him staring at my ass—not in a scientific, detached "Oh, that's an ass" way. But in the "Damn, that's an ass" gaze that men sometimes lose themselves in. I wouldn't make anything of it since maybe it wasn't anything at all, just a look from a ho-hum-looking guy from Colorado. By his just looking, though, my hormones had startled awake and now jiggered through my bloodstream. Couldn't remember the last time I had caught a man admiring my body and me not being offended by his admiration.

So, I did the least erotic task I could manage: I busied myself with measuring water and coffee beans.

He picked up another picture, studied it, then slipped it back in its place. A moment later, he settled on a stool at the breakfast bar. "So when are you gonna tell me?"

I pointed at his right ear. "You have a little soap . . . When am I gonna tell you what?"

He swiped at the lather. "About your sister." He nodded back at the photos on the mantel. "Cute picture of you and her at Disneyland. Big ears, big smiles. How old were you?"

I paused in my step, then restarted. *Sugar, cream, spoons . . .* "I was seven. She was twelve. And who told you that I had something to tell about my sister?"

"Pepe."

I grabbed two mugs from the cupboard, then stared at him.

He had an expectant smile on his lips.

Seconds shimmied by. Coffee burbled into the pot. My stomach growled.

I pinched the bridge of my nose, then said, "There's really nothing to tell. We went to the liquor store that afternoon. She stole a pack of

Starbursts and got caught by the guy who owned the place, Napoleon Crase—"

"Of Crase Parc and Promenade?"

"The one and only," I said, pouring coffee into our cups. "Then, I ran home. Two hours later, my mother stepped through the front door and Tori was still gone. Mom went to go search for her, didn't find her, came back home to call the police and the cops kinda searched for her but . . ." I dumped one teaspoon of sugar into my mug. "I don't remember much about the scene at the liquor store. Her friends were there— they gave statements, but it didn't help."

"Who *is* this Crase character?" he asked.

"Back in the day, he owned only one store," I said. "Crase Liquor Emporium. It was in the torn-down plaza across the street from where we found Monique Darson's Lexus. Then, one store became two stores, then so on and so forth."

I told my partner about Crase's rise in Los Angeles' business world, and I also shared with him Crase's well-documented propensity to date girls young enough to be his granddaughters.

Colin took a sip of coffee, then said, "So, the bad guy gets rich, dates hot girls. Meanwhile, your sister stays missing and you and your family . . ."

I said, "Yeah," then swiped at my sweaty brow. "Umm . . . I don't wanna talk about this anymore." I waggled my head, then released a burst of air. "I'm hungry. You hungry?"

Colin stared at me for a moment before dragging out, "Sure."

Relieved, I yanked open the fridge and said, "I doubt we'll have time for a proper meal today." Hands shaking, I grabbed random items off shelves and pretended to be interested in domestic this-and-that.

So, Colin and I ate our American breakfast as penny-colored light blinked between the kitchen blinds, as the *tap-tap-tap* of joggers' shoes brought Cielo to life. Stuffing your face with bacon, eggs, and sourdough toast was always the most proper response to pain, right?

13

The Darson house was a slate-gray, two-story Spanish-style protected by a decorative wrought-iron fence. A red Maserati was parked in the driveway behind a black Toyota 4Runner and a white Toyota Prius. This neighborhood was a hybrid, too—some houses had been purchased by professionals who mowed their lawns and hosted church potlucks; while other houses were rented by Those People, families with dangerous-looking youths wearing long white T-shirts who sat on the porch all day, smoking cigarillos and chronic, getting shot on the regular, cursing so much you had to bring the kids in and give them baths to rinse off the neighborhood filth.

Earlier this year, I had visited Garthwaite Avenue. Work-related, of course. A fifteen-year-old gangbanger (also a father of two) had been murked on the sidewalk just four houses down from the Darsons.

Before we approached the front door, I clutched Colin's arm. "We will not tell them upfront that she's dead—they'd be too shaken up to tell us anything useful. And we will not mention the belt or the finger-nails."

Colin said, "Got it," and then finished crunching his mouthful of Tic Tacs.

I shifted the growing case file to my other hand and held my breath as I rang the door.

Like any cop, I hated family notifications. You never knew how folks were gonna react. In normal situations, they wailed and sobbed, pleaded with God and the LAPD for justice. In abnormal situations, families wanted to fight me, or they sat on the couch, sphinx-like, and said, "Oh. Okay."

Colin also took several deep breaths as we waited for someone to answer the door. His eyes shifted back to the sidewalk, to the golf club–wielding old couple walking their terrier, to the mother herding three young children into a minivan, and finally to the red Maserati sexing up the Darsons' driveway. The Mas was a fancy car for most neighborhoods, including this one.

A woman wearing a bus driver's uniform answered the door. She could've been my age or a bit older. A pink scarf covered her hair. Her lips, plum-colored from smoking, wore bread crumbs and a frown. She was not pleased that someone was ringing her doorbell so early in the morning.

I showed her my badge and introduced Colin and myself as homicide detectives.

The woman's scowl worsened. "What's this about?"

Colin glanced at me—had she not heard the word "homicide," the biggest clue to what this visit was about?

"Are you the mother of Monique Darson?" I asked.

"Yes," she said. "I'm Angie Darson. What's wrong?"

"May we come in?" I asked.

"Momma," a young woman shouted from inside the house, "who is it?"

Angie didn't answer her daughter and continued giving me the too-early-in-the-morning-for-this-bullshit stink eye.

I glanced past Angie and into the house at that young woman, who was about twenty-one or so, standing at the bottom of the staircase.

Whoever she was, she wore a fuchsia-and-gold Pucci scarf on her head and a silk robe covered in Dolce & Gabbana's logo. "Momma, what's going on?"

"Get your father," Angie said over her shoulder. After the girl had run up the stairs, Angie turned back to us. "What did she do? Is this about Derek?"

I offered a comforting smile, hoping that Colin would write "Derek" (the same "Derek" from Monique's suicide note?) into his pad as soon as possible. "This will be easier if you let us come in."

She stood there, though, unmoving, blocking our way as though we were vampires, thinking about what I was asking her to do. Finally, she sighed and stepped aside. Guess she had heard some sexy things about vampires. "I don't have much time," she snapped. "I'm already running late."

The house smelled of cigarettes, coffee, fried bacon, and toast. The morning news played on the newish LCD television bolted to the living room wall. Old crap was mixed in with new crap—a new leather sofa and love seat alongside a stained corduroy armchair; a new, antique-ish lamp placed atop a tired area rug with shedding tassels; a yellowing porcelain ashtray sitting on a new cherry coffee table. Someone had won the Showcase Showdown on *The Price Is Right*.

A man with long, graying dreadlocks came down the steps as he buttoned his blue uniform shirt. "What's happening?"

The young woman came down behind him and clutched his arm. "They're detectives." She was pretty: high cheekbones, large doe-brown eyes, and perfect eyebrows that looked drawn on. She was bosomy beneath that short D&G robe.

"Are you Monique Darson's father?" I asked.

"Monie?" he said. "Yeah. I mean, yes, Officer. Cyrus Darson."

Dual pearly scars ran like diagonal train tracks from the man's upper lip, across his nose, and into his thick hair. He'd had the locks and those scars for a very long time, and the scars, especially, made me wince—they had been mean and bloody and hydrogen-bomb hot on the day he'd received them.

I nodded at the young woman. "And is this Monique Darson's sister?"

Both father and daughter nodded. He said, "This is Macie, our oldest."

Angie aimed a remote at the television and the screen went black. She sat on the new sofa with her hands clutching her arms. Macie remained on the steps as Cyrus moved to the living room, offering Colin and me a place on the love seat before settling into the armchair.

I opened my leather binder and turned to Colin. *Ready?*

My partner nodded, steno pad in hand. *Time to plow the road.*

"When did you last see Monie?" I asked.

Angie tugged at her hair scarf. "Tuesday evening around six o'clock. I know it was almost six cuz my sister Jolene called. Monie was supposed to be babysitting for her and flaked out."

"Do you know what Monique did instead of babysitting?" I asked.

"She had a date, but she didn't tell me who she was going out with."

"How was her mental state when she left the house that evening?"

Angie scratched her left palm, then flexed her hand. "She was mad at me. We argued cuz she flaked on Jolene, and we said some nasty things to each other, and she drove off."

"Drove off?" Colin asked. "In what type of car?"

"A red Lexus," Macie said.

"Did she carry a purse?"

Angie nodded.

"Do you know what kind of purse?" Colin asked.

"Did somebody steal her purse?" Cyrus asked, eyebrows bunched in confusion.

"She had my red Dooney & Bourke," Macie said.

"Did she have any appointments back on Tuesday afternoon?" I asked. "Nail, hair . . . ?"

Angie shook her head.

Macie shook her head.

Cyrus was still trying to figure out if his daughter's purse had been stolen and that's why two homicide detectives had knocked on his door at seven in the morning.

"Any school event on Tuesday night?" I asked. "A pep rally or a game or . . . ?"

"No," Angie said. "She would have worn her uniform if there was a game. And anyway, she's out of high school."

"So she had on regular clothes, then?" Colin asked. "Because, as you said, she had a date that night."

Angie nodded. "She wore jeans, I think. And them boots that drive me crazy. It was hot as hell outside and she had on boots."

"So she goes on her date," I said. "And what did you do?"

"I ended up babysitting the kids and . . ." Angie reached for the pack of Kools on the coffee table. "Why are you asking us these questions?" She shook out a cigarette but didn't pluck it from the pack.

"I'll explain everything in a minute," I said, "but it's important that we ask a few more questions first."

"What about you, sir?" Colin asked Cyrus. "When was the last time you saw your daughter?"

"Around noon on Tuesday. I had a job out in El Segundo that afternoon. Monie was still in bed when I left."

"And what do you do for a living?" I asked.

"Electrician."

"What time did you get off?"

Cyrus paused, then said, "Umm . . . Around seven."

"You come home after?"

"No."

I waited for him to continue.

Cyrus licked his top lip, then said, "I got a bite to eat and umm . . . Went to have a few beers, and umm, played some pool, and then I came home."

"Around what time?" I asked.

He blinked. "Around two? Two thirty?"

I nodded, then turned my attention to Angie. "And you were . . . ?"

"Babysitting," she said. "Up until midnight."

"Monie," I said. "Is that Monique's nickname?"

Both parents nodded, and Cyrus added, "And we call her Baby Girl, too, cuz she's the baby of the family."

"Macie and Monie are five years apart," Angie volunteered. "When Monie was born, she was sickly—a heart murmur—so she got a lot of attention. Macie wasn't used to sharing space but she loves her sister. Makes sure she never lacks for nothing. Makes sure she never overtaxes herself." Angie looked over to the staircase and to Macie, who nodded—*yes, I take care of my sister, yes, I love my sister.*

"Other than Tuesday's argument," Colin said, "is Monique a good kid? Any behavioral problems?"

Angie gave a smile that warmed the room. "She's a wonderful child. Smart. She was captain of the cheer squad. She was valedictorian at graduation last week. She's going to Cal State Dominguez Hills to become a vet." She held up her hand and said, "Okay, stop. Cops just don't show up to people's front doors to hand out awards for good behavior."

My heart fluttered in my chest as I leaned forward. "There's no easy way to say this, so . . . Last night, a young woman was found murdered at a condo site over on Santa Rosalia Drive, near the old Santa Barbara Plaza. We believe she's your daughter Monique."

"*What?*" Angie took several quick breaths, Lamaze style. "No. Nuh-uh. No."

Cyrus shook his head. "Wait minute, wait a—I don't understand."

Macie understood immediately and covered her mouth with her hands.

I reached into the expandable file and pulled out the autopsy photograph of a very dead Monique Darson. I offered it to Cyrus Darson. "Is this your daughter?"

Cyrus took the photo and peered at the image. The picture shook in his grasp and he whispered, "Yes." He turned to his wife with drooped shoulders. "It's Monie."

Angie's breathing had become shrill, and now she was keening and rocking until finally crying out, "No! *No!*"

Macie flew into the living room and perched at her side. She threw her arms around her mother, but Angie wrestled out of her grasp. "No! Not my baby! Oh, God, no!"

Colin and I sat there in sad silence, noting every action the Darson family made. Studying them as though they lived in a tank and we had just added a bead of liquid mercury into their environment. We watched as Cyrus remained in the armchair like a tree trunk. We watched Macie comfort her mother and suggest that she go upstairs and lie down.

But Angie shook her head—she didn't want to lie down. She gasped for breath, swiped at the air as though wasps were attacking.

Macie ran to the kitchen, returning almost immediately with a handful of paper towels. She handed the bouquet to her mother, who then told her, "Go put some clothes on."

Macie nodded, considered us with despondent brown eyes, then jogged up the stairs.

"How did it happen?" Cyrus asked, now squeezing a chair cushion.

"We believe she was strangled to death," Colin said.

"What?" Angie shouted. "Who did it?"

"We're working to find that out, ma'am," Colin said.

Angie muttered, "No, no, no," and the tears started again. But she stopped. "Where's Butter? Her dog. When she left the house on Tuesday night, Butter was with her. Where's Butter?"

"The dog was not with your daughter when we found her." I remembered that line in the suicide note—whoever killed Monique had asked Angie and Cyrus to take care of the dog. "Can you describe Butter for me?"

Angie rose from the chair and stomped to the mantel. She pulled a picture out of its frame. "Here," she said, handing it to me. "She's a bichon frise."

It was the same dog found on the phone's lock screen.

"You said she was valedictorian?" I asked, trying to lead Angie back into safe territory.

"Excelled at everything," Cyrus said, waving his hand at all the commendations and awards on the walls. "She was supposed to start working at Trader Joe's next week."

I handed them a printed screenshot of the suicide note found on their daughter's phone. "Does this seem like something your daughter would write?"

Both parents read in silence. Angie shook her head, then grabbed matches from the coffee table. With shaky hands, she stuck a cigarette between her quivering lips and finally lit up.

Cyrus frowned. "I'm confused. You said she was strangled. Why would she write this?"

"I don't think she did," I said. "I think someone else wrote it so that we'd all *think* she committed suicide."

Cyrus hugged the chair cushion to his chest. "I don't understand. Who would do something . . . ?"

"Mr. Darson," Colin said, "do you have a good relationship with your daughter?"

Cyrus lifted his chin. "Absolutely. We're very close. I do everything for my girls."

"The Lexus," Colin continued. "Did you purchase that car for her?"

Angie frowned. "Do we look like people who can buy a child a Lexus?"

"Someone here drives a Maserati," I said, thumbing to the driveway. "And a Prius is not a Yugo."

Angie's lips tightened. "We didn't buy the car."

"I believe Von and Monie bought it together," Cyrus said. "V-O-N Neeley."

"And Von is her boyfriend?" I asked, scribbling the name into my binder.

"Yeah," Angie said. "His people got money. They live up in Ladera."

"Do you know of anyone who might want to harm her?" Colin asked.

"Everybody loves Monie," Angie whispered. "She's an angel, always doing good by people. Always helping out when she can. Nobody would ever want to hurt her."

Cyrus shook his head. "Derek would."

Angie glanced at him, then stared at the burning end of her cigarette.

"Derek Hester," Cyrus said to me. "He's a friend of hers. A gangbanger."

"Do you know from which set?" I asked.

"Black P Stones," Cyrus said.

Colin's writing faltered—he didn't know what the hell he was writing now.

"Were Derek and Monique romantically involved?" I asked.

Cyrus snorted. "Hell no. She was better than that thug. They knew each other from middle school. Well, when Derek *went* to school."

Colin flipped through his notebook. "Why do you think she went to the condos that—?"

"So do y'all know who did it?"

Macie stood on the stairs, makeup applied and dressed in red shorts and a white tank that sported the Chanel logo. Her long wavy hair, a weave but a damn good one, had been pulled into a ponytail. She stood there, knock-kneed, a life-sized Bratz doll.

"There are no suspects yet," I told her, then stood from the love seat. "But Macie, I'd like to talk to you outside for a moment." I turned to Colin. "Can you get the addresses and phone numbers for Derek and Von?"

A flush crept up Colin's throat—he was pissed that I was excluding him.

Boo-hoo.

I needed to know the real deal about Monique Darson, and Macie would never spill it in front of Colin or her parents. And I had a feeling that whatever she was about to tell me would tarnish Baby Girl's halo. But hell—who doesn't have a little scum on her wings?

14

Outside, the air smelled of car exhaust and wet grass. It was half past seven in the morning and the neighborhood was now awake. People who had jobs were driving to them, and people with kids were shepherding their little ones to cars and SUVs.

Macie sat on the hood of the Maserati. Her red shorts rode all the way up to there.

I didn't wanna look but those shorts were designed for looking. The "mom" in me wanted to yell, "Put on some damn clothes," but the cop in me, having seen worse, would say, "Meh, whatareyougonnado, kidsthesedays."

Macie placed her head into her hands. "I can't believe this," she was saying. "I can't believe . . . How did she die?" she asked as she tugged at her hair.

"She was strangled."

"No, no, no." Her body went rigid hearing that, but a wave of truth washed over her and knocked down that tightness until she bent forward, almost slipping off the car.

A car horn blew, and Macie peeked from her cocoon to see a Camry carrying little girls with braided hair. They waved at Macie as the driver—decidedly not smiling—sped toward Leimert Boulevard.

Macie forced her lips upward and waved back. "Auntie Jolene and my baby cousins," she said to me with tears in her eyes. "Monie was supposed to watch them on Tuesday night and . . . Who's gonna tell them that she . . . ?" She watched the Camry race to the end of the block, then dropped her head back between her knees.

I leaned against the 4Runner's tailgate, pen and pad ready. "Macie, I need to ask you some things that I didn't wanna ask in front of your parents. I'm old, but I haven't forgotten that young women have private lives, and so I need you to speak as freely as you can, okay?"

She sniffled, then said, "Okay."

"How old are you again?"

"Twenty-three."

Macie had been born the year I had learned to dissect a baby pig in Honors Biology.

"Do you work?" I asked.

She blinked—*work, as in the verb?*—then blurted, "I'm a tutor."

I had only known Macie Darson for thirty minutes, but in that short time, I knew that this girl was no Madame Curie. What subject did she tutor? How to Get Over 101? Advanced Methods in How to Get Paid? If so, maybe I would sign up for lessons.

"So Von and Derek," I said. "Let's stop the bullshit. What's really going on?"

The veil lifted from Macie's face and she gazed past me, checking to see if her parents were standing at the front door. "Monie was datin' both of them. But Mom and Daddy would never believe that their princess was sneakin' around with a banger. Church in the mornin' with Von, freaky-deak in the evenin' with Derek. Ain't nuthin' new," she said with a flick of her hand and another cautious look at the door.

"The difference between Monie and me," she continued, "is that I never hide my shit. Monie, though . . . That girl is a shadow. Von thought he was talkin' to the church girl cuz she was actin' all sweet, but little did he know that she was fuckin' Derek while talkin' on the phone with him." Her shoulders slumped as any remaining lightness left her body. "Is that what you wanted to know, Detective?"

"For starters? Yes. How old is Derek?"

"About twenty-two. Von just turned nineteen two weeks ago."

"He like cheerleaders?"

"What man *don't* like cheerleaders?" she asked with a smirk.

"What about Derek? Did she wear her uniform whenever she saw him?"

Macie tilted her head. "Think about it."

And so I did. "Her uniform has blue in it," I said, and Macie nodded. A tried-and-true Blood would never fancy anything blue, cute girl or not.

"What type of guy is Von?"

She faked a yawn. "A guy who thinks cheerleading is a sin. A guy who hated that she was the squad captain."

That made me pause. How much did Von hate it? Did he detest cheering enough to ask her to wear that uniform on Tuesday night so that he could show her just how much he hated it?

"Did Von know about Derek?" I asked.

"He knew Derek and Monie are friends. Just not how *close*. He figured cuz he has some ends and goes to church that he don't have to worry. Every nigga gotta worry. He's kinda cute in that buttoned-up-music-minister way so he thinks he has a lock on Monie. He don't suspect nothing. And Monie likes that."

"When did you last see your sister?" I asked.

She squinted at the sky, then slowly shook her head. "I'm not even sure . . . She was always runnin' behind me. She'd always pop up outta nowhere."

"Were you home on Tuesday?"

"No. So I must've seen her on Friday cuz me and my boyfriend drove to Pechanga Casino in Temecula. So yeah, I saw her on Friday. But she called me all weekend and then on Monday and Tuesday."

"Why?"

"Random sister stuff. 'Can I wear your shirt?' or 'Do you have so-and-so's number?' Stuff like . . ." A sob burst from her chest, and then another. Her shoulders shook as she hid her face in her hands and wept. Through her tears, she kept apologizing, kept wiping her face with a tired paper towel until the hurt ebbed. "This is hard," she said, offering me a weak smile. "I can't believe this is happening."

"I know. You're doing good. Just a few more questions, okay? Did she mention seeing either Derek or Von this past weekend?"

"Umm . . ." She inhaled but didn't release, bit her bottom lip to keep it in. She hugged herself, forcing out the air, then said, "She was plannin' to break things off with Derek on Tuesday. She was tired of only hangin' out in BPS territory. Can't go here cuz you'll get shot. Can't go there cuz you'll get shot. She wanted a regular boyfriend like Von but not so . . . *boring*."

"So she wanted a yuppie thug," I confirmed. "Was she scared what Derek's reaction would be when she told him that she wanted out?"

Another cry broke from Macie's chest like a clap of thunder.

The suddenness startled me, and I almost dropped my binder.

"I told her to hold off," the young woman said between tears and hiccups. "I told her that Derek would probably be in jail before the summer ended, and that she'd have a better chance at breaking up with him then." She hid her face in her hands and cried, "I miss her so much."

I patted her back, remembering my mother's hands lost in my hair as I had cried, "I miss her," and "I'm sorry, Mommy." I remembered never feeling better afterward, and sometimes, never feeling forgiven.

Macie dried her face with the front of her fancy tank top. "I'm sorry. It's just . . ."

"You don't have to apologize," I whispered, staring at the makeup smeared across the Chanel logo. "It's okay. Take your time."

She exhaled and jiggled her arms, shaking it off. "I gotta be strong for Momma."

Familiar words.

"What about your dad?" I asked. "He'll need you, too."

"But he's . . . weak. Always a little jittery, know what I mean? Momma's the backbone of the family. If she goes down, we all go down. My dad, he's not a man like that." She clamped her hand over her mouth, then squeezed her lips. "I didn't mean . . . I shouldn't have said . . . It's just . . ." She groaned, then hugged herself. "I love my dad, but my mother . . ." Her nostrils flared as she fished for the right word. "You know what I mean, right? Please don't tell him what I just said."

I nodded.

"Ain't strangulation a crime of passion?" she asked. "I saw an episode on *CSI* where this stripper was strangled, and the murderer was her ex-boyfriend."

"It can be," I said, "but not always. Do you think that's what happened here? You think Derek killed Monie? Tell me the truth."

She squinted at me, then lifted her mouth into a stingy smile. "That's a nice ring you wearin'." She nodded at my princess-cut diamond engagement ring. "What's that? Like three carats?"

I nodded. "Your appraisal skills are impressive."

She gave me a fake smile. "Your man a true baller or is he just nigga-rich?"

"A true baller."

"He black?"

"That's the box he checks."

She gave a side of fake chuckle to go along with the fake smile. "You don't know what it's like," she said, a sneer forming on her lips. "You ain't from around here."

"Actually, I grew up on Hillcrest, over in the Jungle. Went to Audubon and Dorsey."

"So you know," she said, shaking her head. "You don't snitch and you don't drop dimes on niggas. Especially if that nigga is BPS."

I leaned closer. "But I'm already looking at Derek for this. All I need from you is an endorsement, a 'Yeah, that fool is crazy, he coulda strangled my sister cuz he didn't want her to leave him.' That's all." I offered a conspiratorial smile and whispered, "Derek was on my list—and I'm sure his phone number is in Monique's phone directory. And I'm sure there are pictures of him, too, on that phone. He was a part of her life, Macie, and your family wouldn't be the only source for me to find that out."

She swiped at her forehead, nervous now, eyes darting up and down the street as though a hooptie filled with twenty Black P Stones toting forty Tec-9s was two houses away.

"Time is passing, Macie," I said. "Your sister's killer is getting farther and farther away." And the type on the reports was already degrading.

Finally, the young woman whispered, "Yes. He could've strangled her. Yeah. He coulda killed her."

"Okay. What about Von?"

"Church boy?" Anxiety lifted enough for Macie to roll her eyes. "That boy goes to confession every time he has a wet dream."

"Did she say *where* she was going to meet Derek on Tuesday?"

"She said something about going to Kingston's."

"The Jamaican restaurant over in Ladera Heights?"

She nodded. "She didn't wanna be alone with him. Not that crowds ever stopped Derek from actin' a fool."

"How do you think she ended up at the condos?"

Macie tried to square her shoulders, but her lips quivered and gave away the show. "I don't know."

"Tell me about Butter."

A smile as bright as the sun washed across her face. "Monie takes

Butter everywhere. She loves Butter. We all love Butter. She's the sweet-est dog in the world." But the smile dimmed as she closed her swollen eyes. "And now, she's gone, too. Miss Butter was the nicest gift Derek ever gave my sister."

"I have a more difficult question," I whispered. "What was your re-lationship with Monique? Any competition? Any jealousy?"

Macie folded her arms, but then rubbed her hand over her heart. She bit her lip, conflicted by what she needed to say.

"Please be honest with me," I said. "That's the only way I can solve this."

She jammed her lips into a grim line and breathed loudly through her nose. "You got a sister?"

My tongue thickened in my mouth. "Yes, I do." *Dead? Alive? Don't know. Please don't ask.*

"Then, you know how it is," Macie said. "We fight over triflin' shit all the time now. She eats up all my strawberries or won't put on a new pa-per towel roll. She calls me all day, literally *all day*. Sometimes, she needs advice. Sometimes, she wants me to be the referee between her, Mom, and Dad. Sometimes, she wants me to drive her and her girls places. And she gets mad if I tell her no. Like *I'm* a bitch for not wanting to be a chauffeur for some high school kids."

"My sister—" *Was I gonna do this?* "My sister was five years older than me and she was a cheerleader and she hated me most of the time."

Macie laughed. "Cuz little sisters are freakin' annoying. Mom keeps sayin' that we'll be friends once we're older—"

"My mother said the same."

Her smile dimmed. "But I'll never know that, huh?"

I shook my head. Nor would I.

"Your parents say they gave Monie a lot of attention."

Macie stared at her shaking hands. "I was cool with that as I got older. She was the baby, the hope of the family." She tugged at her soiled, damp tank top. "Me and Mom used to be really close when I was a kid. She used to take me to Baskin-Robbins over by the mall for ice cream every day after she picked me up from school."

"No more ice cream dates after Monie was born?"

Macie shook her head. "She was sick so she cried a lot. It just got too stressful. We stopped doing a lot of stuff cuz Monie couldn't deal with the situation and Mom couldn't deal with Monie."

"If she was the hope of the family, what were you?"

Macie pointed to her chest, then pushed out a laugh as hollow as a PVC pipe. "I'm the one who needs to marry a rich man. Whatever." But sparks had flown from her eyes, so not "whatever."

"I'm used to my parents treating us different," she said, eyes softening again. "I mean, I'm sure your parents do, too. One kid is always difficult and the other kid is Little Miss Perfect. Except Monie ain't perfect. She likes being two people. All presto-chango, today I'm nice, tonight I'm nasty." Macie frowned and her eyes turned dark and hard. "No. She ain't perfect. Guess being a shadow is catching up to her."

15

After Cyrus signed a consent form to allow Colin and me to search Monique's bedroom, we followed him and Angie up the stairs and down the hallway. This part of the house still smelled of hot water and soap from a recent shower, and a tinny laugh track from *The Nanny* drifted on top of the steam. The sound was coming from a bedroom with a queen-sized mattress and rumpled blue comforter.

We reached a room at the end of the hallway.

"This is her . . ." Angie moaned, collapsed against the wall, then staggered back to the staircase.

Cyrus stood there, staring at his daughter's bedroom door.

"We'll let you know if we have any questions," Colin told him.

"And we'll also let you know if we need to take anything," I added.

Cyrus said, "Okay," but didn't move.

Colin and I doubled down and didn't move, either.

Cyrus's eyes widened. "Oh. Okay. Sorry." He crept back down the hallway, throwing one last glance at us before descending the stairs.

Colin and I gawked at each other—*was that as strange as it seemed?*—then stepped into the bedroom.

It could have been the room of any well-achieving teen girl in America, with dark brown ceiling beams and pink walls covered in posters of Ludacris and Jay-Z, puppies and Black Jesus holding a lamb. The bed had been made, and folded laundry sat atop the pink-and-blue comforter, waiting to be put away. A vase of wilting white roses sat on the nightstand and made the room smell like a funeral home. A deflating foil "Happy Graduation" balloon had floated to the corner near the window and now bobbed on an air current. Blue and yellow pompoms and yellow honor cords, still stiff and bright, hung from a white board filled with a to-do list for the week of June 10. *Go to dry cleaner. Get vacc. for Butter. Smile—Jesus Loves You!*

My head swirled and my heart felt pinched in my chest. Tori's room—*our* room—hadn't been as nice as this. On the day she never came home, a *Right On!* magazine had been left on her bed, turned to the centerfold: LL Cool J. A bag of green apple Jolly Ranchers sat on the pillow, and a half-eaten can of Pringles sat on the milk-crate nightstand. For days, weeks, Mom and I had left it all there. Then, one day, I came home from school and the magazine, chips, and candy had disappeared. And I cried.

And now, here I stood, in another girl's room, tugging at my ear as though it would give milk, my sister still a question mark . . . Did she know that LL Cool J and Ice Cube were now respectable men, actors and daddies?

I chuckled.

"What's funny?" Colin asked.

I shook my head. "Just remembering." My gaze on that lonely balloon, I said, "Ready?"

Colin, his eyes on the roses, said, "Yeah."

Then, we both took deep, deep breaths.

He started searching the closet.

I turned toward the desk.

A pink netbook sat on a tray crammed with photos, paper clips, and a small ferret desk calendar. Beneath it was a yearbook for the St. Bernard Vikings.

I opened the pages and in just minor browsing saw that Monique had been class president, cheer squad captain, and Most Likely to Save the World. The slick pages had been filled with well-wishes from friends. *Never forget me. K.I.T. LAYLA. BFF.* The quote beneath her senior portrait: "The race is not to the swift, nor the battle to the strong . . . but time and chance happeneth to all."

Time and chance: What would Tori be if she'd had the chance to fully run her race? Would she be a psychologist today, like she had planned? Or would she be a stay-at-home mom with lots of kids and photos of her days as Most Popular on mantels and key chains?

Someone had turned off *The Nanny*, and now the only sounds in the house were Angie Darson's muffled cries.

I opened the desk drawer.

A phone charger, pens, cherry ChapStick . . .

Where is it? There has to be one . . .

My eyes swiveled from the lamp to the mattress, from the bedside table to the . . . *bed*.

I grabbed the purple unicorn Pillow Pet that lay against the headboard.

It was heavier than what a purple unicorn Pillow Pet should be.

I unzipped the cushion and stuck my hand into the stuffing. *Yep*.

I pulled out a pink satin–covered journal.

The lined pages were filled with neat cursive and stuffed with ticket stubs, scraps of paper, pressed flowers, a picture of a handsome kid with a big smile standing in front of a church van, and another picture, this one of a naked man, all muscles and menace, tats and scars.

Back to searching the desk.

An enrollment packet from Cal State Dominguez Hills. Random sticky notes, store receipts, and gum wrappers. A framed picture of newborn Monique strapped in a carrier with a five-year-old Macie dressed in panties, kissing her little sister's forehead while placing her hand over Baby Monique's mouth.

I searched the dresser drawers next.

Underwear, shirts, shorts . . . nothing unusual.

My stomach muscles relaxed, and I let out a long breath. In another investigation and search of a thirteen-year-old's room, I had found a vibrator in the girl's nightstand, along with pictures of her and her father doing shit that was illegal in every galaxy on this side of the sun. And after my sister had disappeared, Mom had found rubbers and two unsmoked jays in Tori's hope chest. The condoms and joints didn't make Mom cry as much as the framed picture of our deadbeat dad, also discovered that day.

"Any luck?" I asked Colin.

He had pushed hangers from one end of the closet to the other and was now searching the top shelves. "Nope. I gotta say, though. Girls own a lot of—" A Timex watch box fell from the shelf to the carpet. The top popped off.

Colin plucked a cloth from the box and fluffed it out. "Just a handkerchief." It was all white . . . except for a large yellow stain in the middle.

I narrowed my eyes. "Why put a dirty handkerchief in a box?"

He considered the cloth, then winced. "What's this stain?" he asked, waggling the hankie. "I'll give you three guesses, even though you'll only need one."

I grinned. "Cleanup on aisle 4."

He nodded. "But who's the lucky guy? Von or Derek? Or is it some even older dude she was banging on the DL and was keeping evidence of, just in case?"

"Just in case of what, though? That shit got real and she needed ammo?"

Colin whispered, "Cyrus?"

"Possibly. Or like you said: some other old guy who has a cheerleader fetish."

"I'll bet you a Code Four that this stain ain't snot." He stuffed the hankie back into the box and placed the top back on. "I say we take it. Test it. Just in case."

Like any cop, I liked free lunches, but I wouldn't take Colin's bet.

Because I knew that he was right.

I would tell Cyrus and Angie that we were taking the netbook and the diary. But I would "forget" to mention the soiled handkerchief. I didn't know what that stain was about but I did know that it had OH SHIT splashed all over it.

16

It was a little after nine o'clock when I pulled into a parking space in the station's garage. As I ducked into the building, I squinted up to the sky: the sun was out and doing its job. The squad room was crackling with quiet energy. Luke Gomez sat at his desk with a cell phone to his ear, three-hole punching reams of reports and sweet-talking a woman who may or may not have been his wife, Lupita. Joey Jackson was flossing his teeth while flipping through a stack of fingerprints. As he slid string between his back molars, he said something like, "Search *wahai* for *gwah* trailer's on your *gwehk*."

The room stank of Luke's seven-dollar cologne and sludge only cops called coffee. An open box of Krispy Kreme donuts sat near that pot of so-called java, and from the looks of Luke's belly and sugared mustache, he had eaten at least five of the dozen.

Peter "Pepe" Kim, the tallest Korean-Mexican American in South Los Angeles, was filling in the board—squares of old and new murders and the names of dicks who worked them as well as a few new cases awaiting the assignment stork. All those victims' names—red ink for unsolved, black for solved—and ways they had died, you'd think the Apocalypse was in full swing. Nope. Just another year in the city.

It had almost been fifteen hours since I had caught the Monique Darson case and time was chipping away. My nerves always started to ping around eighteen hours in, so I needed to make some progress before I stroked out. The more time passed, the more witnesses forgot and the more people grew reluctant to talk. How far you got in the first forty-eight hours helped determine whether you would be taking victory laps or playing a sad trombone. But Monique Darson had lucked out today—the A-Team would be searching for her murderer. Each of us turned cases upside down, inside out, and then magnified them to

200 percent. Not to brag, but I had solved 90 percent of the investigations I had led. Pretty good for a girl.

Colin, seated at the desk next to mine, was nibbling on a glazed donut. He licked at the flecks of sugar on his lips and said, "Better get one before Gomez takes it."

The search warrant for the construction site trailer sat near my keyboard . . . which sat near a vase of purple roses. The flowers didn't fit in the squad room with its old computers, raggedy space heater, and the men. But then, neither did I. "So, Cyrus Darson," I said. "What do you think he's hiding?"

Colin snorted. "What do you mean? You don't believe the late-dinner-beer-and-pool alibi?"

"There were a lot of 'umms' in that timeline."

"Think he's getting a little on the side?"

"He's a man, ain't he?" I plucked the small white card from the bouquet.

I miss you. Sorry I've been AWOL. I'll do better. GAN

Oh, crap. There it was.

Greg had sent creamy brown roses when he had been cheating on me with Amarie. And when I had busted him texting her while he was supposed to be watching *Letterman*, he upgraded my Ford to the almighty Porsche. Purple roses . . . Who was the lucky whore now? And what would he buy me next? A space shuttle?

I had last talked to Greg yesterday afternoon around three. He had reminded me to send in the car insurance payment. Then, he had yawned loud and long, and begged off talking because he needed sleep. I had said, 'I love you,' and he had said, 'I'll call you later,' and now I wanted to tear up this new card, drive home, collapse on the couch, and have an ugly cry while eating Doritos and watching *Ghost*.

Right now, though, I only had access to the last two donuts in the Krispy Kreme box. And so, I sat at my desk killing myself with delicious pastries, listening to the frantic pleas of the cuckolded wife within demanding that I Do Something! I wanted to tell her to get bent—hell, I *was* doing something. I was eating.

Lieutenant Rodriguez must have sensed my repressed distress because he charged into the room as I picked up donut number two. He plucked it from my fingers and bit the glazed in half. Then, he shouted, "All right, fellas. Let's have a seat."

Chairs scraped, notepads opened, and all eyes fell on me, the lead detective for *Who Killed Baby Girl?*

I leaned against my desk and cleared my throat. "So . . . A woman is in the delivery room giving birth—"

Laughter filled the room.

Lieutenant Rodriguez rolled his eyes. "Ha-ha, Lou. Let's get serious."

"At least let her tell us the punch line," Luke whined.

I settled on top of the desk, then said, "So the woman says, 'I'm just glad it didn't bark!' "

The room exploded with laughter again. Gallows humor.

I waited for the room to quiet before saying, "My Jane Doe is actually Monique Darson, seventeen years old, just graduated from St. Bernard's last week." Then, I gave a brief rundown about who we had talked to and all we had discovered—strangled with a belt, nails cut, abandoned Lexus, strange suicide note, family notified . . . "Anybody know about any similar cases?"

"Down in San Diego," Pepe said, "they found a college kid in a hotel room."

"Strangled?"

He nodded. "Kinky shit, though."

"Black girl?"

"Not through and through."

"What was she wearing?"

"A bunch of nothin'."

"Was a cheer uniform a part of that nothin'?" I asked.

"Nope."

"Nice hotel?"

"The Omni."

"Well, that's swankier than a condo on the edge of the ghetto," I said.

"I don't think it's related," Colin said, tapping the side of his shoe with a pen.

Pepe and I gave each other the eye.

Lieutenant Rodriguez said, "Keep your finger on it, Kim." To me, he said, "Do you have an idea of who done it?"

I shook my head. "I'd say someone close to the victim, though. She had two boyfriends—both at extreme ends of the spectrum. And the church boy is just as good for this as the gangbanger."

"And she was wearing her high school cheerleader's getup when we found her," Colin added. "And we wanna know why."

"Well, we probably already know *why*," I clarified. "I'm thinking typical role-playing. Submissive character dominated by a partner who likes 'em young and virginal."

"And maybe she realized at the last minute that she was out of her league," Luke said.

I nodded eagerly. "And she freaked out. Did something that made him go cuckoo for Cocoa Puffs, and that was that. Whoever did her? Dude has a temper a mile long and an extraordinary mean streak. And he knows that what he did was wrong—"

"Which is why he made it look like a suicide," Colin added. "And whoever he is didn't mind leaving behind that $300 belt."

"So he's got some ends," Pepe observed.

Colin and I nodded.

I told them that we would talk to *everyone*, even the seemingly innocent ones like Von Neeley the Church Boy. "We don't want the jury a year from now having reasonable doubt because we didn't talk to the butler who, two years before, had killed Miss Marple in the library with a candlestick holder."

"You mean, like the case Joey screwed up?" Luke said with a smile. "Y'all remember: the guy who kept taking dumps outside the home ec window over at Manual Arts, then ended up killing the home ec teacher."

"What?" Colin said, with a reluctant grin. "You're kiddin', right?"

A flush colored Joey's neck. "The kids in the class said it was a fat Mexican guy with glasses. Was I supposed to question every fat Mexican with glasses?"

"Is you is or is you ain't a detective?" Luke asked.

"Never mind that," Lieutenant Rodriguez said. "Just don't fuck up—that's the lesson here."

And then, it was time to hand out assignments.

Joey would retrieve school and medical records.

Luke would pull Monique's phone records, including texts, e-mails, call lists, and bills.

Pepe would set up a tip line and look for any similar crimes in the Crenshaw area. He'd also design the reward flyer, the one with a nice picture of Monique Darson and the offer of $1,000 for information that led to the bad guy's arrest.

Colin would manage the murder book and serve as the liaison between us and forensics.

Besides keeping my hand in everyone's cookie jars, I would get a warrant to examine the Darsons' finances. Monique may have shared a bank account with her parents, and weird financial shenanigans could have precipitated her murder—maybe she had withdrawn a large amount of money from the ATM on the night she was killed.

The group disbursed and Colin grabbed the book from my desk to log in the diary, the netbook, and the soiled hankie found in Monique's closet.

I pulled from the expandable file the plastic bag that held Monique's journal—I'd read it in a quieter moment.

Before leaving the room, Lieutenant Rodriguez stopped by my desk and whispered, "You okay on this?"

I scrunched my eyebrows as I shuffled papers around. "Why wouldn't I be?"

"Don't play me, Lou," he said, straightening the yellowing picture on my cubicle wall: Tori and me at the Redondo Beach Pier. "First sign that there's a conflict of interest—"

"I'll bail. Got it. No need to worry. I will treat Napoleon Crase just like I'd treat anyone else who may have possibly last seen my sister before she mysteriously disappeared and now may be involved in the death of someone else's sister." And then I smiled and gave him a thumbs-up.

He eyed me for a moment, frowned, then plinked a rose. "Aw, shit. Again?" He shook his head and wandered over to the empty donut box.

I grabbed the telephone and held my breath as I punched in a number.

She answered on the first ring. "Well, hello, stranger."

"Mom, I talked to you three days ago." I began to fill out a warrant request for the Darsons' bank records.

"Since I'll be leaving the country next week," Mom said, "I wanted to talk to you. But can I call you back? Martin and I are heading out for our walk."

"Yep."

"Breakfast tomorrow at the marina?"

"Uh-huh."

After "I love you" and "I love you, too," I hung up and finished the warrant request. Then I scribbled *Derek Hester BPS* on a sticky note. Pulled another note: *f-up on Q-tips, rape kit*. And another note: *talk w/tech re computer*. Each sticky went on the frame of my computer monitor.

Then, I typed *Derek Hester* into the crime database's search bar. In his latest mug shot, Derek wore cornrows as neat as a ten-year-old girl's. He didn't smile—but they never smiled. He had the shoulders of a linebacker and sleepy-looking eyes, which had earned him the nickname Sleepy D. He had seven pages worth of priors: from possession of drugs and guns to trespassing, battery, and robbery. He had done a little time at State in Lancaster for dealing, for corrupting a minor, and for a robbery-carjack combo plate.

My body groaned in advance. This visit would require a police radio, a Kevlar vest, a gun in my side holster, and a gun in my ankle holster. Fortunately, the thermometer would just hit a high of sixty-nine degrees today so only a creek of sweat would pour down my back and into a vest that wasn't washable, so it stunk. While I could deal with the reek of a three-day-old corpse, body odor from living people (me included) set me off like a fire alarm.

In his latest dance with the law, Derek had been stopped for running a red light and possession of marijuana. These probation violations had landed him in Men's Central. He had also been dating Monique Darson, a girl under the age of eighteen. And now a *dead* girl under the age of eighteen. But I wouldn't pull the statutory rape card until I needed to hold him for something bigger and deadlier. He had been released from jail a week before Easter and now lived in an apartment on Coco Avenue in the heart of the Jungle. No chances of recidivism there.

"Were there gangs in Colorado Springs?" I asked Colin, who was now three-hole punching a report for the murder book.

He nodded. "Crips, Bloods, a large Mexican gang, and a motorcycle club. Most of them were on the east and south sides."

"You worked west side, right?"

He held up his hands. "Hey, I went where I was assigned." He pointed at the roses. "Those from your husband?"

"Um-hmm."

"Pretty."

"Yes. Very pretty."

He let himself smile for a second, then said, "Zucca Super-Glued the phone and got some prints. Nothing good on the belt, though." When heated, Super Glue fumes adhered to the amino acids found in fingerprints. But this technique was a one-shot trick—if it failed, there were no do-overs. "So now what?"

"AFIS," I said. Automated Fingerprint Identification System. "But that doesn't get me hot. A suspect can explain away his prints—houses are filled with random fingerprints from repairmen, from second cousins, the Pope . . . Semen, though. That handkerchief? *That* gets me randy." I scribbled Derek's address onto a sticky and stuck it inside my binder.

Colin leaned over and tapped Derek's image on my monitor. "So we're having high tea with this guy today?"

"The highest. First, though, I need you to take the laptop and the handkerchief down to forensics. Come back here and we'll drive over together to the Jungle. Make sure you wear your vest—seems Mr. Hester has a quick temper and is known to carry a gun or three."

"Are we gonna call first or just show up?"

"Show up," I said. "Just like the folks from Publishers Clearing House. We'll skip the balloons and big-ass check, though."

Colin leaned back in his chair. "How the hell does a Catholic-school girl on the honor roll get mixed up with a banger?"

"She wanted to walk on the wild side," I said, staring at the purple roses sent by a man who had seemed so . . . *safe.*

Hate to say it, but my sister had more bangers inside of her than the county jail. When she was only sixteen, Tori had dated a Gramercy Crip nicknamed Baby Buddha (he was a quarter Korean). When Baby Buddha was killed on the corner of La Brea and Jefferson, she hung with Big Ant, another Gramercy Crip who had been a preacher's kid in his former life. Mom never had a clue—or maybe she did and had just ignored it, considered it a "phase."

Some girls made it out of this "phase" and went on to marry CPAs, history teachers, and IT guys. But some girls, girls like Tori, girls like Monique, died before seeing the light.

17

On the afternoon of July 17, 1988, Tori collapsed next to me on the living room couch. "I'm bored. This is stupid." She sucked her teeth and threw a cushion to the carpet. "Mom is a straight bitch for making me stay home with you."

Mom had agreed to teach summer school because we needed the money to buy new tires for the car and to pay off a ridiculously high phone bill, courtesy of my big sister. Unfortunately, in the last three days, two guys and a girl had been shot within a three-block radius of our apartment, and Mrs. Kelley from apartment 3 had been raped in our laundry room. Mom, rightfully concerned, had prohibited Tori and me from leaving the house, and she called every two hours to make sure that we hadn't snuck out.

"What do you wanna do?" I had asked brightly. "We can play Monopoly. Or we can watch TV." I didn't mind being trapped at home—I was hanging out with my big sister. She rarely played board games now, and she didn't watch much television with me because she hated every show I liked.

She narrowed her eyes, and said, "You know what tomorrow is, right?"

I nodded, then chewed on my bottom lip. "But . . ." I slowly inhaled, then little by little, let that breath leave my lungs. "Mom will get mad if she finds out," I whispered. "She'll ground us like she did last year."

Tori slung her arm over her head, then raised her other arm, the one that held the gold wristwatch Dad had given her for her thirteenth birthday. "This is what I think of Mom finding out." Her middle finger jabbed the air. "We have the right to celebrate his birthday. So what, he left us? He's still our father. We're still his kids."

"We don't have enough eggs," I said in a small voice. "So we can't make a cake."

She let her arm drop, and then she sat up. "We can still sing 'Happy Birthday,' though."

And so we sang, loud and clear, to the man who had helped make us but hadn't stuck around to see us work.

With that over, Tori and I settled back into the Land of Yawn.

"I have another idea," Tori said, smiling at me with sharp little teeth. "Let's go to the store for some Twinkies. Daddy likes Twinkies."

My heart hammered. My hand found my right earlobe. "Go to the store down the hill?"

"No, Lulu. The store in the bathroom." She rolled her eyes, then snapped, "Yes, Elouise, the store down the hill." She saw that I had started tugging on my ear, so she added, "Don't worry. We'll be home before she calls again. We're just going down the hill. That's, what, fifteen minutes?"

"But what if something happens?" I asked, tugging my ear harder. "And Mom doesn't want you going into another store without her after you . . . you know." I swallowed, then added, "The earrings and that bracelet."

Tori sucked her teeth. "This is different. I boost shit in Crase's store all the time. He's too busy watching girls' asses to pay attention to what I do."

"But—"

"If you're scared," Tori mocked, "just say so. You scared, Lulu?"

Two minutes later I was following my sister down Hillcrest Avenue. The sun was hot and high, and the sky was the color of dirty oyster shells. Tori had tarted up with every Bonne Bell and Wet N Wild cosmetic she owned—strawberry-scented lip gloss, salmon-colored blush, blue eyeliner, violet eye shadow, and a fake mole. She had given me a fake mole, too, and had rolled sticky gloss across my lips. Tori's friends Golden and Kesha, just as painted as my sister, were seated on the stoop of Golden's apartment building. They saw Tori and me walking and decided to join us.

Once we reached Santa Rosalia Drive, Tori dug into her purse and pulled out a crumpled pack of Kools. Kesha and Golden both took cigarettes. Then Tori, eyes narrowed, offered me one, the words "You're just a stupid little baby" ready to trip from her pointy pink tongue if I refused.

I plucked the cigarette from the pack. "Got a light?"

The girls gave each other surprised looks as I waited with the cigarette between my fingers, as I prayed for forgiveness and that He would keep me from vomiting in front of these three bitches because that would be it for me, I would never be cool again.

Tori produced a mint green Bic she had boosted from Woolworth and held out fire for us to take.

Smoke filled my chest and I found it difficult to breathe—but I didn't throw up. I wheezed out a compliment to Golden on her pink L.A. Gear high-tops and listened as she bragged about the twenty-year-old gangbanger who had bought them for her. "All I had to do was suck his dick," she said nonchalantly.

I blushed—I knew what a "dick" was but didn't know anything about sucking one. That day, though, I learned that you sucked them to get shoes, purses, Quarter Pounders, and anything else you wanted. "Just don't bite," Golden told me. "Cuz then he'll hit you."

And then the trio laughed.

18

Pepe found me in the parking garage, sitting on the hood of my Crown Vic of the Day. He said nothing as he pulled a pack of cigarettes from his shirt pocket and sat beside me. He lit up and smoke mixed with the scent of hot grease from the taco stand across the street. "So," he said, then blew smoke into the air. "How are things?"

I raised an eyebrow and laughed.

He joined me. After a few more drags, he said, "Saw the roses."

"Fancy, huh?"

"Gorgeous." He paused, then said, "Can I be honest?"

"Aren't you always?" He had never liked Greg and had always told me so.

"What he's doing," Pepe said. "It's bullshit."

I picked at the cuticle on my thumb. "Yeah?"

"So now, you're gonna throw yourself into the Darson case—"

"Because I'm a good cop."

"Sure. And because you don't wanna deal with the asshole at home."

The nerve over my left eye ticked. "Such language, Peter."

He slipped off the hood and faced me. "I know what it is to lie to myself, Lou. To pretend to be with someone because I don't wanna deal with the truth. Many times, many, many times, I wish I had it easy and could just say, 'Fuck this, this is what I want,' but I can't. You can, though. You're straight and you're married. You can be honest."

"You can be honest, too."

He tossed the cigarette on the ground. "Oh, yeah. I'm gonna tell my buddies in there that I'm queer. And I'm thinking afterwards, we'll go hunting and shit and they'll be cool sharing the showers with me. Yeah. That's easy. And so is climbing Everest without oxygen."

"It's been done: coming out and climbing Everest without oxygen."

"Yeah. And people have died doing both, too."

My eyes swept over Pepe, at the bead of sweat trickling along the scar on his left cheek. A scar he never talked about.

He gave me a slow smile. "Let's make a deal: you reckon with the asshole and I'll call what's-his-face."

I gasped and leaned closer to him. "The guy over at JPL? Rocket Man?"

Colin banged into the garage and yelled, "Lou! Where you at?"

Pepe winked at me. "*An-nyeong*, my sista."

I held up the Black Power fist. "*An-nyeong*, my brotha."

As Pepe headed toward the exit, Colin made a face. "What the hell is 'an' . . . 'an' . . . whatever the hell you were saying?"

"It's 'good-bye' in Korean," I said, standing now.

"You and Pepe got somethin' goin' on?" Colin asked with a sly grin.

"Can't men and women be friends?"

Colin smirked. "Not if she's hot. And I must admit: you're kinda hot."

I rolled my eyes. "You talk to Zucca?"

"He'll keep us posted." Colin's cell phone chirped as he climbed into the passenger seat. He hummed as his thumbs tapped at the keyboard.

"Lemme guess," I said. "A girl?"

"Yep. Met her at Whole Foods on Sunday. Hope you're not the jealous type." He turned the phone to show me her picture.

I squinted and said, "What's his name?"

Colin said, "Ha-ha," but studied the picture again with a teaspoon of suspicion.

"Seriously," I said, suppressing a grin, "she has a five o'clock shadow."

Colin peered closer at the picture. "No. No, she's just . . . the light's weird." Then he shoved the phone into his jacket pocket.

I pulled onto King Boulevard and shifted in my seat—the Kevlar vest pinched at the roll of skin caught between my pants' waistband and the vest's bottom. It also pressed against my boobs in a way that only a masochist would enjoy.

Since Colin was still sulking about possibly picking up RuPaul in the gluten-free aisle, I said, "But he's very pretty. And after some electrolysis . . . You have good taste in . . . whatever he or she may be."

He laughed, then brought out that damned container of Tic Tacs.

Baldwin Village was the government name for my old neighborhood.

But regular people knew it as the Jungle, a used-to-be-nice-place-to-live back in the Sixties, a neighborhood boasting twisty streets lined with banana palms, roomy apartments, and swimming pools. But the Seventies came, bringing with it the Black P Stones and PCP, and now the twisty, sometimes dead-end streets weren't so charming. Shootings in the alleys (so many alleys in the Jungle) behind those roomy apartments caused white folks to flee and middle-class blacks to move to Inglewood. The neighborhood was bad when I was a kid, but in a candy-is-bad-for-you kind of way. Now, though, it was bad for you like swallowing Drano followed by a rat poison chaser.

The police department and the city council had worked together to develop safe city initiatives, to file injunctions, to form task forces and arrest hoodlums for trespassing. They also revoked family members' Section 8 if they harbored gangbangers. Eventually, the rate of serious crime dropped. Unfortunately, it didn't drop for the most serious of serious crimes—homicides shot up 33 percent.

There were rumors that the Jungle would be torn down once the Santa Barbara Plaza was rebuilt. This meant that the twenty-seven thousand residents that resided in two square miles of mostly Section 8 apartments, including four hundred gang members, would have to find another place to live.

One part of me thought that displacing these people was a cruel and unreasonable act. It wasn't cheap to live in Los Angeles—where would they go? Sure, the neighborhood had its share of thugs and crack dealers, molesters and rapists, but there were also day-care workers and janitors living in those apartments, third-graders and toddlers, deaconesses and nurses. And girls in green-and-white cheer uniforms, skirts barely covering their asses, crushed packs of cigarettes in their Swapmacci handbags. Where would people like my family, poor but hardworking and decent folks, live?

But the other part of me was now navigating an unmarked police car up Coliseum Street, passing bangers in long white T-shirts and red denim shorts; passing a chickenhead in run-over flip-flops, her saggy breasts peeking beneath a cut-off tank top; and watching babies run in and out of apartment gates without adult supervision. As I witnessed all of this, I wanted to shout, "Burn it down!"

As a cop, it was my job to yank out the 1 percent who screwed it up for everybody else. But that was hard to do when the deaconess was hiding her Black P Stones grandson in her bedroom closet. Hard to do when the crack dealer was also the nurse's baby daddy. The bad grew with the good just like weeds in wheat.

Despite the circumstances, my heart warmed as I made a right onto Hillcrest Avenue—on that corner over there, Tori and I had found a twenty-dollar bill and had bought bags of potato chips, Snickers bars, cans of soda, and Jolly Ranchers. My friend Kimya (a.k.a. That Little Whore) had lived in those apartments over there. And my father taught Tori and me how to play tennis in that park right there.

I slowed as I reached the green apartment building where I had lived for fifteen years: a few boarded windows, weeds where grass once grew, thugs hanging out in the entryway. "Home sweet home," I said, awed that I had made it out.

Colin's eyes bugged and his knee bounced—this was his first trip to Baldwin Village. "You grew up here?"

"Yep." I accelerated and made a right at the next corner, drove for a bit, then turned right onto Coco Avenue. "Welcome to the Jungle. Keep your hands and arms inside the vehicle at all times."

"This place is fuckin' gnar," he whispered, shaking his head.

I glanced over to my partner. "If that means 'rough,' then yes, it's fuckin' gnar."

Colin swallowed hard and his left hand fluttered to his underarm—making sure that his Sig Sauer hadn't been jacked by the air.

I slapped his bouncing knee. "C'mon. Colorado has poor areas. I saw it on an episode of *Cops*. I'm guessing that's where you saw it, too, since you worked the west side."

He didn't throw the ball back—his Adam's apple kept bobbing and his eyes kept gaping at the ghetto canvas on the other side of the car's windshield.

I laughed, told him that he'd be fine, then grabbed my radio to call Sergeant Gino Walston, one of the gang officers assigned solely to the Jungle. "Hey, Gino-Boy, we're almost there."

The radio crackled and blipped, then Gino responded: "I got another black-and-white roaming the block. Just in case Derek needs to blow off a little steam."

I parked in front of a dingy yellow apartment complex named Sea

Side Village, then said to Colin, "Assume that he's packing. Watch his hands. Keep your mouth shut. And if you do say something, be careful—we don't want him to lawyer up."

Gino and his partner, Samoan Ro, drove past in a black-and-white patrol car, its trunk filled with nine-millimeter submachine guns and shotguns. Both wore their everyday paramilitary gear.

Colin checked the magazine of his Sig, then pushed the air from his lungs.

After Gino and Ro parked near a fire hydrant, I plucked the sticky note with Derek's address and apartment number from the dashboard and whispered, "Lord, be with me."

With cops on the block, the street had cleared. Crack smokers slunk further into dark carports. Middle-school drug runners hustled past wrought-iron gates to not do homework. Homies lounging on the hoods of El Caminos and Regals watched us with wary expressions, hoping that they weren't on Gino's and Ro's dance card today.

"Hell-o-uise." Gino, tall and dark and ex-Marine-big, winked at me. "The party can start now that you're here."

I winked back at him. "The roof is on fire, my friend." I had never dated cops and had no plan to in the future. *But* if Gino and I were to ever score hall passes from our respective spouses, we would destroy each other, then combust into flame, leaving behind a pile of ash and Glock.

"You got my back?" I asked him now.

"Your back, your front, every little finger and toe," he affirmed.

Every step I took, glass crunched beneath my shoe soles. Broken forty-ounce bottles, broken vials, broken crack pipes. The security gate that protected Sea Side Village was wide open. So much for safety. The swimming pool in the middle of the courtyard was filled with liquid the color of the Incredible Hulk. On top of that "water" was a thin film of lord-knows-what rippling with the draft. Flies skimmed across that layer and their buzzing was almost louder than the stereo blasting Lil Wayne.

The music was coming from Derek's place, Lucky Unit Number 7.

I kept one hand on the butt of my gun and used the other to knock on the door.

The stereo cut off, and now the courtyard was left with the buzzing of those flies.

A dog started to bark from inside the apartment.

"A Rott," I predicted.

Colin took a deep breath, then muttered, "Shit."

From behind the door, a man yelled, "What?"

I badged the peephole and said, "We're here to talk with Derek Hester."

A pause, then, "For what?"

"We gon' have a problem, Derek?" I asked. "Open up, please."

The dog stopped barking.

Click. Click. Click.

How many deadbolts could one door have?

Click.

Four.

The door opened and the stink of weed and dog washed over me. The theme music from *I Love Lucy* had replaced Lil Wayne.

Derek was big—six-foot-five, and damn, he could fill a doorframe. One side of his scalp remained cornrowed but the other boasted a big, wavy Afro. A Rottweiler on a red leather leash heeled at his side. Derek made eye contact with Gino and Ro before settling his gaze on me. Poor Colin, the white boy from Colorado, didn't even merit a glance.

I smiled. "Hi, Derek. I'm Detective Lou Norton from Homicide. This is my partner, Detective Taggert. I believe you already know Sergeants Walston and Matua." I placed my hands on my hips, making sure he saw my gun.

Derek didn't respond. His jean shorts hung low on his hips, showing tan boxers. He wore a gray wife-beater and his biceps, bulked up from his fellowship at State, were as big as my head. Stretch marks rippled up to his shoulders and tattoos—BPS, pyramids and stars, Sleepy D— covered his caramel-colored arms.

"We need to talk to you for a moment," I said.

"I'm off the paper," he spat.

"This ain't about probation or anything you've done. I *hope*."

"What about then?"

"Monique Darson," I said.

He squinted at me, making his sleepy eyes almost close. "Monie?"

"May we come in, please? Unless you wanna do this at the station."

He gave me the up-and-down and asked Gino, "She Five-O for real?"

"Naw," Gino said. "She a sandwich artist over at Subway."

Derek sneered. "Sergeant Walston got jokes." Then, he stared at me. "Ain't nothin' scare you, huh?"

"Bees," I said, faking a shiver.

He smirked. "You need to be up in a classroom, teachin' niggas algegras and shit 'stead of bustin' fools' nuts."

"You sound like my mother," I kidded. "Did she call you? Did she tell you to say that?"

He laughed. "You got jokes, too."

"Wednesdays and Thursdays only," I said, doing anything to make him—and his Rottweiler—relax.

Derek tugged the dog's leash. "C'mon, King."

Colin and I entered the apartment while Gino and Ro stood at the open door.

The apartment was clean, too clean. There was no furniture in the living room, just a patio chair placed in front of a forty-inch television now playing the "Lucy Stomps Grapes in Italy" episode. Empty Olde English bottles lined the baseboards around the room. In one of two dog dishes, there was a bone the size of a T. rex's leg. About ten yellow boxes of sandwich bags sat on the kitchen counter.

"You part of the summer lunch program?" Colin asked.

Derek frowned. "What? *Sir*?" He glanced at the boxes, and then at Gino, now stepping into the living room and standing near the television. "They was on sale at Target, *sir*."

The bedroom closet probably hid guns, Baggies of weed, some raw, and some white. But I couldn't wander around without probable cause, and the hospitality shown to us by Mr. Hester thus far didn't warrant probable cause.

"Do you have your dog under control, Derek?" I asked, hand back on my Glock. "Cuz I'd hate to shoot him. I'm an animal lover."

Derek, eyes on Colin, drawled, "King cool."

"Monique Darson," I said, "how do you know her?"

"We friends," he said, focusing on the television set.

"Romantic?"

Gino hit the TV's power button, forcing Derek to focus on me instead.

"Were you in a relationship?" I asked again.

"Somethin' like that," he said in a flat voice. "Not that she wanted everybody to know. Except when she came 'round here. Anywhere else, though? My name was 'Whodat?'"

"When was the last time you saw her?" I asked.

Colin was rubbing something on the filthy shag carpet with the toe of his shoe.

King growled, and perfect drops of spit fell from the dog's gleaming white teeth.

I gave Colin a quick headshake. *What the* fuck, *dude? Stop that.*

"I ain't seen Monie since the night she graduated," Derek said. "Pissed me off. She ain't want me at the ceremony, but I was supposed to buy her a gift? Fuck that. I ain't talked to her after then. Wait—no. I talked to her on Tuesday, like in the afternoon. She wanted to meet me somewhere, but I wasn't down wit' that."

"Mind if I look at your arms?" I asked.

"What for?"

"I have a thing for arms."

He sighed—he knew the deal—and held out his forearms.

No recent scratches or bruises from a fight.

"Thanks," I said, studying his face.

No scratches there, either.

"I hate to tell you this," I said, "but we found Monique last night. She was murdered."

Derek's eyes widened—they were the color of Amaretto and not so sleepy now.

The dog had felt his master's mood change and started to whine.

Colin slowly described Monie's death, like a doctor giving his patient the worst-case scenario. He was good at it.

Derek hid his face in the crook of his elbow. "Aw man . . . Aw man . . ."

"We found her in one of those new condo units over on Santa Rosalia," I said.

"You sure it was her?" Derek asked.

"We're sure," Colin said.

"Did you do it, Derek?" I asked, tenderly.

He gazed at me, his eyes wet. "I ain't do that shit, ma'am. I ain't done nothin'."

"You piss anybody off recently?" I asked. "Do something that would've made her a target?"

His hands were shaking, and he closed his eyes and gritted his teeth. "Naw. I been layin' low since April. Ain't interested in gettin' in no trouble."

I winced. "Dating a minor may now bring you some of that trouble, Derek."

He chewed on his lips and studied the ceiling.

"Where were you between midnight on Tuesday night and two, early Wednesday morning?" I asked.

"My nigga got buried over at Inglewood that day," he said. "I was at his grandma's house out in Gardena, eatin' and shit."

"What did you wear to the funeral?" I asked.

"Why you got to know all that?"

"I have a thing for men's clothes."

He could understand my interest in his arms, but the clothes question made him gape dumbly into the distance. "I wore red khakis, a white shirt, red Jordans, that's it."

"A belt?"

"Yeah. This one right here." He lifted his tank top to show a battered black leather belt. With shorts that low, what had been the point of wearing it?

"You got a picture of you at the funeral?" I asked.

He plucked his phone from his pocket, scrolled through, and found a picture. In it, he stood with a crew of BPS beside a white casket, throwing up signs. He had worn the outfit he had just described to me, down to the belt. If he had owned a Gucci *anything*, this funeral would have been the occasion to floss it.

"I'll need the number to Grandma's house," I said.

"I ain't killed Monie, ma'am," he spat, eyes hot.

King sat up and growled.

Colin took a step back. "Whoa, buddy."

Derek turned to him and snapped, "I ain't yo' buddy, *sir*."

"*Derek*," I said in my CAPS LOCK voice, "relax, okay? I believe you, but I still need to clear your alibi."

He gave me Grandma's name and telephone number, then snapped his fingers. "I got some more proof. Five-O rolled up on me close to midnight for some bullshit." In a "proper" voice, he said, "Failure to signal." Back in his regular tone, he said, "I sat on the curb for like an hour."

"Gardena PD?"

"Yes, ma'am. They followed me back to Grandma's crib," he said, sounding more certain than before. "I'm gon' fight that shit. I ain't goin' back to jail for no bullshit traffic ticket."

I sighed and faked annoyance. "Whatever. Who killed her, Derek? Right now, I don't care if you BPS, if you sling, pimp, whatever. All I wanna know is this: who killed Monique? Tell me the truth. Come on, dude."

"Ma'am, I'm telling you the truth."

In the apartment above, a boy shouted, "Shoot, nigga, shoot!" over man-made gunshots. I recognized the music—*Dirty War*, Greg's game.

"Know anybody who would want to hurt Monique?" I asked. "Like them fools in 18th Street or somebody in the Rolling 60s?"

"Naw," Derek said, his shoulders drooping. "I loved that girl. She was the best thing I ever had. We always talked 'bout escapin' out of LA and livin' like them fools on *Gilligan's Island*." He grinned, probably imagining himself and Monique wearing grass skirts, living off opakapaka and coconut cream pie.

"You watch *Gilligan's Island?*" Colin asked.

Derek frowned. "What? Niggas can't like Gilligan?"

Colin held up his hands. "My bad."

"The Lexus," I said. "You buy it?"

Derek smirked. "Naw, I ain't bought her that bitch car. Probably that nigga Von."

"But you bought the other bitch," I said. "Butter."

He sucked his teeth. "Yeah, but I wanted to get her a *real* dog. A Doberman or a mastiff."

"What do you know about Von?" I asked.

"I know she was with that fool when I called her the night before graduation. That nigga answered her phone like he the boss of shit."

The boys in the apartment above us dropped something heavy.

Colin startled and glanced at the ceiling.

Derek laughed, and said, "This dude here need some Valium and shit to calm the fuck down. He makin' me nervous."

"Did you and Von exchange words that night?" I asked.

Derek sneered. "I ain't gon' waste my time on that buster. Monie, though. I was gon' change for her if she just gave me a chance. Now . . ."

"You and Monique ever fight?" I asked him.

"Yeah, we fought."

"You ever hit her?" Colin asked.

"Why niggas gotta beat on some girl, homie?" Derek asked. "You ever hang a nigga in a tree? You eat fuckin' sushi and cantaloupes for breakfast every day before going to yo' KKK meetin'?"

"Just answer the question, Derek," Gino growled from the door.

"Naw, I ain't ever hit her," he claimed. "She wasn't that type."

"There's a type?" Colin asked.

Derek rolled his eyes. "This dude right here."

"What if I said a witness placed you at the scene?" I asked.

"Then, I would say, 'Bullshit, that fool need glasses,' cuz I was nowhere *near* Santa Rosalia on Tuesday night." He offered a bitter smile and glared at Colin. "Was the witness white? Niggas look alike to white people."

"There's DNA," I revealed. "And fingerprints."

"So?"

"So, if you were with her—"

"Ma'am, I told you I ain't *seen* Monie since last week. I'll take a lie detector test to prove that shit."

"When?"

"Hell, we can do that right now."

"I'll arrange a test then," I said. "Just know that I *will* find out if you were anywhere near her or inside of her on Tuesday night."

"Run that shit," he said without hesitation. "I'm clean." He sucked his teeth and dropped his eyes, now silver with tears. "Don't worry, Monie," he whispered. "I got this."

The way he said her name made me pause. There had been affection in his "Monie." Like the way Joe Q. Citizen without a record would say his girl's name.

Whoever killed Monique Darson now had a price on his head two times. If the State of California didn't kill him, a G-ride filled with BPS would.

19

It was half past noon when Colin and I climbed back into the Crown Vic. "He's dealing," Colin said with great certainty. Then, he folded his arms and nodded as though he'd just discovered Presbyterians on Uranus.

"Now why would you say that?" I asked. "Because there were a hundred boxes of Baggies on his countertop? Because he has seven pages of priors?" I rolled down the window and hoped that air would somehow twist its way between my sweaty torso and bulletproof vest. But the draft only kissed my face and lifted my hair, refusing to go any farther. Prude.

Colin's eyes goggled. "C'mon, Lou. Dude's carpet had more grass seeds in it than a farm in Kentucky."

This section of Coco Avenue was totally clear now—either the noncitizens had been caught up in the Rapture or had rushed home to watch *All My Children*.

"Maybe the seeds were there when he moved in three weeks ago," I said, fastening my seat belt.

"You've *got* to be kidding me."

"Okay, so I bust him after just eyeballing bags and seeds. Then, we get told that he really *is* a lunchroom volunteer at the local elementary school as a condition of his parole, and that those seeds really were there before he moved in. We're Homicide, Colin, not Vice, not Gino and Samoan Ro in the Gang Unit. We weren't there on a drug case or because he's BPS. We went there to determine if he killed the girl, and my gut tells me that he *didn't* kill the girl. We got enough shit to do without being the Weed Patrol." I paused, then added, "And I need him out anyway."

Colin, arms still folded because he was now pouting, muttered, "So he can do a drive-by on whoever killed her?"

I turned the car's ignition. "Murder's out of tune, and sweet revenge grows harsh."

We pulled in front of Crase Parc and Promenade with the sun hidden behind pearly-brown haze. Yellow tape still cordoned off the front of the units, but construction crews had received the okay to keep working. So much noise: the whir of drills and saws destroying wood, men shouting back and forth, the *beep-beep-beep* of heavy machinery backing up. News station field reporters and their cameramen stood in front of the site with microphones clutched in their hands, doing feeds for the three o'clock news. Wide-eyed and sweaty, James Mason, security guard extraordinaire, was pointing back to the condos as he talked to reporter Tricia Yamaguchi, Channel 9.

Zucca had parked his van in a red zone. He and his team were back inside unit 1B, searching for more clues.

A gold Mercedes-Benz was parked a few feet away from the CSI van. I knew that car well. Had passed out in its backseat after nights of serious drinking. Had taken my turn behind its steering wheel during trips to Vegas and Palm Springs. The sedan belonged to Syeeda McKay, my sorority sister, friend, and favorite reporter in the world.

Before being laid off in April, Syeeda had written thoughtful and provocative stories for the *Los Angeles Times*. I was surprised to see her here—she had been following the trail of the Phantom Slayer, the city's most active serial killer. She was now writing a book about that investigation.

"What are you doing in this part of the 'hood?" I asked as we met.

"A girl died here, almost-sergeant," she said. "Where else would I be?"

We hugged.

Syeeda was taller than Lena but still five-foot-four. She was pretty, but not the pretty that made other women want to push her in front of a train. She had big brown eyes, cheekbones sharper than a paring knife, and great hair. She wore a pair of Gucci loafers that I was determined to buy one day but wouldn't—only a fool would wear $400 shoes to crime scenes soaked in blood, crap, and maggots.

She eyed Colin and said, "Hello."

I made introductions.

Colin blushed, smiled goofily, and said, "Nice meetin' you."

Syeeda had that effect on men—she was now dating Adam Sherwood, the lead detective on the Slayer case. And whenever Syeeda was around, Superman Sherwood got goofy, too.

"It's just a regular murder," I said to Syeeda. "Nothing to see here, folks, please move along."

She lifted a freshly waxed eyebrow. "Then why are *you* working it? A woman practically three busts away from HSS?"

Homicide Special Section detectives like Superman Sherwood handled high-profile cases like the Menendez brothers, the Hillside Strangler, and the Night Stalker murders.

To Colin I said, "Could you check in with Zucca? See if he found anything new."

Colin started off, throwing back a last look at Syeeda.

"He has a crush on you," I said.

She smirked. "Who doesn't? He was *almost* cute."

"His looks are . . . *subjective*."

"Steve McQueen."

"But with bigger ears."

She grunted as she thought about Steve McQueen, then said, "So . . . What can you tell me?"

"First of all . . ." I pinched her shoulder.

"Ow! Why'd you do that?" she asked, pinching me back.

"Because," I whispered, "I haven't told anybody about the HSS thing."

"Oh." She offered a sheepish grin. "Oops. My bad. So the case . . . ?"

I eyed her—this would be a delicate dance. If you were careful, planting information via reporter often got results—like witnesses you didn't know about reading the newspaper and coming forward. And reporters like Syeeda knew all the backroom deals, the grudges, who was sleeping with whom, and on and on.

She took a step closer to me. "Give me something that those losers over there in front of the cameras would kill their moms to have. I'll hook you up. Swear."

I already knew that I would give her something, but feigned thinking about it. "I don't think so."

"Why not?"

"Because I don't need an Al Sharpton around here, telling me that I'm not doing my job and protecting the People."

Syeeda rolled her eyes, then pulled from her leather satchel a gold cigarette case. "I don't race bait—I point out the discrepancies in the justice system *because* of race." She plucked out a Newport and stuck it between her lips. "The Phantom Slayer was killing black hookers in a super-poor black neighborhood. As you know, task forces don't get formed for black hookers in super-poor black neighborhoods until reporters like me start snooping around. Twenty years, Lou, since he killed the first girl, and it's only *now* that you all have finally decided to move on it. And *that's* because of my articles. Tell me I'm wrong."

She lit her cigarette with a golden lighter. "I'd hate to think that your case goes unsolved because the suspect is rich and powerful, and can buy his way out of jail."

"Who do you think is rich and powerful and can buy his way out of jail?"

Syeeda stared at me.

To be honest, I wanted *her* to say his name, to breathe life into the idea and make my suspicions real. Speak of the Devil, and he shall appear.

But Syeeda didn't bite. Instead she said, "I don't wanna write that story, Elouise."

"I don't want you to write that story." I chuckled, but didn't mean it.

She chuckled, too, and didn't mean it, either.

In a low voice I said, "This is off-record until I give you the okay."

The group of TV reporters had noticed the print journalist talking to the lead detective on the Darson case.

"The zombies have spotted us," Syeeda said, eyes on the group. "Quickly now."

"We found a semen-stained hankie hidden in Monique Darson's closet."

She scrunched her eyebrows. "Does that mean she was settin' somebody up?"

"I haven't confirmed that yet, but it sounds like blackmail, right?"

Syeeda puffed slowly at her cigarette and stared at a point beyond me—she was thinking, and I liked it when she thought.

"And when we found her, she was wearing a cheerleader uniform."

Syeeda held smoke in her lungs as she processed this new nugget of information.

"And we talked to one of her boyfriends," I continued. "A BPS named Derek Hester a.k.a. Sleepy D, but I don't think he did it." Then, I told her about his alibi, his willingness to take a polygraph, his obvious affection for Monique Darson.

"Are you gonna test his DNA against the hankie?" Syeeda asked.

I nodded. "But I don't think that's him splashed all over the place. He's not explosive enough, no pun intended. Because so what? A thug gets sent to prison. That boy's always in prison. No—whoever this guy is must have some means, some influence. And he shouldn't have been naked with a seventeen-year-old girl."

"Hell, *Derek* shouldn't have been naked with a seventeen-year-old girl."

"True. But I really don't think he's good for this."

Syeeda shot a plume of smoke into the air, but her eyes remained fixed on that invisible target. "Do you know about Cyrus Darson and Nappy Crase?"

I narrowed my eyes. "No. But you do."

"Cyrus Darson was the lead activist against the Santa Barbara revitalization project, including the construction of these condos. He thought the deal was corrupt, that developers would price out the regular people already living and shopping here."

"True so far," I said.

"At one point," Syeeda continued, "there was some back-door dealing between the city and the Crase Group. Certain companies landed contracts while others didn't. And those companies that got a contract had a history of not hiring blacks and women. Crase didn't care about affirmative action—he wanted the cheapest bid. But he did this whole song-and-dance about hiring minorities and in the end, still screwed anybody who had tits and was darker than a paper bag. Cyrus's group gave him the blues, and they showed up at every city council meeting with pickets and bullhorns. They delayed the project for almost two years."

"But Cyrus lost," I declared.

"Yeah," Syeeda said, "and Nappy Crase was pissed because of all the money he had lost. Two years is a long time for money-huggers and thugs like Crase."

"So payback was the murder of Cyrus's daughter? Harsh."

Syeeda sucked her teeth. "You know and I know: that fucker likes 'em young. Easier to woo and easier to beat, especially with his arthritic knuckles."

I clucked my tongue and said, "Hunh."

"I don't get it," she said. "These little girls actin' like they're these sexual sophisticates . . . Old-ass men old enough to know that she's just playing another game of dress-up." She snorted. "Silly rabbit, they don't want your ancient, tired ass."

"Johnny Depp is old now," I pointed out.

Syeeda cocked an eyebrow. "But Napoleon Crase and the rest of his kidney-stone-weak-prostate-buddies ain't Johnny Depp. And c'mon: old Johnny Depp is a world away from *21 Jump Street* Johnny Depp. Which version would *you* choose?"

And for just a second or two, we lusted after *21 Jump Street* Johnny Depp.

"So here you are again," Syeeda said. "You, Napoleon Crase, and another seventeen-year-old girl. *Another* cheerleader. In this part of town."

"Coincidence, right?"

She tossed her cigarette to the ground and smashed it with her shoe. "Einstein said, 'Coincidence is God's way of remaining anonymous.'"

"I have to be careful here," I said. "Rodriguez will throw me off this case if I behave badly."

"But you *are* looking at other people," Syeeda said.

"I am but . . ." I twisted my lips, then said, "But Crase is an evil bastard."

"Crase *is* an evil bastard, so do not underestimate the powers of the Emperor. Bring fire, bring cannons, bring big men with bigger guns. And warrants: bring plenty of those. You got this, Lou."

The construction trailer door banged open and slammed shut.

My gaze shifted to the trailer's porch. A balding white man wearing chinos and a burgundy polo shirt stood there with a radiophone and clipboard in his hands.

Syeeda turned to see the man, too, then said in her best David Attenborough voice, "The hawk spots the lizard. She circles high above the ground, floats on air currents before she swoops in for the kill."

I cracked my knuckles. "The hawk is about to serve a warrant to search that trailer."

"You'll tell me if you find anything exciting?"

"Yep. And you'll tell me if you hear anything that will help me solve this case?"

"Absolutely." She opened her mouth, then popped it close. Then: "Quick question."

"And here I am, thinking I almost escaped."

She leaned forward and whispered, "So, are you off of them now?"

"Am I off of what?"

She smirked.

I poked the inside of my cheek with my tongue, then searched the sky. "Any day now."

She peered at me, then said, "It's your Spidey senses, you know. They're tingling and warning you not to procreate with this man."

"This *man* has been my husband for eleven years," I said with a twisted grin. "Not that you would know anything about being in a committed relationship."

"True," she said, unflinching, "but we're not talking about me. I'll say it again: having a baby to save your marriage is like a sailor fixing that rip on the *Titanic* with needle and thread."

I pulled my fingers through my hair and forced a smile to my lips. "Doomed, am I?"

She stared at me, then said, "You're the one trying to conceive on the Pill."

"Oh, Sy. Stop bein' an old lady, will ya?" I bowed at my waist, wilting beneath her hard eyes. "Now if you will excuse me. I have to see a man about a horse."

After promises of drinks to catch each other up on men issues, I strode toward the bald man and the trailer. Syeeda's eyes burned my back—the hawk was being watched by a falcon.

20

Heavy machinery roared and grumbled, and hot tar made the air sticky with stink. Somewhere, a truck was backing up and its beeping . . . beeping . . . beeping made me want to scream. But the smell of fried meat wafted from the bright yellow and green roach coach parked on the street—those fragrant tendrils of smoke twisted up my nose, to my brain, and Mickey-Finned my jangled nerves. I hadn't eaten since the crack of dawn and my stomach growled just as it had when I stood here eighteen hours ago.

I clipped my badge to my jacket's breast pocket and slipped my aviators back over my eyes. Then I called Colin on the Motorola. "I'm on my way to the trailer. Get over here as soon as possible."

He said, "Copy that."

As soon as that call ended, another call came in—it was Dispatch with Macie Darson holding on the line to talk to me.

"Detective Norton?"

"Hey, Macie. How are you?"

The young woman laughed weakly. "I think the shock's starting to wear off but . . . I'm okay, I guess." She took a sharp breath, then slowly exhaled. "When you have a chance, could we meet to talk again? I may have more information that will help my sister's case."

I clamped a hand over my free ear to block the sounds of growling earth-movers. "Of course. When?"

"Tomorrow morning? Like around ten or eleven? At the Ladera Starbucks." After I agreed to the time and place, she thanked me for doing everything I could to help her family. The sound of a dial tone told me she had hung up.

Poor girl. No one expected to deal with murder on a Thursday morning.

The weak sun beat down on me even though it hadn't hit seventy degrees yet. But the beads of sweat that rolled down the middle of my back and were being half-assedly absorbed by my already soggy bra? Yeah, those beads could give a damn about highs and lows.

I ignored shouted questions from the TV reporters and strode toward the construction trailer. Workers in hard hats and grimy jeans paused in their step as I passed. One of them said, "The LAPD hiring like *that* now?" His buddy added, "I need to serve and protect, cuz *damn*."

But the bald man in the burgundy polo, the one standing where I needed to go, threw an irritated glance in my direction. He clomped down the steps and headed west and to the ongoing construction of the back condos.

"Excuse me, sir," I called out to him. "I'm Detective Elouise Norton and—"

"I don't know anything," he said, frowning. His voice was rough, as though he'd found it soaking in a vat of cement.

I offered him the smile I'd give an IRS auditor. Cold but polite. "First of all, I didn't ask you anything. Second, what's your name? I didn't catch it."

He gave me the up-and-down. "I didn't throw it."

My smile dropped. "Give me your name unless you wanna give it to me at the station, ass-hat." Then I came to stand up against him—I had a good three inches on this guy. And even though I had only attended two Krav Maga classes in the last month, I still had more muscle than this soggy tomato in chinos.

Aware now that I could kick his ass, the man took a step back and cleared his throat. "Hank La Garza."

I scribbled the jackass's name into my pad.

He tried to smile but was too nervous, and his smile was more of a grimace. "It's just that we're behind schedule, Detective, and—"

"A girl was murdered on this site, Mr. La Garza, so right now, I could care less about schedules. My job is to figure out who killed her."

"You don't understand the pressure I'm under," he said, shaking his head, offering me that pitiful grin. "You don't understand the significance of this place."

I snorted and narrowed my eyes. "Am I going too fast here? Am I, like, speaking Farsi or something? Mr. Garza, a girl was found *murdered* on this property."

"All the back and forth," he rambled, still not listening. "The residents wanted the Plaza restored and then they didn't want it. No Walmart in our neighborhood, they shouted, but now you can't even walk into the store cuz it's so damn crowded. We don't need any more bad press, Detective."

"That's why it's important to find out who killed this girl," I said with great patience, "before the goodwill of the community turns and your boss is seen as a money-grubbing leech who cares more about timetables than seeking justice for a dead, seventeen-year-old valedictorian and future veterinarian."

Hank ran his hand over his bald head and muttered, "Crap." He pulled a pack of Camels from his pocket and slid out a cigarette. "Feels like I'm in an episode of *CSI*."

My blood pressure jumped at the mention of that show, but hey, go with it. I pointed to the trailer. "I need to peek in there real quick."

He furrowed his eyebrows. "Why? The trailer was locked up on Tuesday night."

"Are you the only one with a key?"

He nodded and his hands shook as he lit the cigarette.

"So what goes on in there?"

He took a drag and the nicotine made the muscles in his face relax. He lazily blew smoke into the air, then said, "Payroll, administrative stuff, scheduling. I have a secretary—Beverly Leman—who comes in three times a week."

Colin was ambling up the sidewalk toward Hank and me. More muscle.

"Still," I said with a let's-be-reasonable smile, "I need to see. To quiet the niggling in my brain. Cuz in *CSI* episodes . . ." I waited, hoping that he'd fill in the ellipses.

He nodded eagerly. "Evidence can be found everywhere. There was this one episode where a pigeon stole a dead man's ear. And they found the ear in North Vegas even though—"

"Are you stalling me, Hank?" I asked. "Do you have something to hide?"

"No, of course not." His eyes shifted back and forth as he took another nervous drag. "Shouldn't you have a warrant?"

I snapped my fingers. "Oh, yeah." I plucked the warrant from my file, and said, "Thanks for reminding me."

Hank slumped, and his neck and face turned red—he really was a soggy tomato.

Colin, now at my side, introduced himself to the project manager.

"So," I said, "shall we go inside?"

"Guess so." Hank tossed the half-smoked Camel to the ground.

Both Colin and I considered that cigarette sitting there, just waiting to be picked up and placed in an evidence envelope.

If nothing else, *CSI* had taught the world that DNA could be found anywhere—especially on the filter of a smoldering cigarette.

21

Hank La Garza stayed outside—he had been pulled into an argument between a painter and a carpenter. Colin and I would not wait for him. We pulled on our latex gloves and clicked on our flashlights. Then, I opened the trailer's door.

A pretty blonde with long, crinkly hair and longer red fingernails was typing on a computer at a cheap desk.

A calendar of motivational sayings—*If not us, who? If not now, when?*—was tacked on the wall.

A water cooler rumbled in the corner, making the steel office-supplies cabinet vibrate.

At first glance, this construction trailer resembled every construction trailer on every construction site in the world, and a small part of me said, "Don't waste too much time here." But that part of me was wrong.

You can't ignore the smell of bleach.

Or the smell of death.

Colin whispered, "He did her here."

"Yep." My eyes skipped from the pot of African violets on the secretary's desk to the cheap green carpet that covered the trailer's floor.

Someone had used a tub of bleach to clean up whatever bad thing that had happened here.

I wandered over to the desk and stood over the secretary. "You are . . . ?"

She fluttered her clumpy eyelashes at Colin, then said, "Beverly Leman." She was a dainty teacup up top but an old country milking bucket around her hips and thighs. The seams of her rayon skirt were thirty minutes from liberating those thighs from rayon oppression, and I'm sure the boys around the construction zone wouldn't have minded that one bit.

"Ms. Leman," I said, "does the trailer always smell like this?"

She flicked a look at me, then returned her gaze to Colin. "Not this bad. But you know: this ain't the Ritz Carlton."

"True. Ms. Leman, could you step outside, please?"

She didn't say a word, nor did she click the mouse to save her document. In silence, she grabbed her purse from the desk drawer, offered Colin a sexy hair toss, then brushed against him as she wiggled past.

I sniffed—there was another smell on top of the bleach. I closed my eyes as though I stood in a Napa winery, sniffing a glass of very complicated merlot.

"Vomit," Colin whispered in my ear.

"You sure know how to turn a girl on," I said, opening my eyes.

"Just call me the Love Doctor."

"Just do your job, please."

This time Colin directed his attention to the ground. Atta boy.

"Lookie-lookie." He was pointing at a white circle the size of a quarter. Then, he pointed at a smaller circle the size of a dime, and then to an even tinier spot no bigger than a corn kernel.

I stooped to examine the marks but froze—the base of the desk had been bashed in, and that bashing thing had left behind a concave circle of splintered wood. *The back of Monique's head?*

Behind me, Colin said, "Whoa!"

I turned to my partner—he was now crouched before a file cabinet near the watercooler. "What's 'whoa'?" I asked.

"Gimme a picture of Monique's hand," he said.

I rifled though the expandable file, found a photograph, and handed it to him. "What is it?"

He moved aside so that I could see.

A yellow acrylic fingernail was trapped behind the file cabinet. And this nail hadn't been cut but had popped off.

Colin peered at me, his blue eyes sparkling with excitement. He grabbed his Motorola from his belt, and said, "Zucca, you there?"

After a few squawks, Zucca said, "Yep. What's goin' on?"

"We found the primary scene."

I tore my gaze from the fingernail and glanced at the side of the file cabinet. "Holy guacamole," I muttered.

On the gray metal were dried blood drops with upward-moving tails.

I rushed out of the trailer and hailed two patrol officers who kept people from entering the condo.

In less than a minute, those same cops had wrapped the trailer with yellow tape.

A crowd formed, then—construction workers holding greasy Fatburger and Taco Bell bags in one hand, and camera phones held high in the other.

As I waited for Zucca on the trailer's porch, I called Luke and Pepe back at the station and told them to drop whatever they were doing and come over to the condo. Colin searched for Beverly Leman to take her statement and to get a set of her fingerprints we'd use to compare against any we'd find in the trailer.

Syeeda was standing at her car, scribbling into a notebook, looking at me, then scribbling again.

The monster who had caused this racket was watching me, too. I felt his spotlight burn on the nape of my neck like dragon's breath. I took in every face in the crowd as well as gazed at the windows of surrounding office buildings and the fancy houses on the hill.

Zucca materialized before me as though he had found a wormhole that connected unit 1B to the trailer. "What's this about a fingernail?"

"Right this way."

He followed me into the trailer. I didn't even have a chance to explain before he sniffed the air. "Whoa."

"That's what they all say," I deadpanned.

Zucca scanned the carpet. In his mind he was already dropping yellow tents near splotches and splatters, banged-in desks and abandoned fingernails.

"Look for hair in the wood of that desk," I instructed.

Colin was popping up the stairs as I was leaving the trailer. He held up a set of fingerprint cards and said, "I got—"

"Where is Hank La Garza?" I asked, brushing past him.

Colin pointed to the yellow-and-green roach coach—Tito O'Mulligan's Mexican & Irish Cuisine. Hank was sipping from a large Styrofoam cup and laughing with a sunburned man in an orange shirt and yellow hard hat. Laughing as though shit was all good, as though a seventeen-year-old girl had been found dead at a construction site in Norway and not ten yards from where he stood.

"What the hell is so funny?" I muttered as I stomped toward the food truck.

Colin followed behind me. "Is my line 'Calm down, Lou, don't do anything stupid'?" He waved over the six-foot-five, Aryan-big patrol cop who had wrapped the trailer in tape.

"I won't do anything stupid," I snarled. "I'm just gonna go Duke Nukem on his ass."

I reached Tito O'Mulligan's just as the fry cook handed Hank his hamburger.

And I promptly slapped that burger out of Hank's hand.

Someone in the crowd shouted, "Excessive force!"

Hank glowered at his fallen meal. "What the—?"

"You need to go with this officer right now," I instructed, pointing to the big cop. All eyes were on me—including Syeeda's and a few left behind TV reporters. A camera phone was probably recording this confrontation right now, and if I didn't cool down, I'd be on YouTube by three o'clock.

Hank paled. "Why? I didn't—"

I smacked the Styrofoam cup out of his hand and the chances of picking up that burger, kissing it up to God, and claiming the three-second rule was washed away in orange Fanta.

"Let's go," I growled. "*Now.*"

Hank squared his shoulders. "I have rights."

The giant patrol cop who hadn't smiled since *Cheers* went off the air stepped toward him.

"You want rights?" I asked. "Fine. I wasn't arresting you, but okay, I'll read you your rights. You have the right to remain silent. You have the right to an attorney—"

"Stop." Hank lifted his hands in surrender. "All right. I have nothing to hide. I haven't done anything."

"Then this won't take long," I said. "See you soon."

22

Interview room 1 stank of flop sweat from a Hoover Crip who had been questioned in a drive-by shooting that had killed a pastor's wife and her six-month-old fetus. It was a soundproof room that typically ran very hot or very cold, making our guests crazy uncomfortable and willing to talk just to get the hell out. Five minutes into the interview, Hank La Garza had melted through his burgundy polo. His sweaty bald head and wet eyes glistened like reflecting pools as he pleaded with me to believe him. He had sworn that he had never done anything wrong, okay, maybe once or twice he had cheated on his wife, and sure, he tended to do California rolls at stop signs, and all right, he had operated a vehicle while under the influence a few times. *But!* He attended Mass every Sunday and foster-parented a black kid named Jamaal, and so he could never kill anybody, especially a child.

I was sweating like Kobe Bryant in Game 7 of the NBA Finals against the Celtics and my reserve tank of patience had only three drops left. "This is all very touching, Hank, but you need to answer my question. Where were you on Tuesday night, around midnight, to around two o'clock on Wednesday morning?"

Hank's face reddened and he swallowed nervously. "I wasn't anywhere near the condo site."

"So where were you near?"

Hank didn't respond at first, then muttered, "I was with a friend."

"What kind of friend?"

Hank turned the color of a fire engine. He clamped his lips together and closed his eyes.

"A *girl* kind of friend?" I asked.

He dropped his head and muttered, "Yes."

I waited for more, but when a minute passed in silence, I said, "Look, Hank. I don't care about whatever clandestine adventure you're having, but I *do* care where you were on Tuesday night and early Wednesday morning. Or maybe I should ask your *wife*."

"I was at Denny's on Sunset with my friend," he blurted.

"And what's your friend's name?"

Just when I thought he couldn't get any redder . . .

He swiped his mouth and squeezed his lips. "Why do you need that information?"

There was a scratch on the back of his right hand. But it wasn't as angry as the purple welt on his neck.

"Just to rule people out," I said, studying that hand scratch.

"Joanna Palexi." Then, he gave me Joanna's number.

"Okay," I said, setting down my pen, "do you know Cyrus Darson?"

Relief washed over his face—that was an easy question. "Cyrus was against the revitalization. He and his wife would show up to the site with fifty people and form a picket line. Some of my guys threw rocks at them. But that was then. Now Cyrus does some electrical work for us."

"What's your relationship with him?"

"Don't have one. I don't even pay him."

"Who pays him?"

Hank stuck his hands beneath his damp armpits. "Can't say. Don't like the guy all that much. Not too reliable. But Nappy personally hired him, so he comes and goes when he wants. Crase does that sort of thing all the time. His *girlfriend*"—he made air quotes with his fingers—"Brenna Benevides? She's on the payroll as a secretary, but I doubt she knows how to spell or type or do anything *secretarial*. But I hear she provides *other services*." More air quotes, more italics.

"So if I ran Brenna's name through the system?"

He laughed without humor. "I'll just say that she's in there. And she has access to the trailer key—Nappy's copy."

"And do you know where Crase was that night?"

"No."

I watched him—he blinked quickly and licked his thin lips. Either he was lying or dehydrated and moments away from passing out.

"You ever meet the victim, Monique Darson?"

Hank swiped his face. "No." He pulled out the pack of Camels from his back pocket.

I plucked the pack from his hand and slid them down the table. "Can't smoke in here. The scratches on your hand and neck—how did you get them?"

He studied his right hand, then touched his neck. "I'm in construction. I get scratched all the time."

I openly stared at the scratch on his hand to make him nervous.

"Listen," he said, "I didn't have anything to do with Cyrus's kid getting killed. I was with Joanna all night, and we were . . . You know, hanging out and talking, but I swear to you . . . I'll take a lie detector test." He puffed his cheeks and blew out air. "I need a smoke real bad."

"Hank," I said softly, "did you and Joanna kill Monique Darson? Maybe you thought she was a prowler, or a hooker . . . ?"

"No, Detective."

"I don't believe you."

"I'm telling you the truth."

"I have a witness who says that they saw you at the trailer Tuesday night."

"They're lying," he said, shaking his head.

"They said that they saw you that night and you had a jug of Clorox."

"What?" he shouted. "That's a lie."

"If it wasn't you they saw with the jug of Clorox, who was it then? Was it Joanna?"

"Look," he said, "I don't know—"

I slapped the tabletop. "I stepped in that piece of shit trailer of yours, Hank, and I smelled dead girl, and if you tell me one more time that you have no idea—"

"I have no—" He stopped and clamped his lips together. "I got there on Wednesday morning at seven like everybody else and . . . and . . . I don't know, I swear on my mother's grave. I smelled it but I figured . . . I don't know, that it was a squirrel or a—"

"A *squirrel?*" I screeched. "Are you *kidding* me?" I leaned across the table and snarled, "So help me, I will close that construction site down today if you don't answer my questions, you goddamned dingleberry."

"I thought the cleaning ladies, you know, tried to get rid of . . ." His hands clapped both sides of his moist face, Macaulay-Culkin-*Home-Alone* style.

I sat back in my seat and squeezed the bridge of my nose. "Before I left to come spend some special time with you, *Hank*, I talked to Beverly Leman. The cleaning lady comes on Monday and Thursday nights. And guess what that means? There *was* no cleaning lady. So, *Hank*, who the hell splashed bleach everywhere?"

Eyes wide, he manically shook his head. "I . . . I . . . don't . . ."

"Didn't you say you're the only one with a key?"

"I just told you: Mr. Crase has a key."

"Right. Him and his hooker secretary."

He nodded quickly. "Yeah. Yeah. Exactly."

I kept glaring at him—to tease and scare out a "tell," a gesture that suggested deception. "When was the last time Mr. Crase or Brenna visited the site?"

"A week ago," he said.

"Is Brenna always with him when he visits or does he switch up sometimes and bring other young things around?"

"Always Brenna."

"And how long did he stay the last time he visited?"

Hank shrugged. "Just a few minutes. To sign checks, see the progress being made . . ."

"And when was the last time Cyrus Darson came to work?"

"Last Wednesday. I haven't seen him since."

I took a deep breath, then said, "One more time: do you know who may have killed Monique Darson?"

"No, Detective."

"Would you be willing to give us a DNA sample to compare against any DNA found on the victim?"

He nodded. "Yes. Please. What do I need to do?"

I left the interview room and hurried to the alcove where Joey and Colin were watching the interview on closed-circuit monitors.

Joey grinned at me. "*Dingleberry?* What the hell is that?"

"A piece of poop that sticks to ass hair," I said, wincing. "Who wants to take DNA?"

Joey raised his hand. "I'll do it."

"Want me to set up the poly?" Colin asked. "He can do it right after Derek Hester."

"And when is that?" I asked.

"Around three this afternoon."

"Cool. What do you guys think so far?"

Colin stood from the chair and stretched. "I think he's scared of you."

I laughed. "Scared of *me*? I'm sweet as apple pie."

"Yeah," Colin said. "Apple pie laced with arsenic and rusty razor blades."

While a cigar-chomping polygraph examiner gave Hank La Garza a lie detector test, I sat at my desk staring at the DMV picture of Angie Darson. *Three traffic tickets over the last seventeen years.* Clean. I then typed CYRUS DARSON into the computer and hit ENTER.

Misdemeanor trespass—probation.

Misdemeanor false imprisonment—six months in county jail.

Misdemeanor violating a restraining order—one year.

All three charges were almost thirty years old. Had Cyrus been a stalker before he had married Angie? Had a girlfriend dumped him but he had refused to go away, returning to her home, peeking in the windows, trapping her in a bedroom, begging her for another chance, coming back around after a judge had ordered him to stay away?

The officer who had administered the polygraph trudged over to my desk. "La Garza passed," he announced. With the cigar still in his mouth, he slipped a stick of gum between his teeth.

I groaned and slumped in my chair. "You sure?"

"Yup."

"And you asked if he was covering up for Napoleon Crase?"

"Couched in a different way, yeah, I did. And he said no. And there were no indications of deceit in his answers."

I rubbed my eyes and released a long, loud sigh—Derek Hester had also passed his test. "Well, eliminating suspects . . . okay, well . . . damn . . ."

Exhaustion was setting in—my inability to complete sentences was the first indicator that my brain was packing its bags for a trip to Leisure World.

I escorted Hank La Garza back to the lobby and thanked him for coming in.

When I returned, Colin and Joey were standing at the coffeepot, talking about the best rifle to take down elk. They saw the frown on my face and laughed.

"Oh, yeah," Joey said, with a playful sneer. "Lou's a tree hugger. She don't eat nothin' that casts a shadow."

I reached my desk—someone had left an In-N-Out burger and a large soda next to my computer keyboard. I took a big bite from the burger, then said, "Shooting helpless animals is wrong."

"She says with her mouth full of cow," Colin said, sitting back in his seat.

I shook my head. "This guy wasn't killed because I wanted to show how big my dick is. He's dead cuz he's delicious." I finished the double-double in five bites, then pushed the vase of roses farther away from the keyboard and closer to the edge of the desk. Their proximity made no difference—there were pictures of Greg and me tacked all over my cubicle walls, and I wore those rings on my finger, and had a "Sorry, baby" Porsche parked in the garage.

Luke, back from the construction trailer, stood at the board—he was now chronicling Monique's final twenty-four hours alive. "So while you were watching Sleepy D and Hank La Garza tell the truth," he said to me, "Monique's phone records came back, and—"

"Time for an update?" Lieutenant Rodriguez had wandered to our area and was slurping from a Cup Noodles.

I propped a leg on my desk. "Sure."

He jabbed his fork into the cup, then pointed to me. "After this, you need to clock out." He nodded at Colin. "You, too." Then he sat atop my desk and stuck another forkful of noodles into his mouth. "Let's hear it."

Colin started. "It's still too early for DNA results. There's the hankie, the blood found in the trailer, the fingernail, Hank La Garza's cigarette and DNA swab, the rape kit, Derek Hester's DNA that he gave before the lie detector test—"

"Which he passed," I added. "And so did La Garza."

"Any fingerprints on the girl's phone?" Lieutenant Rodriguez asked.

"Only one print," Colin said, "and it belonged to Monique. Zucca did find a few strands of hair, root attached, in the wood of that desk. And he'll get us the 3D scans as soon as possible."

I turned to Pepe. "Anything come over the tip line?"

Pepe took a big bite from his second burger, then said, "One woman claims that her dog can sniff out murderers. All we need to do is find the murderer and she'll bring in the pooch. This other guy—a medium—"

"Can men be mediums?" Joey asked.

"—claims that Monique is talking to him and that for $250, he can connect us with her spirit."

"Total rip-off," Luke said. "I know somebody who'll do it for $175 and a Whopper meal."

"So, no credible tips?" I asked Pepe.

"Not a one. And no serial murders with the same MO. Just a bunch of one-offs, like the one in San Diego."

"So the family," I said. "They're working-class people who spoil their daughters, who love their daughters. Dad is a neighborhood activist who led the charge against the rebuild but landed a job out of it—he's now an electrician at the site where Monique was found. Nappy Crase personally hired him."

Lieutenant Rodriguez slurped his noodles. "Coincidence?"

I sipped my Diet Coke. "His alibi is a little shaky, but Colin checked it out."

"Pann's for waffles at eight," Colin said, "then the Flying Fox from ten to midnight. Can't confirm anything after that."

"You thinkin' *he* did it?" Luke asked.

"We've seen worse, unfortunately," I said, then took another sip of soda.

"Like the monster who thought he was the Messiah," Lieutenant Rodriguez recalled. "Had babies with all five of his daughters. Then killed every one of them."

I nodded. "Also: Cyrus Darson has a record." I listed the charges.

"Sounds like he can't take no for an answer," Pepe said.

"Something he and Crase have in common," Luke added.

"Which is why . . ." I took a deep breath. "Which is why I'm putting Crase down as a person of interest on our big white board."

Lieutenant Rodriguez crossed his arms and dropped his chin to his chest. "Because?"

"Because Monique Darson was found on his property. Because he enjoys being with young women and then committing acts of violence against them. Because, most importantly, he has one of only two keys to that trailer. And the man with the *other* key just passed his poly." My body trembled as I said all of this. My shoulders hunched as I awaited the beat-down from my boss.

Lieutenant Rodriguez lifted his large head, then nodded.

That single gesture caused Luke to write NAP CRASE on the POI section of the board.

"So the phone stuff," Luke said as he handed Colin and me a thin stack of papers. "This is Monique's most recent bill, and the calls and texts she sent and received up until her death."

On every sheet there were highlighted rows of yellow, orange, blue, green, and pink.

"Yellow," he said, "are the most highlighted, and those are calls to and from Macie." He returned to the board and pointed to the seven o'clock time slot. "Macie texted Monique at 7:03 P.M., and then Monique's last call to Macie was Tuesday at 7:05 P.M. and lasted five minutes."

"A lot of pink calls, too," Lieutenant Rodriguez said, looking over my shoulder.

"That's her mom's line," Luke noted. "And as you can see, on Tuesday Angie Darson called Monique several times. The last call was 11:18 P.M."

Calls from Derek were in orange, and there were seven calls over the last week, the final one on Tuesday afternoon lasting for ten minutes.

"Interesting," I said. "She was planning to break up with him on Tuesday."

Blue highlights were Von Neeley's. Just two calls had been made last week—an hour-long conversation on Tuesday of the previous week and an eight-minute call early the following morning, probably before her graduation ceremony.

On every day, there had been a call highlighted in green.

"Who does this green number belong to?" I asked.

Luke grimaced. "Don't know. It's one of those throwaways you can buy without a contract. I tried calling, but it's disconnected."

I called that green-inked number, hoping that the line had suddenly become undisconnected. No luck. "Wanna put that on your to-do list?"

Luke was already scribbling into his steno pad. "Got it."

"And," Lieutenant Rodriguez added, "can you find out where Monique was when she got that late-night call from her mom?"

"Yep," Luke said.

Lieutenant Rodriguez turned to me. "Think this guy's in the wind?"

"Hell no," I said. "He's watching us and sipping tea."

Luke turned back to the board. "I've been filling in our girl's day, including phone calls and text messages, that trip to the pet store, and the last time the Darsons saw and spoke with her. There were five voice mails on Monique's line. Each was left by Angie Darson telling her to call, saying that just because she graduated didn't mean shit, *blah-blah-blah*, typical angry mother stuff." Luke then played the messages for us.

Hey, Monie. Call me.

Where are you? You need to pick up the phone and call me.

Okay, this isn't funny, Monique.

Monie? Please call me. I'm starting to worry, baby. I'm not mad anymore, okay?

With each call, Angie's voice moved from anger to fear. On the last call, she had said, "Please, sweetheart. Just call me and let me know you're okay."

No one spoke after Angie hung up that last time. The sound of the dial tone echoed through the room.

Panic and sorrow washed over me—I wanted to *do* something, to save Monique and assure Angie, but I couldn't. It was too late.

Luke cleared his throat, then whispered, "Let's look at the text messages." Then he handed out more papers. "The usual stuff at first. But then . . ."

I read aloud Tuesday morning's texts.

My cuz is sooo cute!!! Enjoy:)

Glad u made it home

Will call u and mom when I get home after mall

Thinkin of u makes me soo wet

I looked up from the page.

Joey cooed, "Ooh, Lou, say that again."

"Shut up, Jackson," Lieutenant Rodriguez snapped.

At that moment, I was grateful for Joey's stupidity—it had forced back shadows that were trying to seize the squad room.

"That text was sent to Mr. Green Ink," Luke said.

"I wonder," Colin said. "Is Mr. Green Ink also Mr. Hankie?"

No one responded but everyone had the same answer: yes.

Back to the log and the Tuesday afternoon texts.

So yeah . . . He say he dont wanna hurt my feelings. dont believe him at all

Ummm goood LOL

Wahy to end the year with a bang!

So whats up

"Call me when ur alone." I read that text message aloud twice.

Luke nodded. "Again, sent to Mr. Green Ink, at one thirty on Tuesday afternoon, right before that hour-long phone call to the same number."

"We need a name, Luke," I said, still scanning the entries. "Tick tock, my friend."

"I'm working on it," Luke said, "but don't plan a banquet around it."

There were fewer Tuesday evening text messages.

One from Macie at 5:33. *Stuck in traffic Tell mom not to wait for me.*

Macie sent another text a little after seven. *Just gonna stay with max CU tomorwo*

And then Monique sent a series of texts to Mr. Green Ink at 10:32 P.M.

U ready for me?

He texted back. *Always*

She returned his text. *Good*

Where r u?

With Renata

Can you handle this dick tonite?

Ya U think Ill give it up 4 nothin? LOL

Its like that?

U know it

U crazy, What this time?

Surprise me LOL

Ltes meet

Same place?

Ya at 11

At 11:18 P.M., Angie Darson had left that final voice mail.

At 11:20 P.M., Monique had texted Mr. Green Ink one last time.

Im here where u at? LOL

A final text message had been sent from Monique's phone to Angie Darson's phone.

I am ok

But it had been sent at 2:51 A.M. on Wednesday morning—Monique had been far from okay.

Colin asked me to take him to choir practice.

In other words, he wanted to hit a bar where off-duty cops hung out, got drunk, talked about hunting, women, and sex. A bar like the Short Stop over on Sunset, a spot now ruined by hipsters wearing ironic T-shirts.

I shook my head. "Sorry, no. Don't do that anymore."

"Aw, Lou," he said, as he put his feet on his desk. "Don't be so damn granola."

"I'm not—I just don't enjoy hanging out with assholes after my shift ends. Maybe Pepe or Luke will take you."

He rubbed his neck and glanced over to Luke at the coffeepot, who was now telling Lieutenant Rodriguez a foul-mouthed story about chasing a one-legged pimp down the Los Angeles River.

"Not that they would," I said, shouldering my purse. "You haven't been here long enough—no one trusts you."

"Is that a joke?" he asked, his ears and neck crimson.

"Nope."

"What are you about to do?"

"Eat," I said, and headed to the door.

"Mind if I come along?"

I minded—it had taken me almost my entire career to move from being alone all the time to being kinda accepted into the fraternity. I had combated sexism, racism, classism, and jerkwadism, and had finally earned my stripes. So, I had no sympathy for a new fish who had an up on me in three of those four categories.

"I'll buy you a beer." Then, he added, "Hell, I'll buy you dinner. You deserve it."

"Well, thanks." Payday was fourteen hours away and I had just paid car insurance. "Fine. I hate beer, though. A margarita and Jerry's Deli up the street from my condo."

Twenty minutes later, we had parked our cars in the shopping center's lot. The glow of the mai tai–colored sun had tinted fast-moving fog rolling off the Pacific. The sunset made you think life was one big Hallmark store. If you ignored the bereavement, divorce, and "get well" sections, then, yeah, it was.

The air inside the restaurant smelled of pickles, French fries, and fresh-brewed coffee, and almost every table was occupied by customers. The hostess led us to our very own red Naugahyde booth and both Colin and I darted for the east-facing side. We both wanted the view of the entrance, but I won because this was my city.

"I've heard about this place," Colin said, taking in the movie posters, black-and-white-tiled floors, and that drunken sunset beyond the windows. "Movie stars come here, right?"

I said, "Sure," and focused on the television monitor and the closed caption text scrolling at the bottom of the screen—Greta Glick was "live on location" in Baldwin Hills. *Breaking news. Police have found evidence that suggests that seventeen-year-old Monique Darson was murdered here, in this trailer . . .* The camera zoomed in on the construction trailer still wrapped in yellow tape.

Colin said, "Lieutenant Rodriguez told me—"

"I'm off the clock, and I leave work at work," I muttered, even though my attention was turned to my work now being featured on the news.

Colin grunted, then said, "My ex-fiancée—"

"A woman actually agreed to marry you?"

"Best thing that ever happened to her."

"Who *was* this lady?"

He flipped through the pages of the menu. "Police chief's daughter. We'd been together for a while—I'd break up with her, screw around some, make up again, break up again, that kinda thing. Dakota was all right—her teeth kinda drove me crazy."

"Why? They kept scraping against your ego?"

He winked at me. "You think my ego's big, I got somethin' bigger than *that*." He grinned, pleased with his massive . . . wit. "Anyway, it ended when I got caught with my pants down."

I lifted my eyebrows. "Literally? Or . . ."

"So there was this girl I'd been seein' on the side, just talkin' to, really. She was *hot*. I mean . . ." He flung his hand as though it had caught fire. "And so, you know, she wanted me, I wanted her, one thing led to the next, and we went to Cheyenne State Park. And we're there, on the hood of my Crown Vic, going at it, and man . . . Security cameras caught it all."

I was gawking at him now.

"*Technically* I didn't break any laws, but I needed to get the hell out of Colorado before the chief drop-kicked my ass off the side of Pikes Peak."

I laughed. "And then you came *here*? Neptune is more like Colorado than South Los Angeles."

The ancient waitress—her name tag read ALMA—tore my attention away from Colin's tale with glasses of iced water. Great timing, since I had started to shake from hunger and from that boxed-in feeling that everyone in the restaurant was watching me, judging me for stopping for the day, laughing, and having dinner.

"So what'll you have, sweetie?" Alma asked.

I ordered a pastrami sandwich and a pomegranate margarita.

Colin ordered corn beef and a Sam Adams. After Alma left us, he said, "You look lovely tonight."

I snorted. "You're an idiot."

He flushed. "I'm . . . I'm a little nervous, believe it or not."

"This isn't a date."

His flush deepened. "People don't know that. I mean, I'm attractive and you're—"

"And you're an idiot. Just shut up, Colin. Drink your water. Chew some ice."

"Not that you're my type."

I faked a sad face. "Color me disappointed."

He broke into a wide grin. "Don't get me wrong. You're cute and everything. You just wouldn't give a damn about pleasing me."

"Wow," I said, eyes back on the television, "it's like you've known me my entire life."

He leaned forward. "Has Greg—?"

"Change the subject."

"Why so serious?"

"Why is Greg any of your business?" I asked, the indifference now evaporating.

He rolled up his shirtsleeves—there was a tattoo of the Cracker Jack sailor boy and his dog on the inside of his left arm. "We can't talk about work. We can't talk about your husband. What's on Elouise's approved topics list?"

I twisted my lips as I thought, then said, "*American Idol* and . . . that's about it."

Alma brought over a bowl of pickles and green tomatoes.

"These are good." I speared a pickle, bit into it, and shivered as my mouth tingled from brine and cold vinegar. "Add pickles to my approved topics list."

"So your old partner?" Colin asked.

"He was a good guy."

"Yeah?"

"Took me in when nobody wanted to partner with me cuz I was a girl."

"Cuz girls be fuckin' up," he said.

I flipped him the bird and continued. "He was funny. An Italian-American Southerner. Bruno Abbiati. Dude was a hard-ass and he pushed me when all I wanted was to take the bar exam again. He'd say"—I dropped my voice an octave—"'Lou, you need to embrace bein' a gal. Perps think with their dicks and most men could fuck up a one-car funeral because of that, so you better take advantage of that stupidity.'"

"Ha," Colin said. "A one-car funeral."

I stabbed another pickle and bit off a chunk. "Bruno was a dinosaur, but he was a good guy."

"He die?"

"Nope. Parkinson's. The shakes made him turn in his badge."

"Back in the Springs," Colin said, "my partner was ultrareligious. I mean, when we weren't talking about the case he was tryin' to baptize me or read me these fuckin' pamphlets and . . ." He shook his head as he remembered. "I don't miss that guy. He creeped me out. You, though. I don't know *what* you believe, and I'm sure with us workin' together, I'll find out, but you seem . . ."

"Godless?" I asked.

He snickered, then plucked a tomato wedge from the bowl. "How does it feel? With your sister's case being similar to Monique's? With the Crase connection, I mean."

I sang, "'I don't think I can take it, cuz it took so long to bake it' . . ."

"So . . . you feel sad?" he said.

Someone somewhere aimed a remote control at the television and switched to *TMZ*.

"I love this show," Colin said. "I'm thinking of taking that bus tour. You know, to get my bearings."

I held my chin in my hand. "That's a different Los Angeles. Lindsay Lohan and Justin Bieber don't drive south of Pico. But don't let me stop you: take the tour. Just don't try to expense it as education."

"Your friend," he said, "the reporter. What's her name again?"

I smirked. "You really forgot her name?"

He did his squinty-eye flirty thing, thought about it, and added work-the-jaw-this-way-and-that.

"Just ask the question, Colin," I said.

"She go out with white boys?"

"Why? Know any cute ones?"

"Can you put in a good word for me?"

"Sure. When I have something good to say."

He laughed, then speared a pickle. "So was your sister like Monique?"

"You mean, living the double-life thing?" I nodded. "Except Tori didn't really hide it toward the end. Didn't have to since my mother worked all the time and was never home. By then, my father had been gone for a few years."

"The similarities are kinda spooky," he said. "Same age, same race, found in the same spot of town, the scent of Napoleon Crase's cologne in both scenarios."

Tori's bloody Nike sat in the evidence room at the Forensic Science Center, Number 13 in a queue of thousands, each ancient item needing DNA testing. The city council had given the LAPD several million dollars—from federal grants, private donations, recycled cans, change from everyone's car ashtrays—to process backlogged DNA evidence. Sometimes the results came too late, and the victim had already died or the bad guy had already died. Sometimes the results came but not soon enough, and innocent men were freed from prison, finally exonerated by proteins that never belonged to them.

I nodded, then said, "Yep. Damn spooky. And if I had been named after a tiny French general, I'd be worried right now."

"You like him for both, then?"

"Yes," I said, flat and final.

"Then I'll help you. I'll do whatever you need to take the son-of-a-bitch down."

I didn't know if I would take Mr. Shoot First, Ask Questions Later up on his offer—discretion was not his strongest quality. Still, I nodded as my eyes found the silent monitor: *TMZ* cameras were now following Kanye West up Rodeo Drive.

Alma slipped our sandwiches before us. Glistening slices of meat were piled high on kaiser rolls next to steak fries as thick as bamboo poles.

"Is Tori the reason you became a cop?" Colin asked.

"Yep. Typical, right?"

I had not intentionally planned a career with the LAPD—growing up in my neighborhood, you didn't trust the police. They stopped you for no reason. They harassed you in Westwood and Venice and anywhere blacks weren't supposed to be. And they had never found my sister.

I had earned degrees from UC Santa Cruz and then UCLA Law, doing well at both schools. But then I had flunked the bar exam. Twice. I didn't want to leave Los Angeles and take the bar in Nebraska just to pass, so I enrolled in the police academy.

Mom had not been thrilled with my decision and days passed before she started talking to me again. "Why am I supposed to be happy about this? Because now my *other* daughter will be taken away from me?"

But I wasn't "taken" anywhere. I had kept my wits about me as a patrol cop, working downtown and then the neighborhood that I knew, busting people who had sat next to me in algebra and metal shop. When I made detective five years ago, I had never seen such relief in my mother's eyes.

"You think your sister's alive?" Colin asked as he squirted yellow mustard on his corned beef.

I smeared spicy brown mustard on my bun. "The cop in me says she's dead, but the little sister in me won't believe that. The little sister tells herself to keep hope alive, that hope springs eternal, and umm . . . God willing and the creek don't rise."

Colin hoisted his beer and said, "To optimism, a disease worse than herpes."

We toasted.

After two large gulps of margarita, I said, "My mother's more conflicted than I am. She just wants closure. If she found out Tori's dead, then that would be awful, but at least she'd know for sure. Unfortunately, that makes her feel like she's a bad person for wanting closure." I took another gulp, and felt the tequila loosen strings that kept me as tight as a girdle. "At least Monique's mother gets to bury her."

"What does your husband think?"

I nibbled on a piece of pastrami. "He thinks I should let it go, but . . ." Another gulp of margarita. "We don't talk about it anymore. Talking always ends in an argument. To him, I'm 'emotionally unavailable' because Tori takes up the space in my heart that should belong to him, blah-blah-fuckin'-blah."

The meat tasted rubbery now. Freakin' Greg. Ruining my meal even though he was thousands of miles away.

I reached over and jabbed the tattoo on Colin's arm. "Never seen a tribute to snack food mascots on a cop's arm. What's the deal?"

He said nothing for several moments. "You know my father is in the Air Force. That means he goes away for long stretches of time. Being a kid, that was tough, not seeing your dad for months . . . But every time he'd come home, we would sit on the porch, just us two. And he'd pull out a box of Cracker Jack from his rucksack and we'd sit there on the porch, eatin' and talkin'. I'd tell him about baseball or girls I liked or . . ."

His eyes twinkled as he stared at his arm. "Those were some of the best times of my life." He waggled his head and sighed. "So I got a tattoo." He took a long pull from his beer.

"Why did you come to LA, though?"

"Wanted the beach," he said. "Wanted to get away from . . ." He studied his beer bottle, his thoughts lost in the suds there.

"Homesick yet?"

He smiled. "I miss the lightnin', the hikin', mountains . . ." He laughed, adding, "That's about it."

I said nothing as I stirred the slush in my glass. I envied Colin—he had a dad who came back every time he went away. What was *that* like?

"Homicide Special Section," Colin said, sensing that he should change the subject. "That's bad-ass. When should you hear back?"

"Don't know." And I didn't know. It had been a month since I'd completed the final interviews, and there had only been silence.

Colin bit into his corned beef and his eyes rolled to the back of his head. "This is good." He took another bite, and then another.

I watched him eat. Greg gobbled his food the same way, then whined about the meat sitting in his gut like a ball of dark matter.

Colin's cell phone chimed. He wiped his fingers on a napkin, pulled the phone from his jacket pocket, then glanced at the display. He frowned and muttered, "Shit."

"Lieutenant?"

"I wish." He sat the phone facedown beside his plate and stared at the last quarter of his sandwich. "Dakota, my ex. She's been calling all day."

"She wants you back?"

He drummed the table with his fingers and chewed his bottom lip. "Who knows what she wants. She says she's forgiven me. That I should come home."

I forked a piece of corned beef off his plate. "End of relationship haiku."

He counted on his fingers—five-seven-five—and that perfect smile of his peeked from the gloom. "I'm a poet and didn't even know it." He took some of my pastrami.

"Why'd you do it?" I asked.

"The girl in the park?" Beer bottle to his lips, he smirked. "Why is it any of your business?"

"It's not." I raised my glass for another toast. "May you be in heaven a full half hour before the Devil knows you're dead."

25

Tori, Golden, Kesha, and I arrived at Crase Liquor Emporium smelling of sweat, tobacco, and synthetic strawberries. Tori wandered the candy aisle while I grabbed packages of Twinkies and a grape soda. Golden and Kesha quickly purchased packs of Sno Balls and cans of Cactus Cooler, and left the store to talk to three shady-looking guys in the parking lot.

I found Tori still wandering the candy aisle. "You gonna get something?" I asked her. "We have seven minutes left."

Her eyes shifted to the front of the store. "No. I changed my mind. We should go."

As I started toward the cash register with my Twinkies and soda, Napoleon Crase shot from behind the potato chips stand. He grabbed Tori's arm and shouted, "I finally caught you." His face was pockmarked and oily. His Afro tilted left.

Tori cried out and pulled away from him. She shrieked, "Let me go," as two packets of Starbursts fell from beneath her shirt. "Lulu, help me!"

Terrified, I dropped my snacks and screamed. Then, I wet my jeans.

Napoleon Crase sneered at me, and growled, "You better get on, you little *bitch*."

I dashed out of the store. I didn't even stop to explain to Golden and Kesha what had just happened. I ran ten blocks, passed Howell's Bakery, the Laundromat, and the YMCA. I ran against red lights, dodged cars and buses, ignored the world and the people in it. I ran up the hill until I had reached my apartment.

Mom came home two hours later, nerves already jangled from teaching kids who hadn't paid attention during the regular school year. I rushed into her arms and told her everything. Leaving the apartment. Meeting up with Kesha and Golden. Buying chips and soda. Tori stealing and being caught. Leaving Tori behind and running home.

After screaming "What? *What?*" and having me tell the story two more times, Mom raced toward the front door, wild-eyed. "I'm gonna drive around. Go back to the store and see if I can find her. You stay here just in case she comes back." With that, she ran down the stairs, forgetting to close the door behind her.

For an hour, I stood at the living room window, staring out at our apartment complex, hoping that I'd see my sister climbing out of a car or strolling past the mailboxes. For an hour, I prayed and tugged my ear and held my breath.

Mom eventually returned. Alone. "Did she call?"

I bit my lip and shook my head.

Her shoulders slumped. Her purse slid off her arm and landed in the middle of the living room. Then, she trudged to the kitchen, grabbed the telephone receiver from its base, and called 911.

An hour later, Detective Tommy Peet was seated on our couch, taking my statement about all that had happened. "Someone needs to stay by the phone in case she calls," he instructed. "Don't worry. We'll find her. Girls like her disappear like this all the time. She's probably with a boyfriend or something." He left our apartment with a school picture of my sister in his pocket.

For dinner that night, Mom tried to broil round steak, but it burned. I ate two bowls of Cap'n Crunch instead. Then, I helped her fold laundry as we watched a rerun of *227*. At every commercial break, Mom would smile at me and say, "It'll be okay," even though the phone still had not rang.

Tori didn't come home that night.

When questioned, Napoleon Crase said that Tori had been stealing from him for months and that he had ignored it. But today, he couldn't let it slide, so he caught her. He threatened to call the cops, but she begged and cried and pleaded with him not to. She paid for her stolen candy and left the store very much alive. But he couldn't explain the abandoned pack of Starbursts near the Dumpster behind his store. He could not explain Tori's wristwatch—her last gift from our father—found on the asphalt beneath his Cadillac. Nor could he explain the single white Nike Huarache, women's size 6, also found near the Dumpster, seemingly pristine if not for that perfect drop of blood.

26

At home, the damp air smelled of salt and kelp, and my skin tingled from the cold. I lingered at the open garage door. So still. So quiet. Parked cars filled the streets—everyone was home tonight. A dark-colored truck with no plates had pulled into the last open spot a few condos down from mine. I wouldn't have noticed it, but cigarette smoke wafted from the driver's-side tinted window toward me. The driver didn't leave the truck, and even though I couldn't see the face, I sensed him looking in my direction. As I stood there staring, the truck pulled back out of its space, U-turned, and rolled south, away from me and into the fog.

Inside, I stored my guns in the closet safe and took a long hot shower. Ten minutes later, I retreated to the sun deck with my iPad, a glass of wine, and a shipping box from Amazon.

It was almost 9:30, and a small band in the courtyard a block away was playing Bob Marley's "Stir It Up." The thump of bass and drums drifted on the air along with the smells of night-blooming jasmine. A heron with unblemished white feathers alighted on the grassy island across the street, in search of a last-minute snack even though the sun had already dropped behind the Pacific.

I was off the clock but homicide detectives never stopped working—even though we tried to separate home life from casework. We lay in bed, our minds not sleeping. We sat in Adirondack chairs, our minds far from the crossword puzzle or magazine on our laps. We thought about relaxing but our thoughts quickly turned to that missing puzzle piece—*who did it?*

I didn't come out to the sun deck to think about Monique Darson and I had intentionally left her diary on my desk at work so that I wouldn't be tempted to read it during my downtime. But I grabbed my iPad and started swiping around the dead girl's Facebook page.

Monique Darson knew her killer—I was convinced of that. *Who was he?* One of her 2,133 Facebook "friends"?

If I visited every profile, would I find the man behind the green-highlighted telephone number?

Had he left one of countless messages of grief that now filled her Wall?

We miss you!

RIP Baby Girl.

Weeping may remain for a night, but rejoicing comes in the morning.

Monique's last status update had been posted a little after ten on Tuesday morning, several hours before her death. *Rise shine give God the glory!!* She had also posted a picture of her and Butter wearing matching head scarves and similar sleepy expressions.

I tapped on Photos and found more than twenty-five hundred pictures in her cyber albums.

"Geez," I said, rubbing my jaw, "where do I even start?"

At the pictures of Monique in a choir robe? Or maybe the picture taken in front of a Red Lobster. In it, she wore a gray pantsuit and stood beside a young man, tagged as Von Neeley, who wore a bow tie and a three-piece suit.

And then, there was the picture of Monique sitting in the bed of a glittery red El Camino, licking Derek Hester's shoulder tattoo while he threw up gang signs. And another picture of Monique hoisting a bottle of Boone's Farm Strawberry Hill, faded and sloppy, with Derek behind her, his hands groping her seventeen-year-old breasts.

Monique Darson had more lives than Garfield.

But then, didn't we all?

I returned to her Wall.

Relationship: *It's Complicated.*

It was *always* complicated.

There was a back-and-forth about that status change with a girl named Renata Reese.

Number 1 or Number 2? Renata had typed.

Number 7, Monique had answered. *Got me a big baller. LOL*

???

LOL!!!

:(Plz?????

I said its compliated. ROTFLMAO.

Im calling U RIGHT NOW!!!!

Monique had been tagged in a picture of seven black girls, their ghetto booties straining against the denim of their skinny jeans, hands on hips, Miracle Bras working wonders. Two Ed-Hardy-T-shirt-wearing males stood behind them, fingers in some salute that who-the-hell-knows what it was supposed to represent.

Poseurs trying to be hard.

"Let Derek and his BPS homies see you doing that," I muttered.

Whatchu claimin', fool?

Ladera Heights, nigga. 90056.

Pop-pop-pop-pop.

I clicked off the iPad and slumped in my chair. "Enough." I reached over to the side table for my wineglass and took a long gulp of 2007 Sequoia Grove cab. The band had switched to Earth, Wind & Fire and "That's the Way of the World." I grabbed the Amazon box from the table and tore it open. The packing slip said that Lena had sent me this book.

Impostress by Lisa Jackson. On the cover, there was a blonde in a Princess Leia–style dress, looking into the distance. There was a castle in a foggy background, and a glowing . . . lily pad?

Exactly what I needed.

One hundred pages later, I tossed the book on the deck and pulled myself out of that chair. I glanced at the clock on my phone—almost ten thirty—then found Greg's hotel phone number in the recent calls directory.

A woman answered.

I paused, then said, "Is this Room 3133?"

She said, "Yes. Is this room service?"

She sounded young, Japanese.

I squeezed shut my eyes as the Crazies started to claw their way in. "Is Greg Norton there?"

"Yes. Hold on."

I had started rocking in the chair, chewing my thumbnail, tugging at my silver hoop earring.

Greg came on the line.

"Who was that?" I asked him, hot as Satan's skin.

He paused—this was *not* room service. "Who was who?" He paused again, then said, "Oh. No one. What's up? I was just about to call you."

I knew No One. She had been with him that time in New York. She was different from Just a Friend in Toronto.

"What's No One's name?" I asked.

Greg paused a second too long. "Michiko. I told you about her."

"No, you didn't."

"She's just a friend."

Ah. There she was again. Just a friend. Like Angie.

"Michiko Yurikami," he said quickly, attempting to sound casual but coming off as cagey. "I know I've mentioned her."

"She work for M80?"

"No. She . . . She designs purses. Whatever. How's the case going?"

I closed my eyes and gripped the phone tighter. I confessed that Monique Darson's case had injected me with a renewed sense of purpose.

"I know she reminds you of Tori," he said, "but she isn't. Remember that."

And then, we talked about lie detector tests, Lakers season tickets, and the leaking showerhead. I swiped my eyes, expecting my fingers to be wet with tears. But I wasn't crying. *Why wasn't I crying?* I sat there, dry-eyed, trying to figure that out, listening to my husband lie and pretend that we were okay. I sat there as anger instead of sadness poisoned my heart, as the smell of kelp and jasmine curled around me, as the band played on.

27

It is almost midnight and even the lights in Stevie's and Treyanna's house are dark. Renata glances at the clock on her cell phone again, sucks her teeth, then says, "I am so stupid."

She told Big Jay just yesterday that she was more than a booty call. And he had said, "You right, you right," like he did every time. But nothing changed. *She* hadn't changed because here she was, driving to see him this late at night.

If it walk like a booty call, if it smells like a booty call . . .

She climbs into the Taurus and shivers.

Two days ago, Jalen dumped all of the milk from his sippy cup into the backseat, and now the car smells sour.

"Just one more stink," she mutters, shoving the key into the ignition. But she doesn't turn. Not yet. She usually whispers a prayer before she turns the key. *Lord, please let it start this time.*

Tonight, though, she pauses.

If she wants Big Jay to treat her right, then she has to respect herself first. No more late-night booty calls, then getting tossed out of his bed afterward, kicked to the curb an hour after she arrived. She deserves better, especially now. Jalen deserves better, too. And if Big Jay doesn't understand that, then she needs to be ghost.

She stares out the windshield, at her pink house down the block. She and Monie used to jump double Dutch in the front yard. Sit beneath that big magnolia tree with bags of Flamin' Hot Cheetos. They would lick their red-stained fingers and talk about boys and complain about their mothers. The yard is dark now, but silver television light shines in Momma's bedroom window. Momma had pretended to sleep as Renata crept past the bedroom door. Jalen was asleep in bed, next to his grandmother. He acted more like Momma's son than Renata's.

Why hadn't Momma stopped her? Why hadn't she said, "Big Jay ain't gave you nothing except a baby. He ain't good for nothing else." She said those words more than she said "the" and "and."

For Renata, the baby *had* been enough. Jalen was just two years old but he already knew how to spell his name. And he looked just like his daddy, with those wheat-colored eyes and those thick cow eyelashes and the freckles . . . She loves Big Jay's freckles, and the times that he lets her stay in his bed while he sleeps, she counts those rust-colored spots.

Jalen will never know his godmother. Renata will show him pictures of Monie, but that ain't the same as Monie being there. She is alone now, friendless, and sadness sits in her belly like an anchor, pulling her deeper and deeper into the darkness.

A tear slips down her cheek. Her heart—the part that remains— hurts. Her breathing hasn't been the same since . . .

"What the hell am I doing right now?" she whispers. She is not Cinderella, and a pumpkin is more reliable than her fifteen-year-old Ford. And Big Jay sure as hell ain't Prince Charming. But here she is, freshly showered and shaved, sitting in her car, hand on the keys, not turning, not going anywhere.

The world blurs as tears flood her eyes. "Oh, Monie," she gasps.

Tomorrow. She will tell the detective working on her friend's case everything she knows. She'll tell that detective about Von and Todd and—

Tap-tap-tap.

Renata startles at the rapping on the driver's-side window. She dries her face on her jacket sleeve and peers through the fogging glass. "Oh, hey!" She unlocks the door and rubs her hands together as she waits for her friend to join her.

God has answered the prayer she hasn't prayed. He knew that she was lonely, that she needed comfort and would attempt to find that comfort in the wrong place, in the wrong arms. And so He has sent the angel now sitting beside her.

No longer alone, Renata exhales with relief. "You scared me! You don't know how happy—"

The rear door opens and now the Devil sits in the backseat of the Taurus. The gun, the one pointed at the spot above Renata's car, makes her swallow her words. Her underarms prickle and beads of sweat pop on her nose. She moves her mouth but can only say, "Why?"

And she thinks of Jalen and his rust-colored freckles and she wishes she had given him a bath instead of letting Momma—

Friday, June 21

28

She sits on the couch and pretends to watch people her age auditioning for a dance competition. But she can't focus. And even though she wears one of his most comfortable dress shirts—Egyptian cotton, high thread count, the softest material in the world—she is far from relaxed.

He mutters to himself in the bathroom.

A razor blade scrapes against glass.

She closes her eyes and tries to block those sounds.

Scratching. Muttering. Scratching . . .

And she has to pee but she doesn't want to step into that bathroom.

Her mind races—nothing makes sense anymore.

He had tried to explain but his words started to slam and melt into each other until they turned into stew.

Lately, *physically*, he seems . . . *not there*. His arms and fingers jerk and jab a lot at times. He'll be eating something, eggs for breakfast, and the fork would fly that-a-way, sending yolk into the air. And sometimes he moves really slowly, as though he would die if he wiggled a toe. As though his bones would shatter if he walked like a regular person. His speech slurs now and his eyes glaze—and it isn't because of the coke, at least not all the time. And "Lorraine"? Who is she and why does he keep calling her by that name?

Something is wrong.

The door of the medicine cabinet slams shut. A second later, he lurches into the living room holding his mirror filled with white. At least he's moving quicker. He collapses next to her on the couch, being careful not to spill. He slips the mirror onto the coffee table.

She watches him but says nothing. Her bladder pushes against her belly—she really has to go, but the bathroom . . . He threw up and like always, he's left it for her to clean. She jams her hands beneath her butt and takes slow, steady breaths.

He smells sick. Sweet, but not a good, cinnamon-roll kinda sweet. More like a piece of meat inside of him is rotting.

He touches her thigh.

She bristles. Did he notice her flinch?

He bends over the mirror and snorts a line. Satisfied, he sits back and flicks a finger at his nose, nods toward the table.

She shakes her head. "Don't feel like it." Then she fixes her gaze on the television screen.

On a stage in Seattle, a chubby girl rolls around to Madonna's "Vogue."

He hoovers another line, then places his head in her lap.

She lays her hand atop his head, runs her fingers through his thinning hair but avoids his ears—the hair in his ears yuck her out. Then she hears herself say, "I know you told me and everything, but why? I mean, I understand but . . . I guess I don't understand. Not really. She wasn't gonna tell. If you had just let me talk to her . . ."

He doesn't speak.

Her heart races as though she's done three lines. Maybe she should shut up and watch the fat girl voguing and sweating.

He says, "You don't trust me?" His sick breath warms her thigh. Gives her goose bumps, but not the good ones.

She forces herself to smile. "Baby, you know I do. I just like understanding for myself."

He slowly sits up and stares at her. His corneas spin like pinwheels, twirling and spinning. "Come 'ere."

She snuggles against him, changes her mind, and climbs into his lap. She holds her breath as she kisses him.

He strokes her hair and lets his hand fall to her neck. "My sweet angel."

That's when her smile becomes true—she loves his hands. They are almost as strong as his will.

He clasps her neck with one hand. "Don't get soft on me."

"Baby," she coos, "I'm—"

His grip tightens. "We needed to, all right?"

Tighter now . . .

Her body trembles. "Yes."

"You wimping out on me now?" he asks. "After all I've given you? Thought you loved me."

Tighter . . .

"I do," she squeezes out.

The room whirls and something in her neck cracks. Her bladder threatens to release.

"Can I trust you, Lorraine?" he asks.

She nods—her head is pounding.

He releases her and chuckles. "My sweet angel." He bends over and snorts another line.

Air scrapes against her throat and it still feels as though his hands are clenching her neck.

By now, the fat girl on the television has left the building in tears.

He sits back and nods toward the table.

The coke will dull her pain. Clutching her own neck now, she bends over glass too messy to reflect. She takes one long snort and sends that numbing powder into her blood.

29

I startled awake in my dark bedroom, breathing hard and sweating. On the nightstand, the clock's red numbers blinked 3:15. My damp tank top stuck to my skin, and my heart pounded as though I had been running through the Grand Canyon. Someone too short and too lean to be Greg lay in bed beside me, hidden beneath the sheets. I stared at the sleeping figure, at the rise and fall of its breathing. I reached over and pulled away the comforter.

Tori lay there. Her skin was black and leathery, and her fingers were clawed. Creamy white moths fluttered around her body.

I couldn't move. Heat spread like brushfire across my face, and my scalp prickled. I needed to look away, but I couldn't look away. I couldn't scream. I couldn't move.

Tori pointed at me and whispered, "Lulu, help me."

My eyes popped open.

Clang-clang-clang.

I sat up.

Pinballs.

I touched the empty spot in my bed. No Tori. Just a dream.

Clang-clang-clang.

Greg was calling.

I grabbed my iPhone from the nightstand and climbed out of bed.

It was Friday.

After our good mornings and a rundown of the past ten hours (and no mention of Michiko Yurikami), Greg asked, "Breakfast with Mom today?"

"As is custom."

"Tell her that I bought her a couple of kimonos for her cruise."

"She'll like that," I said. "She's really into this Martin guy."

"Everybody needs somebody." Then, he paused and said, "I miss you, Lou."

My response: "I . . . *weruisfdakldsj*." Or something.

Then, as I grabbed a crisp white shirt and khaki Calvin Klein pant-suit from the closet, Greg and I talked—about the extraordinary time difference between Los Angeles and Tokyo, about going on vacation to Hawaii or Jamaica once he returned, somewhere with lots of rum and lobster. His promises of a romantic getaway pushed me deeper into the sad little sinkhole I had spent the night in. And despite my designer gear, I didn't feel fly. And no matter how much eye makeup and lipstick I found in my makeup bag, I wasn't Max Factor and therefore not skilled enough to hide the train wreck of emotion dogging my face.

During breakfast with my mother, I decided to say as little as pos-sible about the Monique Darson case. I also decided that I would not utter the words "Monique" or "the Jungle" or "Napoleon Crase." Instead, I would let her jabber on about her upcoming trip to the Bahamas, about shenanigans in water yoga class, and about the stray pit bull that had been terrorizing her Inglewood neighborhood.

And so it was.

"That's when I told Carol that we should just shoot the dumb dog ourselves." Mom smiled to herself and brought the coffee cup to her painted lips.

Mom was as tall as me, but she had been a wisp of a woman since the Bad Time. The big smile she'd worn before then, the one that had shown strong, perfect teeth, had been shelved for ages, only making appearances with the Hale-Bopp comet. But on this morning, there it was, speckled with toast crumbs and slick with melted butter.

"By the way," she said, "I think I'm going to retire from the school board next year. The thrill of being a paper-pushing administrator has lost its luster."

I sipped my coffee. "Paper cuts getting too dangerous?"

"You laugh, but remember what's-her-face Cecilia? She got flesh-eating bacteria after stapling her pinkie." She leaned forward, elbows on the table, chin in her hand. "So how is Gregory? Still in Japan?"

"Still in Japan." I faked a smile, then used my fork to jab at the square of hashed browns on my plate.

Mom tugged her right earlobe—a habit I had inherited—and said,

"How are you supposed to be trying to have a baby if he's always traveling?"

I eyed her, then gathered potatoes on my fork.

"Is there a new way I don't know about?" she asked, a smile in her voice. "Internet conception or some such thing?"

I lifted my eyes but not high enough to meet her curious gaze. "It takes time," I said to her silver-polished fingernails. Then, I stuffed my mouth with potatoes.

She waited for more, but when I didn't speak, she sat back in her chair. "He's not stepping out on you again, is he?"

I didn't dare move, not a bit. Just hoped that the T. rex named Georgia would move on and find new prey.

"Somebody has to sacrifice—"

"So it's my fault again?" I shot. "*I'm* the reason *he* has a pecker problem?"

Mom narrowed her eyes, not caring that the couple at the next table was now clutching their pearls. "Do you want a family or not? Or do you plan on playing cops and robbers until you die? I *wish* your father—"

"I wish, you wish, if wishes were fishes, just stop, Mom." Something inside of me burned, and by the end of this soul-killing experience, I would be a half-pound lighter.

Mom reached inside her purse and pulled out a folded newspaper. She opened it, then slid it before my plate. She tapped the story below the fold. *Southland Teen Found Strangled to Death*.

I shivered as my eyes skipped over a story I had already read.

"Some things stuck out as I read," she said. "First: the girl was found in the Jungle. Second: Napoleon Crase's name. And last: this is *your* case and you didn't tell me."

Now, my eyes met Mom's—she was seconds away from crying. I swallowed, but the lump in my throat remained. "I didn't . . . It may be a coincidence."

"Elouise—"

"And I didn't want to give you false hope."

That bright smile she had worn earlier had died. But then, she had come to breakfast to ask about the Bad Time, so maybe the smile had never been meant to stay.

She reached across the table and grabbed my wrist. "Tell me the truth, Elouise. Did he kill this girl, too?"

I opened my mouth to speak, but nothing came.

Those tears quivered in her eyes, waiting for the right word to force their fall.

"I'm working on it, Mom," I said. "Every single day, I'm working on it. Twenty hours a day. As I sit here with you, I'm thinking about it, looking at it in every way possible. I told you that I'd fix everything and bring Tori home, that he'd hang for it. And . . ." Now, my eyes burned but I forced that smile I gave whenever she was about to lose it. "I got this, okay?"

A single teardrop tumbled down her bronzed cheek. She squeezed my hand and let go. "Okay." She dabbed at her eyes with a napkin, then exhaled.

"As much as I would like to stay here and gossip," I said, "I gotta get going." I pulled two twenties from my wallet and dropped them in the center of the table.

"What's on your to-do list for the day?" she asked, now checking her makeup in a compact mirror.

"Playing cops and robbers, what else? You staying for a while?"

She nodded and gazed out to the marina. "It's always so beautiful here. I'll just sit and watch the boats for a while."

I leaned over and kissed her cheek.

She tugged a lock of my hair and told me that she loved me.

Guilt ate at my heart as I left her there. Strange. Didn't think there were any good parts of me left.

As I left the marina, I committed myself to scheduling a come-to-Jesus heart-to-heart with Greg, a state-of-the-union conference call to determine whether we should remain married or . . . do something else.

Would I actually follow through and have this difficult conversation, though? Really: how many of these talks had I planned and had then postponed? Jesus was probably tired of receiving appointment notices, only for me to send cancellations five minutes before the meeting's start. Fortunately, as I was committing and then doubting myself, my iPhone rang and pulled me from My Personal Problems and into a world of Somebody Else's Problems.

Two minutes later, I ended my call with Angie Darson and trudged into the squad room at half past eight.

Colin was already seated at his desk, talking on his cell phone.

Seeing him there, smiling and fresh-faced, sent fire and ice crackling through me. "Angie Darson called," I told him, even as he continued to talk to whoever it was. "We need to drive over to the house." I grabbed Monique's diary from my desk and lumbered to the garage.

Colin caught up with me at the Crown Vic and offered to drive. "Sorry about that. I was talking with Jen." He slipped behind the steering wheel, which he started to tap. "Jen's the fox from Whole Foods, remember?" *Tappity-tappity-tap*. "After I left Jerry's last night"—*tappity-tappity*—"she called and we hooked up. And now I can truly say that Jen is *all* woman. *Whoop-whoop!*" He glanced at me and his smile dimmed. "What's wrong, partner? You okay?"

I studied the single blue bird on the cover of Monique Darson's pink satin diary. "Are we gonna leave the garage anytime soon?"

He waited a beat, then started the car. "You wanna talk—?"

"No, I don't wanna talk about it." And no matter how many times

Colin looked at me as we drove, I refused to discuss all that was bothering me.

At every other stoplight, he'd say, "You'll feel better if you do."

But I kept my mouth shut. Even though I wanted to cry and throw things and curse, I couldn't bring myself to talk about Greg, about last night's phone call, and about Michiko Yurikami.

Because with talking came enlightenment, and with enlightenment came acknowledgment, and I didn't want to acknowledge *that* right then. And so I thumbed through Monique's diary as Colin drove, looking for any trace of Napoleon Crase—his initials, pictures of him, telegrams from him, *something*—as the Big Baller in the girl's life.

The pages were filled with Typical Teen Girl font—big loops, circles, and sometimes hearts over every i and j, leaning-to-the-left cursive that made the eyes of anyone older than twenty cross and fall out.

June 1. Can't believe I'm almost done with high school! Woo hoo! ... to celebrate, He told me that He'll take me to whatever restaurant I want. I'm thinking Gladstones in Malibu b/c I want LOBSTER! For real tho? Don't know how that dinner will happen since we are a BIG SECRET! Ssh.

June 12. Dress from Nordstrom. Mom put it on the card and told me not to tell Daddy and Macie. It's not like I don't deserve it. How many times does a girl graduate as valedictorian from high school? And Macie doesn't need OUR money anymore so she needs to SHUT UP and enjoy Max as long as she can.

June 17. I love Him. He scares me sometimes. He's just so passionate about things. But I love Him. I do! I want to be with Him all the time but I can't and so I keep finding excuses to call Him, to stop by His office, to touch Him, to sit in empty parking lots in the middle of the night just to be with HIM. I read that the human brain isn't fully developed until the age of 25. For me, that's 8 years from now, so the part that tells me, 'Don't do that! it ain't all there yet,' and I know it's not there bcuz it's getting a little crazy-intense with Him but I refuse to back away, to run back home to Mom and Dad and church ... And this whole situation with Mom ... tired of it, over it. Not going to spend ink writing about it. But I will say this: I'm soooo hungry!! My stomach is seriously rumbling right now and I want a double-double animal style and a chocolate shake but I don't want to smell like grease and onions. And He likes me skinny. Tiny tits. Small ass. Narrow hips. Derek is always telling me to "eat a sammich." I want to tell him, Nigga, learn to say the word. SAND-WICH. If tonight doesn't go right, if He tells me what I THINK He's going to tell me, and say those words I've been dreading since our first time together, then I don't know what I will do. That's a lie. I know. And if my plan doesn't work? Then Life will never be the same. FOR ANYBODY.

I turned to the next page, bookmarked with a slip of torn paper.

73881 Don Tomaso Drive. An address in Baldwin Hills, an affluent African American neighborhood that overlooked the Jungle.

Who did Monique know at this house?

My fingers flew across the car's computer keyboard as I typed in the address.

A few seconds later, the results blinked on the screen.

"Well, gee whiz." I *think* I said this aloud—my heart beat so loudly in my ears that I couldn't hear anything else. "So I just found something interesting: an address in Monique's diary. I just looked it up. Guess who lives there?"

"Attila the Hun."

"Also known as Napoleon Crase."

"Get the fuck outta here," Colin shouted, wide grin on his face. "Let's go on over there and kick his *ass*, man."

I studied the torn slip of paper. "Now, why would a seventeen-year-old girl have an old man's address in her diary?"

"Girl Scout cookies? Magazine drive?"

"Mister, can I paint your curb for ten dollars? Oh, and I'll wear my cheer uniform if you say yes." I slipped the address back into the crease.

"What the hell are we waitin' for?"

I took a deep breath, then said, "I need more than this."

Colin gawked at me.

Before he could protest, I held up my hand. "If I screw this up, shoot my wad just cuz I found an address in this girl's diary and he and his lawyer come up with a reasonable explanation, then he's gone. And I'll go back to hunting for something else to get him on, but by now, he's in Venezuela or someplace, laughing at me and beating up the high school girls of South America."

Colin didn't want to, but he nodded.

"I *will* have Napoleon Crase lying on a stainless-steel table," I said. "Trust."

Colin parked in front of the Darsons' house. Before he opened the car door, he touched my arm and said, "We're partners, correct? We got each other's back, right? I know we just started workin' together and, *technically*, you don't know me from a jackrabbit, but you can trust me, okay?"

I forced a smile to my face and squeezed his hand. "It's too early in the day to talk about bullshit, Colin, and we have a killer to find right now." I squeezed his hand again, then dropped my smile as he climbed out of the car.

31

Police theorized that Tori had intentionally run away from home because she had fallen in love with Li'l Tee, a Piru Crip wanted for a homicide in Compton. My mother, willing to believe anything if it brought her daughter home, had searched through Tori's diary to support the cops' theory. She found only one reference to Tee, a.k.a. Terrell Jones. *November 16, 1987. Tee is the most ignorant, backwards person in the whole world. I wish he'd just GO AWAY!!*

I tried to help and told Mom, "She liked this guy named James. She always talked about him on the phone with Golden."

"Do you know him?" Mom asked, her eyes bugged. "This James? Do you know him?"

I shook my head, then added, "But he's on the football team." I showed Mom a picture of James in the student newspaper. Broad-shouldered, cornrows, hazel-colored eyes—Tori's type. "She talked to him on the phone, like, a couple of weeks ago," I continued. "She told Golden she was in love with him. That he was gonna take her with him when he made it into the NFL."

Mom shook her head. "But she doesn't mention him in her diary."

Still, Mom told the police about "James on the football team" and his plan to whisk Tori away. But the cops never questioned James, preferring their original idea of Tori on the lam with Terrell Jones. It didn't take long for detectives to find Terrell. He hadn't seen Tori in months—as Inmate No. 638493 since January 1988, he hadn't seen many people.

After that lead fizzled, Detective Peet returned to our apartment to interview Mom again. He tried to avoid eye contact as much as possible. "Was your daughter a virgin?"

I was peeking from the hallway and saw Mom's eyes widen with shock.

She gasped, then said, "I don't know what that question . . ." She took a deep breath, then said, "As far as I know, Victoria . . . yes. Although I still don't understand—"

"Who were her boyfriends again?" he asked.

Mom pulled out a list she had created while scouring Tori's diaries for Li'l Tee references: Lawrence Bales, Alan Dorsey, Samuel Griffith, Derrick Alexander, Royal Fisher, and Mikey Duncan. Mom had also placed football player James Kinney on the list.

Detective Peet reviewed the names, then whistled. "Your little girl got around." He stuffed the list into his jacket pocket and considered his notepad. "Did she use drugs?"

Mom shook her head. "No."

"Has she been in trouble before?"

"Not with the police," Mom said. "At school . . . Well . . . She's had some trouble—"

"Did you ever hit her?" Detective Peet asked. "Punish her? Chastise her? Embarrass her for misbehaving? Do something that made her run away?"

"No."

The detective flipped to a clean page in his notepad. "What about your husband?"

Mom clutched her neck, then dropped her gaze. "He's away."

"Away. Of course." Detective Peet gave Mom a stupid smile, then stood from the couch. "I'll keep in touch. I may want to talk to your husband later on."

He had been in our house for only eight minutes.

32

Angie and Cyrus Darson sat silently on the living room couch. Their eyes skipped from Colin down to their tight fists, to the coffee table, then back to Colin. Their red-rimmed, hollowed eyes told me that they had not slept. Angie had lost weight overnight and seemed shrunken and skeletal in her droopy cable-knit sweater. Cyrus hadn't shaved— salt-and-pepper stubble had overtaken his face and his dreads hung at his shoulders like clubbed snakes. The house stank of burnt toast and cigarettes, which had snuffed out the more pleasant scents of the roses, lilies, and hydrangeas sitting on the mantel, on the sideboard, and on the dining room table. The mail had piled up, and a tower of envelopes and catalogs teetered on the coffee table. Other than our voices, the muted roar of the clothes dryer was the only sound in the house.

Around seven that morning, the Darsons had claimed Monique's body from the county morgue. Macie had refused to go into the building and had wept in the car.

After Cyrus told me all of this, I had started to ask questions about Monique's life . . . including *that* question. Neither he nor Angie had answered it yet, and now here we sat, in uncomfortable silence.

I turned to Colin. "Can you . . . ? Umm . . . Can you call Dr. Brooks? He should have test results by now. Thanks."

Colin's lips flattened and the muscles in his neck flexed. "Sure," he growled, pissed with being dismissed from another interview *again*.

I offered him a barely there what-can-I-do shrug and a comforting smile to the Darsons. Once the front door closed and Colin was out of the house, I asked *that* question again: "So, other than Derek and Von, do you know of any other men Monique may have had a sexual relationship with?"

Cyrus hunched over—talking about his dead daughter's sex life was transforming him into an armadillo.

"I told her 'be careful,'" Angie said, taking the scenic route to a response. "I knew she was active—and she wasn't a ho about it, so don't get it twisted—but I wasn't interested in becoming a grandmother anytime soon. I ain't Renata's momma, all excited about taking care of somebody else's babies." She rubbed her arms, then closed her eyes. "I know I'm not answering . . . She ain't mentioned nobody else."

"Did you know what *type* of relationship she and Derek had?" I asked.

"She didn't *have* a *type* of relationship like that," Cyrus said. "Not with him. We would've put a stop to that immediately—we don't allow gangbangers in this house and Monie would never be interested in boys like that. No. We didn't know." He looked to his wife for an "amen."

But Angie was biting her thumbnail and tugging at her sweater.

Cyrus narrowed his eyes. "You *knew*?"

She gave a hesitant nod. When Cyrus hopped up from the couch and stormed around the living room, she shouted, "What was I supposed to do, Cyrus? She's a grown woman."

"What the *hell*, Angie?" Eyes wide, he held out his hands. "You let our baby date a *thug*? A *felon*?"

"The girls date a whole buncha people," she shouted back. "Am I supposed to know every boy that Macie talks to? That ain't my job no more!"

"I talked to Derek yesterday," I said. "He's no longer a suspect."

Cyrus shook his head. "That doesn't matter."

"For me, it does. Part of an investigation is not only identifying suspects but eliminating them as well." Since neither parent responded, I continued. "I *do* know that Monique was seeing an older man. She called him a 'big baller' on her Facebook page. And she talked to him on the phone at least once a day. Has an older man that you don't know visited sometime over the past several months?"

Both parents shook their heads.

"Can you keep a list for me from now on? Like, who sends a card, who shows up at the funeral service and so on?"

A zombie nod from Angie.

Cyrus had hunched over to support himself on the sideboard. He used one of his hands to rub his left temple.

"Mr. Darson," I said, "are you okay?"

"Headache," he muttered, with his eyes closed.

"He hasn't slept," Angie explained. "Nobody has." She turned to him. "Baby, you want an aspirin? Or—?"

He waved her off. "Let's just . . ." He groaned, stood upright. "What else do you need, Detective Norton?"

I pulled from the expandable file a copy of Monique's phone records. "Do either of you know this number?" I pointed to an entry highlighted in green.

"No," Angie said. "Who does it belong to?"

"We don't know," I said, "but we will soon." I slipped the records back into the folder. "One more thing. Cyrus, you were against the Santa Barbara redevelopment efforts. You protested at the site for more than a year and attended city council meetings and—"

"He's a community activist," Angie said. "What Crase and them was doing was wrong, bringing in outsiders to rebuild our neighborhood without hiring people *from* the neighborhood. So yeah, we picketed. Us and about three hundred other people from Leimert and Crenshaw and Baldwin Hills."

Cyrus threw a weak glare in Angie's direction—he was still agitated that she knew their daughter was screwing a banger.

"We were influential, too," Angie continued. "We knew we hit a nerve, cuz Crase started sending thugs to try and scare us. Throwing rocks and jumping people, late-night phone calls, sleep with the fishes BS. But we didn't back down, even though it had gone past arguing. People were getting hurt now. If there was nothing shady going on, why was Crase and them doing this to us?

"And so, other people started asking questions. *Were* they gonna hire minorities once the shops and theater and hotel opened? *Were* there gonna be black businesses? *Were* the police gonna be around to keep the knuckleheads out? *Would* our schools get some of that tax revenue?"

"And you two led all of this?" I asked.

Angie gave a weak smile. "You do what you gotta do. What's right is right."

"And now, you, Cyrus, work at the same condo site you had protested."

"Yeah," Angie said, "and at least twelve percent of the guys down there come from the community."

"I'm truly impressed," I said with a nod. "Cyrus, where were you working before?"

He picked at a scab on his elbow. "Here and there. Whole lotta places."

I waited for more but he didn't speak. "Like where? Who gave you a 1099 at the end of the year?"

Angie held up a hand. "Why is that important, where he worked?"

I offered her an assuring smile. "We need to consider everyone in your circle as potential suspects. Including past employers and co-workers."

Cyrus swallowed, then said, "Can I get you that list later today?"

"Sure," I said, "but let me just put this out there, though. I don't care if you worked under the table, that you didn't pay taxes on income. Whatever. I'm not the IRS."

My assurance didn't offer relief—his jaw remained tight as an oyster.

"So no hard feelings from the Crase Group after the protests?" I asked. "Napoleon Crase has let bygones be just that?"

"Why wouldn't he?" Angie asked.

"Because," I said with awe, "he and his investors had spent more than thirty million dollars on this project, and because of you, it all stalled for more than a year. He's rich, but he ain't so rich that he wouldn't notice a couple of million missing from his checking account because of a few neighborhood malcontents."

Angie started to rebut my argument but stopped. Instead, her mouth slowly fell open.

Because with talking comes enlightenment . . .

"What are you . . . ?" she whispered. "You don't think Napoleon Crase had something to do with Monie, do you?"

Cyrus gaped at me. "You're kidding, right?"

I wanted to mention Crase's address found in Monique's diary, to show that I was far from kidding. No—that discovery could possibly wend its way back to the Devil himself.

"Crase is an older man," I said instead, counting off fingers. "He's rich. He wouldn't want his name out there as a pedophile. And Monique—"

"Would never sleep with Napoleon Crase," Cyrus shouted. "Never in a million . . . That's . . . that's *sick*."

"But then you thought she'd never sleep with Derek Hester, either," I pointed out. "Never in a million years."

"And when she was about to expose him, he killed her," Angie murmured.

"It's certainly a theory I'm considering," I said. "Again: everyone is a suspect." To Cyrus, now pacing near the living room window, I said, "Have you ever seen Napoleon and Monique together? Has he ever met her? Has he ever called the house and she answered the phone?"

"No," he shouted. "No, no, no!" He clamped his hands over his eyes. "I refuse to believe any of this. He'd never do anything like what you're suggesting."

I wanted to put Cyrus Darson and a dish of Super Glue into one of Zucca's airtight chambers to see if Napoleon Crase had been handling him lately.

"He has a history of dating very young women," I said, holding up a finger. "He has a history of *assaulting* those very young women," I added, holding up a second finger.

Angie had started to whimper as the idea of Napoleon Crase and her daughter expanded like foam in her mind.

"Angie," Cyrus said, "Nappy Crase would never . . . He has a girl-friend. Several girlfriends."

"I wouldn't call Brenna Benevides a *girlfriend*," she snapped. "She's a whore, and that's the truth." She turned to me. "And she looks like she just stopped wearing training bras last week."

"What numbers do you have for Napoleon Crase?" I asked. "Give me everything. Assistant's number, fax, Twitter handle, anything and everything you have."

"I'll get it." Angie, grateful for having something to do, hopped off the couch and hurried to the den.

Alone now with Cyrus, I said, "So how long have you known Crase?"

"Long time," he said, then swiped his mouth.

"Was your relationship always adversarial?"

He shook his head.

"Not until you became an activist and blocked his progress?"

He said nothing.

"Your record."

His shoulders jerked back as though I had just reined him in. "What about it? All that was a long time ago."

"I understand. But is it possible that someone from your long-time-ago . . . ?"

Cyrus crossed his arms.

"You get that scar during one of your stints in County?"

"Did I get it in County? Yes, that's where I got it."

I paused, just to let the lie stretch its legs. "Is there anything else in your past that I should know about? Again, I just want to find out who killed Monique."

He shoved his hands into his pockets.

"I know Crase is, like, your boss or whatever. And I know that he probably sponsored that television over there and your wife's brand-new Prius, but you cannot protect this man. Do you understand me?"

Cyrus folded his arms and said nothing.

"He may have killed your daughter, Cyrus. He may have murdered Monique."

He stared out the window, as silent as a sphinx.

"When bad people don't get what they want," I said, "they destroy. You blocked Napoleon Crase for more than a year, and now he may be trying to destroy you . . . starting with your children."

"I know that," he spat. "You don't think I know that?"

I slipped over to stand behind him. "You want me to solve this case, you gotta help me. Right now, though? I'm putting together a puzzle without a picture."

Cyrus Darson didn't speak and refused to give me the help I needed—even though that meant the Bad Guy going free. Again.

33

Cheap phone to his ear, he stands on the veranda with the city sprawled before him. Usually, he is a deliberate man—he eats the same breakfast each morning, takes three different routes to work on alternating days, and chooses the type of woman he beds. Lately, though, he knows he has been acting too impulsively. And life is getting a little messy because of his rashness. He must do something to regain control. Which means he must to do something about her. *Now.*

Just an hour ago, he had cruised the streets behind the wheel of his truck—west on Florence, north on La Brea, east on Century, east, south . . . He had found another Boost Mobile store in the worst part of South Central, one in between a liquor store and a fish market. There were lots of people going in, lots of people coming out; dealers and gangbangers in the parking lot selling and buying dope and whores; poor people everywhere, so many people, like sand at the bottom of the ocean.

He had purchased the disposable phone with cash. Had used the name "Ato Zee."

The saggy-tittied salesgirl didn't get the joke and didn't care enough to ask for his identification—hell, everyone knew Benjamin Franklin.

And now, with the new phone to his face, he dials his angel's number. The line rings . . . rings . . .

He paces and watches a police helicopter circle over a Culver City neighborhood miles away.

"Hello?" Her voice feels like warm buttered rum. Just hearing it makes his heart throb, makes his pulse slur one beat into the next.

"Hello, my queen," he says. "You amaze me."

No hyperbole. She has done everything he has asked of her. She believes everything he says. Her commitment runs deep, and now he knows how Hitler felt as Germans did all kinds of shit in his name. Even then, though, some had seen the so-called light and had betrayed their Fuhrer. How had that happened?

And can it happen to him? Could his angel, his right hand, betray him?

Of course she could. Of course she will.

He must do something about her. *Now*.

"What do you want this time?" he asks. "You deserve something extra-special."

"Umm . . . Surprise me," she says. "I'm easy to please. You know—"

A shot zigzags from the front of his head to the base of his skull. The pain left by the fiery trail knocks him to his knees, makes him clench the phone so tight it cracks. Hurts so bad he can't even scream. His body shakes and the city dims . . . dims . . .

A slight moan trips from his lips and his hands loosen. Tears well in his eyes and now he hears her, still on the phone, calling his name.

Light-headed, he struggles to kneel, dull sharpness still lodged in his shoulders. He lifts the phone to his ear and tells her, "Hold on." He grabs a filled water bottle and shakes it. He twists off the cap and plucks a long-handled cotton swab from the couch cushions. He dips the fluffy end of the swab into the cloudy liquid, then sticks the wet cotton up his nostrils. In just seconds, his face numbs and the pain lessens and he wishes he could shoot cocaine directly into his brain instead of snorting it and swabbing it.

"You okay?" she asks, her voice shrill. "I'll come over—"

"No," he says, weakly, "I'm fine."

"I'll do anything for you," she whispers.

"Die for me?"

She pauses, then says, "Yes. I love you."

He smiles—he must do something about his angel before her change, and his, comes.

34

Outside the Darson house, Colin sat on the hood of the car, texting on his phone.

"You drive," I told him, then slipped into the passenger seat. As soon as he turned the ignition, I jabbed the heat button—another cool June day in Los Angeles.

In silence, he pulled away from the curb and out onto Leimert Boulevard.

"Cyrus Darson knows something," I said. "And I don't know what that is or why he's keeping quiet, but I *do* know that he's protecting Napoleon Crase."

No response from Colin.

"Any word from Brooks?" I asked.

"Monique had HPV," he said, as though he'd said, "A car has wheels."

"Shit," I said, eyebrows raised. "Did she know?"

He nodded. "She'd gone to the doctor right before graduation. Dr. Brooks is faxing you the lab tests. She didn't have any alcohol, weed, or any other controlled substance in her system, but he did find semen. There hasn't been an immediate DNA hit on that yet. Lieutenant's bumped up all of our DNA requests to Priority."

I playfully punched him in the arm. "See? That's good stuff. I told you Brooks would have something."

Colin's knuckles whitened as he gripped the steering wheel tighter.

I tapped my earring. "You mad at me?"

He jammed his lips together, then pushed out, "Nope."

"If you got something to say, spill it or squash it. I don't have time or patience for bullshit."

He considered me with fire-filled blue eyes. "You sent me away."

"Excuse me?"

"The interview with Monique's parents," he said. "You sent me on an errand like I was your kid or some shit."

I ran my fingers through my hair, then tugged a lock to make sure that I was awake and that we were really having this conversation. "Have you ever taken classes in body language?"

"Yes."

"Then you know—"

"That they were embarrassed. I know—"

"Especially in front of a funny-talking white man wearing cowboy boots."

"Funny-talkin'? Who are you callin'—?"

"Put on your big girl panties, *Detective*, and get the fuck over it, okay? I'm done talking about it." I crossed my arms and glared out the passenger-side window. "Get on the 10 West, then exit on Cloverfield."

Colin accelerated, his jaw tight, and roared up Crenshaw Boulevard as though the street had just called his first cousin a whore.

Since I had no one to talk to, I ran Von Neeley's name through the car's computer. *No priors.* Not even a parking violation. The boy was as clean as the Mormon Tabernacle on Christmas morning.

Colin exited at Cloverfield, and we were soon cruising the clean streets of Santa Monica, an ocean-side town still lost in morning fog. I could barely pick out Yahoo! over there and Universal Music Group over there. A few more blocks down Colorado and we reached the service department of W. I. Simonson Mercedes-Benz.

Colin parked at the curb.

"You can take the lead," I told him.

He gasped. "Well, gee whiz. I'll get to send *you* out to make copies?"

I shot him a glare that could sour milk.

He blanched, because that's what men do with that glare.

"Keep it up, smart-ass," I spat. "You think you don't have friends in Southwest now, just keep pissing me off."

He slumped in the driver's seat and rubbed his mouth. "All I'm sayin'—"

I climbed out of the car before he could explain. *Didn't he hear me?* I was in no mood to kiss boo-boos and hand out juice boxes. There were worse things in life than being sent from a living room. Being murdered, for one.

Von Neeley, the young man from Monique's Facebook albums, stood behind the Enterprise Car Rental desk in the service department's waiting room. Handsome, clean-cut, no earrings or visible tats. Today, he wore blue slacks, a blue necktie, and a white dress shirt. He was so shiny that he probably bled Windex; so clean, he probably peed Lysol. Right now, he had three customers in line—a sixty-year-old cougar who should not have pulled on those clingy yoga pants this morning; a blond chick who rocked her pair; and a twink with frosted hair, a goatee, and Elvis Costello glasses.

"A little crowded," Colin observed.

"We'll wait," I said, and wandered to the coffee bar.

Colin followed me and grabbed a complimentary muffin from the basket. Then, we plopped on the leather couch to watch CNN.

And as we sat there with giant muffins and cups of French-roasted coffee, fancy people with fancy cars left their keys with very clean repairmen wielding clipboards and wide smiles. I could have sat there all day.

Ten minutes later, Von had placed each of his customers into a courtesy car, bidding each to have a blessed day.

I fixed a second cup of coffee and watched as Colin moved toward Von. I didn't know what Colin was saying until Von's "Can I help you?" smile faded. That's when I joined them.

Colin introduced me as his partner, and then the three of us wandered out of the building and to the employee parking lot. We stopped near an older-model gray Mercedes that had never seen dirt in its life. "This your car?" Colin asked the kid.

Von nodded. "Yes, sir."

"Mind if I look in?" I smiled to take the edge off the question.

"No, ma'am," Von said. "Go right ahead."

I opened the door and was quickly enveloped in New Car Smell wafting from a tin of freshener in the ashtray. Not much to see: CDs, an open pack of Juicy Fruit gum. No blood. No dog hair.

I closed the door and gave Colin a slight headshake. *Clean.*

"When did you hear about Monique?" Colin asked.

Von licked his lips. "I guess you guys had just left the house yesterday when Macie called me and . . . Yeah, yesterday."

"When was the last time you talked to Monique?" Colin asked.

"We were together on Sunday," Von answered. "After Mass, I went over to her house. That was around one o'clock."

"And what did you two talk about?"

Von's eyes watered as he scanned the sky. "I wanted to see her that night to talk about our future. I'm supposed to fly down to Belize tomorrow with our church—we're building houses and an orphanage. Before I left the country, though, I wanted to get some things straight with her."

"What kind of things?" I asked, scanning his face, hands, and neck for scratches or bruises. *Clean.*

"I was gonna ask her to marry me," Von said. "We'd wait until after she graduated from college to get married, but that's what was supposed to happen."

"Did you propose?" I asked.

He shook his head, shoved his hands deep into his pants pockets. "It didn't feel right. Her phone kept ringing, and she kept answering."

Colin and I glanced at each other. We had studied the phone records and so we knew who had been calling—a Blood who yearned to be Gilligan.

Von laughed bitterly. "Yeah, I know about Derek. She used to throw him in my face whenever she wanted something. Pit us against each other like we were dogs. Drove me crazy cuz she was better than that, better than being his girl. But it's hard to compete financially with a dealer, you know? I tried, though."

"Is that why you bought her that Lexus?" I asked.

He sucked his teeth. "That wasn't me. Homeboy got it for her."

Colin and I looked at each other again—Derek didn't buy the Lexus, Von didn't buy the Lexus, so who bought the freakin' Lexus?

"Was Monique seeing anyone other than you and Derek?" Colin asked.

Von glared at the sidewalk. "No."

"Do you know anyone who could've killed her?" Colin asked.

"Derek," Von muttered.

"Anyone else?" Colin asked.

He shook his head.

"Did you kill her?" I asked, voice soft. "Maybe not intentionally, since you say you loved her, right? Maybe because you were jealous of her relationship with Derek? If I can't have her, no one can, that sort of thing? Maybe you hit her a little too hard or . . . ?"

A teardrop slid down Von's cheek. "No, ma'am. Never. I loved Monie. I wanted to spend my life with Monie. I stayed in California for college just so I could be *near* Monie."

Von's "I loved Monie" was Splenda compared to Derek's C&H Pure Cane "I loved Monie."

I bristled, cuz boy, I hated artificial sweeteners. And I hated men like Von Neeley, the "nice" guys who always wanted to pray with you, who always offered you blessings and put-on smiles. Men who always told women how to live, what to wear, who to sleep with, all in the name of God. Whores and thugs in the shadows, many of them, who committed the worst acts of violence against women and children. Men's Central was filled with huckster-holy men who had hooker problems, free-flying fists, and "sex addictions." I had thrown my fair share of these assholes in jail myself and so I knew one when I saw one. And Von Neeley was definitely a Jerk-in-the-Lord trainee.

"So why should I believe that you loved Monique?" I asked Von now, a little heat in the question. "That you'd never hurt her?"

"Because," he said, "I'm not that type of guy, ma'am. I'd never—"

"You two ever argue?" I interrupted.

"Yes, ma'am."

"Did your arguments ever get physical?" I asked. "You ever touch her?"

He shook his head so hard, he almost gave himself whiplash. "No, ma'am. Never."

"Did you ever *threaten* to hurt her?" I asked. "You know: just to scare her?"

"No, ma'am."

If he called me ma'am one more time . . .

"I heard that you hated Monique doing the cheerleading thing," I said.

Von jammed his lips together, then said, "I think it sent the wrong message."

I nodded. "So did you ever try to convince her to stop?"

"Many times."

"How did you do that?"

"Just . . ." He shrugged, "I talked to her. Prayed with her."

"Argued with her?"

He nodded. "A few times, but nothing . . ."

When he didn't finish his sentence, I said, "Nothing what?"

He bit his lip and didn't speak.

By now I knew that Von Neeley did not kill Monique Darson—he was a jerk and a liar, but he wasn't violent. Still, I needed his alibi to cross him off the list, just so I could tell Lieutenant Rodriguez that I had followed every lead. But the little fucker kept lying to me and refused to go quietly into the night. So, I squinted at Colin, then crossed my eyes.

My partner gave me a small smile—he, too, knew that Von Neeley was not our guy—then reached into the case file. He pulled out a head shot of Monique Darson on the coroner's table, eyes closed, lips purple, neck broken. He held it up for Von to see.

The kid groaned and dropped his eyes to the sidewalk.

"This is what happens when you let anger take over," Colin said, matter-of-factly. "You're smilin' one minute, she says somethin' hurtful the next minute, somethin' like, 'Derek fucks better than you ever will,' and then, *BOOM!* You blank out and lose time. Next thing you know, your hands are wrapped around her neck and she ain't breathin'."

Colin considered the photo, then peered at Von. "You didn't *mean* to do it. It just . . . *happened.* Is that the deal, Von? Man to man, be honest with me. Did she set you off and shit just . . . *happened?*"

Von's shoulders were shuddering as he tried not to cry. "No, sir. She said stuff like that all the time, hurt me to the core. But I never reacted."

"*Never reacted?*" I asked too loudly. Okay, I was done—with him, with men. Greg thought I was some ignorant housewife, oblivious to his late-night phone calls to skanks at home and abroad because I was mesmerized by a dick and a Porsche; Colin, another arrogant snot, thought he knew Los Angeles and criminals and everything better than me. And now, *this* kid thought I was a stupid bitch with a badge. He was about to see how stupid I could be.

I crossed my arms and took a step closer to Von. "A girl tells you that another man is a better lover than you and you *never* reacted? Bullshit."

With pleading eyes, Von whined, "No, ma'am. I didn't."

"Then, why didn't you?" I asked. "What kind of man is cool with hearing bullshit like that?"

Von's mouth moved, but no words came.

"I have her diary, Von," I continued. "And I've read about your little temper. She wanted to break up with you, and she was scared shitless what your reaction would be. Why would she be scared?"

He shook his head and his shoulders slumped.

"You threaten her?" I asked again.

"No, ma'am." His head dropped—he was getting tired now.

"Where were you on Tuesday night?" I asked.

"Out with friends, ma'am."

"*Stop*—!" I took a deep breath, exhaled, then said calmly, "Stop with the ma'am thing, all right? It means jack-shit to me. So which friends were these that you were with?"

"*Fr-fr*-from *sc-sc*-school," Von stuttered. "We all drove up to CityWalk to *s-s*-see a movie."

"What time was the movie?"

"Eight o'clock."

"Where did you park?"

He blinked. "Huh?"

"Which lot did you park in?" I asked, trying not to smile. "Which level?"

He wet his lips, and said, "P3?"

"Is that the Frankenstein level, the Dracula level, or the Wolf Man level?"

"Umm . . ."

"I'll need your friends' names and numbers."

"They didn't see the movie with me," Von said. "We just met up for nachos at El Camacho."

I narrowed my eyes. "So you saw a movie all by yourself. Which movie?"

Von blinked. "The new Superman movie."

"That's a lie," I said with a smirk, "but I'll let it in just cuz I'm easily entertained. So the movie let out at, what, ten o'clock? What did you do after nachos at the Mexican place?"

He bit the inside of his cheek, then said, "Just hung out."

"By yourself?" I asked, hands on my hips.

"Yes," he said, eyes on my badge.

"Where?"

He crossed his arms. "I just chilled out, you know? Hung out by the fountain, went into a few shops . . ."

"You're *still* lying." My temples throbbed, my stomach ached, and I wanted to vomit—this kid had given me cramps. "Why won't you just tell me the truth and let me go on my way? Why do you insist on lying to me, Von Neeley?"

Von licked his lips again. Bet they tasted like Lie.

Colin touched the boy's shoulder. "Look, son. We're gonna find out everything you did that night, down to how many times you took a piss. Wanna know why? Because my partner here? She ain't gonna let go until she hears the truth. If you don't wanna be ripped apart, then I suggest you start talkin'."

Von swallowed and his Adam's apple bobbed like a buoy on the ocean. "I was with this girl Margo on Tuesday night," he whispered.

"Is Margo a hooker?" I near-shouted.

Colin stifled a chuckle.

Von lifted his chin with pride. "No, she's not a hooker. She's a youth minister like me."

I rolled my eyes and said, "Hooker. Youth minister. I don't care what you call her, but I'll still need her contact information."

"Why?"

I sneered at him. "None of your business."

He backed down and recited Margo's phone number.

"Is Pastor Margo of age?" I asked.

His eyebrows scrunched. "Huh?"

"Your *other* girlfriend, the one we found dead the other night? She was a minor, Von."

"So you broke the law," Colin said. "Bad deal for a youth minister. Could get you a few years in the Big House. You're a handsome kid, too, so your dance card will be filled quick as spit."

"Margo is nineteen," Von said, then moistened his lips.

"And you were together all night?" I asked. "Doing God's work, I suppose?"

He kinda nodded.

"And *where* were you ministering to each other?" I asked, tired of this *Degrassi-High*-Teenage-Love-Affair bull crap.

Von pinched the bridge of his nose, then shoved his hands into his pockets. He now stood before me like a delinquent standing before the school principal. "We went to the Jet Inn over on Slauson."

The Jet Inn Motel charged by the hour. The rooms boasted round mirrors on the ceilings and dried blood and semen on the carpets, on the walls, in the air . . . If Zucca sprayed luminol in the Jet Inn's parking lot, the entire building would glow like a float in Disneyland's Electrical Parade. Astronauts at the International Space Station would see it from their kitchen window.

"The Jet Inn," I said, shaking my head. "Wow. Do better, Von. She's a youth minister—she *at least* deserves the Travelodge over by the airport."

"Will everyone have to know about me and Margo being at the motel?" Von asked meekly.

"If this case goes to trial," I said, "yeah, they'll find out."

"We'll probably need to talk to you again," Colin said, pulling out his business card.

"I'll take a lie detector test if you want," Von offered.

"Right now," I said, "we want a DNA sample."

Von's eyelashes fluttered like a hummingbird's wings. "Why? I didn't do anything."

"Which means you'll be eliminated by your DNA." I marched toward the Crown Vic.

Von trudged behind me. Once we reached the car, I opened the trunk and grabbed the DNA kit from the nest of flares, sweatshirts, and spools of barrier tape.

Von shook his head. "I'm not sure I wanna do that. The DNA thing."

I paused—hadn't expected *that* response.

"Why not?" Colin asked. "If you're innocent, you got nothin' to worry about."

"Me and Monie," Von said. "We were . . . We had unprotected sex, and so you could find . . . you know . . ."

"Sperm?" I shouted.

He blushed, nodded, then said, "But that doesn't mean that I killed her."

"When was the last time you and Monie had sex?" Colin asked.

"Like around June tenth."

"You're fine," I said. "Sperm can live up to five days in the best conditions." And since Monie's cervix was not in its best condition, Von's little guys had probably shattered upon impact.

"Maybe I should talk to a lawyer," the kid said.

Colin and I exchanged looks.

Von nodded. "Yeah. I think I'll talk to a lawyer first."

And that was that.

I dropped the DNA kit back into the boot and gave the trunk's lid a good slam. Then I stomped over to the kid and snarled, "Go ahead and get your lawyer, but know this: I *will* expose you for what you are, whether you killed her or not, since you seem to care more about your reputation than your dead girlfriend. You are a liar and a hypocrite, and I hate liars and hypocrites. So get your lawyer, Von Neeley. I'm getting your DNA and I'm talking to Margo. *And* I'm sure there are security cameras at the Jet Inn and I'm almost positive that they'll have tape of you and a woman who is not your wife checking in at the front desk. So you, Von Neeley, you have a *blessed* day."

And then I stomped to the driver's side of the Crown Vic and slammed my body behind the steering wheel.

Moments later, Colin climbed into the passenger seat. We sat in silence until he shouted: "Sperm?"

I laughed, even though my head was filled with buzzing and white noise. "Thanks for joining me on my gleeful quest to destroy that little jerk."

"Anytime, Detective." Colin lifted his palm. "High-five."

And we slapped hands, feeling like partners for the first time in four days.

35

I dropped Colin back at the station, then drove to meet Macie Darson.

The Starbucks in this part of black Los Angeles was a known hub for Old Playas, the sixty- to seventy-year-old men who had a lot of cash in their pockets and the need to recapture their swagger and holla at the Fine Young Thangs wiggling past in spandex dresses; old men who sipped strawberry margaritas at the T.G.I. Friday's next door in their pressed slacks and shiny Stacy Adams or velour tracksuits and bright white Adidas, the keys to their Caddy or BMW on the table next to that too-sweet margarita or J-with-soda, sucking in their guts, wanting to "get some soon" cuz their sugar was up, damn margarita, or their pressure was down or they had only two hours left on their Viagra high.

But at almost noon, the Old Playas were either at work or sitting in a doctor's waiting room. And now, only a handful of that tribe sat at the chess benches outside the coffee shop.

Macie Darson occupied an outside table, cigarette between her fingers, hunched forward as though her stomach hurt. A whisper of a white dress barely covered her thighs . . . and the rest of her. She was dressed more for midnight than high noon.

But then, I couldn't judge—I never left the house without a bra and a gun.

"Macie," I said, "how are you?"

She gave me a Mona Lisa smile. "Better now that you're here. You're gonna solve this. Any minute now. I know it." She moved her Louis Vuitton bag from the chair and sat the purse at her feet.

A two-thousand-dollar bag on the ground. Kids.

"Thanks for coming, Detective Norton."

"No problem." My iPhone vibrated—a text from Lena. *Where u at?*

To Macie, I said, "Hold on for a sec." I texted Lena back, *Ladera Sbucks w/a wit*. She replied immediately: *Nearby c u soon*. I slipped the phone on the table and turned my full attention to the young woman in white. "Heard that you had a hard time at the morgue this morning."

"I couldn't go in there," Macie whispered. "And I felt bad cuz I knew Mom needed me. But I don't wanna remember Monie like that. I don't want my last memories of her . . ." She bit her lower lip and closed her eyes. "I know: I need to be stronger."

"Macie, don't push yourself to feel something you don't. The worst thing that could ever happen *has* happened. You're supposed to be sad. You're supposed to mourn."

"Thank you. I needed to hear—"

A car horn blew.

Over in the parking lot, an old man behind the wheel of a gold Jaguar waved to Macie and shouted, "You gon' be here tonight?"

Macie pulled on a cute smile, the one reserved for Old Playas, and shouted back, "Not tonight, Willie. Family stuff."

The old man said, "Okay, then." He honked again, threw another wave, and zoomed toward the grocery store.

Macie plucked that smile off her lips, Mr. Potato Head style, and dumped it back into the tub. She absently swiped at a purple scratch that ran from her chin down to her left armpit.

I winced and pointed to the injury. "How did you do that?"

She considered the burning end of the cigarette. "I have no idea. Since all this started, I've been having nightmares, and every time I wake up, I find new scratches or bruises. Look." She showed me her calf, smooth and brown except for the greenish blotch the size of a sausage patty. "And I don't even remember bumping into anything." She took a quick puff, then tapped off the cigarette's ashes. "Mom wants me to go to the doctor to get some Valium. Maybe I will—I've been chain-smoking these things to relax . . ." She held up the cig. "Whoever killed my sister needs to get caught before I end up falling off a cliff or getting lung cancer."

"I'm working as fast as I can."

"I know." She cleared her throat, then opened her hand to reveal a tiny square of paper. She dropped it on the table before me, then slowly exhaled as though it had weighed a ton.

I picked it up—the paper was moist. I unfolded the square to discover a list written in thin, scratchy cursive:

1. *Von Neeley*
2. *Derek Hester*
3. *Byron Delbridge*
4. *Malcolm Koll*
5. *Keith Skinner (maybe gay)*
6. *Todd Wisely*

Each name had a phone number beside it.

"And who are they?" I asked.

"Boys Monie had been kickin' it with since her junior year. I thought . . . You know, since our last conversation . . . I don't wanna be scared no more."

"And I don't want you to be," I said. "Thank you for making this list." The names had been a gift and a burden, a combo pack of rejuvenation and exhaustion—so many boys to talk to, but then . . . *so many boys to talk to.*

Macie's smile widened and her eyes begged for more encouragement.

So I said, "This is very helpful. We need as many leads as possible, and maybe one of these guys will be the one." I considered the names again, then asked, "Are most of these guys . . . *older?*"

Her eyebrows scrunched. "Huh?"

"Seems that your sister preferred dating older guys. Like Von and Derek: they're both a few years older than—"

Flickers of anger flashed in Macie's eyes. "Are you sayin' that Monie asked for it cuz she likes older—?"

"No," I said, holding up a hand, then shaking my head. "No, no, no. I'm only trying to form a profile of possible suspects. Your sister did nothing to deserve this. Okay?"

With that explanation, Macie's eyes cleared and her shoulders relaxed.

"So where are you off to, looking so fancy?" I asked, slipping the paper into Monique's expanding file, hoping to lighten the moment.

She tossed the cigarette to the pavement, then grabbed a crumpled pack of Newports from the handbag. "Shopping for a nice dress for Monie's service."

"Your mom going with you?"

"No." Her iPhone chirped from the table. She peeked at the display and a new smile, a more genuine smile, found its way out of that Mr. Potato Head bucket and onto her lips. "My boyfriend Max is taking me. I saw a dress at Neiman Marcus a month ago. Hope they still have it."

"A dress for you or for Monique?"

She flinched. "For . . ." She flushed and covered her mouth. "For my sister. We were together when I saw it and she said she really liked it and I couldn't buy it for her right then, but Max, he told me to get it and that he would pay for it."

"What's Max's last name?"

"Yates." She squinted at me, wondering why I needed that information.

"And did he and Monique get along?"

Macie plucked a cigarette from the pack, lit it, and took a long drag. "They got along fine, I guess. They didn't hang out."

The smoke writhed toward me and mingled with the scent of fresh-brewed coffee. Reminded me of mornings with my father. And with Tori.

My facial expression must have changed because Macie asked, "You okay?"

"Yeah. Just . . . thought of something."

"Something about my sister?"

"No. Something about mine. Kind of."

"She live in LA?"

I blinked at her, then heard myself say, "Don't know."

Macie tilted her head. "Y'all not close?"

With each breath I took, my stomach ripped into confetti-sized pieces. "She was kidnapped a long time ago. We never found her."

Macie covered her mouth with her hands. "So you *do* know how I feel. Except . . . I know where my sister is."

I tried to smile. "Yeah."

"Are you still looking for her?" she asked. "Are you still looking for the person who took her?"

I nodded. "But . . ."

"No 'but.' You *have* to learn the truth, Detective Norton. *Please*. I'll never stop until I know, until whoever did this . . . I guess that's why I made that list." Her eyes dropped to the table, then found mine. "Don't ever let them tell you 'enough.'"

I inhaled, then said, "You're right. Thank you." Then I shook my head to clear it. "So: where did you meet Max?"

"He helped me get a good deal for my Maserati, and he hooked up Monie with the Lexus."

"He works at a lot?"

"Uh-huh. NC Posh Auto on La Cienega."

"That's Napoleon Crase's dealership," I said, thrilled with having one more spoke in the wheel.

Macie rubbed the bruise on her calf. "They have nice cars."

"Yeah," I said, finally scribbling into my notepad. "We've been trying to figure out who got Monique the Lexus. So where was Max on Tuesday night?"

Macie killed the cigarette on the sole of her shoe. "With me in Temecula." She stared at the dead cigarette, then said, "Even when we got back to LA on Wednesday morning, I told him to drive me around. Mom and Monie had been arguing all weekend and I didn't feel like going home and being pulled into it. Monie was already sending me a million text messages."

"What were they arguing about?"

Macie laughed bitterly. "Everything. School. Laundry. The dog. Money . . . Monique is a sweet girl, but she's a brat, too. And when she got the Lexus, she thought her shit didn't stink for real." She stared into the distance and a shadow darkened her face. "All of a sudden, Von wasn't good enough for her. Neither was Derek—no shit, right? He was never good enough. She wanted to be like them girls on that *Basketball Wives* TV show. And Todd Wisely? Dude on the list? He plays for UCLA." Macie reached for the pack of cigarettes again. "Todd's been in trouble before—he's always roughing up his girlfriends. But he's the star point guard for the Bruins, so trouble? What trouble?"

Got me a big baller.

"Does Todd live in Los Angeles?" I asked, my heart pounding.

"I think so."

"When was the last time Monique talked with him?"

"Not sure. He's gonna be a senior this year, and he didn't want any-body knowing that he was kickin' it with a high school girl." Macie offered a wicked smile. "Especially his girlfriend. She's a"—she hooked her fingers—"*model*. If you hadn't told me that a man killed my sister, I woulda said that this chick, Gabriella Simone, did it."

"Gabriella Simone," I said, writing in my pad. "What a name."

"Uh-huh. And she's a bat-shit-crazy, wannabe-Tyra-Banks bitch who officially dates Todd. I know for a fact she was pissed cuz he was creepin' on her with a fuckin' *High School Musical* cheerleader."

I pulled out Macie's list and found the phone number by Todd Wisely's name—it didn't match the green highlighted number on Monique's phone records. None of the numbers on Macie's list matched that mysterious number.

"Monie thought she was bad," Macie said, rolling a new cigarette between her fingers. "But I always told her: watch your back. There's always somebody out there who's worse than you."

36

On day six, my sister still hadn't come home. Detective Peet called and asked Mom to bring me to the police station. I don't remember much—fear keeps it hidden—but I was led to a small, dark room where six men stood against a wall. Even though they couldn't see me, their eyes somehow found mine in the glass. My knees weakened and I suddenly needed to pee.

"Do any of them look familiar?" Mom had asked me.

Eyes squeezed shut, mouth clamped into a hard line, I shook my head.

"You sure?" Detective Peet asked.

I nodded.

"Elouise," Mom said, "this is very important. Are you sure?"

Both adults asked me this more than once. *You sure? You sure?*

I was sure. None of these men in the lineup had been at the liquor store that day. And other than Napoleon Crase, I didn't know who else could've taken my sister.

Back at home, Mom stormed around the kitchen, throwing pots and plates in the sink. Her yellow sweat suit hung off her thinning frame—she hadn't eaten with Tori away, and now shadows darkened the hollows of her cheeks and beneath her eyes.

I sat on the couch in the darkening living room, knees drawn to my chest. I cried without making a sound as guilt ate away at my spirit. *I shouldn't have left her. I shouldn't have left her . . .*

Mom rounded the corner to see me huddled on the couch. She sat beside me and slung her arm around my shoulders. "It's gonna be okay," she whispered. "Don't cry, Lulu."

Her words only made me cry harder.

Our hopes of the police finding Tori diminished as days passed, and we rarely heard from Detective Peet. The man Mom had been seeing, her Valentine's Day date, stopped calling after she stopped answering the phone and going to church. Unable to focus on prepositions and noun-verb agreement, Mom took a leave of absence from school, never returning to the classroom afterward, and took to sitting on the living room couch. She didn't cry or watch television. She didn't flip through *Ebony* or through one of her thick paperback novels. She just sat, barely blinking, staring at her knees.

On Day 23 without Tori, I crept into the living room, now being haunted by my catatonic mother. I perched beside her on the couch, and touched her wrist—warm skin. The scoop in the center of her clavicle dipped—alive. The whites of her eyes had darkened to eraser-pink and tissue lint clung to her peeling nose. Her hair had been braided into two plaits, but both had started to unravel.

"Want some Kool-Aid?" I asked her. "Or a sandwich?"

No answer.

"I wrote in my journal today." I was now seeing a shrink who specialized in siblings of the missing and dead. Dr. Christina Sherrod spoke in whispers and platitudes. *Something good will come of this. Everything will be okay. We need to do what we can do.* For homework, I had to write about my feelings that prior week. My last entry had delved into a recurring nightmare: waking up in the apartment alone, the door locked from the outside, and me, trapped, screaming for help.

My mother still didn't respond, and for an hour, we stayed like that: Mom and I on the couch. Once the living room darkened, she stood and trudged toward the hallway without a word.

Later that evening, I fixed her a ham sandwich, a pile of potato chips, and a glass of punch. I put it all on a tray and carried it to her bedroom. I nudged the door open with my foot. Drawn curtains made the lightless room even darker. Mom lay somewhere in her bed, a boulder beneath the comforter.

"Mommy?" I whispered into the darkness, "I made you some dinner."

I stepped into the hot, musty room and turned on the bedside lamp.

Mom's head poked out from the covers. She blinked from the sudden light. Bottles of Tylenol, Bufferin, and NyQuil—our entire medicine cabinet—crowded the nightstand.

"You sick?" I asked. "Need me to call the ambulance?"

Mom grunted. "No."

I frowned. "I'm gonna put these up." I sat the tray on the carpet, then grabbed the bottles from the nightstand. I left the bedroom to restock the bathroom's medicine cabinet. When I returned, Mom was lying on her back, staring at the ceiling. She held a fist to her chest as tears rolled back into her hair.

"I made dinner." I watched her cry until I found the courage to whisper, "Momma, what do you want me to do?"

Mom opened her mouth, and her jaw squeaked. "Be good," she whispered. "Just . . . be good."

I nodded, even though that request confused me. *Wasn't I already good?* "You have to eat something," I said, then stroked her clammy forehead.

She winced from my touch.

I snatched away my hand, not wanting to hurt her anymore than I had.

The telephone rang, and we both startled from its angry shrill. We stared at it with wide eyes, neither of us moving to pick it up. Finally, she grabbed the receiver from the cradle.

"Hello?" She sat up and unclenched her fist. She held in that hand too many pills to count. She looked at them, then threw the pills across the room.

My heart pounded as the tiny white disks scattered on the carpet. I was moments away from screaming, moments away from totally losing my shit. *What was she gonna do with those pills?*

"Okay," she was saying to the person on the phone. "Okay . . . Okay . . . Okay . . . Bye." She hung up.

I closed my eyes and waited to hear.

"That girl they found?" she said. "It ain't Tori."

I nodded, then tried hard to swallow.

The vein in the middle of Mom's forehead bulged. Still calm, she said, "Go watch television."

"I'll fix it, Mom," I whispered. "I promise. I'll fix it."

"Go watch television, Elouise."

I hesitated before leaving a bedroom with carpet rich with drugs. I left, though, and as soon as the door closed, Mom screamed. Not a wail heard at funerals, a wail filled with hopelessness and sorrow. No. She made a warrior's cry full of rage and frustration. Certain that she would drop to her knees for those discarded pills, I ran back down the hallway and threw open the bedroom door.

Mom stood in the middle of the room. Her pink nylon gown hung off her body like molting skin. Her breasts stood high, firm, and full. She held the telephone, but she had ripped the phone jack from the wall, and now it sat dumbfounded in the doorway. She screamed again, then hurled the telephone—base and receiver—at the large mirror connected to the dresser. The mirror didn't break, but it fell forward and pushed perfume bottles and a jewelry box to the carpet in a wild crash.

I shrieked through it all, and closed my eyes as Mom whipped past me, leaving the bedroom for the bathroom. She swung her arm across the countertop, and everything—toothpaste tubes, lotion bottles, the big jar of Vaseline—crashed to the tile floor. She screamed again, then kicked the bathroom door with her bare foot. The door banged against the wall, and the doorknob cracked the plaster. Mom shouted, then, screamed and cried out to the ceiling, "Why? Oh God! Why?"

Unable to stand it, I covered my ears with my hands. I crouched in the hallway until Mom's cries became sobs, until sobs became whimpers. She stripped off her nightgown and, with swollen red eyes, stared at her reflection in the mirror. Her chest heaved as she panted, as she tried to catch her breath.

Too scared to move, too scared to speak, I watched her from my spot in the hallway. I couldn't tear my eyes away from my mother's body. Couldn't look away from the jagged scar beneath her belly button, or from the stretch marks that traveled like bumpy highways from her waist down to her thighs. Mom moaned, then leaned against the counter. She muttered, "Okay then," and stepped into the bathtub, pulling closed the plastic curtain. The shower knobs squeaked, and water pelted the porcelain walls. Steam licked the ceiling, and the fragrance of melting soap drifted out to the hallway. "Did you eat?" she asked.

I hugged my knees tighter.

Mom poked her head from behind the curtain to look at me. She frowned at what she saw: a thirteen-year-old girl with red eyes and a runny nose, in a tight ball. "We're going out to dinner," she told me. "We need to get out of this place. I need to . . . Go get dressed."

We ate at Sizzler that night. Mom gave me her cheese toast and the pineapple slice that came with her Hibachi Chicken. She asked me about school and friends, my latest journal entry and visit to Dr. Sherrod. As we drove home, she kept the patter light and trivial. Before we climbed out of the car, though, she turned to me. Her eyes glistened with tears as she tried to smile. "I'm sorry, Lulu," she whispered. "Please forgive me."

Unsure of a proper response, I nodded.

We never mentioned those pills, the dark, or her tears ever again.

37

After Macie had flitted away to buy dresses at Neiman Marcus, I sat and drank a cup of coffee: tall drip, lots of sugar, nothing fancy. A silver Range Rover rolled past with Lena behind the wheel. An Old Playa in an Adidas tracksuit who had climbed out of his Corvette thirty years ago, and was finally making his way out of the parking lot, passed my table. He winked at me and said, "Why is a fine young lady like you sitting out here all alone?"

"Just enjoying the sun." I stretched so he could see my badge and gun.

Nothing to see here, old man, keep it moving.

His eyes widened and he nodded his farewell as he shuffled to join the crew at a chess table.

"Elouise!" Lena, dressed in a zebra-print skirt and matching sunglasses, a black tank top and silver python stilettos, *click-clacked* to where I sat.

I lifted my sunglasses just to appreciate all of her shine. "Looks like you were baptized in the River Beyoncé this morning."

"And you, *ma chérie*, look like stir-fried shit. Extra-crispy."

We hugged.

She settled in the chair abandoned by Macie, then used my napkin to wipe down the table before setting down her Birkin bag. "My ex-mother-in-law is sick. Diabetes. Or, as she calls it, the Sugar. She begged me to drop by since she's *convinced* that she's dying of *the Sugar*." She sat back in her chair and fanned her face. "She hasn't talked to Chauncey since his wedding. Not that she accepts that he's, once again, a married man."

Lena's ex-husband, Chauncey, a former sports agent, had fallen in love with someone else. And now Chauncey and his husband (a personal trainer ridiculously named Brando Gooch—who smartly took Chauncey's last name of Meadows) owned a gym in Connecticut. He had found his happily-ever-after and Lena had been left with baseball jerseys, a few signed basketballs, and accidentally discovered love letters written by the man who had stolen her husband's heart. Lena had made millions in the divorce, but that hadn't mattered—she had loved Chauncey and he had dogged her after they had been together for fifteen years.

"What's going on with you?" she asked. "And what's the deal with all of this?" She waggled her fingers at my face. "You got the Sugar, too?"

"Oh. Lots of stuff goin' on." I twisted my wedding ring and tried to smile.

Lena folded her arms. "Spill it."

I waved my hand. "Nothin' new to spill, really. Just same ol', same ol'. Did you send Chauncey and Brando Gooch Meadows a gift?"

She rolled her eyes. "I still refuse to believe that they sent me an invitation. Fuckers." And then she launched into a medley: her ex-mother-in-law's weekly dialysis treatments, selling a signed Derek Jeter jersey on eBay for three times its worth, Chauncey's wedding pictures on Flickr, which then led back to the pitiful health of her ex-mother-in-law.

Lena sighed, then said, "Chauncey's always acted like he was the center of the universe, but when he was with me, he treated her better. When he was with me, I would have made him move her into the house. When he was with me . . ." She stopped, puffed out air, then bit her lip. "N'importe quoi."

But with ragged breathing, misty eyes, and a twitching nose, Lena's feelings for Chauncey were far from "whatever."

I drew in air, then said, "How . . . ? When Chauncey did what he did, how did you feel? I know: I was there and saw you and how everything exploded and you threw books and phones and everything at him and then he filed the restraining order . . . But that was then. Looking back now, how . . . ?"

Lena didn't speak for a moment, then said, "Bamboozled. Didn't see it coming. *You* didn't see it coming. This man had never flirted with another woman, so another *man*?" She tapped the table with her fingernails and chuckled to herself. "And when I found out that his mistress was a 'mister.' Again: you were there. And you were there when the Santa Monica Police Department came to the house."

Humiliation. Fear. Anger. And five stitches for Chauncey above his left eyebrow.

"You didn't want to give him a second chance?" I asked.

She smirked. "Did he ask for one?"

"If he had asked, what would you have done?"

Lena gazed out to the parking lot, then gave a one-shouldered shrug. "I would've forgiven him. I wanted what my parents had back in Brooklyn. You know: church on Sundays, taking the kids to ballet and karate on Wednesdays, pizza night Fridays. And he had promised me all of that. And even after . . . everything, I still wanted him to keep that promise."

"But he didn't keep that promise."

She forced herself to smile. "But he's keeping it with someone else. Doesn't matter that it's a guy he's keeping it with. I just care that he ain't keeping it with me."

I leaned forward, elbows on the table, chin in hand. "I think that Greg—"

The Motorola squawked from my hip. "Lou, you there?" It was Colin.

I grabbed the radio and toggled the switch. "Yeah, one minute."

Lena gaped at me. "You think that Greg is *what*?"

I squinted at her but didn't speak.

Her eyes widened. "Oh, shit, Lou!"

"But I can't talk about it right now."

"When can we talk about it then?"

"Soon. Swear." I toggled the radio as Lena continued to gawk at me.

"How was your coffee date with Macie?" Colin asked.

"She came half-naked, and I think I caught a cold by proxy."

"The girl has a crush on you."

"I'm a sexy beast. Who can resist? Check a name for me?"

"Yep."

"Max Yates. Y-a-t-e-s." To Lena I said, "This may take a while."

She pointed at me. "You *will* tell me what Greg is up to."

I rolled my eyes. "I think you already know what he's up to. And/or into."

Kiss-kiss, hug-hug, and she *click-clacked* back to the parking lot.

The radio squawked, followed by Colin's voice. "A trio came up with that name. Two are old white guys. One is African American."

"The black guy," I said. "How old is he?"

"Twenty-four."

"Got any priors?"

"A couple of parking and speeding tickets. Nothing serious. So who is Max Yates?"

"Macie Darson's boyfriend. Works at Crase's car dealership."

"The Darson girls certainly like the guys with the cars that go boom."

"Don't they? He's the one who hooked Monie up with the baby Lexus."

"Great. Mystery solved. So: Renata Reese."

"Monique's BFF."

"Want me to go over and talk to her? It'll give you some time to breathe."

"I tried breathing once. Highly overrated. Don't think I'll try it again."

He said, "Ha," but didn't mean it. Something was up.

"Sure," I said. "Go talk to Renata Reese. Anything else?"

"You got a delivery. From your hubby."

I tugged at my earring. "Yeah? What is it?"

"The fanciest muffin basket I've ever seen."

"Hunh."

"Luke wants to know if he can have one."

I said, "Sure," again, then added, "And you take one, too, and anybody else who wants one." Nothing says, "I'm boning a Japanese girl at this very moment" like a basket of fancy muffins.

Colin shouted back to Luke, "She says you can have one." Then he came back on the line. "So, Renata Reese."

The world had blurred before me and I swiped at my eyes. My lungs filled with air and I pushed it all out in a single huff. Also, I had been sitting in one space for too long. "I'll go with you," I said, standing. "Watch you work. See if you've learned anything."

Moving again, and filled with caffeine and sugar, I drove to meet Colin at a dingy pink house around the corner from the Darsons. Another homicide detective stood with him on the sidewalk. Thomas Jefferson (mother had high aspirations for her little black boy) was taller than me and had skin oilier than a skillet in a soul food joint. Neither he nor Colin was smiling.

"Hey, Jeff," I said. "What's going on?"

"Hello, Elouise." Jefferson glowered at me as though I had been shopping for shoes as the levees broke and the city flooded.

"Renata's gone," Colin said.

I cocked my head. "By your tone, it doesn't sound like her departure was planned. And with Jeff here . . ." I peered at Jefferson with new eyes. "Oh, crap. Is she dead?"

"Don't know," Jefferson said. "My LT sent me out since your team is all over the city. Anyway, the girl's mom can't find her. Her car's still parked here but she's been missing since around midnight. And it looks like there may be blood inside the car. The mom saw that and called it in."

"So there's blood but no body," I said.

Jefferson nodded. "I'll show you."

Colin and I followed him down the block to where two patrol officers kept a small group of onlookers at a distance. A mint green Ford Taurus, as beaten as a gypsy cab in Beirut, was now surrounded by yellow tape. There were scratches in the paint. Black scrapes on both fenders. A missing left headlamp. A dent the size of a man's foot in the driver's-side door. And several drops of blood on the inside of the driver's-side window.

"You look in the trunk yet?" I asked Jefferson.

"I was just about to when Taggert drove up," he said, pulling on latex gloves. "The mother is looking for the extra set of car keys."

And we stood there, staring at the beat-up Taurus, not saying much but hoping that the congealed red droplets on the window had come from a cherry Slurpee and not from Renata.

A thin black woman in an emerald green pantsuit hurried from the pink house. She had keys in one hand and the tiny fist of a butterscotch-colored toddler wearing a diaper and a Raiders shirt in the other.

"That the mom?" I asked Jefferson.

"Yeah. Her name's Nova West, and that's Renata's son, Jalen."

Nova West looked too young to be a mother but was obviously old enough to be somebody's grandmother. She held out the car keys long before she reached the yellow tape. Jefferson thanked her and patted the top of Jalen's head. Nova threw a look at me and then an anxious look at the Ford Taurus. She smelled of soap and flowery perfume—I'm sure she had been expecting to go to work like she probably did every Friday morning.

Jefferson unlocked the car door and pulled an inside lever. The trunk sprung open and we clicked on our flashlights and huddled around to look inside.

A plastic bag of bottled water. Old *Vibe* magazines. Fast-food containers. Clothes . . .

I stepped back and said, "Okay."

Jefferson sighed, relieved to find trash in the trunk instead of a dead girl.

I peeked beneath the car and threw light on the slick asphalt. "Did it rain last night?"

"Fog," Colin said, "but no rain."

"Maybe the sprinklers kicked on this morning," I said, staring at a dark puddle that should not have been there—especially since the rest of the asphalt was dry.

Colin peered beneath the car, noticed the puddle, and whispered, "Fuck . . ."

Jefferson was clearing out the trunk and placing all of the contents on the sidewalk. "Nothing's here."

"Unfortunately, I think you're wrong." I returned to stand at the trunk. "Let's move that rug."

Jefferson pulled out the black square of carpet and then the plank that hid the spare tire compartment. He took a step back and muttered, "Oh, shit."

No spare tire. Just a young black woman curled into a fetal position. She was a beauty-shop blonde, a tiny girl who had been so cute in those photos on Monique's Facebook page. Now, though, the freckles on her nose and cheeks lay flat and lifeless. Now, those twinkling green eyes stared dully at her knees. Her mouth was open and the inside of her lower lip was crusted with darkened blood. There were brick-colored holes the size of salt tubs above her right ear and the middle of her neck.

"What is it?" Nova West shouted from the perimeter. "What? Tell me!" She sounded far away—like she had been hollering at us from the Darsons' porch around the corner.

We heard Nova's shouts but didn't answer her. We stood there in silence, staring at Renata Reese, who had been stuffed in the back of her car like a bag of old clothes. After we had all thought about that and had said a prayer to whichever deity had allowed this to happen, Jefferson toggled the switch of his Motorola and said, "I'm gonna need the paramedics and the coroner out here."

Ten minutes later we were joined by three more detectives, more uniforms, an ambulance, and an air unit.

Even though this was Jefferson's murder, Colin and I still needed to talk to Nova about a dead girl not her own. But the grieving mother had collapsed on the sidewalk. A neighbor lady cuddled Jalen as she carried him back to the dingy pink house.

"We'll talk to Nova later," I told Colin as we moved away from the crime scene.

There had been so many questions I had wanted to ask Renata. *Why was Monique at your house on Tuesday night? What time did she leave? What was her mood? Did she say who she was meeting that night? Was it any of the guys on this list her sister made? What do you know about Todd? Do you recognize this phone number highlighted in green?* Those questions would now probably go unanswered.

"When do you think it happened?" Colin asked.

"Last night. When no one was around."

"Wouldn't someone have heard?"

"Oh, yeah. Because gunshots in this part of Los Angeles are precious and rare things."

Colin chewed on that for a moment, then said, "Think her murder is related to Monique's?"

I glanced at the helicopter now making tight circles in the sky. "I don't wanna think that, but I will if I have to."

Colin glanced back at the Taurus. "Maybe Renata knew something. Maybe she was planning to tell us but he—"

"*He?*"

"Mr. Green Ink. Maybe he wanted to stop her before she talked to us."

"Maybe."

There was nothing more for Colin and me to do on Sutro Avenue. Jefferson had his own team, and I had my own murder. I told Colin to hang around for a moment, just in case the other detectives needed context, then climbed into my car. It would be a twenty-minute drive to Cal State Los Angeles, and I would spend each of those moments holding my breath.

After my visit, I would slowly drive back to the squad room, my speedometer never moving past thirty-five. Maybe the muffins would be eaten by then. Maybe the cellophane would be stuffed in the trash can and the crumbs swept from tabletops and Luke's mustache. Maybe then I would get to pretend that those muffins never came.

Maybe.

38

Before I crossed the threshold of the Evidence Storage Unit, I switched my phone to vibrate and slipped it into my jacket pocket. In many ways, this place was a cemetery—parts of the dead were stored here, and that demanded respect.

It was freezing in this room where cold cases came to get colder. Not because they had been forgotten but because DNA and biological specimens like blood, spit, and semen degraded in heat.

Janice Feinberg, the unit's civilian manager, looked up from the computer monitor. "Good afternoon, Detective." She regarded me without a smile; but then, she never smiled. Probably because she had watched over these boxes of Dead People's Things since 1966— from Robert Kennedy's murder to the infamous forty-four-minute North Hollywood shootout. With no break in the action, why would Janice Feinberg smile?

Since making detective, I came to the unit once a month to check on the status of evidence for any of my open cases: the spit on a coffee cup, the splash of semen on a dead nurse's smock, that perfect drop of blood on my sister's shoe.

And each time I visited, Janice Feinberg was seated at the same desk, with the same pair of glasses on the end of her nose, her slate blue eyes on the computer monitor, which had been the only change in her world.

My phone vibrated and I pulled it from my pocket.

Zucca had texted me. *Hair in desk is Monique Darson's.*

My response: *Great & awful news.*

Phone tucked away, I started the familiar trek to row KK.

There were so many boxes. Too many. How were we supposed to right all these wrongs?

Back in my patrol days, I had asked then-Sergeant Rodriguez that same question and he said this to me: "You eat an elephant one bite at a time."

I reached row KK and found Tori's box on the third shelf from the bottom. It was lighter now and fingerprints had been left on the dusty lid. I pulled off the top—the white Nike Huarache was gone. The unopened packet of ancient Starbursts and the gold wristwatch had been left behind.

Hope burst in my chest and I grinned, even though I was surrounded by Dead People's Things.

Maybe now I would know.

Maybe now Napoleon Crase would be charged with Tori's murder and then connected to Monique Darson's death.

Maybe now I could give Greg that space I had saved for my sister. *And then?*

Then, I would live happily ever after.

I considered the log sheet taped to the front of the box.

05/11 LLJ Nike, white.

Forensic scientist LLJ was now examining Tori's shoe.

But . . .

What if the DNA test proved that Napoleon Crase *didn't* do it? That the blood belonged to someone else and that person was *not* in the National Crime Information Center? Humans were only separated genetically by 0.5 percent of our total DNA. Not much, but enough to determine the innocent from the guilty.

I tugged at the small silver hoop in my left ear, not wanting to be in this room now, not wanting the shoe to be in LLJ's possession. My hands shook as I held that box, shook as though someone had been imprisoned behind my rib cage and was now grabbing the bars and trying to break out.

Not knowing: you can imagine the best of scenarios when you didn't know. For more than twenty years, that blood on Tori's shoe belonged to Napoleon Crase. For years I thought, *If only they could examine it . . .*

Now that they were, there was a chance I had been chasing a shadow all this time. Now there was a chance that the sun would shine into that dark place and show me . . . nothing. Now there was the chance I'd realize that all this time I had been Don Quixote dressed in a Calvin Klein pantsuit.

I shook the evidence box again. A boulder had lodged in my throat and I couldn't swallow.

Maybe I should retrieve the sneaker before LLJ runs a swab over the blood. Steal back that shoe and destroy it just to keep my imagination intact.

It had been so long since Tori's disappearance that my hatred for Napoleon Crase had become a part of me. Not to have it anymore would be akin to losing my hand.

39

The purple roses were dying.

But then I had neglected the bouquet, relegating it to the edge of my desk since its arrival on Wednesday. No new water. No sunlight. No love. And now the petals resembled the new scales of a molting dragon. Unfortunately, the flowers weren't dead enough to throw away. Like many things in my life.

My eyes wandered back to the computer screen. The same screen that said *1 result* for Napoleon Crase's "secretary."

Brenna Benevides, a pay-to-play girl, had been busted for prostitution every other year. Her government name was Oleta Brown and she specialized in sex games that, literally, took your breath away. She was stunning even in her mug shots. One parent had been black and the other parent was some kind of Asian. Brenna had long, shiny hair; big boobs; high cheekbones; and lips that men loved. In her industry, though, she was a senior citizen at thirty-one years old.

My iPhone vibrated on my desktop.

Syeeda's picture flashed on the screen. "Hey," she said. "What's going on with the Darson case?"

I opened the PDF of Monique's autopsy report that Dr. Brooks had just e-mailed, then slumped in my chair. "Hello, dear friend. I'm well, thanks for asking."

She snorted. "We've known each other since 1993. We can skip the foreplay, sweetheart. I forwarded an e-mail to you. Did you read it?"

"Is it the Daily Candy Shop-Til-You-Drop e-mail thing?" I asked, scrolling through my inbox. "Or is it . . . ?" I clicked on Syeeda's last message—three PDFs.

Letter of Protest.

Special Events Permit.

A picture of Angie Darson, picket sign in one hand, a bullhorn in the other.

"Okay," I said. "So what is all this?"

"Behold," Syeeda said, "the power behind the anti-Crase, anti–Santa Barbara Plaza revitalization movement."

I scrunched my eyebrows. "The Darsons. I know this. And? So?"

"Not *the* Darsons. *Angie* Darson. Cheese and bread, dude. Look at the shit I sent you."

I sat up in my chair and eyed the three PDFs. And then, I *saw*. "She's the contact on the letter. She's the contact on the event permit. She's the one leading the march."

"And *he*?"

My eyes scanned the documents again. "*He* is nowhere to be found." I rubbed my thumb across my lip. "She's the one pushing Cyrus into this role of community leader, and he's . . ."

"Just not into it, obviously."

"Interesting," I said.

"Wanna know what's even more interesting? The last approval for Crase's project went before the city council in April. The Darsons didn't show up."

"Really?" My attention turned back to Monique Darson's autopsy report. *Remarks: Decedent originally presented to this office as a suicide victim. Contusion . . . 0.25 inch linear fracture . . . occipital bone . . . no hematoma . . . laceration with abrasion of scalp . . . presence of the post-mortem ligature mark suggests that suicide in this case is highly improbable.*

Suicide: that had been the initial thought only two days ago. So much had changed since.

I yanked a dying petal from a rosebud. "Do you know anything else about Cyrus Darson? He's not talking straight to me and that pisses me off."

"What's he being shifty about?"

"Who did he work for before Crase?"

"Is my finding out predicated on you giving me an update?"

"Yep."

Syeeda huffed. "Fine. I'll call you back."

I crumpled the rose petal in my palm—there was no crunch, still some give, still some meat. Again: just like many things in my life.

In the spirit of "Please like me, please?" Colin had pizzas delivered for lunch. Over greasy pepperoni pizza slices and cans of Coke, the Who Killed Baby Girl? team huddled around the whiteboard for a midday update.

"So where are we?" Lieutenant Rodriguez asked as he folded his slice in half.

I told them about my meetings with Cyrus and Angie Darson, and then with Macie. I told them about finding Monique's best friend, Renata, stuffed into the spare-tire compartment of her Ford Taurus.

"I'll make sure Jefferson shares info with you," Lieutenant Rodriguez said to me. "Make sure you do the same."

After only taking two bites of pizza, the dough and cheese sat in my stomach as heavy as a gold bar. "During my meeting with Macie, she gave me a list of potential suspects. Well, more like the names of guys Monique had dated over the last two years." I passed the list to Pepe. "I've only had a chance to hit one name: Todd Wisely."

"Any reason you're starting with him?" Pepe asked.

"He plays basketball for UCLA," I said. "And he's twenty-one years old."

" 'Got me a big baller,' " Luke said.

"Exactly. But Todd's been at training camp up in Arrowhead since last week. He was nowhere near Los Angeles on the night Monique was murdered."

"Says who?" Lieutenant Rodriguez asked.

"Says Todd. Says his coach. I talked to both a few minutes ago."

"So Todd is out," Lieutenant Rodriguez said, ticking off his fingers. "And the church boy is out—"

"*Possibly,*" I said. "But not definitely."

Lieutenant Rodriguez continued. "The gangbanger's out."

"Yeah."

"So we *may* have two people of interest?" he asked, two fingers in the air, a screech creeping into his tone. "And those two are Napoleon

Crase and Von Neeley. After three days working this case? *Maybe two?*"

I cleared my throat as heat prickled my armpits. "I'd like to send a few vice cops over to Santa Rosalia to see if any of the girls or the tweakers saw anything that night."

Lieutenant Rodriguez nodded. "Anything else?"

"A little more on the Crase angle," I said. "I found his home address written on a slip of paper in Monique's diary. Macie, her sister, bought a car from his dealership—and so did Monique. That's where the Lexus came from."

"Anybody see Crase with Monique Darson?" my boss asked. When I didn't answer, he crumpled his napkin and tossed it into the wastebasket. "Lou, I put you on this because you *usually* get results."

"Pepe called Crase just a few minutes ago," I said. "Asked him to come down today for an interview. Nothing formal. Just to talk. No lawyer needed."

Lieutenant Rodriguez turned to Pepe. "And is he coming?"

Pepe nodded.

"It's just gonna take a little more time," I said, my nerves jangled, my voice sounding wary even to me. "The lab will come back with prints. A witness will come forward. And there *will* be blood." I forced a smile to my face, clinging to optimism like a junkie clutching the last eight ball in the galaxy. "This case is solvable," I said. "Everybody repeat after me. *This case is solvable.*"

They all played along.

This case is solvable.

This case is solvable.

This case—

My desk phone rang. Grateful for the interruption, I grabbed the receiver.

"Lou!"

"Zucca!" I said. "Please tell me that you have good news."

"I have good news. First, the acrylic nail found in the trailer belonged to Monique. So she definitely was attacked there. And I got a print off her underwear."

"*What?* A print? How?"

"VMD."

Vacuum metal deposition. Lovely. Zucca had placed the panties into a vacuum chamber where gold was heated to the point of evaporation. He then reduced the pressure inside the chamber, causing a very thin film of evaporated gold to spread over the fabric. He heated zinc next and that attached to the gold, but only in the spots where there were no fingerprint ridges. Those left-behind fingerprint ridges couldn't be "lifted," but they could certainly be photographed. In a way, it was like a reverse X-ray.

"I'm dancing," I told Zucca. "You can't see me dancing. No one can see me dancing, but I'm freakin' Lord of the Dance jigging on the inside right now."

Because girlfriend-beating Napoleon Crase's fingerprints were in the system.

He laughed, then said, "A fingerprint tech is about to feed them into AFIS to get possible matches. Shouldn't take too much longer. As for DNA from the victim and on that handkerchief: still out on that. And the high-tech guys still haven't gotten around to the victim's netbook. Sorry. We're just really jammed."

Despite the DNA delays, I still couldn't help but smile as I hung up. Couldn't help but picture my shiniest pair of handcuffs clamped around Napoleon Crase's wrists. "Zucca got a print," I announced to the room. "Shouldn't be too long now."

"Okay. What about that mystery phone number?" Lieutenant Rodriguez asked, not placated by this recent development.

"Still working on it," Luke said. "The provider is slower than a snail in a snowstorm."

Joey laughed. "Say that three times."

Luke said, "Slower than a snail in a—"

"So what's next?" Lieutenant Rodriguez asked, ignoring them.

"Next up," I said, "Napoleon Crase comes in for an interview this afternoon."

"According to his secretary-slash-girlfriend," Pepe said, "he's been in Chicago all week. He flew back this morning."

"Tread carefully," my boss warned. "And keep looking at *everybody*. No fuck-ups. *None*. What about the press?"

"The press release is done," Joey said, "but no one's demanding answers right now."

I had three voice mails from reporters; fortunately, none of them worked for major dailies.

"What about your friend?" Colin asked me.

Joey laughed. "Oh, yeah! Sexy Sy." He turned to Pepe for a high five. Pepe left him hanging.

Meanwhile, I glared at Colin for bringing up Syeeda.

Lieutenant Rodriguez considered both of us, then focused on me. "And what are you going to tell Miss McKay if she asks?"

"We're pursuing all leads at this time," I said, unblinking.

Lieutenant Rodriguez grabbed another slice of pizza from the box. "You better go find some leads to pursue, then. We don't wanna lie to the press now, do we?"

40

Napoleon Crase needed to *feel* something. He needed to step inside interview room 1 not as a self-made man and not as BFF to the councilmen of black Los Angeles. No. He needed to come in as a human, vulnerable and uncertain of his fate. And he needed to confess that he had been involved in the death of Monique Darson and the kidnapping and murder of Victoria Starr.

I wanted to tape autopsy pictures of the Darson girl along the room's wall, mixing in a few shots of her laughing, posing with Butter, and accepting her high school diploma at graduation just a week ago. On one of the walls, I wanted to tape up pictures of Tori, too. Shots that I had plucked from our family photo albums long ago: high school graduation, baptism, church fashion show. I wanted to tape up area maps, the condo site circled in red, just a block away from the old liquor store, also circled in red.

But I couldn't contaminate the interview. Any lawyer worth his degree would claim intimidation and false confession. So the room had to be stark, bare, blank.

I could, though, bring in a folder that held my eight-ball pictures. And those pictures, I hoped, would pound the man into a true confession.

Colin pointed to the camera bolted in the upper north corner of the room. "Is it good?"

Pepe nodded. "Yeah. Luke put in a new tape and made sure that the microphone was working."

"And I brought provisions for our guest." I waggled a bottle of water and a disposable cup wrapped in plastic.

Pepe said, "Good luck," then squeezed my shoulder before he left the room.

Colin and I waited for Napoleon Crase in the crowded lobby. My partner took my hand more than once. "You're doin' the ear-tugging thing. Keep it up and you'll tear your earlobe." He paused, then said, "You sure you don't want me in the room?"

I nodded.

"Because I'm here."

"I know."

"And you sure you wanna do this?"

"Do what? My *job*?" I frowned at him. "You think I'm being irrational?"

His bottom lip disappeared "I just . . ."

I snorted. "Weren't you the one ready to go over and kick his ass?"

"Yeah, but—"

"Colin, I spent my entire teenage life writing in a journal and nightmaring about what this man did to my family. You would do whatever it takes to stop those dreams, dreams that I *still* have, wouldn't you?"

Colin scratched his jaw and didn't speak for a long time. Then: "I enjoy working with you, Elouise, and . . . And I don't really wanna start over with a new partner, know what I mean? But you do what you have to."

At three o'clock sharp, a chauffeured Maybach pulled up in front of the station.

Colin grinned at me. "He's kidding, right?"

I stared at the car's passenger climbing from the backseat. The old man wore a tailor-made Italian suit and so much gold that he could be seen twinkling from the stratosphere—fancier than the green chinos and brown short-sleeved shirts he wore during my childhood. I glimpsed Brenna inside the Maybach. Well, I glimpsed her long legs, one manicured hand, and the egg-sized diamond on her finger.

Napoleon Crase, gaunt and crinkly, opened the station's glass door, and his cologne (pine forest and musk) wafted in on top of the draft. Had the weight loss been the result of the diet recommended by his proctologist? Or was Brenna Benevides into yoga and vegan macrobiotics, and therefore so was he?

Colin and I met Napoleon Crase in the middle of the lobby. I introduced my partner and without thinking, I offered Crase my hand.

We shook—my stomach lurched and the rest of me went stiff. I tried to keep my Scowl of Disgust stored in its bin, but its tail end muddied the feigned, it's-not-personal, just-doing-my-job cop smile.

"I don't have much time," Crase said, glancing at his gold Rolex. "I have a meeting at City Hall in an hour." His voice was still deep and craggy, like canyon walls as tall as Mount Everest.

I wiped my Crase-contaminated hand inside my pants pocket. With each step, that soiled lining burned my leg.

We escorted the businessman deeper into the building.

Crase's eyes never stopped moving, and he was already sweating as he took in the commotion of the Southwest Division. The angry mother demanding information about her jailed son; the tired grandmother holding a pink slip from the bail bondsman; an adolescent Hispanic girl translating for her bleeding father.

And through more chaos: ringing telephones, undercover cops wearing black ski masks, screams from the drunk tank . . .

We arrived in the quiet of interview room 1. Crase cleared his throat, then said, "Busy today."

"The days are longer now," I said, easing into the interview. "That means more time to hang out, more time to drink, more time to get in fights. Please have a seat, Mr. Crase." I plopped into the chair across from his.

He thanked me and sat with his hands folded on the table.

"Have you ever had to do something like this?" I asked. "Be interviewed by the police?"

He smiled. "A long time ago."

I faked a smile of my own—his last domestic assault had happened just last year. Not much of a "long time ago." "Well, I certainly appreciate you coming in to talk with me. It's very important that we turn over every rock in this case, big and small."

He offered a nod full of understanding.

I waved my hand over the bottled water and cup. "If you'd like coffee, I can get you some, although I must warn you: it's horrible."

He chuckled and unscrewed the bottle cap. "Water's fine."

I leaned forward. "So we're here to talk about Monique Darson, who was found Wednesday evening, murdered in a condo unit on Santa Rosalia Drive."

He crossed his legs and glanced at his watch again.

"And we wanted to talk to *you* because there's a connection—well, a few connections between you and the victim."

He lifted an eyebrow. "Because she was found on my property."

I pushed away the notepad and pen—he'd talk more freely if he saw that I wasn't taking notes. "First things first. Where were you on Tuesday, June 18?"

He narrowed his eyes as he thought, then said, "For most of the day, I was at home, packing for my trip to Chicago."

"Which home is this?"

"73881 Don Tomaso Drive in Baldwin Hills."

The same address found in Monique's diary.

"And what time did you leave for Chicago?" I asked.

He pulled a handkerchief from his chest pocket, then said, "Car service picked me up sometime that evening and drove me to LAX. And my plane left around ten or so, on United Airlines."

"How did you find out about Monique Darson's murder?"

He paused, then said, "I believe that my project manager Hank La Garza called."

"At what time?"

He reached for the bottled water. "I don't recall."

I opened my folder and selected the autopsy picture of Monique Darson. I slipped it before him. "Do you recognize this young woman?"

He nodded as he poured water into his cup. "That's the young woman you all found at my condominiums. I've started a scholarship fund in her honor."

"That's nice. Had you ever met her before?"

He shook his head. "No."

"You sure?"

"I'm not a liar, Detective, and I resent the accusation."

I let my arms relax and took slow, easy breaths. "Mr. Crase, I'm not accusing you of anything. People forget. Misremember. Is there any reason why Monique Darson would have your phone number in her cell phone's telephone book?"

His eyes widened. "No."

"What about your address?"

"Absolutely not."

"Has she ever been to your home?"

"No."

"Is there any reason why your DNA would be found—?"

"She was found on my development," he interrupted. "I walk through those units all the time, checking on the progress, meeting the workers . . . I've sneezed a few times from the dust." He gave me a knowing grin. "I don't have to tell you, Detective, that we're both shedding skin and spit as we sit here. So yes: there may be some of my DNA on Miss Darson."

I nodded and gave a lopsided smile. "Let's change gears, then." I took a sip from my own cup of water.

Napoleon Crase did the same.

I opened the folder and selected the only photo left: the high school picture of Tori, circa 1988. Feathered hair, fuchsia lipstick, and blue eyeliner. I slid it before him "What about this girl? You recognize her?"

He glanced at the picture and his body jerked. After catching his breath, he said, "I have a meeting downtown in an hour. Will this take much longer?"

"You mentioned that you had a meeting," I said. "Thank you for your time."

Crase swallowed. "I do not know her, Detective." His shirt collar was darkening with perspiration.

I pulled out the ancient witness statement from the folder and read aloud Napoleon Crase's words.

As I read, his eyes never left that photo of Tori. "Care to revise your answer?" I asked.

He dabbed at his forehead with the hankie. "I remember her now."

I waited for more but he didn't elaborate. "There's a connection between these two girls, sir. Maybe you can tell me what that is."

His nostrils flared. "My land."

"What happened after you caught Victoria Starr for stealing candy?"

"I let her go," he said, firmly. "But then she came back to vandalize my car, and I scared her away. Where she went after that and who she ran into was not my problem. And I was cleared—I had proof that I had nothing to do with her disappearance. I'm completely innocent."

"*Completely* innocent?" I asked, eyes narrowed. "In the past, you've been arrested for domestic abuse."

He flicked his hand. "Misinterpretations."

"Says you or the court?"

He didn't answer.

I didn't speak.

We sat in silence.

Twenty seconds passed . . . thirty seconds . . .

"Victoria Starr," he said, shaking his head. "If she had been a good girl—"

"Are you saying that girls who boost junk food are justifiably murdered?" I asked. "Are you saying that she deserved to die for stealing thirty cents' worth of candy?"

Crase didn't speak, but the vein in his forehead throbbed.

"Did you create a scholarship fund in light of Victoria's abduction?" I asked. "Did you put up any 'Have you seen her?' flyers? Did you publicly express any remorse? Do anything for the girl's family?"

He smirked as he drank from his cup of water.

"The watch found beneath your car," I said. "Any idea how that got there?"

"No idea," he said.

"She'd stolen from you before this final time."

"Yes."

"Could you have taken the watch as payment for her prior thefts?"

He laughed. "I don't need some teenager's cheap watch."

I bristled at the insult to my father's gift, then took a deep breath. "Let's return to Monique Darson. Why would someone strangle her, and then leave her there at your condo site?"

"I don't know," he mumbled.

I shifted in my seat. "Would you be willing to help us out today?"

He held out both hands. "That's why I'm here."

"Then you'll give us a sample of your DNA? It's a quick, harmless procedure. Just a swipe of cotton swab on the inside of your cheek."

He stared at me, then said, "I'll have to discuss that with my attorney."

"Because?"

"Because," he said, arms crossed, "I discuss *everything* with my attorney."

"Fair enough. Back to your flight to Chicago: if we checked the passenger manifest for United Airlines flights between ten and midnight . . . ?"

"You'll see that I had a ticket," he completed.

"Will we see that not only did you *buy* a ticket, but that you actually *boarded* the plane?" I asked.

"Absolutely." Then, he drank another cupful of water and wiped his mouth on the handkerchief.

"Better?" I asked, eyeing that hankie. "Can I get you something else?"

"I'm fine. Thank you."

"What's your relationship with the Darson family?"

"I don't know the Darson family," he said.

"Cyrus Darson," I said. "The man who vehemently opposed your development plans and then suddenly changed his mind. You don't remember him?"

Crase laughed and nodded. "Oh, yes. Him. Yes, I do know him. He put up quite a fight."

"Until he didn't," I said. "Why do you think he surrendered so quickly?"

Crase frowned. "*Quickly?* All of that nonsense lasted two years or so. As for surrender: maybe he finally realized that the neighborhood needed it. That property values would increase with the building of Crase Parc and Promenade."

"Or maybe because you gave him a job," I pointed out.

Crase crossed his legs. "He's a talented electrician who needed work, Detective Norton. That has been my position this entire time: redevelopment brings jobs to the community."

"You do anything else for Cyrus Darson? Give him gifts? Money?"

"*Bribes*, you mean?" He waved his hand. "Darson is incorruptible, not that I offered to corrupt him. He's an honorable man and I am very sorry for his loss. I created a scholar—"

"Right. You mentioned that. Brenna Benevides is your companion, yes?"

He gave me a hard smile and waited.

I didn't respond and just let my comment hang.

"Are you wondering what a young woman wants with a seventy-year-old man?" He sneered. "I'll tell you what she wants. Money. A fancy car. A diamond necklace." He waved his hand, bored now with the conversation. "That's what all women want. You know how they get it? Sex. And if we were all honest, we would admit that marriage is just a more acceptable form of whoring."

I cocked my head. "You think?"

"And then, when it comes time to collect, women get scared and wanna change their minds."

I squinted at him. "And sometimes, bad things happen."

"Yes, Detective. Sometimes, bad things happen." He placed his index finger on the picture of Tori. "I can tell you from firsthand experience that this one whored for 7-Ups and Cheetos."

My chest tightened as I held my breath. My hands shook and the nerves around my right eye jumped. "Is that right?"

"And I wasn't the only one, either. She gave head to any man with five dollars in his pocket."

My stomach burned and my fists clenched.

"Guess she learned it from her momma."

I pushed away from the chair and stood, seconds away from lunging across the table and punching him in the throat.

But Crase didn't move. And *that's* what made me freeze.

He just sat there with that Chiclets-tooth smile. "You think I'm blind? I'm not. You're taller. Got a badge and a gun, but I remember you, little girl. Except today, you're not peeing in your pants."

I scowled at him, speechless, my nails cutting into my palms.

He glanced at his watch again. "You've been very polite and very impartial, but we should end this now. If you have any more questions, you can talk to my lawyer. You have a pleasant afternoon, Elouise Starr." He stood from his chair, nodded a final farewell, and strode out of the room.

41

Napoleon Crase had recognized me.

Back in the squad room, I threw my pen and it flew through the air like a javelin and hit the whiteboard.

"Easy, Lou," Colin said, as I stomped past him and to my desk.

I whirled around and shouted, "I should've strangled that old bastard. Let him see how it feels."

"He just wanted to piss you off," Pepe said, his eyes filled with concern.

"And if you had touched him," Colin said, "he would've pressed charges and gotten you thrown off the case."

"I've already put in a request for the passenger manifest," Pepe said, trying to calm me down.

"And I left a message for Hank La Garza," Colin added. "He never mentioned during your interview that he called Crase to tell him about Monique Darson."

"And Crase left that cup behind," Pepe said. "There's DNA all over that."

"We'll see who's smiling next year this time," Colin said.

I grabbed my purse from the desk drawer.

"Where you goin'?" Colin asked.

I hadn't stopped moving. "Out."

He said something else and Pepe said something else, too, but I was already out the door. Cool air washed across my face as I stormed to the parking garage and to my car.

I sat in the dark, stuffy Porsche and stared at the concrete wall before me. My muscles tightened again and my eyes filled with tears, and then . . .

Boom.

A sob, and then another, escaped from my chest until I freely wept. I rested my head upon the steering wheel and tears, spit, and snot dripped down my neck, wetting my shirt. My eyes only opened to let more tears fall. And for ten minutes, I cried.

Minute eleven, I found napkins in the glove compartment and dried my face. Then I glanced at my reflection in the rearview mirror and startled at the defiant smile on my lips. Relief: that's what I saw. Crying had served a purpose. Like a controlled burn in a forest. Like a release valve on a pressure pump.

After driving around the block three times, then pulling into the drive-thru at Krispy Kreme, after inhaling three glazed donuts and guzzling a cup of coffee, I settled down and returned to the station, ready to take the next step toward solving the Darson case.

As soon as I stepped into the squad room, Joey hustled over to me with a folder in his hands. "Macie Darson's in number two with a possible wit named Bernice Frater. And I gave Miss Frater a slice of pizza and a Coke—looked like she needed it."

I thanked Joey, and said, "And who says the LAPD doesn't serve?"

"You okay?" Colin asked.

I tapped a fist against his heart, then opened the file folder: a six pack that included Von Neeley's DMV photograph as well as five pages of priors relating to one Bernice Frater, Macie's newly discovered witness. Back at my desk, I reviewed Ms. Frater's record. *Solicitation. Trespassing. Possession of heroin. Possession of drug paraphernalia* . . . A regular at Seventy-seventh Street Division's women's jail, Bernice would most likely celebrate her twenty-fifth birthday behind bars.

Ten minutes later, I stood before the closed door of interview room 2. I shifted Monique Darson's file to my other arm and opened the door. The smell immediately slapped me in the face, and my eyes watered from the cloying stink of body odor and alcohol fumes.

Macie Darson and a chickenhead who hadn't bathed since President Clinton's inauguration sat at the table. Macie had changed into a tight black T-shirt (Gucci logo this time), a fuchsia miniskirt, and black-and-pink platform heels. She held in her arms a bichon frise with matted yellow hair.

The unfortunate woman seated next to Macie was Bernice Frater. That was her government name. On the streets she was known as

Sunshine. Today she wore a ratty sundress, although "sundress" was too positive a word to describe the material covering her breasts and thighs. Her hair was also coming out in patches, and her skin was dry and scabby.

"Macie," I said, sitting across from them. "Twice in one day?"

"I guess I'm just eager," Macie said. "I hate sitting around and not doing anything. And with everything happening with Renata now . . ." She clamped a hand over her mouth and her eyes glistened. "Do you think . . . ? Am I next? I don't wanna die, Detective. We have to find this man."

"And we *will* find him."

"But Renata—"

"May not be related to this case," I said, the words hollow in my ears. "We can't jump to conclusions, all right?"

Macie hesitated, then nodded. "Yeah. Okay."

I held out my hand for the dog to sniff. "And is this Butter?"

"Sure is!" Macie closed her eyes and snuggled the animal as though she had wished upon a star for her very own pooch. "I wanted you to meet her. The pound called the house this afternoon. Someone saw her on Stocker Boulevard and brought her in."

On cue, Butter barked, squirmed, and whined in Macie's hold.

I scratched the dog's head. "I'm so glad she's okay."

"Yeah," Macie whispered, "but she just makes me miss Monique more."

I took a deep breath and smiled at Sunshine. "Hello."

The woman kept her gaze on the table.

"And who do we have here?" I asked, leaning forward to catch the woman's eye.

"This is Sunshine," Macie said, touching the woman's hand. "She . . . *works* near the condo site."

"Hi, Sunshine. I'm Detective Norton."

No response.

"Bernice?" I said louder.

The woman flinched and immediately started to pick the scab above her left elbow.

"Since all this started," Macie said, "I've been driving up and down Santa Rosalia, asking people if they saw anything strange on Tuesday night and . . ." She gasped and her eyes bugged with worry. "Oh no! I hope you don't mind. It's not like I don't think you're doing your job. It's just . . . I have to *do* something."

"I understand." And I did understand Macie's need to *do something*. I had hated waiting for the cops to find my sister. Well, to *not* find my sister. And even though I had joined their ranks and understood the hurdles that every investigation presented, I still resented the LAPD for not trying hard enough to bring Tori back. Because that's all I had wanted: bring back my sister, dead or alive.

"Anyway," Macie continued, "Sunshine saw something and I asked her to come tell you."

I cocked an eyebrow. "She did? Wow." I turned to the witness and said, "Well, thank you, Bernice. I need as much information as possible. So what did you see?"

Sunshine stopped with the nitpicking and bit her lower lip.

"Sunshine," Macie said, "please tell Detective Norton what you told me."

The woman said nothing, and now her entire lip had been stuffed inside her mouth.

Macie turned to me, desperation in her eyes. "She said—"

I held up my hand. "You can't tell me, Macie. She has to."

Macie's mouth moved, but no words came. The hope that she had possessed just a minute ago dimmed with the realization that she had entrusted that hope to a heroin addict. "She was scared to come here. She thought you'd arrest her because she . . . you know."

I pushed a smile to my face. "No, no, no. Don't you worry about any of that, Bernice. You are *not* in custody. You're a possible witness. You are free to go at any time. But before you go, I hope you'll help us out."

Sunshine hugged herself and started to rock in the seat.

"Want some more pizza?" I asked her. "Another soda? You can have as much as you want. Or if you don't want pizza, I could give you a couple of dollars so that you could get whatever you want."

Like another eight ball of heroin.

Solving murders by any means necessary.

Sunshine's eyes brightened. "I want the money." Her voice was raspy from years of inhaling toxic chemicals.

"Then, I'll give you money," I said.

"I saw this guy," she said. "At the condo. He was with a girl."

"When? Around what time?"

"On Tuesday," she said. "I ain't got no watch but it was late. All the stores was closed."

"Where were you?"

"Taking a nap near that trailer."

"Were you alone?"

She nodded and picked at a scab on her cheek. "The guy was talking to that girl."

"What did he say?"

Sunshine took a deep breath, then pushed out: "That he would buy her one of the condos when he got his contract to play basketball."

I glanced at Macie. "Yeah?"

Macie, her face bright again, nodded.

"What did he look like?" I asked Sunshine.

"He was tall. He was black. He wore a diamond earring and a light blue tracksuit with a yellow stripe up the leg."

Bruin colors. She was describing Todd Wisely, who had supposedly been at training camp in Lake Arrowhead. Unless the coach had lied to me. Wouldn't be the first time a coach covered for a misbehaving player. Either way, his picture was not in the six-pack that Joey compiled for me.

"He drive a car?" I asked.

"A gray BMW," she said, "with black rims."

"Where was it parked?"

"By the driveway close to the trailer."

Even though Todd wasn't in my lineup, I still reached into Monique's file and pulled out the photo compilation. I slipped it before Sunshine and asked, "Do any of these men look like the man you saw that night?"

Her eyes skipped across the photographs of Von Neeley and the four men who were actually Vice cops. Her fingers hovered over Fake Dude Number Four, but then she pulled back her hand. "Don't know. It was dark."

"It was dark," I repeated. "But you saw that he wore an earring. And you saw the yellow in his tracksuit . . ." I let her sit and ponder awhile longer. When she didn't speak, I said, "You don't have to be afraid, Bernice. We won't let him hurt you. I promise."

Sunshine hunched over and her soul returned to that place where junkies loitered and napped.

I tapped the table once, then withdrew the sheet. "Thanks for coming in, Miss Frater. I know this is difficult, so I really appreciate it. Macie's family appreciates it, too."

"I should drive her back," Macie said.

Sunshine leaned toward Macie. "Is Lockjaw gon' give me the money?"

Macie gave me a what-do-I-say-to-that? look.

I stood from my chair. "Bernice, a promise is a promise."

I gave the woman thirty dollars of my own money, then escorted her, Macie, and Butter down to the lobby.

"Lockjaw?" I whispered to Macie.

"That's what they call you on the street," she whispered back. "Once you're on a case, you don't let go." She thanked me again and exited the station. Sunshine scuffled behind her, in a hurry to get a fix sponsored by private citizen Elouise Norton.

42

Legs twisted beneath him, he opens his eyes to see the dimly lit ceiling. His fingers clutch at strands of carpet.

How long has he been out?

The dim blue digital numbers on the DVR say 10:13 P.M.

Twenty minutes.

The bones in his neck click as he climbs back onto the couch. He blinks—sounds like his eyes are smashing cornflakes.

He reaches out to the coffee table for the swatch of gauzy, blue material—a memento from his last excursion—and rubs it between his thumb and forefinger. He closes his eyes as he remembers the girl struggling beneath his hands. But the image of Nikita morphs into an image of Samantha, and then Mirna . . . Katie . . . So many.

He stares at the television—the ten o'clock news is on.

Car chase. Bank robbery. Child dying after swallowing a thumbtack at school.

LIVE FROM SAN DIEGO pops on the screen. An Asian reporter stands near the Omni Hotel. "Authorities state that the girl was found after the hotel maid came into the room to clean . . ."

He cannot tolerate sounds anymore. The noise from the television hurts his head. Age is a bitch and he wishes he could strangle her, too; but he can't and he needs to hear this news story.

The reporter continues: ". . . has been identified as nineteen-year-old Nikita Swenson, a sophomore at Chapman University." A picture of Nikita, a wholesome girl posing with a rose to her cheek, fills the screen.

His angel returns to the living room but stops in her step. "You're awake." She holds a bag of frozen peas and a glass of brandy. She inches forward, then slips the icy bag around his left hand and whispers, "The swelling is getting worse. And your blackouts . . ." Her eyes flit to the television, to the reporter now interviewing a sweaty-looking detective asking the public for help. "What happened?"

He says nothing, just stares at the TV. The police will look at the phone numbers of the hotel guests and will reach one phone number and call it— but the line will be disconnected. They will stop at one name in the computer: Peter Kurten. They will search and discover that Peter Kurten killed thirty people over a span of fifteen months back in Germany during the summer of 1929. And he has come back to life to kill sexy little Nikita.

Maybe he should stop.

No. He can't stop. He doesn't have much time left.

His mind races. *Stop. Do more. Stop. Do more.*

He reaches a compromise. One more girl. His angel. And then the detective.

"The cold will make your hand feel better." She slips the peas on his hand, then offers him the high-ball glass of brandy. "This will help, too."

He stares at the drink.

She takes a sip, then offers it to him again.

He takes the glass and gulps it down. His stomach warms. Delicious.

She perches on his lap and tugs at his zipper.

He shakes his head—he can't tonight.

"Please?" she whispers.

The bag of peas tumble to the carpet as his swollen hand finds her neck. His thumb rubs the scoop where her pulse beats against the skin.

She closes her eyes and whispers, "Tighter."

He obeys—but the bulge in his pants . . . the detective put that there. The detective with her long, breakable neck.

"You'd never hurt me," his angel whispers. "You need me."

He says, "Yes. I need you." He kisses her, then pulls her T-shirt over her head, unclasps her pink bra.

Will he miss her when she's gone?

He doesn't miss the others. And even though his angel now wears a sapphire ring, the ring he took from the Mirna of Cal State San Bernardino, she is no different from others.

Detective Elouise Norton—she is different. And a kill like that only happens once in a lifetime.

43

It was a nice night for catching up: filling out reports, making copies of reports, three-holing and stapling those reports, and slipping them into binders and file folders. Colin and I did all of this over foam cartons of one-dollar Chinese takeout and bottles of Diet Coke. Puttin' on the Ritz, Southwest Division style.

In between the eating, sipping, and stapling, Colin learned that Max Yates's alibi had checked out.

According to a Pechanga Casino customer service rep, Yates and Macie checked in on Friday, June 15, ordered room service on Monday morning, June 18, and on Tuesday night, June 19. Yates checked out of the hotel on Wednesday morning at 10:03 A.M.

As Colin worked the murder book, I studied the Darsons' most recent bank statements. The expression on my face must have been a strange one because Colin said, "What do you see?"

I narrowed my eyes. "Last March, Cyrus Darson's account saw this crazy infusion of cash. Ten thousand dollars, seventy-five hundred dollars, twelve thousand dollars."

"He win the lottery?"

"Don't know."

"Maybe it was payment for services rendered."

"There haven't been any other large amounts like that in his account since then. But that's not the only WTF moment I've had. So I've also been scanning city council meeting minutes for all Crase-related activity and I saw that in April of last year, a month after Cyrus Darson wins the lottery, the city voted on building approvals—specifically, the building of Crase Parc and Promenade.

"According to the minutes, there were no protests—Darson and the neighborhood group never showed up to City Hall. I mean, it was the most important council meeting *ever.* The renovation got the 'all systems go' that day and Darson's a no-show? But now, looking at these banks statements, Darson's lottery winnings had started to arrive in March, just a month before that crucial vote."

"You thinkin' Darson was bribed?" Colin asked.

"*Something* happened. Strange, right?" I flipped a page in the bank statements and scanned the entries. "Okay, this is interesting: a thousand dollars deposited on the twentieth of each month." I flipped back to the end of the prior year. "A thousand dollars, deposited on the twentieth of every month."

"Maybe it's his salary for something," Colin suggested.

"He told me that he worked 'here and there.'" I looked up from the statements. "Something's going on with Mr. Darson."

By ten thirty, Monique Darson's book had been updated. Unfortunately, as the binder thickened, I still lacked enough evidence to make an arrest.

Then, Colin and I made phone calls.

Nova Wheeler, Renata's mother, had been placed on bed rest by her doctor and couldn't talk to me. The old woman that had answered the phone hung up before I could say "good-bye."

Margo, Von Neeley's sidepiece, had been doing just fine when I rang, but she refused to come to the station for an interview without legal representation. "I been praying on it and God told me to call a lawyer." Since when was God acting as a referral service?

And in all this time, not once did pinballs clang or Greg's picture and cell-phone or hotel-room telephone numbers brighten my phone's display. *No bueno.*

I caught Colin staring at me after my last voice mail to Greg. "What are *you* lookin' at?"

He waggled his pen between his fingers. "Nothin'."

That's when his cell phone rang from his shirt pocket. He plucked it out, glanced at the screen, grimaced, then placed the phone facedown on his desk. The ringing stopped and a *swoosh* sounded seconds later— the caller had left voice mail. Colin stared at the phone for several seconds, then turned back to the murder book.

My gaze settled on the picture of Greg and me in scuba gear, preparing to dive somewhere off the coast of Cozumel. *Smiles, everyone!*

Colin's phone rang again. Again, he didn't check for the caller.

"Is that the chick from Whole Foods?" I asked.

He stapled a crime scene photo onto a divider. "Nope."

Swoosh. Another voice mail.

I cleared my throat, then said, "Can I ask you a personal question?"

His jaw worked for a moment, until he gave a curt nod.

"Did you love what's-her-face?" I asked. "Colorado?"

Colin, eyes still in the big blue binder, said, "Yeah. I loved her."

I twisted in my chair for a bit, then asked, "Did you do what you did intentionally, so that *she'd* have to end it?"

Colin pulled at his lower lip, then sighed. "As Sun Tzu said, 'The supreme art of war is to subdue the enemy without fighting.'" Then, he met my eyes and for a quick second, his cockiness had been subdued by sadness.

I ran Todd Wisely's name through the computer. He came back clean, but a simple Internet search turned up three news stories about him doing bad things to strippers, a Chihuahua, and one very unfortunate mailbox. "How is it that I'm reading all of this, yet he has a clean record?"

"He got slapped on the wrist those times," Colin said, coming out of his momentary funk. "Most college basketball players gotta live by a code of conduct. If Todd had been convicted of domestic assault or vandalism or whatever, he would've been kicked off the team for conduct unbecoming of a player. Then, the season would've been in the crapper. Betcha the DA or the judge is an alum and took it easy on him. And the team probably has great lawyers on retainer, a cleanup crew who deals with shit like that all the time."

UC Santa Cruz, home of the Fightin' Banana Slugs, was my alma mater. Sure, we had athletics and cheerleaders, but we were also Division 183 or something. So sports: yay?

"Try calling him again," I said.

Colin grabbed the receiver and punched in the number Macie had scribbled on that list. After waiting and waiting, Colin hung up. "Still no answer from Mr. Wisely."

"That's the fifteenth time you've told me that," I said, closing my carton of chicken fried rice. "And frankly, I'm tired of hearing it."

"Frankly, I'm tired of saying it." His cell phone rang—the ringtone was the first few bars of some Maroon 5 song about needing something to believe in and *la-la-la*. This time, Colin picked up the phone but still didn't answer. He waited until the *swoosh* sounded before he smiled and said, "Jen, the chick from Whole Foods? Just sent me a picture." He held up the phone to show me the photograph. "Hot, huh?"

The blonde in the small screen had big hair and wore on her face every color of paint Sherwin-Williams sold.

I winced. "Just promise that you won't feed her after midnight."

Colin's brows furrowed. "Huh?"

I had just showed my age and wit with the *Gremlins* reference, and he didn't understand it. Good things were always wasted on the young.

"So Todd Wisely," I said.

"What about him?"

"Let's go pay him a visit. Sunshine put him at the scene. Macie put him on her list. He's a big baller. And I'm curious."

"About?"

"How it feels to consider some guy other than Napoleon Crase as the Evil One."

Colin smiled. "You may enjoy it and never come back."

I laughed. "I doubt it—Crase is the wind beneath my wings. Saddle up, cowboy."

"Right now?" He consulted his watch. "This late?"

"You turning into a pumpkin at midnight?" I stood and stretched like a cat on a carpet, flexing the tips of my toes and fingers until they cracked. "Since when do we allow potential murder suspects to catch *Letterman*? Are we in Kennebunkport or are we in South Los Angeles?"

And hell, it had been a decent enough time of day for someone—maybe even Todd—to wrap his hands around a child's neck and squeeze until she stopped living.

44

Todd Wisely and his family lived in Carson, sixteen miles out of downtown Los Angeles. In the 1920s, oil had been discovered in this part of Southern California. Refineries opened and job seekers and their families followed. Almost one hundred years later, Carson was still a city of oil production; a city that stank of methane, its unofficial flower; a city shrouded in sherbet-colored refinery lights and giant plumes of steam.

Only a few homes on Todd Wisely's block glowed with television light—and someone was still watching the boob tube in Todd's living room. The Wisely house was not the original tract home that had been built in the 1970s. It had been remodeled into a five-bedroom McMansion with lush plantings and a waterfall—too much this-and-that for such a small plot of land. A Bruins flag hung above the front double doors. UCLA bumper stickers had been plastered in the rear windows of the two Lexus sedans parked in the flagstone driveway.

After knocking and waiting, knocking and waiting some more, the front door opened and a draft of onions rode out to greet us. Weezy Jefferson, all bosoms, wig, and fake eyelashes, stood there wearing a blue-and-yellow tracksuit similar to the one Sunshine had described Todd wearing on Tuesday night. But Weezy knew as much about exercise and conditioning as I knew about horse husbandry in Kazakhstan. At half past eleven, she was not pleased to see two strangers standing on her porch.

I identified myself and Colin, then asked to speak with Todd.

"Todd is not here," she said with a frown.

"And you are . . . ?" I asked.

"His mother, Gerri Wisely."

In the background, I heard a very excited man preach about God's plan for His children. Plants—ferns, orchids, and something carnivorous-looking—filled the foyer and beyond, crawling everywhere and sucking up all of the oxygen meant for us highfalutin homo sapiens.

"Do you know where he'd be, Mrs. Wisely?" I asked. "We've tried calling him all night but we've had no success . . . which is why we drove here tonight. It's very important that we speak with him immediately."

She crossed her arms. "About?"

"The murder of his friend Monique Darson."

"Is he a suspect?"

I held her gaze. "We'd just like to speak with him, please. We're talking to all of the victim's friends."

She said nothing at first, just tapped the door with her fingernails. Then: "Do you show up this late to *all* of her friends' houses?" Weezy was acting hard, but her jaw muscles twitched and the left eyelash fluttered too much—fear lurked beneath her pissiness. Because *murder*? Who the hell wants *that* on their porch at almost midnight? She touched her wig with a shaky hand and the gold five-point-star ring on her finger caught the porch light.

"You're an Eastern Star?" I asked, nodding at the ring.

Her eyes lit and her chin lifted with pride. "Yes, I am."

Yahtzee!

"My grandmother was an Eastern Star," I said. "She was the . . . Who's the officer responsible for the initiations? The conductress? Yes, she did that in a chapter back in Brooklyn." I sniffled. "Rest her soul."

Gerri Wisely's bosom lifted to follow her chin. "I'm Worthy Matron of my chapter."

"Oh, wow." I dropped my eyes, all *golly, gee whiz*. "I've always been interested in joining. I have such warm feelings about Eastern Stars, you know, because of my grandmother. Before she died, though, she asked me to join. But I'm just a cop "

"Oh, sweetheart," Gerri Wisely the Worthy Matron said, "you're a relative, first of all, and second, *all* distinguished women are invited to apply."

"Even a gun-slinging wretch like me?" I asked, sad-eyed.

"You *are* a detective," she said with a soft smile. "You keep our neighborhoods and families safe from—"

Colin cleared his throat and said, "I hate to break this up—"

"Oh. Yeah. Sorry." I offered Gerri Wisely an embarrassed grin. "I'm forgetting why I came to your house so late at night. And again: I apologize for the lateness."

"Todd said he was going to a party over in Inglewood," she shared. "At some club called Metro."

I thanked Gerri Wisely for her help and promised that I would check out her chapter's Web site once I had a free moment.

"So the Eastern Star whatever," Colin said as he pulled away from the curb. "Was that a lie?"

"My friend Lena's grandmother was the grandmother I never had." I tossed him a smile. "Like my dorm-room Malcolm X poster said, 'By any means necessary.'"

The traffic on La Brea Avenue was a delight. Cars jammed the streets—most of them filled with drunken revelers, male and female, standing in the sunroofs of their cars. A few of Inglewood's Finest had pulled over the worst offenders, but there were so many sinners—the cops' efforts were equivalent to putting out a forest fire with a baby's bottle filled with milk. Bass boomed from car stereos as some so-called rapper muttered on top of the beat, "The hat, walk with it, walk with it, The hat, get low . . ." Somewhere in New York, KRS-One and Chuck D were sobbing into their Fuzzy Navels and Cool Ranch Doritos.

As we got closer to Metro, more people—young women wearing booty shorts and cheap stilettos, and their male counterparts, sporting baggy shirts of color (couldn't wear white T-shirts to clubs), flooded the streets and sidewalks. A few members of a bike club revved their custom-made Harleys at the curb.

"Oh, goody," I said. "An FFA convention."

Colin snorted. "*Future* Felons of America? How much you wanna bet that a few of these cats are current members—"

A gray BMW 630i with black rims shot from Market Street and swerved north onto La Brea Avenue .

"That our boy?" Colin asked, speeding up to get a better view of the rear license plate.

I ran the sequence through the computer. "That's his car. Don't know if that's him behind the wheel, though." The Bimmer's windows were blacked out. Not only could I not determine if Todd was driving, I couldn't tell whether there were other people in the car.

"This could be bad," Colin said.

"Shit." I grabbed the radio and requested backup just in case somebody was feeling large like Ferrigno.

At Manchester Boulevard the BMW picked up speed and shot through the red light.

I said, "Shit," again.

Colin turned to me. "Well?"

I rubbed my forehead. "Damn it. Didn't feel like having an adventure tonight."

Colin said, "Oh well," then hit the siren and floored it. Off we went, also blasting through the red light, almost clipping an Altima that wouldn't move the hell out of the way.

The Bimmer was now traveling at least sixty miles per hour in a thirty-five.

"We don't want him going down the hill," I said.

La Brea Avenue northbound cut between Baldwin Hills and Kenneth Hahn park. It was a twisty son-of-a-gun, one of those Autobahn stretches of road where a car could get away from you, flip, bang, and kill you dead.

Colin sped up. "Thinks he knows we want him to stop?"

The Bimmer cut a quick right into a gas station but didn't stop. It then sped out of the station, cracked a nearby bus stop bench, made a left, and roared west on Slauson Avenue.

"I think he knows," I said.

Two patrol cars, sirens blasting, lights swirling like crazy, joined the chase.

My heart pounded—I rarely participated in car pursuits now, and I wondered how this one would end. I thanked God that I wore Kevlar today, and for the first time in a long time was grateful for the vest's pinching at my hip—it was very possible that whoever sat behind that steering wheel wanted to die by cop tonight.

The BMW swerved into the parking lot shared by a McDonald's and a Home Depot.

A second later, Colin also jammed into the lot.

The BMW screeched to a stop near the store's entrance.

Colin and I hopped out of the Crown Vic, guns drawn and trained on the Bimmer's driver's-side door.

The officers in the two patrol cars—two Hispanics, two blacks, none of them acquaintances of mine since they worked graveyard—also had their weapons drawn.

"Get out of the car!" Colin yelled. "Get out of the car *now*!"

Nothing.

Sweat rolled down my temples and my back. *Please God, let this be quick and bloodless*. I grabbed the car's PA system microphone and said, "Open the door. Step out of the car. Hands out so that I can see them. Do it *now*!"

Nothing happened.

I repeated my order.

A moment later, the driver's-side door swung open and the noise of T-Pain's autotuned crap rode out on acrid smoke.

I smelled it from where I stood. "He hot-boxin' in there?"

"Yep," Colin said. "I'm gettin' a contact way back here."

A long leg clad in denim left the car and a $200 Air Jordan landed on the asphalt. A long arm, the wrist shiny with a Rolex and a thick gold bracelet, hung in the air. The rest of Todd Wisely followed. He slowly placed his large hands on the top of his baseball cap–covered head.

"Anybody else in the car?" I asked over the mike.

"No," Todd Wisely shouted.

Officer Two crept toward the passenger-side window. With one quick move, he opened the door and pointed his revolver into the darkness. "Clear," he shouted.

Todd Wisely snickered. "Y'all fucked with the wrong—"

Officer Number Three did the honors—he spun the big baller around, wrangled one large hand and then the other behind his back.

And T-Pain said, "Yeah, god damn, you think you're cool, you think I'm not—you think you tough . . ."

Saturday, June 22

45

I gaped at the handcuffed ballplayer seated across from me. Not because he was a wonder to behold. No, unfortunately. Beneath the fancy clothes and diamond stud earring, Todd Wisely was an average-looking kid with skin the color of a Hershey's kiss, lips darkened from smoking shit on his downtime, and high cheekbones courtesy of some Native American great-great-grand-something. His eyes were rheumy, the whites the color of rhubarb. He had that combative tilt to his chin, that swagger anyone could master if he watched Season One of *The Wire*. Height—six-foot-six—was the only gee-whiz thing about Todd Wisely.

But if anyone owned a Gucci belt, it would have been this kid. And until today, my handcuffs had never brushed against a genuine Rolex.

"You're telling me . . ." Awed, I shook my head. "You ran from us cuz you was ridin' dirty?"

"Yup." He crossed his long legs, then uncrossed them.

"Not cuz you killed Monie."

"Yup." He was staring at something behind me, maybe a rainbow or perhaps a unicorn.

I turned in my chair—hell, I had waited all of my life to see a unicorn. But there was nothing behind me except a dirty wall. Facing him again, I said, "Why can't you look me in the eye, Todd?"

He folded his arms and intentionally held my gaze. "I'm lookin'."

"You're displaying defensive behavior," I said. "What do you have to be defensive about? This ain't a TV show and you ain't Stringer Bell, so stop with the bad-ass-thug routine. You're from *Carson*, son."

No response, and so we sat there in silence. Forty seconds later, he said, "Ma'am, I didn't kill Monie. I was in Vegas on Tuesday night."

"You got proof?"

He smirked. "My word is bond."

"Your word is turd. Show me a receipt or stop with that noise."

"I don't have a receipt on me," he said. "Let me go home and I'll find you one."

I waved my hand. "Let's move on to tonight's never-ending game of *Pole Position*."

"You didn't have to chase me."

"You didn't have to run. We just wanted to talk to you and now look." I ticked off fingers: "Vandalism, reckless driving, failure to stop . . . You fucked up, my friend."

"Whatever. I didn't kill Monie."

"When was the last time you talked to her?"

He shrugged. "Don't know."

I narrowed my eyes. "Come on, Todd."

He shook his head. "We weren't a couple. I didn't call and check in with her like she was my girl, cuz she wasn't."

"Fine. Where were you late Tuesday night, early Wednesday morning?"

"Like I said: I was in Vegas at the craps table in the Venetian."

I sighed. "So if you were in Vegas and didn't kill Monique Darson, why did you run from us tonight?"

He glared at me. "Already told you." His high was quickly fading and he was becoming prickly. "Why you keep asking me that?"

"*Because*," I shouted, standing up, "you don't seem to be pissed off enough with what I'm accusing you of."

"I don't?"

"If someone accused *me* of murder, well, I'd be shouting and banging my fists against the walls, acting like a crazy woman cuz I. Didn't. *Do*. It." I held out my arms and shook my head. "But you . . . You're sittin' here in the cut, like I just accused you of nibbling too many grapes in the produce section."

He grunted and slumped in his chair.

"Probably cuz you're high, right?"

His mouth twisted into something that should've been a sneer but was too lazy to be that aggressive. "Yeah. Somethin' like that."

I sat back in my chair. "Monique was a cute thing. A flirt, I hear. She liked big ballers—you're a big baller, aren't you? Does Gabriella know that you had sex with a seventeen-year-old girl?"

"That's my private business."

I pulled Monique's autopsy photo from the expandable file and slapped the picture on the table before him.

Todd pushed the photo away without looking at it.

I moved the picture back. "You killed her, didn't you?"

This time he sat up and boomed, "Why? Cuz I *fucked* her? And? So?"

I laughed. "*And* the age of consent in this beautiful state of ours is eighteen. *So* you can go to jail. Even big ballers like you. Hate to pull you from the Matrix, Todd, but you're not the special snowflake your mom has told you that you are. That UCLA has told you that you are."

"Then I'm mistaken," he said with a smile. "I didn't have sex with her. We just held hands."

"Does your mother, the Worthy Matron of her chapter of Eastern Star . . . Does she know that you, her precious boy, committed statutory rape?"

"I didn't *rape* her," he said, his eyes hot.

"The law says you did," I retorted. "Consent or not."

His eyes shimmered with angry tears.

"Tell me the truth, Todd, or else—"

"Or else you're gonna beat it out of me?" He threw me a sullen glare. "That's what the LAPD do, right? Serve, protect, break a nigga's neck?"

I poked out my bottom lip and touched my heart. "That really hurts, Todd. I've never, not ever, taken a flashlight to somebody's head." I paused, then added, "But never say never, right? We all fall short of the glory of God." I leaned forward, almost knee to knee with him now. If he wanted, he could land one square punch to my face. *POW!* Right in the kisser. And then, it would be on like Donkey Kong, as we used to say back in the old days. "There's DNA on Monique's body, Todd. Will that semen belong to you?"

He swallowed and his Adam's apple bobbed. "I didn't do it. I was in Vegas."

"Vegas again?" I groaned and rubbed my temples. "When I called you yesterday afternoon, you told me that you had been at Bruin Woods. I called your coach and he told me that you had been at Bruin Woods."

In a small voice, Todd said, "He was mistaken."

"Not mistaken. He *lied*. And you *lied*. So which story do you wanna go with, cuz frankly, I'm bored with this now. The mountains or the desert?"

He didn't speak and a tear rolled down his cheeks.

I leaned forward, knee to knee again. "C'mon, dude. It's two in the morning. *You* got shit to do. *I* got shit to do. So let's end this, all right? A witness placed you at the scene on the night Monique was killed."

He shook his head. "Then your witness must be a crackhead cuz I wasn't *with* Monie on Tuesday night."

I resisted laughing since my witness was indeed a crackhead. Instead, I said, "There's DNA on—"

"I want my lawyer," he said, eyes on the table.

Well, damn. That shut me up and slapped the grin off my face. "So it's like that?" I asked.

He smiled. "Boom."

A *digital photograph with world champion boxer Floyd Mayweather taken on June 18 at 11:38 P.M.*

A bank statement showing an ATM withdrawal of $300 on June 18 at 9:55 P.M. at the Venetian Hotel and Casino in Las Vegas.

Surveillance camera footage at that ATM in the Venetian.

These three items had been spread before me on the table in interview room 1 by prominent Los Angeles defense attorney Jeremy Lowenstein. "Sports Stars in Trouble" was his specialty—just as Colin had figured. His slicked-back brown hair and blue pin-striped suit had been the second- and third-fanciest things this room had ever seen, with Todd being the first. And Lowenstein smelled good, like butter and warm sugar. I thought of having him stand on my desk for the rest of the day, like a human air freshener, but he already had a job—the Fixer. And he had done it well.

The attorney tapped the bank statement. "I think this proves it, Detective Norton. Mr. Wisely is innocent of murder. As you can see, he wasn't even *in* California when Monique Darson was killed."

"Why did he lie to me?" I asked.

"Why does it matter?" Lowenstein said.

"The other charges—"

The defense attorney waved his hand. "No problem. I'll have those dropped by the time morning rush hour ends. I don't know who your witness saw, but it certainly wasn't my client."

My stomach burned—the beginnings of an ulcer my doctor had warned me about two months ago. I tried now to block the pain with positive thoughts—*it doesn't hurt, that's just gas*—but staring at Lowenstein's evidence only made the burning worse.

The sun was coming up somewhere beyond the walls of interview room 1, and I had been awake for twenty-four hours. In that time, I had found a dead girl in the trunk of a Ford Taurus, had led a car chase down La Brea Avenue, and had lost $30 to a heroin addict who had fingered the wrong tall black man driving a BMW who was no longer a suspect, whose attorney had threatened me with a wrongful arrest suit even though his client had fled from the police, vandalized city property, and had enough OG Kush flowing through his veins to put a family of zombies to sleep.

Damn. I needed a drink. A mimosa or three. It *was* almost time for breakfast.

46

So Todd Wisely walked. He spent two hours in the bucket and now had a fish story to tell. Technically, he had to post bail and still answer for the lesser charges. As a homicide detective, though, I couldn't care less about those offenses.

The squad room was noisy with third-shift dicks and their shifty-eyed witnesses. Colin had left a sticky on my computer monitor. *Catching a nap in the cot room.* I plopped into my chair, arms heavy, muscles sore. I leaned back and closed my eyes as the clatter of doors opening and closing, the whimpers of crying relatives and the rhythmic clack of nightsticks rubbing against Sam Browne belts, melted into its own kind of silence.

A knock on my desk pulled me from that place called Sleep.

Lieutenant Rodriguez stood over me. "In my office. *Now.*"

I glanced at my desk clock: almost seven in the morning.

By this time Pepe, Luke, and Joey had arrived and had been joking by the coffeepot, telling some story about a shopping cart, a peg-legged goat, and a transvestite hooker. As I left my desk, they stood in silence— the favored child was about to be torn a new one. That didn't bode well for *anyone* this morning.

Lieutenant Rodriguez was seated behind his desk. "Close the door."

I did as he asked, then stood before him like a sixth-grade trouble-maker.

He said nothing as he stared at me—over the last fifteen years, a vampire named Los Angles had sucked almost all of his life away, leaving his eyelashes as gray as his eyes.

I waited and forced indifference into my expression.

Finally, he said, "What the hell was that?"

"What the hell was *what?*"

"You collared one of the best players in the NCAA on a *hunch?*"

I squinted at him. "I shoulda let him run away cuz he shot 223 points in a game once upon a time? Are you *kidding* me?"

"I expected better—"

"You're acting like I randomly rolled up on a Boy Scout."

"PC?" he asked.

I gawked at him, then said, "You want probable cause? Fine: he was speeding away from me, and that may have been an indication of guilt, running away because he murdered my victim."

He shrugged. "That's it?"

"Since when do I need more?" I asked, hands on my hips. "And when we drove out to Carson, it wasn't my intent to arrest him."

"Oh, really?" he said, as he rearranged the picture frame of his twin girls with the Matt Kemp Dodgers bobblehead. "Forgive me if I don't believe you."

"Did I come to you and ask that you sign an arrest warrant for one Todd Wisely? No. Because I only wanted to *talk* to him since a witness placed him at the scene. *Talk*, just like I've done with—"

"You trusted a known heroin addict—"

"Mary Ford," I said, holding up a finger, and then, two more fingers. "Calvin Hasan, Guillermo Acosta."

"Yeah? What about them?"

"Two alcoholics and a hooker," I said, "who all witnessed murders, who told me what I needed to know, who helped get three killers off the streets of Los Angeles."

Lieutenant Rodriguez exhaled, then rubbed his eyes.

"First, you tell me to use kid gloves with Napoleon Crase," I said. "And *now*, you want me to baby Todd Wisely. Are there any rich people I can piss off? Treat like I treat the gangbangers and the crackheads?"

"That lawyer Lowenstein is an asshole who will—"

"I don't care about Lowenstein and his agenda." I glared at the wall and at a picture of Lieutenant Rodriguez shaking hands with Tommy Lasorda.

"That's your problem," he shouted. "*Eww. Politics.* You don't care. You *should* care."

"Dude was high as fuck," I yelled back. "He was a danger to the community. He had three Baggies of weed in his jacket *and* two

Costco-sized tubs of Ecstasy and Viagra in his trunk. Fine: he didn't kill our girl, but goddamn, he's an asshole who could've hit and killed *your* family. But I guess you'll forgive him for that since he's gonna play for the Lakers someday."

Lieutenant Rodriguez pounded his desk with his fists. "Damn it, Lou! You want us to have a black eye? You want folks screaming about racial profiling? You want your reporter friend writing an article about how Southwest Division targets more black men than any other race?"

I rolled my eyes. "The BMW's windows were so freakin' dark—another offense—that I couldn't see inside the car. So at that time, I didn't know *who* the driver was or *what* box he checked on the last census."

Lieutenant Rodriguez sank in his chair and tugged at his mustache. "Lowenstein threatened to call the mayor."

I laughed. "Good luck with that. Ain't the mayor in Maui right now, helping himself to the local lady reporters?"

"Be careful."

"I'm always careful. I even restrained myself from stomping in Crase's head yesterday. But I guess that doesn't count."

"You're letting this affect your judgment, Lou."

"*This?*" Confused, I shook my head. "What is 'this'?"

"Sometimes you focus on one thing until you can't see anything else," he said "And sometimes, that changes everything about you."

I closed my eyes and forced myself to smile.

"I just want you to be as good as you can be," he said.

Dumbstruck, I gaped at him. "So caring about something makes me a horrible person?"

"No. Caring about something too much that it affects your judgment is a problem," he said. "And to be honest, I'm three seconds from pulling you off this—"

Someone knocked on the door.

Lieutenant Rodriguez called out, "Yeah?"

Colin poked his head in and said, "Sorry to interrupt but we have a visitor. A relative of Monique Darson."

To my boss, I said, "This isn't personal, Lieutenant. I'm just doing my job."

But maybe I *did* care too much. But that's who I was; that's what I did. For many people, Greg included, that wasn't good enough. Sometimes, I wished that I could read something horrible in the newspaper and say, "Wow, that's too bad," then drive down the hill to buy a handbag and a Frappuccino. But I can't, no matter how hard I try, even when I'm doing just that. One day I will luck out. One day, a callus will form around that part of my heart, and then I will stop caring like some cops, and then I will be as good as I can be. This will lead me to Hell, but at least I won't care only because I can't.

Before we returned to the very popular interview room 1, Colin squeezed my shoulder. "You made the right call, partner. Todd was a danger."

But his support didn't silence the noise in my head—which sounded like a middle school orchestra was warming up during basketball practice. All squeaks, squawks, and echo. Colin said something else, but I couldn't hear him over the clarinets.

A woman the color of peanut butter was seated at the table, hunched over a cup of coffee. She wore jeans and a blue postal worker's shirt. She had a mustache and the loveliest hazel eyes in the world.

I introduced myself and shook the woman's hand.

She said that she was Freeda Duffy, Monique's cousin. "But y'all can call me Free."

"So," I said as Colin and I sat across from her, "why are you here so early in the day?"

"I work graveyard at the post office," she said, "so I'm just getting off. I had been plannin' to talk to y'all when it was more convenient, but it's been four days now and it ain't been the right time yet, so here I am."

I didn't say anything—my head still buzzed with that school-orchestra-gymnasium noise.

Colin kicked my leg to get me started.

I opened my mouth, but no words came.

So, he started. "Well, we certainly appreciate you stoppin' by." He cleared his throat and said, "Detective Norton?"

Wide-eyed, I stared at him like a child who had forgotten her lines during the Christmas pageant.

Colin winked at me, then turned to Freeda. "So what can you tell us, Miss Freeda?"

"Monie and me was together on Tuesday afternoon," she said. "Like between one and four."

Colin said, "Yeah?"

"Even though I'm older than Monie and Macie, Monie and I was real tight. I drove her places before she got that car, anytime Macie wouldn't drive her. Anyway, she and Macie was fussin' with each other over the phone on Tuesday."

Colin nodded. "Macie mentioned that to us."

"Did she tell you that they was arguin' about Max?"

I lifted an eyebrow—*that* woke me up. "Really?"

She laughed. "Of course she didn't tell you. I only heard one part of the conversation—Monie's side—but Monie had called Max that afternoon and Macie answered his phone. Monie tried to play it off like she had dialed the wrong number but Macie was like, 'Why you got my nigga's cell number anyway?'"

I leaned forward. "Do you think Max and Monie had something going on?"

The woman took a long sip of coffee. "I don't *think* so but if they weren't sneakin' off yet, it was only a matter of time before they did. Them two was gettin' real close. Right before she got that Lexus, he picked her up from school in his Bentley a few times."

"Like how many times?"

"Three or four."

"What color is that Bentley?"

"Midnight blue with, like, glitter in the paint. And right before Monie left the house on Tuesday night, she made sure she brushed Butter. I asked why she was gettin' so crazy with the lint brush, and she told me, 'Max hates dog hair in his car.'"

My heart stopped—Max had been in Temecula, according to Macie, according to Pechanga Casino and Resort.

"Wasn't Max out of town with Macie on Tuesday?" Colin asked, reading my mind.

"I don't know who was where," Freeda said. "And Monie only said this to me about Butter, in that by-the-way way. Not braggin' or nothin' but more worried, and so you talk yourself to death to calm down, know what I mean?"

Guess we needed to speak with Max Yates in person after all.

"Did Macie know Monique was planning to see Max that night?" I asked. "Or *any* night?"

Freeda laughed. "Hell no. She woulda killed Max *and* Monie. Macie too busy bein' fabulous and spending Max's money to see him dump shit right under her nose. That girl is clueless."

47

The phone on my desk chirped, and the sound startled me. I wasn't asleep, nor was I awake. I had been existing in a state akin to screen-saver mode. Fully alert now, my gaze landed on the dead purple roses Greg had sent me days ago. When the phone chirped again, I grabbed the receiver too quickly and almost knocked over a cold cup of coffee, my fifth cup in an hour. "Lou Norton, Homicide."

"Hey!" It was Zucca, and he sounded too damn cheery for nine in the morning. "You sound like a gravel truck. One of them days?"

"One of them *weeks*." I rubbed my eyes, remembering too late that I wore eyeliner—eyeliner that I had applied yesterday morning. "What's up?" I grabbed the small compact mirror I kept in my desk drawer and . . . yep. Raccoon eyes. Lovely.

"Field trip! Come down to the center. I have fresh coffee and as-sorted pastries."

I glanced over at the pot of steaming crude only cops called coffee. "Assorted, huh?"

"Don't make me beg." He paused, then added, "Although I've been told by various ex-girlfriends that I'm extra sexy when I beg."

"They tell you that before or after you pay them?"

"Ha-ha. See you soon."

I left a sticky note on Colin's monitor. *Going to see a man about some spit.*

As I grabbed my purse, Lieutenant Rodriguez came to stand at my desk. "I've been thinking."

Here it is: my dismissal. I squared my shoulders. "Yes, sir?"

He rubbed his jaw, sighed, then said, "Bring Crase in for another in-terview. A formal one. I'll join you."

A smile found the edges of my mouth. "Yes, sir."

I waited for my boss to return to his office before calling Crase's home.

He picked up the phone on the first ring.

I introduced myself again, then said, "We would like you to come back in for another interview." There was steel in my voice as though our prior conversation had not left me a wrathful, volcanic Gila monster.

He paused before saying, "It's Saturday."

"It is Saturday."

Another pause, then: "I won't be available until Monday."

"Because?"

"Because I'll be bringing my attorney with me, and that is when he will be available."

I didn't speak, pissed at the delay.

"You have my word, Detective," he said, amused. "I have no reason to run. Ten o'clock, Monday morning." And then, he hung up.

I muttered a curse or three, then slammed down the receiver. I had no choice but to wait until Monday.

It was almost ten o'clock when I pulled off the 10 Freeway and into the parking lot of the Forensic Science Institute. I lifted my face to the June sun—so bright, so warm, so alive. I didn't want to leave it. The sun made me feel like I was wrapped in a lover's arms, a lover I hadn't seen in years, and his breath on my neck made me sway. But Zucca wanted to show me something, damn him, so I entered an ex-boyfriend of a building with fluorescent tubes of cold light and central heat.

I found Zucca, clad in his white lab coat, in a brightly lit laboratory crammed with microscopes, computer monitors, and millions of vials and tubs of chemicals. He had brewed a fresh pot of coffee, and as he had promised, the pastries were assorted—from glazed to cinnamon to pink-frosted. None of this lifted my spirits, though, or made me forget that I hadn't slept and hadn't eaten and hadn't even taken a shower. But I faked it as all women are taught to do in that special fifth-grade assembly where boys weren't allowed.

"This was worth the trip," I cooed before taking an enthusiastic bite into a sweet roll. "Good, very good." I sipped from my cup of coffee. "Strong and rich. Just like I like my men. Or something."

He grinned, pleased that he had pleased me. "First: toxicology came back on that DNA we got off Monique Darson." He handed me the report. "Cocaine. Also, a mix of acetaminophen, aspirin, and caffeine."

"Excedrin?"

"Yep, and a lot of it. Somebody has a problem."

"One of many."

"Let me show you something else," he said, leading me to his workstation. On the monitor, there was a black-and-white graphic of twelve bars. Yellow flags of jargon like TPOX and CSF1PO sat atop the rectangles.

I pointed to the monitor. "Let me guess: I'm looking at Monique Darson's DNA."

He nodded. "First, I tested all the blood found in the condo against the semen and saliva found on her body and that handkerchief. Same DNA. I ran it through CODIS to look for a match."

"And?"

"Nothing came back," he said, eyes on those bars. "No matches in the database."

I tossed the rest of my sweet roll in the trash and snapped, "You called me down here to tell me *that*?"

He blinked at me, wounded. "Of course not. I called you down here because . . . The DNA from your sister's shoe also came in."

"It did? And?" All feeling had left my face. I held myself so tight, my body vibrated from the strain. I willed my mouth to open. Willed my thoughts, swirling like falling leaves, to land into a coherent order.

He clicked his mouse and a new CODIS graphic sat atop Monique's. "There were no matches in the database for that DNA, either."

I kicked the desk—anxiety had morphed into anger because that meant Napoleon Crase . . . "Damn it, Zucca!" I shouted, near tears.

"No matches in *CODIS*," he quickly added, startled at my outburst. "But there *is* a match." As I tried to tuck in my pissiness through controlled breathing, Zucca minimized Tori's results, then moved them next to Monique's. "I could bore you with the specifics, go on and on about indexes and PCR analysis and STR loci, but all you'll care about is this: you find the man who killed Monique Darson, and you'll find the man who killed your sister."

48

He finds an empty bench near the library, a place he has always found too closed-in—all those walls of books everywhere. The sun shines bright and hot in this part of Southern California and he regrets wearing a sports coat. He had wanted to fit in with the academics but in this weather, even the oldest professors were wearing short-sleeved polo shirts. There aren't many students around, though, to wonder about the old guy in the wool jacket.

Spring semester has ended and pretty coeds in tight groups giggle and roam past him with nowhere to go. None of the tanned beauties look his way. *Bitches.* Their dismissal of him makes his stomach burn. Makes his skin stretch until he thinks his chest will rip apart at any moment.

His head hums and he reaches into his jacket pocket for the pill case. He opens it, plucks three white disks from the many, and pops them, dry.

There she is . . .

He watches her through the library's glass door.

She's organizing books on the return cart. She's dyed her hair cinnamon. And it is longer than before. She wears gym shorts and a UC Irvine tank top. When she stoops, the muscles in her twenty-year-old thighs stand out like jungle vines.

At one time, he liked Elvia's athleticism. But soon her strength made loving a challenge. She started to keep up with him, had stopped being scared, had wanted to switch roles and force *him* to submit. And so he stopped calling her. Every now and then, he follows her around the city to see who she's conning. The current boyfriend plays soccer and drives a red Fiat.

As he watches her, burning spreads from his crotch and down through his legs, forcing him to stand and move away from the bench.

Elvia pushes open the library door and steps out into the sunshine.

He stuffs his hands into his pockets and saunters along the path.

She ambles behind him, now talking on the phone. She's saying something about beer and chicken wings.

He casually glances over his shoulder.

She looks at him and her eyes brighten with recognition. "Oh my . . ." To the person on the phone, she says, "Let me call you back."

He stops in his step, cocks his head, and smiles. "Well, well, well."

"Oh my *gosh*," she says, coming in for a hug. "What are you doing here?"

She feels so soft. And her hair and skin smell like honey and almonds. "Just met a friend for coffee. Two old guys remembering when."

She touches his cheek. "You're not old."

He pretends to blush and drops his eyes to the pavement. "You wouldn't want to have a drink with an old not-old guy, would you?"

She bites her lower lip. "I'm meeting a friend right now at Hooters, but . . ." She smiles. "What about drinks later tonight? At that little place you'd take me to all the time?"

That "little place" served twenty-dollar cocktails and appetizers made from strange animals that had lived in swamps prior to their deaths. The music was something Moroccan, chaotic, loud. He hates that "little place." But he takes her hand and kisses it. "Anything for you."

"How about eight?"

He nods. "Sounds good."

She tiptoes to kiss him on the lips. "I've missed you."

He kisses her back. "I've missed you, too." His hand slides up to her neck and his thumb strokes the cartilage near her clavicle.

She steps back. "I have to go meet my girl."

"Enjoy the wings," he calls out, then watches as she struts away from him.

Wings and beer.

What kind of last supper is that?

49

You find the man who killed Monique Darson, and you'll find the man who killed your sister.

Zucca had seen my hesitation after he had stated this. I then told him that my number-one suspect, Napoleon Crase, had now been exonerated by DNA. But then, the scientist went *tap-tap-tap* on his computer and into CODIS. No DNA samples had ever been taken from Napoleon Crase. "So that cup you collected during his interview?" Zucca said. "That cup just became extremely important. I'll let you know when we finish analyzing it."

This also meant that Todd Wisely, Derek Hester, Von Neeley, and any of Monique's high-school aged sweethearts were too young to be Tori's murderer. Napoleon Crase, though? He was *juuuust* right.

I was getting there! And as the saying went, by perseverance, the snail reached the ark. And now, I saw that blessed boat on the horizon.

It took one phone call to the Department of Pensions and a request signed by Lieutenant Rodriguez to obtain the address of retired detective Tommy Peet. And by two o'clock, I had pulled in front of Peet's home in Torrance, a beach city twenty miles south of Los Angeles. An American flag hung above the clean-swept porch of the ranch-style house. The green Bermuda grass had been freshly mown.

A small white man with a pug nose answered the door. He saw the expandable file in my arm and the gold shield on my hip and he smiled. After introductions, Peet asked, "Where you stationed?"

"Southwest," I said. "Just like you were. And I'm actually here to ask about an old case of yours. It may be related to a murder I'm working now."

Peet invited me into a living room filled with Montgomery-Ward-ish brown furniture. *Fox News* played on a new large-screen television while a tumbler filled with melting ice and a slick of brown liquid sat in the holder of an armchair. There were no doilies on the coffee table. No copies of *Women's Day* magazine left in the creases of the love seat. No sweet smells of perfume or potpourri or pot roast cooking in a Dutch oven. No pictures of a wife or a child, no pictures at all except for the one above the mantel, the one of a younger Tommy Peet in his dress uniform, not smiling for the camera.

Back when I was thirteen, I had thought Detective Peet was a big man, at least six feet tall, and as wide as a barn door. Back then, his nose hadn't been so red, and he had worn his hair slicked back like he did now. Today, though, his hair was all gray and as fine as an eaglet's. As I sat across from him, I expected a light to shine in his blue eyes. I expected him to say, "Hey, you're that tall-for-her-age black kid with the missing sister, right?" But there was no recognition. A good thing or not, I didn't know.

"Back in 1988," I said, "you worked a missing child case." I handed him a copy of Tori's incident report, then summarized the case as he slipped on reading glasses.

"I've been retired for fifteen years now," he said, still reading. "I don't know how I can help."

"Do you have any theories about what happened?" I asked. "Were there suspects? Persons of interest?"

"We talked to a couple of gangbangers, a few football players, and another guy that was in love with her."

"Anyone else?"

He rubbed the stubble on his jaw. "If you're looking at Nappy Crase, we cleared him."

"How?"

"His alibi checked out. He was in the store, and he never left the store until closing around midnight. There was a security tape that confirmed this."

"I hear that Crase likes them young."

The old guy shrugged.

"And I hear that he plays patty-cake with their faces."

Another shrug. "I was investigating a kidnapping and possible murder. Didn't care who Crase banged and how he banged 'em."

"Even if he banged 'em so hard, they stopped breathing?"

"No reason for me to think that."

"What about the others?"

"What others?"

"There were other people at the store that day. I have their state-ments." I reached into Tori's folder again.

"Don't need to see them," he said, giving me a dismissive wave. "I took those statements, remember? Look, the missing girl was trouble. She dated hoodlums and she slept around, and got in trouble all the time. She was shoplifting and Crase caught her and let her go. She saw a group of guys—"

"Guys? Who were these guys?"

"Some kids who weren't around by the time I got to the store that night. No one knew them, and they were miscellaneous anyway. The last place the Starr girl was seen was the liquor store's parking lot about an hour later. She was standing by Nappy Crase's Cadillac. Meaning, she went back there, I'm thinking, to vandalize his car."

"Who saw her standing there?"

"The girl's friends. One of their names, I think, was Golden."

"You took a statement from Golden. Did you ever follow up with her after that?"

"No need."

I let that statement hang in the air—of course there had been a need. Golden had been one of the last people to see Tori alive.

And Tommy Peet's face and neck flushed—he knew that *I* knew that he hadn't done his best work on this case.

"Did Nappy Crase see Victoria?" I asked. "Standing by his car, I mean?"

"Yeah, and it pissed him off, according to this Golden."

"And then?"

"And then Golden went home. Victoria was still in the parking lot when she left."

"So Victoria got caught, Crase released her, she came back an hour later. After Golden left, what did Victoria do next? Just stand there in the lot by the car until the Rapture?"

"Don't know."

"Did you care?"

The old man tugged at his floppy ear. "Honestly? At the time, I *didn't* care. The city was different back then. The culture was less . . . *politically correct*. And just weeks before I caught the Starr case, I had been looking for another missing teenage girl who hadn't really been missing. And truth be told, I thought the Starr girl was doing the same thing."

"And Victoria's wristwatch?" I asked. "The one found beneath Crase's Cadillac?"

"He said he didn't know how it got there."

"And you, of course, believed him."

"The girl had been standing near his car—even her friends said that. She could've dropped the watch by accident. Or she could've left it there intentionally. There were a lot of ways that watch could've gotten there."

"Many ways," I said, nodding my head. "Like: it could've come off her wrist during a violent struggle with Napoleon Crase."

Peet dropped his head and took off his glasses. "It haunts me, that case, and I'm lucky if I don't think about it twice a day. The mom seemed really nice. Like she had tried real hard to keep her kids on the right path. But sometimes . . ." He rubbed his hands together, Lady Macbeth style, then exhaled. "I don't see how the Starr case is related to what you're working on now. Unless they bused in some white kids from Brentwood, black girls get dead in the Jungle all the time. Why you got such a hard-on for Crase?"

I blinked away the tears in my eyes and made my fingers sift though the expandable file as a distraction. "The DNA found in the current case matches the blood in the Starr case. The girl I found, Monique Darson, was murdered at Nappy Crase's new condo development, not far from the old liquor store. All I need now is a positive DNA match from Crase, and to get a warrant for *that*, I need to have all my Rockettes in a row."

"Crap," Peet muttered. "So it's possible that there's a connection."

"Yep." I stood from the couch and offered him my hand. "Thanks for your time."

He walked me to the door without speaking. After I left, he would probably pour a finger or two of Scotch into that tumbler.

Anything to forget.

Colin met me at Napoleon Crase's car dealership located on La Cienega Boulevard. NC Posh Auto was adjacent to Beverly Hills and socioeconomically far from the Jungle. In seven miles, the streets changed from liquor stores, kidney dialysis centers, and fried fish joints to Thai cafés, bridal shops, and car dealerships that sold preowned Jags, Bimmers, and Benzes, oh my.

"You're grinning," he said as we walked to the lot. "You been rollin' around in pow all day?"

I said, "What the hell is 'pow'?"

"Powder," he said. "Light, fluffy snow."

"Ah. Zucca had great news," I said, then told him about the matching DNA from Tori and Monique.

"So we're lookin' at old guys, then," Colin said.

"Absolutely."

"Which means Napoleon Crase . . . ?"

My smile grew ten times.

"So you're drooling," he said. "What now?"

"Gotta think about that. LT is back on my side for now—don't wanna screw that up and have him kick me to the curb just when I'm about to sing my solo."

He patted my back. "Good job. And Max Yates?"

I shrugged. "Might as well talk to him since we're here."

Not many customers were car shopping this afternoon. A young Japanese couple stood near a blacked-out Maserati. A teenage boy slobbered over a yellow Ferrari.

A Persian man in a shiny shark-blue suit met us at a purple Aston Martin. His name tag said BEHROUZ and he wore a smug smile even though he wore that suit. He said to Colin, "Buying the little lady a car today?" Before Colin could respond, Behrouz turned to me. "We have every luxury car made, no need to go elsewhere. Don't worry about payments—we'll work it out. Don't let this guy tell you no today." He gave that smug smile again.

I badged him and his smile lost its shine . . . unlike that suit. "Is Max Yates here today?" I asked.

Behrouz sighed with relief. "Yes. Yes. I'll get him for you." He hustled to the sales office hidden behind one-way glass.

I waggled a finger at Colin and said, "I'm not letting you tell me no today."

He grabbed my finger and tugged. "As though I'd dare." Then, he plucked the container of Tic Tacs from his pants pocket and dumped thousands of little candies into his mouth.

I winced. "I think you have a Tic Tac problem. You should see someone."

As he crunched, little shards of candy flecked the sides of his mouth. "Tic Tacs, sex . . . I got a million problems, Lou."

I leaned for a closer look inside the Aston Martin. "No wonder Max could hook Monique up with any car she wanted. So many just sitting here, doin' nothing."

Since the recession, people had been losing: jobs, homes, fancy cars. What had seemed easy to do in 2000—$700 for a car note, $500 for registration, insurance to cover it all—was now equivalent to deep-sea diving without an oxygen tank. Gas prices were too high, car registration fees had increased, and with the city's growing pothole problem, you needed new tires every three hundred miles. Many cars ended up in lots like this, wearing LIKE NEW! and ONLY 10,000 MILES! signs. Pretty hookers with gimpy legs and missing eyes.

Max Yates strolled out of the sales office in a suit that didn't shine, that didn't have strings hanging from its hems, and that had taken a tailor a month to sew. He had acorn-colored skin and smog-colored eyes. He was tall but needed to hit the gym to ward off the belly starting to droop over his waistband. He grinned to show white planks of porcelain teeth. A gold Rolex heavier than my head flashed from his left French cuff. He moved as easily and unhurriedly as a pillar of smoke.

"That guy's smooth," Colin whispered.

"That guy's *old*," I said. "Macie didn't tell me that Max is old enough to remember the last episode of *M*A*S*H*."

And this—Max Yates's age—changed everything.

I glanced at my partner. "I thought he was in his twenties when you ran his name in the computer."

"This dude ain't the dude in the computer," Colin said. "Is it just me, or do you also think the Darson girls got some daddy issues?"

I snorted. "Show me a girl who *ain't* got daddy issues and I'll show you where they buried Jimmy Hoffa."

"This guy your type?" Colin asked.

"No," I said, "but he kinda looks like the dude you picked up at Trader Joe's."

"Whole Foods," Colin corrected.

Max stood before us now, but not so close that I wouldn't have to speak a little louder. "How may I help you, Officers?" His voice was raspy and slow, his accent a mix of school and street.

And his voice made every hair on my arms bristle. I flashed my badge again and said, "I'm Detective Norton from Homicide. This is my partner, Detective Taggert."

Max offered us a sad smile, and those strange eyes of his turned soupy. "You're here about Monie, right?"

"We're talking with people in her immediate circle," I said. "And since you're dating her sister, we thought maybe you could help."

Max nodded. "Of course. I'll try my best, Detectives."

"How was shopping at Neiman Marcus?" I tried to take a small step toward him, but somehow Max Yates moved back—without moving.

"Neiman Marcus." He rolled his eyes. "Did Macie tell you? She's disappointed because that dress she wanted? They didn't have it anymore. I told her to find another dress—there were millions of them there. But she wants what she wants. And that means she left the store empty-handed." He cocked his head and said, "Here someone is, offering to buy something for you, and she remains spoiled and singular-minded. I just want to help her but . . ."

"Kids these days," I said. "But then, you're rather generous with the Darson girls. You gave Monie the Lexus, right?"

He nodded. "I wouldn't say 'give.' The note was ridiculously low, something she could handle once she started her job at the store. But it wasn't free. Macie and I wanted to do something nice for her after doing so well in school." His eyes dropped to the asphalt and he slowly exhaled through his nose. "Monie was a good kid and Macie misses her. The last few days, she's been all over the place. Emotionally, I mean, especially after we heard that Renata died. Macie's gone from playing Colombo to crying, starving herself, and vowing revenge." He bit his lip and exhaled again. "Are the two cases—Renata's and Monique's—connected?"

"Not sure yet," I said.

"Are there any suspects in Monie's case?"

"We're looking at a few people," Colin said.

"Let me guess," Max said. "Von and Derek."

Colin crossed his arms.

Max made a self-satisfied grunt. "Isn't it strange? The thug seems more upset by this than the good boy. Have you noticed that or am I being too harsh with the young Reverend Neeley?"

Yes, I had noticed Von's reaction, but now that no longer mattered.

Still, I said, "People display grief in different ways. Moving on: what was your relationship with Monique?"

He frowned. "Relationship with Monique? Well, we didn't really interact. But if I was hard-pressed to say *something*, I guess I'd say that she was like a little stepsister to me. Annoying. A bit spoiled just like her sister. Always on the phone. Seventeen." He winced. "I'm forty-two years old. I'm no longer accustomed to the noise of teenagers."

"How did you and Macie meet?" Colin asked.

"She was looking to buy a car. I hooked her up with the Maserati. Afterwards, she invited me to coffee."

"How about Macie and Monique?" I asked. "Did they get along?"

Max leaned against a shiny LIKE NEW! Escalade. "Macie lost patience with Monique all the time. They bickered over family business. I didn't get involved. Just let them fight it out."

"Were you ever alone with Monie?" I asked.

He narrowed his eyes. "What do you mean, *alone*?"

"Just like I asked. Not a trick question."

His brow furrowed. "Certainly. If Macie went to the bathroom, and Monique was with us, she and I were alone. If Macie left to retrieve something out of the car, again . . . But Monique and I were never *alone-alone* for long periods of time."

My eyes held his gaze. "So you like dating young women?"

"As opposed to old women?" He chuckled. "Who doesn't? No offense."

I said, "None taken. Oops, I lied."

"Look," he said, the cultured accent dropping some, "Monique was a good kid but she was off-limits. Girls that age worry me. A lot of them are looking for father figures. Some of them think it's exciting, being with an older man, and they think that, all of a sudden, they're sophisticated and worldly. Most of them? I'd say that most of them are playing tea party and dress-up."

"And do you like playing tea parties and dress-up?" I asked, remembering Monique Darson's cheerleader uniform.

Max rolled his eyes. "Macie and I were together on Tuesday night up until Wednesday around one in the afternoon. We had been in Temecula for a long weekend. Stayed at Pechanga. I lost $5,000 at the craps table." He said this carefully, as though one misspoken word would launch every Patriot missile in the United States.

"Yeah?" I said. "And if someone said that you were in Los Angeles on Tuesday—?"

"Detective Norton, your insinuations—"

"*Insinuations?*" I said. "I'm sorry—I didn't mean to *insinuate*. So I'll ask you straight out like old women tend to do: did you and Monique have a thing going on?"

"A *thing?*" He laughed. "No, we did not have a *thing* going on."

"You sure about that?"

"Yes."

"There's DNA."

His eyes sparkled. "Wonderful. Hope it helps you catch whoever killed Monique."

I nodded. "I hope so, too. What did you drive to Temecula?"

Bored with me, Max Yates shoved his hands in his pockets. "A Bentley Continental GT."

I spotted two black Bentleys parked near the sales office. "One of those?"

"Neither of those," he said, his jaw tightening.

"Where's the one you drove?" I asked.

"At the mechanic's. Highway 15 is a rough road and I think something happened to the struts."

"Good mechanic?"

"The best." Max smiled, but those smog-colored eyes were flat and lightless. "Rudy's Tires and Automotive over in Mar Vista. I can get you his business card."

Behrouz and his three-day suit crept over to us. "Mr. Yates, you have a call. Val Agranov from the Lakers."

"We have a contract with the team," Max explained to Colin and me. "Providing cars for some of their *lesser* players who can't afford their own $450,000 Bugattis. I need to take this call, if you don't mind."

"No problem," I said, handing him one of my business cards. "If we have any more questions—"

"Please stop by anytime," he finished as he glided away from us. "Anything to help." He held the card to his nose, then patted the Persian on his shoulder before disappearing into the sales office.

51

Golden Lee never overcame. She lived on Coco Avenue, down the street from Derek Hester, in the same ghetto apartment building that she had lived in back in the Eighties. One of Tori's friends, Golden had been the one with the MIA daddy, the two brothers and stepbrother in jail, the always-pregnant mother who shot smack into her tired veins, and the grandmother who had been a hood-rat back in the day, who had borne seven kids before she had reached thirty, who had found Jesus in her fifties and had raised each of her thirty-eight grandchildren, including Golden, since then.

Even as a child, Golden had been "thick," with an ass like a well-fed donkey's. She had green eyes and lips that always smelled of tobacco and strawberries. She had introduced Tori (and me) to beer, cigarettes, Black P Stones, tattoos, abortions, and porn.

Mom had made valiant attempts to end the friendship between Tori and Golden—like she had with Kimya and me. But Mom was always working, and so she had as much power as a light saber found in the discount bin at K-Mart.

Hard living had taken its toll on the woman standing in the doorway of her apartment: blotchy skin, a stringy weave that had worn away her hairline, flabby arms with caked-on deodorant in hairy pits, and a perma-scowl that only Jesus could fix. But then, four kids ages two through twelve ran around in the filthy apartment. They were climbing on furniture with stuffing popping from its seams, watching music videos with half-naked video hoes wiggling fat asses in the camera lens, stomping on bags of Cheetos and Skittles, McDonald's and Popeye's, as far as the eye could see. And even though Golden had to be forty-three years old, her belly was swollen and the poor tired stork would soon arrive. Looked like Golden used birth control like I used Viagra—never.

Hell, I'd scowl, too. And then I'd find a gun. *Pop.* One in the melon.

Golden frowned at my badge. "Don't tell me. JaVonte's ass finally dead." She said this as though I had just told her that she could save money on a new long-distance calling plan.

I blinked. "I don't know a JaVonte, ma'am."

She folded her arms. "Then it's Kenyon? Ro-shaun?"

"Are we talking about your children?"

She rolled her eyes. "My baby daddies."

I said, "Ah," then told her the reason for my visit.

She suggested that we remain outside to talk. "Last time a cop came in, little Trey took his gun out his belt. Trey only six but he know his way 'round shit." She said this with a glimmer of pride. Then she recited all that happened on that summer day in 1988: strolling down to the store, Tori being caught, her little sister Lulu running home.

Lulu was standing in front of her—guess she didn't recognize me, and after Napoleon Crase's interview, I was fine with that. I had never liked Golden and had always felt like my guardian angel had abandoned me so that the Devil could drag both Golden and me to Hell.

"I'm interested in what happened *after* Crase let her go," I said, louder now since a stereo from another apartment began blasting Tejano music.

"Me and Tori went off with these guys we knew," Golden said. "We had just met one of them like the day before. We had sex with them at that park over by Dorsey High School. Man, that was a long time ago." She laughed and shook her head. "Anyway, we went back to the store after that, to the parking lot. Tori and her guy, the new one, said they was driving to Baskin-Robbins for some ice cream."

"Ice cream. How wholesome. And then?"

"That was the last time I saw that dude. Didn't know something had happened until the next night when Kesha Tee called me." She paused, then asked, "They ever find Tori?"

"No," I said and scribbled on the notepad. "What was the name of the guy you were with?"

"Antonio Robinson," she said. "He my oldest boy's daddy. He in jail now. Tonio, not my son. Tonio always in jail. Like County got a rewards program."

I chuckled. "And the other guy? The one Tori was with. What's his name?"

She thought for a moment, then slowly shook her head. "I don't remember his name. Like I said: that week was his first time he hung out with us. And the last time, too."

The apartment door flew open, and a girl of about fifteen stuck out her head and yelled, "Momma, Kobe busted his head open."

I moved faster than Golden into the apartment, being sure to first secure my gun.

The living room smelled odd, uncommitted to just one type of stink. Pee, fried eggs, lilac air freshener, and a crappy diaper. The kids had turned off the television and were all huddled on the carpet around a two-year-old boy. Kobe's chubby face was slick with tears, mucus, and a trickle of blood.

Little Trey—I knew it was him because a barber had sheared LIL TREY into his hair—sidled closer to me.

Golden took her time as she brought over a battered first-aid kit, its cover smudged with old bloody thumbprints. She yawned as though she carried a box of saltine crackers instead of lifesaving interventions. To baby Kobe she said, "Your momma gon' kill me."

I paused. "Kobe's not yours?"

She crinkled her lips. "He one of my grandbabies."

Little Trey moved closer to me. "Hey, lady," he said, his breath hot and wheezy. "Lady, what's your name?"

I ignored the boy and applied gauze soaked with witch hazel to Kobe's forehead. The gash wasn't deep, more blood than bite.

"Hey, lady," Little Trey said again. "Lady. You got a gun?"

More pressure applied to Kobe's forehead, a swipe of ointment, a bandage, and a pat on the boy's back, and I was out the front door.

Golden thanked me for cleaning up the toddler, then said, "I wish I could remember dude's name. Oh, well." And then, she closed the door. The volume on the television returned to normal, and Golden screamed, "You just as stupid as your goddamned, jailbird daddy."

Grandmas never run out of hugs or cookies, do they?

52

Colin would fill out the profile on Max Yates since we now knew he had done the Hustle at his school's homecoming dance. And I would prepare for my Monday morning interview with Napoleon Crase. I called Pepe, and he agreed to roll past Crase's Baldwin Hills home every now and then, just to make sure that my very special guest didn't get a late-night hankering for empanadas in Argentina.

Home was where I had left it a day and a half ago: a mile from an ocean I rarely visited. That would change, though. With the new developments in Tori's case, I would soon have the bandwidth to let the sun shine in.

I grabbed the phone from the kitchen charger and retreated to the sun deck. Someone in the neighborhood was barbecuing—smoke mixed with the salty air—and I decided to invite Syeeda and Lena over for grilled steaks and wine after talking with Greg.

It was now early morning in Tokyo. My husband would just be waking up. He would find cartoons to watch on the television, then complete a hundred sit-ups and a hundred push-ups. He would then drag himself to the bathroom, shave and shower, then pull on a T-shirt and jeans. He would eat waffles and corned beef hash for breakfast.

His line rang . . . rang . . .

Worry reared its head.

Maybe he's with Michiko. Ha-ha.

Worry didn't think that my joke was funny and cocked an eyebrow.

"Hello?"

"Hey, you," I said to my husband.

Worry's eyebrow remained cocked.

"Hey, you," Greg said.

Was it the connection or was he whispering?

"Did I catch you at a bad time?" I asked.

He didn't speak at first, said, "Huh?," and then, "No. I just got out of—"

"Honey, you coming back into the shower?" That was not my question, nor was it my voice *asking* that question. Had Japan's version of Just a Friend just asked my husband to fuckin' wash her back?

"Who the fuck you with?" I shouted, already knowing who the fuck he was with.

I was pacing around the sun deck now, a starving cheetah ready to throw herself at a stupid hippo. Don't remember half of what I said, but the bulk of words heard by Greg and my poor neighbors had been the four worst profanities in American English, including the dreaded C-word.

"Calm the hell down, Elouise," Greg warned. "I can explain—it's not what it seems."

"There's some great explanation about why another woman just asked if you, who she called *honey*, were coming back into the shower?" I screeched. "She just busted you out, asshole."

I pictured him wearing his black Calvin Klein boxer briefs, hunched over in bed, his bourbon-colored eyes squeezed shut, his hand on the washboard stomach he paid too much attention to as a married man.

"She's just an associate," he said.

"She designs *purses*," I spat. "How the hell is that associated with video games?"

He had no answer. Because those two things? Purses and video games? Not associated.

After we concluded our vicious shouting match, after he admitted to sleeping with Michiko Yurikami, after he shouted six times, "It didn't mean anything, it didn't mean anything," I pressed End Call and collapsed in the chair. No more strength. No more resolve.

That was it. No more.

I loved him.

I hated him.

What if he meant it, that it didn't mean anything?

No. It meant something, it meant everything. My husband was a liar and the truth was not in him.

The phone rang, but it wasn't a pinball machine and I answered.

"What's up, lovely lady?" Lena said.

I opened my mouth to speak and a sob broke from my chest.

"Oh, crap," she said. "Lou, what's wrong?"

I squeezed out, "Greg . . . *gurgle-gurgle.*"

"I'm on my way," Lena said.

Maybe Greg's affair was my fault. Being around me seemed to send people to far-off places where I'd never find them, emotionally or physically. Unlike Tori, though, I would not search for Greg, not this time. I would not beg him to be my love, beg him like I had begged my father to come back to me. Greg Norton would not break my heart. But then, he couldn't break something that had been shattered years ago.

53

How can she afford to live in a fancy place like this?

He sits on a park bench in the middle of Cielo. People perch at other benches and hunker over wrought-iron tables with their coffees, boxes of sushi, and copies of *Fifty Shades of Grey*. A jazz band plays "My Favorite Things" as the sun starts its descent behind the Pacific Ocean a mile away. And most important: her condo is right over there.

He followed her home and parked down the block. In his rearview mirror, he watched as she eased the Porsche into the garage. Thinking about it now makes him simmer—as a taxpayer, he abhors seeing a public servant behind the wheel of a sports car.

The band ends the song. A few people clap. Children splash in the fountain.

Heaven.

He takes a breath, exhales, breathes in, out, in . . .

Something is wrong, very wrong, and in quiet moments like this, even when the spider is sleeping, he can smell it, taste it, *see* it.

He doesn't have much time.

Stay cool. Keep it together. Be smart.

But if he were being smart, he wouldn't be here, at this place.

At a bench across from him, a soccer mom in short-shorts and a tank top eyes him. Her son, a boy she calls Jack, is jumping off a lawn chair and into the shallow fountain.

He yawns—women of a certain age bore him. They smell like slow-cooked pot roast and fading antiperspirant. They drive minivans and buy organic beets, fat-free yogurt, and firming creams. This one here needs to go home, redecorate her kitchen for the fifth time, and screw the UPS guy.

The door to the detective's sun deck opens and Elouise Norton steps out. Phone to ear, she looks beyond the courtyard where he sits. Her hands jab the air. She's shouting into the phone.

He wishes the band would can it with their jazzy *Sound of Music* selections just so he could hear. But they now play "So Long, Farewell," and he can only wonder about the conversation Detective Norton is having.

"You look familiar." The soccer mom is now standing over him. This one smells of suntan lotion and coffee. A diamond pendant hangs in the cavern between her giant breasts. She flashes whitened and capped teeth, and asks, "Don't you have a son that goes to WNS?"

He blinks at her, annoyed. "What?" Why is she talking to him? And what the hell is WNS?

Stay cool. Keep it together. Act . . . normal.

He forces light into his expression and says, "No." From the corner of his eye, he sees Detective Norton still pacing the sun deck like a madwoman.

Soccer Mom says, "Oh," and then chuckles. "You look really familiar."

Twenty years ago she would have been his type. Pretty. Racially ambiguous. A whore. Now, though . . .

"Wish I could say yes." He waggles his ring finger—he only wears the gold band on occasions like this.

She peers at the ring but the flirtatious smile doesn't dim. "You *can* say yes." She bites her lip as little Jack pushes a girl half his size into the fountain. "I won't tell if you won't tell."

Desperate housewives, indeed.

54

After she sat bags of barbecue on the deck table, Lena poured me a glass of Riesling.

In one gulp, I finished it and hiccupped.

Syeeda sat in the Adirondack chair beside me and offered a tissue from the box on her lap.

I shook my head—I wanted to *feel* the burn of tears against my skin. I wanted to *feel* the pain.

Lena poured more wine for me, for her, and for Syeeda.

"Are you surprised?" Syeeda finally asked.

I muttered, "No," and a tear plopped into my wineglass.

Syeeda dabbed tissue against my face.

"It still hurts," I whispered. "I love him. I didn't get married to . . ." I clamped my lips together—I couldn't say *that word*. Had it come to *that word*? I drained the glass and hiccupped again.

Lena sat a plate of ribs on my lap and this time poured cabernet sauvignon into my empty glass.

I glanced at her. "You haven't said anything."

She kicked off her snakeskin stilettos and settled into the chair with a glass of wine. "You know what I think. I told you after the second chick that he'd do it again. And he did it again. And now, he's done it again after doing it again *that* time."

My eyes dropped to the plate. Just an hour before, I had craved barbecue, and now that I had it . . . Fucking Greg. Ruined everything. My desire for ribs. My quest for a fairy-tale ending. "It's my fault," I said. "I'm never—"

"Don't!" Syeeda shouted. "No! There's no excuse for his behavior. Don't let him do this, Lou."

"And stop ignoring all the bullshit," Lena added.

"I'm not," I countered.

Syeeda rolled her eyes.

"I'm trying to weigh the pros and cons—"

"Con," Syeeda said, "he's cheated on you more than once."

"Pro," I shot, "he knows what I've been through."

"Con," Lena said, "he knows what you've been through and he *still* cheated on you more than once."

"If he didn't want to be married," I said, "why hasn't he pulled the trigger? If he wants to fuck around, *why* is he married?"

"You need to ask *him* that," Syeeda said.

"I wasn't there for him," I argued. "I'm barely home. And even when I *am* home, my mind is—"

"No, it's not," Lena snapped. "Not *once* have you come to this house with one of those effin' . . . dead people folders. Not *once* has somebody's momma called here to ask about her murdered son. You *never* left his side even when he screwed around on you. When he got laid off and didn't know what he was gonna do, you were there for him and this is such *bullshit* that . . . that . . ." She hopped up from the seat, pacing and flapping her hands. "I'm three seconds from exploding and ruining my favorite pair of python Louboutins. That's how ridiculous this is."

"And his hours weren't nine to five, either," Syeeda pointed out. "He worked just as crazy as you. Except when he was fucking around."

"Maybe *you* should've fooled around, too," Lena muttered into her wineglass.

"With the new guy," Syeeda said. "Detective Funny Face."

Lena nodded. "*Especially* with Detective Funny Face. Want me to call him?"

"Bang, bang, that's dead," I said.

"Why?" Lena asked. "You're a man, he's a—"

"Easy, there," Syeeda said, taking Lena's wineglass.

"First," I said, "I'm married—"

Lena gave that point a raspberry.

"Second, I'm Colin's superior and—" I gave my own raspberry. "And *sixth*—"

"*Third*," Syeeda corrected.

"I ain't got where I am, fightin' the Man all this time, to have a . . . a . . ."

"A sexy, forbidden *liaison amoureuse?*" Lena asked.

"Exactly. And with a guy I wouldn't date in any other situation. If he was freakin' . . . freakin' . . ."

"George Clooney," Syeeda said.

"Or . . . or . . ."

"Harry Connick Jr.," Lena said.

Syeeda and I gaped at her.

"He sings so pretty," Lena said.

"Then I'd be all over that," I said. "Quicker than a tick on a dog." I poked at a rib, tore away a chunk of meat, and ate it. "It's good," I said, chewing.

Lena said, "Yeah."

"Elouise," Syeeda said, "go ahead and cry. Go ahead and give up. You don't have to be the tough cop all the time. You'll be okay. *We* won't leave you. Right, Lena?"

Lena nodded. "Shoop shoop, my sista."

My phone, lost in the mess of barbecue bags and wine bottles, rang. Not pinballs but Darth Vader's theme from *Empire Strikes Back.*

"Who the hell is that?" I asked.

"I thought Greg deserved a new ring tone," Syeeda explained.

Tears filled my eyes. "But I *like* Darth Vader."

"Shit, Sy," Lena said, holding out the phone. "Change it before she melts."

Syeeda fumbled with the phone, which rang again—whooping Ewoks. She beamed. "Everyone hates Ewoks." And the Ewoks whooped again. Syeeda glanced at the phone's screen and held it out for me to take. "It's Greg again. Wanna talk to your devoted son-of-a-bitch?"

I stared at it, then shook my head.

She tossed the ringing phone back into the trash.

"Eleven years," I said.

"I'm sorry," Syeeda whispered.

Lena stroked my hair. "*Désolée.*"

After eating the whole side of a cow, drinking a vat of wine, and inhaling a chocolate cheesecake, I lay my head in Syeeda's lap. The smell of seaweed rode atop the marine layer and twisted around us like cold, damp bandages. And I cried until I could no longer see the moon in the sky. Cried until I fell asleep and awoke in that dream-place where Tori was alive, Greg was in love with me, and no one was ever murdered.

55

Elvia, a Mormon but not a very good one, has dated a lot of men. Slept with more than half of them, too. Not that they're just *any* men—they are all well-off, older guys who never grumbled if she ordered expensive cocktails and the filet mignon instead of cheap wine and sirloin. She paid her lovers back in full—her bedroom skills were off-the-chain. Or so they said. Her talents helped pay the bills.

And now, Chi is back in her life, right in time for a summer vacation in St. Thomas, a closet filled with Burberry, and a check for fall tuition.

She eases the small BMW into the parking lot of the Crowne Plaza Hotel. Her heart pounds—from the drinks and from the anticipation of being with him again.

Her girlfriends turn up their noses any time she says that she is seeing Chi. "He's so . . . *old*," they say.

"Who wants to fuck somebody's grandpa?" her girl Zsa Zsa had said earlier at Hooters.

Elvia had rolled her eyes. "He's not *that* old," she snapped back. "And *biologically*, he's no different than the frat boys that go here. In the end, a dick is a dick."

True.

Kind of.

Chi's dick is surrounded in graying hair just like the graying hair on his chest. And his muscles are softening. And he always wakes up in the middle of the night to pee.

But he gives her trinkets in turquoise boxes and takes her to restaurants with French names.

He takes his time in bed and he doesn't need his parents to put forty dollars into his checking account so that he could feed her.

And all she has to do is let Chi play his little choke games. No problemo. She does that for Rodolfo all the time and he takes her to no-star restaurants.

Zsa Zsa could be such a jealous ho. But then, haterz hate.

The stilettos kill her feet as she rushes from the parking lot to the elevator bank. Up, up, up until the car reaches the twenty-first floor. A moment later, she wanders the carpeted hallways.

There.

Room 2109.

Back at the lounge, Chi had given her a hotel room key. She now slips the card into the reader. *Green light. Click.* She pushes open the door and steps into the room.

No bright television. The curtains are closed. "Hello? Baby?"

"Hey." He stands in the bathroom doorway.

"Hey, yourself," she says, closing the door behind her. "Miss me, *papi*?" She moves over to him and runs her hands up his bare chest and through that graying hair.

He takes her right hand and kisses the palm, sucks her middle finger. He pulls her close, nuzzles her neck, and whispers, "I thought we'd try something different tonight."

Sunday, June 23

56

Syeeda and Lena had decided to stay overnight, and together, we killed three more bottles of wine. Ewoks whooped all night but neither friend would let me answer. The phone chirped with text messages, too, but Lena silenced the ringer, then stuffed it deep into my purse. "If your boss needs to reach you," she said, "he can call that monstrous Motorola thing they gave you." She paused, then added, "Not that you're sober enough to work as a crosswalk guard right now."

We all stretched out on my bed. "Life is always better in the morning," Syeeda said as I fell asleep on her shoulder. "Like Orphan Annie sang: the sun will come out tomorrow."

All night, I dreamed wine-soaked dreams about trudging through a vast parking lot, crying, eyes on the asphalt, searching for something I had lost, but not knowing what it was as Greg followed behind me without speaking. And then I dreamed about Tori and Monique, holding hands, leading me to a crevasse filled with sharks.

Other than the headache and sour gut filled with liquor and meat, other than lingering memories of betrayal and cursing and crying, I awoke clinging to promise—tomorrow happened and the sun came out and Syeeda made omelets.

But then, I remembered the betrayal and the cursing and the crying.

Tomorrow, tomorrow . . . Go screw yourself, Tomorrow.

Greg had left twelve of the sixteen voice mails on the machine, and I deleted each one without listening to them. Since he claimed that I was never there for him, so be it.

Fucker.

After a late breakfast and several cups of coffee, I showered and changed into "formal" leggings that I paired with a light cashmere sweater and riding boots. Being hung over meant that I couldn't tolerate the clinch of a buttoned waistline or the scratch of linen or wool against my skin.

Weather-wise, it was a perfect Sunday. Crisp and fresh smelling, like God had arranged cirrus clouds and a light breeze just for me.

Syeeda and Lena ushered me to the car. "You sure you need to go in?" Lena asked, my chin in her hand. "It's almost noon. What's the point?"

"And what would she do instead?" Syeeda asked. "Lay in bed and write bad poetry while gulping wine from a box." She pointed at me. "Stay busy and don't go buying Franzia. I did it once. Let's just say that they won't let me back into the Sport Chalet over on Olympic."

"Yeah," I said. "Okay."

"And we'll take you out to dinner tonight," Lena said. "Japanese fusion at Chaya."

I said, "Yeah. Okay."

Both made sad faces.

Syeeda took my hands and squeezed. "Lou. Sweetie. Want us to stay with you?"

"No." I forced a weak smile onto my lips. "I'll be okay. I'll stay busy and I'll think about that cream of cauliflower soup and avenging dead girls and . . . and Angela Bassett in *Waiting to Exhale*."

Lena scowled and thrust her head forward. "Get yo' shit, get yo' shit—"

"And get out!" Syeeda shouted, pointing that-a-way.

My friends hugged me, kissed my cheek, and promised that life would straighten out.

With sisters like that, life could possibly happen like that.

I climbed into the Porsche and pulled out my phone.

He answered on the first ring. "Where the hell are you? I've been calling and texting you all night."

"One word: Greg. Another word: wine. And one more word: lying, cheating mother—"

"Got it." Colin paused before saying (with great caution), "So, where you off to?"

"Going to grab an unmarked and then visit a possible witness. And then I shall wait with bated breath for tomorrow. Don't forget: Crase is coming in the morning, and with his lawyer. So be prepared for anything. Wait: aren't you off right now?"

"Are *you* working?" he asked.

"Yes."

"Then I'm working, partner. Anyway, Zucca called. He's been looking for you."

I turned the Porsche's ignition and revved the engine "You handle Zucca, and I'll call you in about an hour."

Twenty-five years ago, the busted windowpanes of Crase Liquor Emporium had been filled with signs advertising bottles of Courvoisier and Oscar Mayer salami, three packs for a dollar. Twenty-five years ago, cars had pulled in and out of the bustling parking lot, and customers had purchased six-packs of Bud-Miller-Coors, bags of pork rinds, and single rolls of toilet paper. Kids would flock here before and after school, pockets heavy with silver, teeth ready to crack sunflower seeds and rip into jumbo dill pickles. Twenty-five years ago, travel agencies and Afro American art stores had lined this street. It was already dying in the mid-1980s, but the riots of '92 had ensured its death.

Today, black fingers of char climbed the remaining walls. Thigh-high weeds hid a parking lot chocked with broken beer bottles, crushed crack pipes, and transients. Now, Santa Barbara Plaza was an urban Pompeii, a land of Used to Be . . . and the last place I had seen my sister alive.

It was almost one o'clock and the sun beat down on me—finally felt like summer as I clicked on my flashlight and stepped inside the ruined building.

My skin tightened. The hair on the back of my neck and arms rose.

Stepping into a crypt.

I shone my flashlight before me.

The counter and cash register used to be right there, the candy stands right there, and the skin magazines right—

An unseen glass jar rolled across the grimy floor.

I swung the light to the left and toward that sound. "Hello?"

Critters scampered beneath the piles of trash. A horsefly brushed across my ear. A family of earwigs scurried around my boots.

Something scratched up on the roof.

I shone a beam of light to a ceiling lost in spiderwebs and mold. A fine rain of grit fell on my face.

My neck burned and the skin beneath my right big toe itched.

Gravel crunched.

Is that a footstep?

My neck stopped burning and started throbbing. A flea or a spider had bit me.

A creature hidden near the rusted candy stands scurried through the trash.

Someone was watching me from the darkness. I could feel it. Man or beast, I didn't know.

I eased my Glock from its holster.

The smell of cigarettes drifted in the air.

Man.

My eyes moved from rusty wire racks to burned plyboards. "Hello?"

No answer.

I could hear myself breathe, could feel the bite's heat spread across my shoulders. I turned back toward the dilapidated soda cases.

Napoleon Crase had grabbed Tori near that pile of empty Schlitz cans. I had been standing nearby, and had run into the rack of pantyhose, seeing nothing, everything a blur as I darted out onto the sidewalk and jammed up the hill in urine-soaked blue jeans.

Tears filled my eyes as I remembered Crase grabbing Tori's arm and Tori crying out and . . . the other guy, the one standing at the counter, eyes as wide and frightened as mine . . .

I stepped back and my boots crunched glass. I clenched my toes as though that would quiet my steps. I stood and listened to the scratching, to the faraway roar of cars and buses. I moved forward, gun held out before me. Slowly . . . forward . . .

To my right, a blink of light.

Just a reflection of my flashlight in a broken mirror.

Past a deli case, past cobwebs black and heavy . . .

Forward . . . slowly . . .

The smell of animal and human shit wafted in the air.

There was a door ten yards away.

I stopped in my steps.

What's that?

I tilted my head to listen.

Crying?

I held my breath to block the sounds of my pounding heart.

Where?

"Hello?" I cried out. "Police. I'm here to help you!"

The crying stopped.

The insect bite on my neck hurt like hell now, but I didn't touch it—scratching would distract me.

Maybe that sound wasn't crying. Maybe those were kittens or . . .

Click.

My shoulders jerked and my Glock rose higher.

I knew that *click.* It was the hammer of a revolver being cocked. And it had come from the same direction of the crying, which was . . . *where?*

Bang. A door slammed, and the floorboards beneath me vibrated. I hurried to the door in front of me and twisted the knob. Threw it open—a descending staircase—and dodged to my right as the stink rushed past me. I crept down the stairs and reached another door. I held my breath and twisted the sticky knob. I counted to three, then threw open the door, gun arm still out.

It was a storage room and there were mounds of trash and the nests of the homeless everywhere. Swipes of old blood or something else stained the walls. Broken pipes and malt liquor bottles, scraps of aluminum foil and a child's Red Flyer wagon . . .

Dim sunshine shone through a high, rectangular window that looked out to the deserted parking lot. The window frame banged against the wall. Whoever had just been here had piled trash onto trash onto the little red wagon to reach that window. Outside, in the dirt lot, a pair of men's work boots, running now, was vanishing in puffs of dirt.

Gone.

57

I sat in the Crown Vic for a long time, in front of Crase's abandoned store.

Something bothered me.

Max Yates. He was like a popcorn kernel stuck between my two back teeth.

During our talk at the car dealership, he had mentioned being forty-two years old.

But when Colin searched for "Max Yates" on our system, the three hits had been two old white men and a young black dude we had assumed to be Macie's boyfriend. No forty-something-year-old man.

How was that possible, a man Max Yates's age . . . ?

I typed his name into the car's computer.

Same three hits, none of the men being the man I had met.

But he *had* to be somewhere. A driver's license would, at *least*, put him in the DMV's database.

And why had Monique been calling him, as Freeda Duffy claimed?

And was it mere coincidence that he worked at Crase's dealership?

I closed my eyes and pictured Max Yates. That expensive suit. His easy gait. Those eyes. His smile. Teeth like . . . white Chiclets.

My eyes popped open and my fingers shot across the keyboard again. I bit my lip as I waited for the results.

MAX CRASE: ZERO (O) RESULTS.

Kesha Thompkins had been Tori's "rich" friend back in the Eighties, the girl who drove a pink Suzuki Samurai and wore Guess? and a different Swatch watch every day. She and Tori had been summertime friends— every June and July, Kesha lived with our neighbor, her grand-mother Mrs. Cornelius.

Today, Kesha lived in a Mediterranean-style home in View Park, a neighborhood of modest black wealth. Here, Benzes and Camrys, speedboats and RVs were parked in driveways while couples walked their dogs past manicured front lawns. Across the street from Kesha's house was a postage stamp–sized park where an old Chinese man led a group of seniors in practicing Tai Chi.

I rang the doorbell.

A dog barked. A pair of child's shoes pounded against the hardwood floor. The front door opened.

Kesha was older, but in twenty-five years, she hadn't changed much. Same flawless dark skin; longer hair, but cut in the same blunt shag she'd worn as a teenager; and the same ten-seconds-from-crying, big brown eyes. A seven-year-old boy with those eyes clung to her leg as a Weimaraner bounded through the foyer. She frowned, annoyed to see me on her porch. But once I showed my badge, relief washed over her face. *"Finally,"* she said. "I didn't think y'all were gonna follow up. I know it's just a home robbery to you—"

"I'm . . . I'm not here about a robbery," I said. "I'm from the *homicide* division."

Kesha frowned. "Homicide?" She touched her son's head, then told him, "Sweetie, take Ollie outside. We'll make cookies in a minute."

The boy gave me a doleful look—a strange tall lady with a gold badge was keeping him from cookie dough. But he was an obedient child and he scampered with Ollie down the hallway and out to the backyard.

I had thought about telling Kesha my maiden name, telling her that a childhood summer friend of hers had been my sister. But then, what good would that do? She would leave out important information just to avoid hurting my feelings or to make her role in Tori's disappearance less than it was. And I didn't want that, so I remained the anonymous detective, innocently working the cold case of a missing and presumed dead girl named Victoria Starr.

Kesha turned back to me. "Homicide? In *this* neighborhood?"

"No." As I summarized the case, she nodded. "So you remember then?" I asked.

"Oh, yeah. I'll never forget that day."

"I talked to the detective who had worked the case. He said that after Napoleon Crase caught Starr, he let her go."

"That's right," Kesha said. "I told that detective what I knew and he didn't seem interested—and I was just a kid anyway, so . . ." She shrugged. "Anyway, Tori was terrified. I mean, I never seen that girl cry so much and so hard. She really thought my uncle—"

"Your uncle?"

"Nappy," Kesha said. "He and my mom are siblings. Tori thought she was going to jail, but he was just scaring her. Cuz Starbursts? Ha-ha. People stole worse from him. The cops questioned him that night. Stupid. Like he'd kill a seventeen-year-old girl for stealing candy."

I tried to nod in agreement but my head refused to complete the gesture. So now, my chin was stuck in the "down" position. "So where did Tori go after he released her?"

"She started to walk home. She lived on Hillcrest, next door to my grandmother."

"What happened next?"

Kesha shrugged. "For some reason, she came back to the store."

"And you saw her?"

"Yeah, and I told her that she shouldn't stand next to my uncle's car and . . ." Kesha gazed past me to the park as she remembered that day. "Tori moved away from the car, but said, 'He told me to meet him here.'"

"Who told her that? Who was 'he'?"

Kesha slowly shook her head. "Don't remember."

I narrowed my eyes, unable to tell if she was lying to me now. "Who was there that afternoon?"

"Me. Golden. Tori. Tori's little sister, Lulu. These guys named Tony and Cyrus—"

"Cyrus?" I blurted.

She nodded. "Cyrus Darson. He went to Dorsey with us."

My skin tightened—Tori knew my victim's father. "And was Cyrus in the same grade as you and Victoria?"

"Yeah. He was one of those kids who stayed on the fringes—he wanted to be a part of our little group, but . . . He was weird."

"And did he know Tori?"

She rolled her eyes. "He was in love with Tori. He worked in Nappy's liquor store and he'd see Tori boosting all the time, but he'd never bust her." Kesha's eyes fixed on someplace far beyond me. "He had this way of disappearing even if he was standing right there. Spooky. He and my uncle were very close, like father and son. Which bothered my cousin *a lot*."

"Napoleon Crase has a *son?*"

She nodded. "Vincent."

"Crase?"

"No. He uses Lorraine's—his mom's—last name, Yates. And he got in trouble a long time ago, so he goes by his middle name now and that's 'Maxwell.' He was visiting that week when Tori disappeared—during the school year, he usually stayed with Lorraine in Chicago. But then, she'd send him out here whenever he'd get into fights or flunk a class."

"You have a picture of your cousin?" I tried to smile nonchalantly as I added, "I have pictures of you, Golden, Cyrus . . . Just trying to put all the players onstage for that day."

She hesitated for a moment, then said, "One moment." She hurried down the hall and made a left, out of my view.

Heart racing, I turned to watch the old people move their limbs slowly through space.

"Here you go," Kesha said, back in the doorway. As she thrust the picture at me, glass crashed to the floor somewhere in her house. The dog barked as though the house was on fire.

Kesha whirled around and shouted, "Ryan, what happened?"

The boy shouted back, "Nothing."

Another glass object broke.

The dog barked again.

Ryan shouted, "Ollie went number one on the rug!"

Kesha apologized, told me she had to go.

I thanked her, then quick-stepped back to the car. With trembling fingers, I looked at the picture she had given me of her cousin.

Those eyes. His smile. Teeth like . . . white Chiclets.

Barely breathing now, I slowly typed *Vincent Yates* into the computer.

One hit.

The Chicago DMV's picture of Vincent Yates loaded.

I stared at the image of the man who had been with my sister on the last day of her life.

And possibly, *probably*, had been with Monique Darson as she breathed her final breath.

58

I called Zucca's office but no one answered. I paged him—still no answer. I called his office again, this time leaving a message. "I know you've been calling me and calling me, but I'm here now, and I need you to run something for me. That fingerprint off Monique Darson's underwear. See if you can get into Chicago's DMV files so you can compare it to a 'Vincent Yates.' I think he's our man."

Shit. Shoulda called Zucca earlier. But earlier today, I didn't know the truth behind the names.

I called Macie Darson next.

Macie didn't pick up.

I called the Darsons' home phone, hoping that even Cyrus answered—especially since he had been at the store on the day Tori was taken.

Angie answered, though, sounding brighter today than she had all week. "I left you a message at the station," she said. "We wanted to invite you and Detective Taggert to Monique's service. This coming Thursday, eleven o'clock, at our church. And then, we're having supper at the house. Think you guys can come?"

"We'll be there," I said. "I'm trying to reach Macie. Is she there? Or Cyrus?"

"No. I haven't seen that girl since yesterday. And Cyrus is out running errands for the service." She paused, then asked, "Is something wrong? Oh, Lord, what happened? I can't take anymore."

And just like that, Angie's mood darkened. Good job, Lou.

"Nothing's wrong," I said. "Everything's fine. I'm just following up on something," I said this carefully, as though I had been creeping through a glen of bear traps.

What to do now? Sit on all of this or go talk to Napoleon Crase now to get more information about his son's role that day at the liquor store? He wouldn't have his lawyer with him, which meant anything he said to me now could be thrown out of court tomorrow, which then meant my career as an LAPD homicide detective would be . . .

I sped out of Kesha's neighborhood, radio to my lips as I called Colin and told him about my newest discovery. "The last known address for Vincent Yates a.k.a. Max Yates is in Long Beach." Twenty miles south of Los Angeles.

"I'll have units to roll out there," Colin said. "And I'll meet you at Napoleon Crase's house right now."

As Colin signed off, Zucca's voice came over the Motorola. "Got your message," he said, "and good news: it looks like a match, but I need the tech to confirm it. She's working on it now. Stay put."

"Yeah," I said, even though I was not staying put. In fact, the world was rushing by in a blur as I charged into Baldwin Hills.

It was almost six o'clock when I rolled past 73881 Don Tomaso Drive, an elegant Georgian home of red brick, white shutters, and stately weeping willows that edged the brick walkway. Napoleon Crase, in sweatpants and a sweatshirt, held a garden hose and watered a perfect lawn.

I made a U-turn at the end of the block and parked fifty yards away, in front of a ranch-style house still trimmed with Christmas lights.

Neighborhood men were washing cars, their radios turned high to sportscasts or R&B. Teens skateboarded as joggers and walkers moved up and down the sidewalk. The sun hung high in the sky. It was Sunday evening, the first weekend of the summer. Everyone was out and about.

Colin wasn't here yet. Just Napoleon Crase and me.

My radio squawked and Zucca's voice came back on the line. "Alexa just finished with the analysis."

I closed my voice and said, "And?"

"And: it's a match. I'll fax it to the car."

A second later, the Crown Vic's telefax whirred and spat out side-by-side photographs of two thumbprints left by Max Crase a.k.a. Vincent Yates.

I didn't smile as I headed toward Napoleon Crase, fingerprints in hand.

He didn't look too thrilled seeing me, either.

"I'm looking for your son," I said.

He let the garden hose splash water near my boots. "Pardon me? My son?"

"Vincent or Max, whichever name he prefers today."

He stared at me as his eyes twitched. "Why do you need to speak with my son?"

I held up the fax and watched his eyes scan the fingerprints there. "We have reason to believe that Max is involved in Monique Darson's murder." I paused, then swallowed. "And that he's also involved in my sister's murder."

Crase dropped the hose and stared at me with sad eyes. "Those fingerprints could have been planted. Or . . . or . . ."

"I also have several witnesses that placed him at the liquor store that day," I added. "Witnesses who stated that my sister was with him after you let her go."

Crase swallowed, but lifted his chin in defiance. "None of this proves anything."

"We have the DNA results from my sister's case," I said. "And we have DNA from Monique Darson's case now, too. And they match."

Crase's eyes filled with tears.

"We need to end this, Napoleon," I said, my own eyes watering. "It's been too long."

He opened his mouth to speak, but dropped his head instead. His shoulders slumped and he slowly exhaled. Finally, he met my eyes. "I think we should talk about this inside."

I nodded, plucked my radio from my hip, and toggled the mike. "Hey, Taggert."

"I'm not too far," Colin said.

"I'm going inside to talk with Mr. Crase. Copy?"

"Copy that."

I left the one-way audio on so that Colin could hear everything being said.

I followed my nemesis into the dark foyer, where the heavy air stank of sweat and cologne. Heavy curtains kept natural light from reaching the inside of the house. But my eyes slowly adjusted to the lack of light, and now I could make out shapes. Empty, green bottles of Excedrin littered the floor alongside soiled and bloody cotton swabs. Each step I took left behind a trail of crushed pills.

"Elouise Starr."

I turned to my right and toward the man's voice. I could see two forms sitting in an armchair.

In the dim light, Max Crase's eyes glistened like a wolf's. He held a backpack shotgun (short-snouted but deadly), now pointed at me.

I immediately pulled my Glock from its holster.

"My mom said you called." It was Macie. She stood near the living room window and sounded too damn cheerful to be sitting in a filthy, dark living room, next to a man with a gun.

"Yes, Macie," I said, gun trained on Max. "And I need you to come with me."

Crase turned to his son. "She claims to have proof, Vincie."

"Fuck her proof," Max said. "Tell her to talk to my lawyer."

Max and Macie laughed as she crept toward me.

I cocked my head. "Will shit be funny when you take your stainless-steel ride to Hell? Cuz that's what I'm talking about here if you don't cooperate, Max. Death penalty."

I had a choice: look at Macie or keep my eyes on the shotgun trained on my chest. I chose number two.

Max and Macie laughed louder. Standing beside me now, Macie slowly lifted her right arm—she held a .22 and had it pointed now at my right ear.

"Macie," I whispered, "you don't want to do this. Put the gun down, okay?"

She slowly reached for my Glock and took the gun from me.

I kept my hands up.

A tear tumbled down Napoleon Crase's face. "Vincie, I'm too old for this shit, all right? I'm tired of cleaning up after you and . . . It'll be okay. You're not well. They can't kill you for something you have no control over."

The old man turned to me. "We will tell you the truth, Elouise, and you will work something out for all of us." He chuckled and waggled his head. "I mean, you still need information from us. And we won't talk about it unless it is for the good of *all* of us. Of *course*." Even though he had regained some of his swagger, he still swallowed a little too hard, seemed a little too eager.

"Are you fucking *crazy*, Napoleon?" Max shouted, his eyes blinking hard now.

Crase whirled around and pointed at his son. "Shut up! *Now*."

Macie giggled as she placed her gun and mine on the couch cushions. "Baby, your dad talkin' to you like you a punk."

"I'm *done*," Crase shouted at him. "You think you can handle—?"

"I didn't ask you for shit!" Max yelled back.

Macie sneered. "You done, Napoleon? Be done, then."

This little tête-à-tête was getting a little too loud now. "Let's just calm down, all right?" I said with forced calm. "We can talk about all of this—my sister, Monique, deals with the DA—later, okay? I would just like Macie . . ." I motioned for Macie to leave her boyfriend's side and to walk toward me.

Max grinned. "I think not."

"I'm staying," Macie said with a smile.

I stared at the young woman—there was no fear in her eyes. "Well, then I will come back and we can discuss all of this later." Live to fight another day, as the saying went.

"I think not," Max repeated.

I squared my shoulders. "You're holding me against my will?"

He kept that grin.

The doorbell rang. "Open up, Max. Police." It was Colin.

"Oh, shit," Macie said. "Another cop?"

Crase raised his hands. "Let's . . . let's . . . We don't want . . ." He turned to me. "We'll cooperate, Detective Norton. We don't want this thing to escalate—"

Max cocked the shotgun. "This bitch gotta go."

Crase cried, "Vincie, don't!"

Colin kicked at the door.

Max took two steps, then stopped.

BAM!

He missed me—*Lord only knows how he missed me*—and the slug exploded against the front door, sending shards of wood flying through the air.

Colin shouted in pain.

I heard a loud thump—my partner was down.

"Fuck," Max shouted, where light now streamed in through a pancake-sized, splintered hole.

As the gunshot rang in my ears, I quickly pressed the emergency button on my radio so that Dispatch would send backup.

"What the *fuck* did you just do?" Crase yelled.

The grin on Macie's face dimmed and she gawked at me.

I took a step toward Max, my hands flexing, hot air venting from my lungs.

Max pointed the shotgun at me.

I stopped in my step.

"What the *fuck* did you just do?" Crase yelled again.

Max squeezed shut his eyes. "Will you just—?"

"Just what?" Crase screeched. "You a cop killer now? You want us all to die?"

"Max," Macie said, "maybe—"

"I need to think. I need to think." Max's smog-colored eyes were now all black. His facial muscles and fingers twitched. The tendons in his neck stood out against the skin and his pulse pounded like a metronome set on supersonic.

"Vincie, please," Crase pleaded. "Just tell her what happened. Just tell her about Monie, about Tori, and the others. Let's be done with this."

"You keep talking," Max said, his voice high-pitched. "Just . . . just . . ."

"If I was you," Macie said to Crase, "I'd—"

"Shut. *Up!*" Max screamed, his finger flexing on the trigger.

Napoleon Crase, crying now, held out his arms to me. "You don't understand, Detective. He's sick. He needs help. He had a tumor in his brain." His finger pointed at his forehead. "When he was little, it was the size of a nickel. We had them take it out, but . . . but it came back. He's sick. He ain't right. He doesn't mean it—"

Napoleon Crase pivoted and grabbed for Max's shotgun.

Max was quicker and took one side step. He turned the shotgun on his father and pulled the trigger.

Boom! Another deafening explosion shook the room.

Macie shrieked.

The old man, his guts spilling onto the floor, crumpled where he stood. The smell of gunpowder mixed with the odors of warm urine and fèces as Napoleon Crase's dying body voided itself. He gurgled and frothy red bubbles dribbled out of his mouth as he took his last breaths.

Outside, sirens wailed. A helicopter thundered above the house. The flickers of red and blue strobe lights brightened the living room walls.

Max gaped at the shotgun in his hand—the game had changed now. The explosion had yanked him from his rabbit hole. No more tremors. No jerky motions. He clenched his jaw, though—he was making great effort to control something within himself. His gaze finally met mine, and he croaked, "I see darkness, and I see you." He grabbed Macie and jabbed the shotgun's barrel against her jaw.

"You don't understand," Macie was saying to me, tears in her eyes. "You don't understand."

"Help me to understand, then, Macie," I said, eyes trained on Max.

"It's not his fault," Macie cried. "It was Monie—she made him do it."

"Put it . . . shut . . . down," Max demanded. "Can't . . . nothing now."

He sounded like a scratched vinyl record, skipping and dropping words.

"We talked about our sisters, remember?" she said, desperately. "But I didn't tell you everything. About how Monie *really* was, for real. I'll tell you, and then you'll see. You'll see that it wasn't Max's fault."

Max's finger flexed on the trigger again. Perspiration glistened on his forehead and a bead of sweat slipped into his left eye.

"Monique stole from me," Macie said, arms at her sides, hands clenched into fists. "Shoes, money, purses. And she stole my mother and father away from me. And she was trying to steal Max, trying to steal the love of my life, and I wouldn't let her . . ." Tears in her eyes, she shook her head. "I didn't see it at first, and I'd always bring her along whenever me and Max went to the movies or to dinner. We called ourselves the Three Musketeers cuz our names . . . Then, I noticed that she would try and hold his hand. She'd kiss him every time she saw him. She started calling him, throwing herself—"

"She wasn't doing any of that alone," I said. "Max—"

"No." Macie closed her eyes. "No."

"I have proof, Macie. I have phone records and text messages. And your sister kept a handkerchief—"

"No," she shouted. "She made him give her clothes, money, that car.

And she told him that she'd tell everybody that he raped her if he didn't break up with . . . We had to do something. It wasn't right what she was doing to him. What she was doing to me."

Max stroked her face with the barrel of the shotgun.

Macie's mouth opened and closed and teardrops rolled down her face. "I . . . wanted to catch her so we left Temecula and Max told her to meet him at the trailer cuz that's where she always met him and . . . I waited in the car . . . he went up and he came back and told me . . . She started fighting him and . . . he squeezed too hard. He didn't mean to."

"It was an accident then," I said. "We can work this out, Macie. We—"

"I was so scared," Macie whispered. "But he didn't mean to."

"Okay, Macie," I whispered. "Okay. Just . . ."

"You love me, right, baby?" Macie asked Max, her eyes closed as the business end of the shotgun grazed her right temple. A sob escaped from her chest. "We're partners, right, baby? To the end, right?"

"Max," I said, shaking my head, "please let her go."

"You promised to take care of me," she said to Max with a lovesick smile. "Remember? You said that, remember, when I was clipping her fingernails? You said that you would make it up to me."

Max kissed the top of her head. "Ssh . . . Ssh . . . Ssh."

Macie closed her eyes as he comforted her. But Max kept his eyes on me.

I shook my head. "Max. Please don't. Just—"

His shark eyes hardened as he fired again.

BOOM!

The gunshot echoed through the house.

Macie was dead before she hit the floor.

Max's skin and hair were now slick with sweat and his lover's blood. "Feel better," he said with a sigh. "Too . . . noise. Hard . . . think."

Heart racing, I forced myself to take controlled breaths.

He smiled at me, his teeth bright white against all that red. "I'm . . . ," he said as he stepped toward me, his shirt now drenched in the blood of the people who had loved him. "Think . . . remember."

I stood there—was I awake or was this a dream?

The thirteen-year-old Elouise knew that this was very real and she lay there, in that apartment back in the Jungle, crying so hard that she couldn't breathe. The Now-Lou, though, the one standing in this big house with two dead at my feet and a madman with a shotgun just a few steps away, with the blood of two people soaking the soles of my boots, felt that decades-old knot loosening in her belly, felt that rope burning away. No more anxiety. No more fear.

Blood everywhere.

Max stood an arm's length away from me now, and his breath—smelled like ripe barley, copper, and dying tissue—was hot on my face. "I'm . . . me," he wheezed, "me and you . . . like me and your sister." He smiled, then pushed out words that slammed against each other: "*She-likeitroughdirtyyououlikeitroughdirtyLu?*" No breaths, no pauses.

"Yeah," I said. "I like it rough and—" My left hand shot out and the heel of my palm struck his nose. And then, I struck his nose again. Bone broke beneath my strikes. Warm blood gushed over my hand and wrist.

He cried out in pain.

I grabbed his right wrist and twisted.

Another crunch.

He shrieked again and the shotgun fell to the floor.

I wrapped my arm around his trachea and clasped my slick hands together and pressed.

Max Crase weakened in my guillotine choke.

And I kept pressing.

And he weakened even more.

Pressing . . . Pressing . . .

And I didn't let go even as big men in black burst through the door and windows.

59

Despite the beating he had received at my hands, Max Yates did not die that night.

An ambulance had rushed Colin down the hill and to the closest hospital emergency room. "Bullet hit his left arm," Lieutenant Rodriguez told me. "That didn't knock him out—yeah, the slug's impact decked him, but he fell and hit his head on one of the steps. *That* knocked him out. A couple of stitches, a couple of pills, and some ice, and the cowboy will be okay. He was more worried about leaving you."

Fog swept over Don Tomaso Drive like ghosts, blurring red lights, blue lights, and klieg lights. My windbreaker did nothing against the chill that had set deep into my bones. I sat on the hood of a patrol car, arms clutching my shoulders, unable to stop shivering.

"Shock," an EMT told me as he wrapped a wool blanket around my shoulders.

My iPhone vibrated in my pocket but I didn't move to answer it.

A few yards away, lieutenants and sergeants talked. I had stopped listening. Couldn't hear anyway over the chatter of my teeth. So cold. But I thought about Colin, remembered how he had cried out like that, but I had been unable to do anything to help him. I wanted him to be sitting beside me now, crunching on his damned Tic Tacs . . .

The phone vibrated again and the muscles in my arm creaked as I pulled the device from my pocket.

Cyrus Darson had sent me a text message with an embedded video.

One of us would have to notify him, tell him that his surviving daughter had been killed by the same man as his youngest daughter, that Macie had, unwittingly, lured her own sister to her death . . .

I tapped the Play icon.

Cyrus Darson was sitting in a truck, his face wet from the tears still falling down his cheeks. "Detective Norton . . . Elouise . . . Lulu."

The world around me dimmed.

"When you came to the house that morning to tell us about Monie, and you said your name was Elouise, I knew then . . . I had memorized Tori's face and I saw her in you, and I knew you were her sister. And I knew that it was just a matter of time until the truth . . ."

My hands shook and I gripped the phone tighter to keep it from dropping to the asphalt.

"I don't even know how to start," Cyrus Darson said. "There's just so . . . much." He tried to chuckle as he wiped his nose. "Maybe I should say that I'm not the best father in the world. Not the strongest or the smartest. One of my girls is gone and the other . . . She's ruining her life and that's not her fault. Not Angie's fault. I should've . . ."

A sob burst from his chest and he clamped his hand over his mouth. "Vince . . . I was there when he . . . We . . . Tori was standing by Nappy's car and we grabbed her and forced her down to the storage room and Vince made me hold her arms down and I thought we were just going to . . . to . . ." He sniffled and frowned. "She either ignored me or she used me. She always treated me like I was beneath her but I loved her, and I hated her because I loved her and I just wanted, *for once*, wanted her to feel the pain I felt.

"He made me hold her down, hold Tori down, but she kept fighting and there was broken glass there and she grabbed a piece and . . ." He touched his scar and let his finger drift along its bumpy path until it stopped in his dreads. "She hurt me again and so I hurt her. After, I thought we were gonna let her go. She promised that she wouldn't tell, that she wouldn't go to the police but Vince . . . She wouldn't stop crying, so he wrapped his hands around her neck and . . ."

Cyrus Darson whimpered as he remembered, then whispered, "And she stopped crying. She stopped." His shoulders shuddered as he swiped his hands over his wet face. "It was happening too quickly, all of it, and I couldn't . . . it felt like . . . I wasn't me. It was like, like I was watching me from some other place and I couldn't believe what I was seeing."

He looked into the camera. "She was so beautiful, even then, even as she lay there. And while all of it was happening, I thought maybe now, maybe now she would love me.

"Nappy was like my father and I would do anything for him and that meant cleaning up after Vince and . . . I didn't say anything back then because he took care of my family. Made sure we had everything. He bailed me out every single time I . . ." He shook his head, then dried his face on his T-shirt, then moaned. "Vince has never let me forget. And I can't prove it, but I know he killed my baby. And because of him, Macie is headed in the wrong direction.

"Angie . . . she thought that I was a good man. She knew that I hated Nappy. She thought it was because of the redevelopment shit, because he was a vulture who hurt his own people. She had no clue that we, that I . . . And I didn't want her to know about my past or about the money he gave me each month, so I let her think that my hate came from that place. Nappy knew Angie was strong, that if she found out about everything, we would *all* go down."

Cyrus Darson let out a breath, then let his head hit the headrest. "An uneasy alliance. Everybody had something on everybody else. But Angie is good. Better than what I deserve. She fills the spaces in me. There are so many spaces in me. And I don't expect her to forgive me. I won't ask. I just know I can't live with this. I *won't* live with this."

He stared into the phone's camera for hours, it seemed, then said, "I saw you today, Lulu, at the old store. And that's where you will find me after this. Your sister is there, too, in the storage room. I know this is true because I helped bury her there." Then, he lifted a revolver and stuck the barrel in his mouth.

60

By the time we left Napoleon Crase's blood-soaked home and drove down the hill to the Santa Barbara Plaza, Colin had been stitched up—forehead and arm—and had forced a uniform to drive him to the plaza. I pulled him into a hug, careful not to smash his taped-up arm or his bag of Vicodin. "Next time," I whispered, "get the hell out of the way."

He laughed, then said, "Next time, take the fucker's shotgun from him."

We found Cyrus Darson's Toyota 4Runner in the former parking lot of Crase Liquor Emporium. After he had sent me his video message, the man who had raped and helped murder my sister pulled the trigger of his revolver and blew off most of his head.

I said nothing as I stood there, looking at the mess he had made.

Lieutenant Rodriguez assigned Luke and Pepe to work the scene and to tell Angie Darson that she had lost her only living daughter and her husband in one bloody night.

I didn't want to go home, and Colin couldn't drive and shouldn't have been alone anyway with a head injury. I told Pepe that I'd stay overnight with Colin at his place, and then drove my partner to Glendale.

We didn't talk much as the world passed by in a blur. He winced each time I hit a large pothole. He napped when he wasn't wincing.

As soon as I crossed the threshold of his apartment, I smelled spilled beer and tennis shoes. He didn't own a lot of furniture, just a sixty-inch television and a futon in the living room, and in the bedroom, a mattress on a box spring. Suitcases lined the bedroom wall, and clothes spilled out of them like intestines.

"Mind if I shower?" I asked, letting my "away" bag slip off my sore shoulder.

Colin guided me down the short hallway to the bathroom. He

twisted the shower knobs and stood with me as steam filled the tiny space. He brushed my cheek with his thumb.

I flinched, then caught my reflection in the fogging mirror. There I was. No eyes, no mouth. Just my darkness, a shadow of me. Disappearing.

"I'll be outside," he whispered.

I said nothing and didn't move until he had closed the door. I stared at my hands: blood crusted beneath my fingernails and stained the lifelines crisscrossing my palms. I kicked off my boots and slowly peeled out of my bloody sweater and leggings. I stepped into the shower, grinded my teeth as hot water stung my skin. And I stayed there until the world around me turned white.

Colin was seated on the futon, drinking a bottle of Sam Adams and staring at the dark television. His pill vial sat open on the coffee table.

"Beer and pills?" I asked, sitting next to him.

He rested his head on my shoulder. "Is there another way?"

I scoffed. "Yeah. The old-fashioned way: vodka."

My body hurt and my mind . . . numb. Too much had happened and so my brain had triggered the safety switch, and I was too tired to find the reset button. The emotions would be there the next day, along with a new set of matching baggage—*fa-la-la-la-la*, Christmas gifts for cops.

"LT called," Colin said. "Angie Darson ain't doing so good."

I sighed, then closed my eyes. "Where is she?"

"In the psych ward at USC."

"Poor lady."

"And . . ."

"And what?"

He took another swig of beer. "They cracked opened Max Yates's skull. Surgeon found a tumor the size of a walnut."

I pushed my damp hair away from my forehead. "The Charles Whitman defense then?"

The shooter on the tower at the University of Texas had killed thirteen people and wounded thirty-two others. A brain tumor had been pressing against the part of the brain that controlled rage, fear, and anxiety. That's why he killed—that's what some doctors and attorneys said.

"He gonna live?" I asked.

Colin lifted the bottle to his lips. "Probably not."

Neither of us spoke for a long time.

"What do you think?" Colin asked.

I paused, before saying, "I'm a cop, not a neurologist."

He grunted, not satisfied. "And Napoleon Crase?"

I took a deep breath, held it, then slowly released. "He could've ended all of this a long time ago. And that would've . . ."

Would've what? Saved Monie? Saved Macie? Cyrus? Yes. But Victoria Starr, my sister, would have still been lost.

I sat up. "Max Crase was in control when he lured Monique Darson to that condo." I ran my hands through my hair, then let my head fall back onto the couch. "I can't say that was true for Tori . . . or the others. But for Monique, for Monie, he deserves . . ." I shook my head. "Shit."

"Yup." Colin offered me the beer bottle.

I took it and guzzled the rest.

"Thought you hated beer," he said.

"Well, you offered."

He looked up at me, his eyes searching mine, looking for a sign that I was as okay as I sounded. "You okay?"

"Are *you* okay?" I asked him. "Since you were the one who got shot today."

He smiled. "It's all good. Chicks dig scars."

"Indeed."

Then, we closed our eyes and fell asleep.

Monday, June 24

61

On Monday morning, I awakened with my head in Colin's lap. He was watching the highlights of a baseball game on mute. Once he realized that I was awake, he turned the channel to a home gardening show. "Cuz you ladies like those kind of shows, right?"

I checked voice mail: Greg had left more messages than I could count, each one seeped in a different mental state. Fear: of losing me. Anger: from being ignored. In love with me all over again. Jealousy. Sadness. And on and on. With the blood of others still trapped beneath my fingernails, I no longer knew if Greg Norton fit into my life. I was not the same Lou he had left almost twenty days ago. A better Lou? A worse Lou? I did not know. Guess we would both find out.

The doorbell rang and Colin groaned as he shuffled to the door.

Pepe stood there holding a brown paper bag from Noah's. "I brought breakfast." And as he laid out bagels, lox, and cream cheese on the kitchen counter, he said, "Luke and I went to see Angie Darson this morning."

"Medicated?" I asked as I fixed a pot of coffee.

"Heavily."

I fixed a plate for Colin, then joined him and Pepe in the living room. We ate slowly, eyes on the television and on a couple house hunting in Costa Rica.

After the episode ended, Pepe said, "We should head back."

Colin aimed the remote at the television and the screen went black.

I frowned. "Where the hell you going? You're on the injured list."

He stood and readjusted his arm sling. "I won't be runnin' after no crackheads today, but I'm good. Let's roll, partner."

Outside, at our cars, Pepe hugged me, then said, "Damn, Lou. I saw

Max Yates's face last night as they were loading him into the rig." He tousled my hair. "You fight like a girl."

I smiled, then climbed behind the wheel of my Crown Vic.

We drove back over the hill and to Santa Barbara Plaza. The sun shone bright and made these urban ruins more beautiful than what they deserved. For an hour, we waited until our entire team had assembled: Joey, Pepe, Luke, Lieutenant Rodriguez, Zucca and his team, and forensic anthropologists from Cal State Los Angeles.

While I waited, I pictured myself emerging from the store's basement four hours later, dusty and exhausted. I imagined lifting my face to the sun as warm tears sluiced down my dirty cheeks. Imagined taking several deep breaths before pulling out my phone and calling my mother, saying to her that I had kept my promise, that I was bringing Tori home.

After so many years, I wanted to live that moment more than I wanted to see God.

Minutes before eleven o'clock, we all clambered into the store, then trudged down the steps and into the basement's storage area. We wore masks with aerators to filter out the smell and to protect us from kicked-up dirt and fecal matter.

Portable light stands set up and burning bright, Zucca handed me a whisk broom. "Shall we?" he asked.

I chose a patch of ground near that rectangular window. I dropped to my knees and started to sweep away dirt and garbage. The others found their own parcels and did the same. After much sweeping, I found a small, metal trapdoor.

Work stopped. The room fell into uncertain silence.

I tried to yank open the door.

No give.

Colin tried.

Still no give.

Zucca used a crowbar and the hinges loosened.

I grabbed the door and pulled the handle.

The videographer turned her camera toward the hole.

I pulled again and the door creaked opened.

The cops stepped back—I did, too—and kept flashlights trained on the darkness. The anthropologists took the best positions, kneeling around the door. One scientist, a woman named Olga, motioned for me to come back. "Look," she said, pointing into the darkness.

I glimpsed a round brown object half-buried in a pile of dirt.

Olga used a hand spade to gently dig around that object. Then, she gradually pulled it free.

It was a shoe. A Nike Huarache.